CRITICAL MASS
THE NADIA PROJECT

thank you!

Live your Destiny

Cyrus Keith

MuseItUp Publishing

Critical Mass © 2014 by Cyrus Keith

All rights reserved. No part of this book may be reproduced or transmitted in any form or by any means, electronic or mechanical, including photocopying, recording, or by any information storage and retrieval system, without permission in writing from the publisher.
The characters and events portrayed in this book are fictitious. Any similarity to real persons, living or dead, or events, is coincidental and not intended by the author.

MuseItUp Publishing
14878 James, Pierrefonds, Quebec, Canada, H9H 1P5

Cover Art © 2012 by Delilah K. Stephans
Layout and Book Production by Lea Schizas
Print ISBN: 978-1-77127-656-6
eBook ISBN: 978-1-77127-255-1
Production by MuseItUp Publishing

*To Cynthia Marie,
who always gave more than she got.
Thank you, little sister.*

Acknowledgements

Thanks to the ones who believed I could. To those who didn't: Greetings from the slopes.

Chapter One

It had been dark for some time. The rain had moved on, leaving the pavement with a sheen that whispered with every passing car. Scud clouds overhead trailed the thunderstorm like remoras behind their shark. The moon cast its wan light between them, a pitiful challenger to the flickering neon of the street below.

The city's diurnal population was at home and in bed. That left the nighthawks, those who thrived in the hours between sunset and dawn. They worked, played, lived, and loved in dark hours. And some of them died there.

The crowd at the Tap Tavern began to thin out about one in the morning. By ones and twos, they filtered through the front door and into the street, fanning out to home, to work, or to other purposes known only to them. By two o'clock, only the closing crew remained, a couple of vague shadows moving beyond the frosted glass of the large windows flanking the door.

A small brown coupe sat parked across from the alley mouth in the dark of the early morning. Traffic was lighter now than it was at eight o'clock, but was still busy enough to conceal the lone occupant seated behind the wheel. With stubborn, unhuman will and deadly purpose, the figure waited for the rest of the lights to go out in the tavern. At ten minutes after three, patience was rewarded. The glow behind the picture window extinguished. A side door opened and shut, and a shadow separated from the building and shambled down the alley.

The coupe's door opened, and a compact, athletic figure emerged into the dimly lit street. The young woman glanced both ways and trotted across, following the figure up the alley. With silent skill enhanced by superhuman agility, she sidestepped cardboard boxes and cats alike. Despite the deeper darkness, she could see as if the way was lit by a full moon. Her hearing, finely tuned on top of her superior talent, picked up every whisper of paper, every scuttle of tiny feet, every rustle of a wing. She didn't have to see her quarry; she should be able to hear him, as long as he didn't suspect—

Halfway down, she stopped. Something wasn't right. She turned her head, tuning, homing—there it was! Someone breathing—

He broke from behind a dumpster and took off at a dead run, scattering rats and garbage across the wet pavement. Even with Jenna's enhanced reflexes, he had a modest lead before she could take up the pursuit.

Block after block he led, dodging and darting to avoid her grasp. But she wasn't that eager for a fight. Not yet. She would wear him down a bit first. She changed her breathing to maximize endurance and followed for a while, not catching up but not falling back, either.

He showed some gumption, that was for sure. That, and training. She gave him a little more room to test his evasion technique, and no surprise, he showed her some tricks that she already knew, most likely picked up from the same instructor. She lost view briefly, twice, but picked him up again just as she had the first time, flushing him like quail from a thicket. No human could have picked him up, but Jenna was no human; she was better. The deadly chase went on, block after block. The man breathed in ragged gasps as desperation overtook him. A hand clutched at his side. There was no way he was getting away again.

An angry flash came over her at the thought of the betrayal that put them both in this situation, and Jenna put on a burst of speed. After three years, every suspicion was confirmed. This was the man who'd tried to kill them. *Time to play.*

Drawing a telescoping baton from her pocket, she caught up to him as he tried to duck down another alley. He spun with a snarl, a hand darting for his pocket. She closed in before he could draw his pistol, and went to work with the baton. Jenna broke his wrist with the first blow, and the second knocked him senseless. Stabbing out with her free hand, she grabbed his shirt and hauled him down, dragging him into the shadows.

He lay panting, whimpering in pain and fear as Jenna brought her face down close to his and hissed, "Let's talk about Tahiti, Hamet."

His eyes shot wide, and he began to gibber in a Middle-Eastern tongue. She placed a knee on his broken wrist. His complexion paled and he fell silent, teeth clenched in agony. "In English. I know who you work for."

"I didn't know it was you," he blurted, a grimace pasted on his features. "None of us knew. We just had orders—" He moaned as a spasm gripped his broken arm. She grabbed it and gave it a light twist. She was rewarded with a howl as the man bucked off the pavement.

She shoved him back down, brandishing the baton in his face. "Orders from whom?"

"You know as well as I." He moaned. "You get orders. You follow them. You don't ask questions."

"Is that right?" She snapped the baton down on his hand. A satisfying crunch echoed off the wall, accompanied by a shriek which was cut off by her wadded up bandana.

It got worse before it got better. Jenna didn't like that part of the job, but two things drove her on: justice, and vengeance. Jenna had to find out why The Pinnacle wanted one of their own dead, and Anna Spielberg deserved payback. Now, after three years, she was damned well going to get it. Occasional shadows drifted by the end of the alley, but at this hour and in this neighborhood, no one was going to get involved.

Hamet was tougher than she gave him credit for. By the time she got the information she wanted, there wasn't much left of him. But the answers came. They weren't what she wanted to hear, but the truth needed to be told. When she finally snapped his neck with a sharp twist from a rear naked choke, it felt anti-climactic. The trail she'd followed on her own for the last three years had finally come to its end. And with that end came the realization that Jenna had been trying to avoid for longer than that. Not all was well with her employers.

There were divisions among the Council. Not on the surface, for outwardly they still seemed to operate as united as ever in their cause for world peace. But underneath the placid veneer were machinations and plots. Whispers of sabotage and power plays chased each other through Jenna's mind as she strode from the alley and back up Seventh Avenue.

Somewhere in the power struggle, someone upline had made a mistake. They issued a kill order on the wrong person, and not just because of who Anna was. Dr. Spielberg had dedicated her life to the purpose of world peace. She saw it happening within just a few more years. It wasn't even that they tried to wipe out a seven-year-old girl as well. Sofi was as harmless as they come, a sweet, shy little thing with as much deadly potential as a pink frosted cupcake. Their worst mistake was in messing with someone assigned to Jenna Paine's protection.

As Jenna stalked away from the body, one thing hung in her mind: she would find out who on the Council issued the kill order on Anna. And when she did, they would face the full fury of a woman scorned.

Chapter Two

The next night, across the country, behind elaborately carved wooden doors, a centuries-old tradition unfolded as a single candle floated through darkness. A head, face hidden by a hooded cloak, glided beneath the single flame to the center of The Pinnacle's Council chamber, where waited a candelabra. As the lighter's candle touched the first wick, a chime, high and sweet, sounded. Once, twice, through seven times it rang, for each candle on the gold stand. On the seventh chime, two doors opened, one at each end of a dais raised at one end of the room. The lamplighter retreated through a massive double door at the other end of the chamber as two files of red-robed figures entered.

Overhead lights dimmed up, leaving the high ceiling concealed in darkness as the files of hooded people split up, filling rows of cushioned seats along the sides of the room. On the crimson-curtained walls behind them hung priceless masterpieces of Renaissance art, silent witnesses to the hallowed proceedings initiating before them. Van Gogh stared across at Reubens in silent consultation. Wyeth and Remington compared notes on wild grandeur with Leonardo.

The last seven to enter the chamber wore hooded scarlet robes similar to the others, with the singular exception of gold braided trim at the hems and along their daggered sleeves.

The low murmur of pleasantries stopped, shut off as if by a switch, when one of the Seven stepped up to a dark-stained wooden podium.

He raised a small gavel and brought it down with one sharp rap on a massive, dark-stained oak podium.

"Brothers and sisters, the Vision lives!" he announced in a booming voice.

"The Vision lives!" responded thirty-four voices in unison.

He punched a fist straight out. On the third finger glared a gold ring, ornately carved, set with a huge ruby. "*Praestat facere rex...*"

The others raised their own fists, adorned with similar rings. "It is better to make a king..."

"*...ac esse rex!*" He lowered his hand to his side.

"...than to be a king!" After completing the response, hoods were drawn back and the assemblage took their seats. These were the gods of finance and power. Oil magnates and shipping moguls, media giants and software tycoons met here and discussed. And decided. And what was decided, happened.

The leader produced a tablet computer and laid it on the podium. "We will begin with old business."

A slim figure on the dais stood and flipped back her hood. Long, straight black hair framed a triangular face with high cheekbones. Her golden complexion highlighted round, dark eyes. The wrinkles beginning to appear around her eyes and mouth only accentuated her beauty, making her look more distinguished and graceful than matronly.

The man at the podium never turned around. "The floor yields to Sirdar Karina Hattangadi of the Eastern Bloc." He stepped back.

She strolled forward and took the podium. In flawless English, she began. "Thank you, Mr. Bowman. I report: Thanks to Congressman Brady's ceaseless efforts, House Bill 3413 has come to a successful vote. A similar bill is on its way to the floor of America's Senate. President Collins has issued an order banning drilling in the last major oil preserve in the Great Plains. House Bill 3413, if passed, effectively seals America's reliance on Eastern oil for the foreseeable future."

She fixed the congregation with a determined look. "The bottom line: we now have exerted sufficient influence in America's legislatures and environmentalist groups to ensure the flow of petroleum though the Middle East exclusively. In the interest of peace, no single country may be allowed to achieve self-sufficiency again. All nations must realize we need each other. So far, we have kept the legislators and environmentalists from knowing about our grand plan, or about each other's role in it. This time we managed to work both ends against the middle, and it is yielding untold profits in progress toward The Vision."

A hooded man along one of the side walls rose. "Your Highness, what if HB 3413 fails to pass?"

"We have a team ready to go at a moment's notice, targeting three deep-water rigs in the Gulf of Mexico. Casualties will be held to a minimum, but the spill damage will ensure a public outcry against offshore drilling for generations to come." This brought nods and mumbles of approval from many in the room. "By the time those wellheads open again, we may be able to eliminate our need for petroleum products. At the very least, our plan for world unity will be too far advanced to stop." She withdrew and sat, drawing her hood back over her head.

The man who opened the meeting stood again and took the podium. "Thank you, Your Highness. I report: Bowman Communications continues to mitigate the fallout from Oregon and The Czech Republic through our newspapers, magazines, and television outlets. As long as we keep up this level of coordination, we will continue to maintain our secrecy behind an illusion of impartial reporting. Our informants in military and civil law enforcement agencies have been effective in weeding out any files and nuggets of information anyone can connect with us. Our secret is safe, and our Vision remains on track."

He dragged a stylus across the touchscreen on his tablet, consulting another set of notes. "Our influence on college youth is increasing by leaps and bounds through the Global Unification Alliance. A new paradigm on citizenship is emerging, replacing the old out-moded nationalism: world citizenship. Soon, so-called immigration laws will reflect that new citizenship, and the time will be ripe for us to complete our takeover."

Behind the podium another hooded figure stood; a short, round male. Bowman moved away again. "The floor yields to Mr. Bruce Wilkes."

Wilkes withdrew his hood as he stepped forward. Silver, buzz-cut hair gleamed in the dim light. He cleared his throat and paused before speaking. His refined British accent and basso-profundo voice commanded attention. "What glowing reports, thank you. Thank you all." When he smiled, his pencil moustache curled at the ends, making it look more like a sneer. "With all due respect, Mr. Bowman, ladies and gentlemen, not all is so rosy. We have a problem. The NADIA program has proven to be a dismal failure. It has taken well over ten billion dollars and thirty-plus years to initiate. We did experience some early successes, but its later stages yielded disastrous consequences. I'm afraid this program has run its course."

The smile faded as Wilkes' voice grew an edge. "The only question now is how to clean this mess up. We have several loose ends, most notably the NADIA unit itself. Mere months after it was brought on line, it dropped off the grid, only to reappear with scrambled programming. Then it disappeared again, and without quick thinking by one of our top agents, would have fallen into hostile hands."

He paused long enough to let that sink in, and heaved a dramatic sigh before continuing. "Speaking of this top agent, her own existence presents a threat as well, as I understand she was the prototype of the NADIA program, and has been engaging in questionable activity between assignments. We must erase every loose end and start over with our enforcement program before something else goes wrong."

Another man spoke up from one of the "peanut galleries" along the walls. "We have another problem, Mr. Wilkes."

Wilkes stopped, fixing the man with a stony glare. "I beg your pardon, Mr. Frost?"

"Dr. Anna Spielberg is deceased, killed by her own hand."

"I beg your pardon, sir, but under which rock have you been hiding? One of your own security teams discovered this three years ago."

"Her daughter is still missing, Mr. Wilkes."

"A small matter. Simply hack the police and medical facilities near her last known location—"

"Has it occurred to you that she bears a striking resemblance to her mother? Anna Spielberg has had no partners since her husband's death. Her medical records show a hysterectomy when she was thirty. Now, how do you suppose she could have obtained a young child so similar in appearance?"

Wilkes grabbed the edges of the podium. His voice remained calm, but his knuckles were white. "What problem would that present?"

Frost stepped into the center of the room. "The team that found Dr. Spielberg's body also found a pair of data transfer units similar to those used in her laboratory to transfer the personalities of dying people into living bodies."

Bowman stood. "Mr. Frost, you're out of order! How is this news meaningful after such a long time?"

Frost strode right up to the base of the dais. Turning to face the assembly, he spread his arms wide. "I detailed this knowledge in a timely manner, through channels. But perhaps someone" —he looked over his shoulder at Bowman— "may have lost my report. Therefore, I submit directly to this grand assemblage that I have information of a threat dire to our goal and mission. If I may be finally heard—"

"You will be allowed to speak in good time. Now, sit and wait your turn."

A tall, slim man came out onto the floor. "If Mr. Frost has such vital information, perhaps we should hear him now."

Bowman grasped the gavel and raised it. "I will have order in this hallowed meeting place!"

Choruses of "Let him speak!" were shouted down by others saying, "Let him wait!" After the gavel banged several times, the pandemonium slowed and stopped as everyone turned to the podium.

Bowman spoke in calm, patronizing tone. "Well, Mr. Frost, since you seemed to have hijacked our convocation, perhaps we should let you get it out of your system once and for all." He nodded at Wilkes.

The Englishman backed away from the podium. The look on his face would have melted uranium, but he nodded. "I yield the floor to Mr. Frost."

With a swagger that bordered on insolent, Frost ascended the lectern. "I believe Dr. Spielberg copied herself into a clone body to disappear for her own ends. Why would she choose to leave our fellowship but to mean us harm down the road? Her knowledge could set our mission back a hundred years. This child could expose us."

"It would be nice to know who signed the erase order on Dr. Spielberg," purred Bowman. "Perhaps the issue was taken up by someone below the boards?"

"Maybe the same person who smothered my reports for three years." Frost turned to lock Bowman's eyes in a contest of wills. The immoveable object met the irresistible force for tense seconds before the silence was interrupted from the floor.

"So where is this child?" a woman asked.

"Unknown. But on the day Dr. Spielberg died, one of our agents saw the doctor in the company of the construct known as NADIA Five."

The room erupted again in chaos. Above the din, John Bowman's voice boomed, "Order! Order!" What seemed an eternity later, the last of the protestors' voices died down.

"Mr. Frost, I'll take the floor, please." Bowman stepped back up to the podium, displacing the smaller man, who retreated to his seat. "Histrionics are not the solution to our problem. Our answer is obvious, and the situation plays more into our hands than you may realize. If they are together, we may take care of both situations in one precise strike."

Sirdar Hattangadi rose again. "Am I to believe you intend to carry on these attempts to recapture the NADIA—?"

"I want them found," Bowman said in a low growl. "I don't care what rock they're hiding under, Mr. Frost." He stabbed a finger on the podium. "Just bring them both to me, right here. Put our top agents on the job."

Frost stood. "You want us to bring them back alive?"

Bowman froze him with an icy glare. "I don't care *how* you bring them back, as long I can identify the pieces."

Chapter Three

The sound of a whinny through the trees made Nadia Velasquez put her screw gun down on the workbench. She looked out through the open garage door and down the packed earth driveway to the curve where it disappeared to connect with Route 78. A moment later, a tawny shape made its way through the jackpines and around the bend.

A tall, rangy man in jeans and a black T-shirt halted his buckskin outside the garage and dismounted. He tossed the reins over the hitching rail beside the door before taking off his wide brimmed leather hat to drag the sweat from his brow with a red kerchief. Tossing his black ponytail over his shoulder, he dragged a saddlebag off the stallion's back and strode into the garage. His leather-brown face wrinkled with a grin. "Bo-joo, Dee."

Nadia stripped off her right work glove and extended her hand with a warm smile. "Bo-joo, George. How's every little thing?"

"Good, thanks. I got some rabbit and venison in a cooler bag here. Wilma made a tea blend for you. I stopped and picked up that brandy you wanted, too."

"Oh, thanks so much! I have some beans and tomatoes for you in the kitchen, and I finished this week's newspaper column."

He nodded to the collection of pine boards on the workbench. "What you got going on there?"

"It's going to be a bird feeder. Sofi was supposed to build it with me, but..."

George nodded. "Yeah, she's off with Sammi again, isn't she?"

Nadia sighed and turned toward the kitchen door. "Ten years old, going on thirty. What a kid, right?"

George followed her into the modest kitchen and unloaded the saddlebags onto the counter next to the fridge. Nadia set out two plastic grocery sacks full of produce from the garden so he could pack them into the bags.

She put two large carrots on the counter. "Those are for Dally, just for putting up with you."

George cocked an eyebrow and pointed at her. "Hey, white squaw, brownies and horses go way back. Dally *lives* to serve me."

Nadia laughed with him. "Whatever you say, Geronimo. Tell Wilma I said hi, and if you see my daughter in your wanderings, tell her I want her home. Oh, before I forget..." He waited while she dashed into her home office. She grabbed a thumb drive from her desk and put it in his hand. "Tell Wilma, in next week's column I want to highlight the Redhawks' volleyball squad, unless she has another project for me." Nadia walked him back through the garage door to the buckskin's side. The horse nickered and tossed his head when she approached, extending his muzzle so she could stroke it as she held out another carrot. "One for the road, fella."

George threw the saddlebag back over Dally's rump and swung back into the saddle. "Okay, Dee. See you Wednesday." He wheeled the horse around to leave. "You know, it'd help if you got a phone up here and a wireless internet connection."

"So you keep saying. You guys know how I like my privacy. It's quiet here. I want to keep it that way."

George shook his head and nudged Dally into a brisk trot, waving as he rounded the bend and disappeared back among the jackpines.

* * * *

Dinner was cold on the table when the back door opened. Nadia put down her book and crept to the doorway leading to the kitchen. Sofi had the refrigerator door open, fishing out a can of cola. She wore black tights and a black long-sleeved jersey in spite of the late summer heat. Her hair was cut short again, and this time it was black with bright purple highlights.

Nadia lifted a letter from the cedar credenza in the living room and walked into the kitchen. "Did Mr. Weesaw see you today?"

Sofi flinched, ever so slightly, before answering. "No." She took out fixings for a cold venison sandwich before closing the fridge.

"I left your supper on the table."

"Oh. I thought that was yours."

"Oh, come on, Sofi. If that was mine, I would have eaten it already, don't you think? Now, why are you just coming home at eight o'clock at night?"

"I said I was going out with Sammi."

"I told you to be home in time for dinner, young lady—" Nadia bit back the rest of the response. This wasn't what she wanted to talk about. She took a deep breath before holding up the letter. "This came from the school."

Sofi shrugged and smeared whipped dressing on one slice of bread.

Nadia sensed the oncoming storm, but it was too late to avoid it, so she pressed on, heart thumping. "I told you not to sign up for sports."

"It's just volleyball. Everyone else plays, why can't I?" She laid a thick slice of roast venison on the bread and peeled the paper from some pepperjack cheese.

"Because..." *Careful, woman. Watch your mouth.* "Because you're only ten, and you're smaller than all the other girls."

"I'm bigger than Shelly Weesaw, and her dad's going to let her play." The girl's movements became more deliberate, her fingertips unsteady as she laid the top slice on her sandwich. "I can work out. I can get bigger."

"I said no, and I mean no."

When Sofi looked up, her blue eyes blazed hot. "Give me a good reason why! I want to know."

"Because it requires a physical, that's why!" Nadia wadded the permission slip into a ball and tossed it into the waste container. "You can't play because it requires a physical."

"And what's so bad about that?"

Think fast, Nadia. "You have…a condition."

"Is that why you won't let me join the chess club, too? Afraid I'll have a heart attack from moving all those huge plastic pieces around?"

Sofi jumped when Nadia slammed her palms on the table. "Don't you understand? Are you that stupid? You're a ten-year-old girl with an IQ of one hundred and sixty-five. You can't stand out!"

Sofi threw the sandwich across the kitchen. It landed with a splat against the wall next to Nadia and slid to the floor. "WHY? And what gives you the right to tell me *anything*? You're not my mother!"

"No, I'm not your mother. But you've called me 'Mom' for three years, and you're a minor child living under my roof. I think that gives me a right to say just about anything that needs to be said."

Sofi's hands balled into fists. "I *hate* you!" she bellowed, and stormed out of the kitchen. Nadia stood frozen until Sofi's bedroom door slammed.

Nadia sat at the table and buried her face in her hands. *Ten going on thirty.*

* * * *

Ten minutes later, the sandwich was scooped up and in the trash. Nadia stood outside Sofi's bedroom door, staring at a hand-scrawled cardboard sign that said, "KEEP OUT!" *Damage control. Why does it always come down to damage control?*

Things were so much easier when Sofi was seven. She accepted Nadia's word readily and did her part to blend in to this small community. As it was, they were "eccentric," simply preferring their privacy. That's what most people moved to the Upper Peninsula for anyway, right? To get away. From what or who was nobody's business, and for the most part no one asked questions. They bartered from their small garden for most of what they needed, and Nadia's job as a columnist for the local weekly paper picked up the rest of the slack. Sure, that meant a lot of rabbit and venison instead of beef, but that came with the cost of security. A cost that was quickly growing against a small girl.

She rapped lightly on the door and stepped back. A muffled, "Go away" pointed to the cardboard sign taped to the door. By the sound of things, Sofi'd been crying, and she was hiding under her covers. Again. *I swear, sometimes she's twenty, and sometimes she's five.*

"I'm coming in, honey." Nadia opened the door and slipped inside. A black light bulb burned in the floor lamp in the corner, throwing lurid slashes off of Day-Glo patterns painted on the walls. What wasn't painted pink, yellow, or orange, lurked in black shadow. A dark lump under the blankets betrayed Sofi's location.

Nadia sat on the edge of the bed. A sullen, half-hearted challenge fought its way through the quilted cotton. "I said go away."

"I know, but I thought you might be hungry." She reached up with a gentle hand and pulled the blankets back. Sofi's skin looked charcoal gray in the UV lamplight. When the girl opened her eyes, the whites stood out stark and blue, the irises an eerie black. Shining tracks ran down her cheeks. She looked up from the pillow, a pathetic frown pasted on her face. She didn't flinch away when Nadia brushed a tear from the corner of an eye.

"Sofi, I'd like you to eat before you go to bed."

"Do we have to talk?"

"Not if you don't want to." Nadia got up and went into the kitchen, leaving the bedroom door ajar. In a short time she had dinner warmed and brought it back in with a fresh glass of soda over ice.

Sofi sat up and accepted the plate. Several bites disappeared in silence. Nadia watched as she ate, all prim and proper like a little lady. The child took a drink from the glass, and when she put it back on the nightstand she looked up, meeting Nadia's gaze with disturbing evenness.

"Why did my real mom have to die?"

Nadia clenched her teeth for a minute before answering. *Would she understand the truth today? She's smart enough, God knows. But can she handle the emotional implications? How do you ask a ten-year-old to wrap her brain around the fact that she's a non-human and her mother built her to be a repository for her own mind and knowledge? What good would it do to tell her now? None.* "Sofi, we talked about this. The bad people—"

"The bad people were going to get her anyway, so she gave me to you and killed herself before they could? You've been telling me that since we moved up here. What kind of sense does that make?"

Damage control... "Your mother wanted to make sure you would be taken care of. And, I think, she got tired of running away."

"Are we running away?"

Nadia shifted uneasily. "Why do you ask that?"

"Mom, get real. We don't even have a phone. You have no internet. I'm surprised you even let us have electricity. We're still hiding from them, aren't we? You don't want them to track us down. If we could call Jenna, she'd take care of them like she did—"

"Jenna *is* one of the bad people, Sofi."

"No! She saved us from them, on the island!"

Nadia pulled the empty plate away and set it on the nightstand. "Honey, I'm trying to tell you—"

"Then don't lie to me! Jenna's *not* one of the bad people. If she was here, things would be better."

"How? How would it be better? You don't know about Jenna—" *Dammit, be careful, Nadia. Not too much!* Nadia bit back the rest of her response and stood with the plate. "I'll get these washed up."

Sofi stared into her lap, her hands limp. "Why won't you tell me everything, Mom? I just want to know."

"Honey, if I told you everything, you'd only be in more danger. Please, let me protect you."

"When are we going to stop hiding?"

Nadia stopped at the door. "I don't know, honey. I wish I did." She glanced at Sofi. The hurt and confusion in her eyes was almost unbearable but she had to be strong for both of them. "Good night. I love you." She closed the door behind her, leaving Sofi in her blacklit sanctum.

On the way to the kitchen, the question lingered in her mind: *When are we going to stop hiding?*

Chapter Four

Jon Daniels lay in bed and watched the little rainbow speck on the ceiling dance in time to the crystal wind chime swinging gently in the bedroom window. A stray gust through the open pane danced a brief tango with the curtain and brought in a fresh breath from the flower garden. *Her* flower garden. The sun was just coming over the tops of the trees, and the day was warming quickly.

He sat up and stretched, and then once more touched the place where Nadia used to be. It had been three years, but he couldn't seem to fight his way free, no matter how he tried. He knew he should move on. Everyone told him he needed to get back out, start dating again. But he couldn't help but feel like he was cheating whenever he tried. She was still out there, and she never said goodbye. She never said it was over, so it wasn't over.

He wondered if Nadia thought of him as much as he thought of her. *Does she feel this same empty spot? Does she dream, too? Who's there to talk her down?*

A light knock on his bedroom door snapped him out of his train of thought. A few polite seconds later, it opened. A pretty, petite Japanese-American woman poked her head through. Her black spiked hair sported bright fuchsia tips today, and she topped it off with a comb that had a head shaped like a tiny Japanese fan. "Hey, Bunny's fixing French toast—you want?"

"Yeah, sure. Thanks, Hushi." She ducked back out, closing the door. Jon shrugged into a shirt and hitched up his pajama bottoms before shambling into the kitchen. He grabbed his coffee cup from the hook on the wall and poured a cup of the strong, dark brew before sitting at the table. "Hey, Bunny."

"'Mornin' Jonny." The spindly little man pushed his coke-bottle glasses up on his nose and turned back to the stove. A sizzle later, he tossed a couple of thick slices of egg-battered Texas toast onto a plate on the counter.

Hushi swooped in and set it in front of Jon with a smile before turning to trade a quick kiss with her husband. "I'll stop by Irving's to see if they need anything from town."

Bunny brushed the tip of her nose with a fingertip. "Be careful, sugar." She bustled out the door into the summer sunshine, a tiny Animé character in a riot of hot pink and electric blue.

Jon finished his plate in silence and nursed his coffee over yesterday's paper. He got halfway through before laying it aside and spent several silent minutes brooding and doodling his fingertip through the ring of cold coffee where his cup had sat.

Bunny finished frying the French toast and took his place at the table. He forked down a few bites before saying anything. But he seemed to know exactly what Jon was thinking. Again. "You know, you coulda gone after her."

The conversation was getting old, but they'd gone through it so often it became the equivalent of their morning script, yet one more endless circle in a life of endless circles. "What good would it have done? Besides, I'm not the kind to chase after a woman like some love-struck teenager. If Nadia decides she wants me, she'll come back."

"So you're just gonna mope around here like some love-struck teenager instead? Jon, you gotta get a hobby—"

Jon slammed a hand down on the tabletop. The dishes jumped and clattered back down. "Then give me something on The Pinnacle, Bunny! We've been chasing ghosts for too long, and I'm tired of dead ends. The last breakthrough we had was a vague list of names that we couldn't attach to *any* of their activity over the last three years. I'm reading these—" He gave the newspaper a backhanded slap. "—and watching the world go to hell in a handbasket because of their insider schemes and poison propaganda, but I can't draw a direct line to anyone. Give me someone *solid* to go after so I can end this stalemate!"

Bunny held up his hands, palms out. "Whoa, Jonny-boy, slow down. I got names, as near as I can figure. I just ain't caught 'em with their hands in the cookie jar. You're the federal agent. That's your job."

Jon pushed his coffee cup away with a sigh. "I think I've had enough of this. Thanks for breakfast." He shuffled back down the hall to shower.

* * * *

Ten minutes later, Jon walked out the Kalinskys' front door into the sunshine of a Virginia summer day. The flower garden tantalized his nostrils again with its clean, fresh aroma. The soft buzz of honeybees faded behind him as he made his way across the clearing. When he reached the tree line, he turned around. White clapboard siding glowed happily in the sunshine. Green and yellow shutters flanked the windows. Wildflowers lounged in their beds around the foundation, the garish color combinations another of Hushi's unique touches. And at the far edge of the clearing, under the hardwood canopy, he could see the flower garden Nadia had built, now wild and overgrown, but still blazing with color.

Uncle Mike's cabin sat there, once upon a time. Right on that exact spot. The land was a gift to Bunny and Hushi. It wasn't as if Jon was using it for anything anyway. But all the same, there were a lot of memories there. Jon grew up with his uncle, spending every summer out here in the valley of the Shenandoah from his twelfth year to the day he left for college. Uncle Mike left the old wooden cabin to him, but it burned down in a Pinnacle attack not long after Mike was murdered. He'd helped put up the little cottage and moved in at Hushi's insistence. It only made sense, as he operated out of here anyway. *I guess it looks better for Hushi than if it had stayed a bachelor pad.*

A narrow footpath wound through the trees, shaded and cool in the late summer heat. A rabbit said hello by way of scurrying through the underbrush to parts unknown. A squirrel overhead chirred its irritation at an invading starling. Jon breathed in the woods all the way to the far end of the path where it emerged in front of Irving's cabin.

Jimmy DeBartolo sat on the porch in a creaking rocker, whittling. In his gnarled fingers, the body of a bird was taking shape. Jon paused to admire the work, noting how steady Jimmy's hands were, despite the outward ravages of age that had taken so many of Jimmy's generation already. *The devil knows he's going to have a fight on his hands when he comes for Jimmy, so he's just putting it off until the old coot's softened a bit. Like that's ever going to happen.* Next to the old man, against the wooden siding under the shelter of the porch, leaned a worn but sturdy Garand combat rifle. He looked up as Jon approached, and his wrinkled face split into a huge, toothy grin. "Hey, Jon."

"Morning, Jim. Another quiet day."

Jimmy's flint-hard eyes scanned the woods as he answered, "Thank the good Lord for that."

"How's Papa today?"

Jimmy grinned wider. "'Bout ready to kill Beth, I think."

"I think I'll say hi before I head downstairs."

"Okay, if you really want to. I'm gonna take a walk around."

The old man rose and picked up the rifle before stepping past Jon and onto the packed earth in front of the porch. He shifted it to an easy grip in his gnarled hands and slunk off through the woods with an easy, well-practiced stride. Seconds after he reached the tree line, he disappeared as if he were only a ghost in John's imagination. The only evidence of his presence was the half-formed wooden sculpture on the seat of the rocking chair.

Damn, I'm glad he's one of ours. I'd hate to be on that old man's bad side. Jon stepped through the screen door and into Irving Ratzinger's living room. Irving's easy chair, threadbare and sunken, hunched in its corner, empty. The comfortable clutter that defined the man's life was neatly arranged around it, the photo of his beloved Hilda within easy reach. Hilda's prize smallmouth bass leered from the wall above the old TV in the opposite corner. Irving's collection of dog-eared paperback westerns loitered on their shelves, separated from his how-to books and his Foxfire Series. Everything here made this cabin a home in every sense of the word.

Everything except one. The smell of Irving's latest culinary masterpiece was noticeably absent in the air. Even though it had been three months since the heart attack, Jon's nostrils remembered the scent of Irving's apple strudel, among other delicious creations from "Papa's" kitchen. How many glazed rolls had he washed down with German roast coffee around that table over the years? Not nearly enough, came the answer from Jon's stomach.

A woman's voice came from down the hall, frustration tempered by a good humor. "Lay back down, you old fart, and let me get your meds in."

Jon chuckled, imagining the struggle taking place as he made his way to Irving's room. When he opened the door, Papa was struggling to get out of bed. Beth Nelson was trying to wrestle him back down. She looked over her shoulder at the creak of the door hinges, a tuft of curly brown hair dangling in her eyes. In spite of the effort she was exerting against the old man in the bed, she smiled.

"Can you help me out here? I have to give him his shot."

Irving grabbed her wrists and sat up again. His German accent was thicker when he was this tired. "I said I was all right, young lady, and I want to get up." Beth twisted her arms free and pressed on Papa's chest again. He began to sweat with exertion. She was just plump enough to give her a weight advantage, especially with Irving's weakened condition, and the strain began to show.

When Jon decided enough was enough, he stepped in and touched Beth's shoulder. She let go of Irving and stood. "Papa," he said, "you know the shot makes you sleepy. So take it and get some more rest. Beth can handle lunch when you wake up."

The old man lay back, pouting. "The way she cooks? I'd rather eat my left shoe!"

Beth's eyes popped; her mouth gaped. She snapped back in mock indignation. "I'll have you know, sir, my meals are perfectly well-balanced examples of excellent nutrition—"

"That taste like old tires!" Despite the rough tone of Irving's voice, the twinkle in his eye told Jon he was just being difficult for the sake of mischief.

Jon said, "We can't all be gourmet chefs, Papa. You've had a rough time the last couple of months. It's not going to kill you to let someone else take care of you for a while. Besides, Beth's been a nurse for..." He shrugged, looking at her. "At least a month. When was it you took that correspondence course again?"

Beth threw a half-hearted punch at Jon's midsection, easily dodged with a laugh. "Thanks a bunch, you jerk. I'll have you know I got my RN from Stanford ten years ago." She turned back to Irving. "Please, Papa, I have to give you this shot. Donna says a couple more weeks and you should be as good as new. Or at least as good as before your heart attack."

Irving paused while he mulled it over. "Can I have it in my chair?"

"If Jon can move your monitor into the living room, I don't see why not." She gave Jon a coy smile and blinked her eyes.

"Gee, how can I say no to that," said Jon with a grin and a wink to Irving. "Let's go, then."

Five minutes later, they had the little man dressed and reclining in his easy chair. He settled back with a whuff of exertion. "Thank you. That room is too much like a hospital. I had to get out."

Beth clipped the pulse/ox monitor lead to his finger and prepped his arm for the injection. At Irving's request, Jon gave him the framed picture of Hilda to hold in his other hand. The needle slipped into his arm, and seconds later, he closed his eyes.

Beth gave Jon a quick hug. "Thanks. I got it now."

He squeezed her back. "How's he doing?" he whispered.

"He's obviously gaining his strength back. I think the Cardimase is doing exactly what Donna and Hushi designed it to do. Give Papa another couple of months, and he could have a young man's heart again." Beth shrugged and turned away. "If we don't run into any major side effects."

"Let's hope that doesn't happen. Look, I just came in to say hi before I head down to the bunker. If anyone wonders where I am, I'm working."

"Okay. Lunch will be at one." Beth walked into the kitchen and started a sink for the breakfast dishes.

Jon left the cabin and its sleeping owner, strolled around the back, and entered the weather-beaten woodshed. His hand found the lever in the darkened corner with the ease of habit. The secret door opened on silent hinges, and he followed the stairs down to the underground bunker that served as an emergency shelter, as well as the command center for their operation.

He hit the light switch at the bottom. In the glow from the overhead fluorescent, the common room revealed itself. Wood paneling lay over the concrete walls, providing some modicum of comfort. Crouching against the left wall was a small workbench under a four-foot by six-foot corkboard cluttered with photographs, printed sheets, and napkins scrawled with notes. A couple of wooden chairs sat next to the bench, at the edge of a large throw rug. Off to the left, a concrete-lined hallway led into gloom.

A flip of a switch at the end of the hall lit up doors on the left and on the right. At the far end of the tunnel, another staircase went up. Jon entered the first room on the right and turned on the light. A small counter and fridge greeted him. On the counter sat a coffee maker. He started a pot and walked back out into the common room.

Eleven people taunted him from candid photos tacked on the corkboard. Next to each was a printout. Jon put a finger on each photo as he named them out loud, a ritual he engaged in every time he came down: "John Bowman. Armando Lopez. Bruce Wilkes. Vladimir Kuznetzov. Bernadetta Caglioni. Noor Ah'halaami. Sirdar Karina Hattangadi." Four other photos were pegged to the board in a separate group. "Jenna Paine. Walter Brady. Alan Whitfield. Mark Boyle." Whitfield's and Boyle's pictures had thick borders drawn in red marker.

Footsteps on the stairs interrupted his thoughts. Bunny came around the corner and joined Jon at the board. Today's T-shirt said BYTE ME. When he spoke, his Brooklyn accent came through strong, showing how many late hours he'd put in on this data. "Whaddaya think, Jonny?"

Jon waved at the top group of photos. "I think we're up to our elbows in alligators. These people have more power and influence than most kings do. Are you positive these are the ones who built Nadia?"

"They're the ones who put in the order. I'd stake my life on it. They're all tied into the Global Unification Alliance. They dump tons of cash into it, on the order of billions a year, but they refuse to take a bow for all their little Boy Scout good deeds for the day. They're clients of Twin Oaks Spa, and none of them ever go there without at least two others."

The skinny little man touched a fingertip on the note beside each picture as he recapped. "Wilkes owns more ships than most third world navies. There ain't a thing comin' across the Atlantic that he don't approve. Lopez moves oil and cattle all over Mexico and beyond, and for some reason all the drug cartels leave him be."

"Maybe he's moving more than cattle and oil."

Bunny scowled deeper. "Or maybe they're all afraid of him, Jonny. Ever figure that?" He went on with his litany. "Kuznetzov started in electronics engineering and got into arms dealing about twenty years ago. Rumor is the Russian mob is his little lap dog. Caglioni owns Aeritalia Airlines and Itamax Clothing. Miss Noor Don't-Even-Ask-Me-How-To-Pronounce-It is a secret majority holder of Vandalore Industries, and a half-dozen other major conglomerates. She *farts* dollar bills, Jonny. In secret, of course. And our friend the Sirdar swings a bigger stick in OPEC than anyone wants to admit. She's a sly one, that."

Bunny sat in one of the chairs and spun it so he faced Jon. "Bowman we know. Dude *owns* the news. He paid Nadia's hospital costs from the time she came alive 'til Twin Oaks released her. So he knows about her, and he was the one who sent her to Iran to 'interview' President Javad."

Jon interjected, "That implicates him in the murder of President Bello in Nigeria, because another NADIA was used in that assassination. We have the video to prove it."

"But to bring him down, Jonny, we have to bring Nadia forward, show the world that she's an artificial person. So unless you wanna give her up, you gotta catch him some other way."

"We need one more person on our side, to get through his mask." Jon fingered the photo of Jenna again. "If we can turn her, she may help."

Bunny shook his head. "That's like reasoning with a rattlesnake. You met her twice, and you're lucky to be alive."

"Exactly. She doesn't want to kill me for some reason. I think I could talk with her, if I could just find her."

"If you're an example of what she does to people she likes, I'd hate to see what happens to people she *don't* like."

"You've seen it, Bunny. Mark Boyle, the man who took the girls hostage. She popped his head with one shot. I wouldn't be so sure she didn't do Whitfield, too."

"Still think she had somethin' to do with that breakout in Vegas?"

Jon nodded. "The Air Force thought they had Nadia. Three dead Air Commandos and a crashed police car later, and suddenly they have nothing. Jenna and Nadia have similar builds, and they had the same hair color and style then. I think that's too much of a coincidence, don't you?"

Bunny pushed his glasses up on his nose with a nervous finger. "You sure you wanna get within ten miles of that?"

"We have to start somewhere, Bunny. I can't touch the big wheels yet. The OSI wants solid proof before they can call out the dogs. Jenna could be just what the doctor ordered." Jon went into the kitchenette and filled two cups as the conversation continued.

"So you want I should change my search to her?"

"We've hit nothing but dead ends on the others. We sure couldn't lose."

"What would the Doc say?"

"I'll make it right with Donna. She's the team leader, but I'm still the chief investigator."

"Okay, buddy, it's your neck. Myself, I wouldn't feel safe on the same *land mass* as that woman."

Handing one cup to Bunny, Jon took a sip from his, swishing the brew around in his mouth before answering. "I didn't say I'd feel safe, Bunny. But she's our best chance."

"Suggestion—if we can't find her, there's one sure way to get hold of her."

"Do I even want to ask?"

"We get her attention and let her find us."

A vague sense of dread rose in Jon's chest as he sighed and rubbed his neck. "Yeah, I was afraid you'd say something like that."

Chapter Five

Sofi sat on the cliff's edge and dangled her feet over. Two hundred feet below, Lake Superior slammed into the polished stone base and fell back in undulating fury. Her eyes scanned the horizon, watching the big ships ply the waters of the Great Lakes waterway. She could recognize each freighter by its outline, even at great distances. Her best friend Samantha Webster joked that Sofi had binoculars for eyes. Sofi only knew she could see farther and pick out more details than anyone else.

A couple miles out, the *Mary Danforth* cruised by with another load bound for Cleveland. To the west, a familiar silhouette followed in *Danforth's* wake. She was the "new kid on the block," having just launched this spring. Sofi turned to look over her shoulder at the red-haired girl lying prostrate in the grass behind her. "Sammi, where is the *E.M. McSorley* bound?"

Sammi tapped the screen on her tablet computer a few times and read, "Gary, Indiana. She's hauling iron pellets for U.S. Steel." Sammi was two years older than Sofi, and stood almost a head taller, but they both knew who the real leader was between them. Sofi was tiny, but she was smart, smarter than some grownups they knew. It was Sofi who had figured out how to hack into the Munising Freight Yards' database and access manifests and destinations for all the ships that plied that port. She then delegated the job to Sammi, mainly because the task bored her.

A fresh gust blew a stray, neon blue lock of Sofi's hair into her eyes. She brushed it away with a sigh. "I wish I was on her."

"Why?"

"Because at least she's going somewhere besides here."

Sammi made lazy circles in the air with her feet as she tapped on the touch screen. "On *that* thing? Wouldn't you rather be on a yacht? That's just a stinky old freighter."

"I'd take a bathtub, if it took me somewhere else."

Sammi picked a blade of grass and held it between her thumb and forefinger, brow furrowed in concentration as she spoke. "This isn't such a bad little town."

"Have you ever been outside it?"

"Why would I want to?"

Sofi turned her back on the ships to face her friend. A shoreward wind gusted up and over the cliff edge, bringing with it the fresh, crisp scent of the churning surf beneath. She closed her eyes and imagined another place with surf, and a tinge of salt in the air. "If I'd told you the places I've seen, you'd never believe me."

Sammi chuckled. "Like where?"

"Tahiti, for one. Budapest, Prague, Berlin. Places you only see on maps. I've been to those places. I want to go again."

"When were you in Tahiti, silly?"

"I was there with my mother. They have this thing where you can swim with dolphins in the ocean."

"What else? You can read that on a tourist pamphlet. Tell me something you'd know only from being there."

"Okay, smarty—" Sofi's voice caught as a memory crashed into her brain, her last day in Papeete. Jenna fighting the men who'd shot her mother. Jenna pulling the limo into the emergency room. Mother and Sofi, both painted in Mother's blood as the doctors pulled them from the car... Her arms prickled and a hot wave rushed through her. *I could tell you. I really could. But Mom said that would bring the bad people back.* Her mother, lying dead in the apartment in Prague as Nadia packed a suitcase for Sofi. *"Come on, honey. It's time to go."*

"Well?" Sammi gave an impatient shrug.

"Nothing," said Sofi. "You just... Nothing. You wouldn't believe me." She stood, brushed grass and pine needles from her jeans, and stretched. "I better go home and face the music."

"Why are you so sure you're in trouble?"

"Oh, come on. You know Mr. Medawis sent a George-Gram. I'll bet Mom's reading it now."

"Wait." Sammi shut down her computer and rose. She slid a smartphone from her pocket and handed it to Sofi. "Here. It's a present."

Sofi held out a hand to receive it. In a small, grateful voice, she said, "Thanks." It felt warm and heavy in her hand.

Sammi fetched a wall charger from a pocket on her computer case and handed it over as well. "Now we can talk whenever we want to. I'll cover your minutes from my allowance."

"Why?"

Sammi tucked a stray lock behind an ear. Her smile was simple, but held a hint of sadness as well. "I just want someone to talk to, sometimes. Dad's too busy, and Juni's too stuck up. I don't have anyone else. My number's already programmed in."

"Okay. I'll call you later, then." *Mom's going to kill me.* Another voice spoke up, a niggling little whisper. *Not if she never finds out.* Sofi stuck the phone in a pocket and tucked the charger in another, pulling her jersey down to hide the bulges. A warm thrill ran through her middle as she turned toward the trees. Mom wasn't the only one who could have secrets.

* * * *

Sofi came out of the woods, following the game trail that ran past the back door. It wasn't that she was sneaking in, hoping to avoid a confrontation altogether. She knew that wasn't going to happen. The girl just wanted to put it off as long as possible, especially after having such a good afternoon with her only friend. Besides, there was no way she could sneak in the screen door. The spring made this nasty stretching, pinging noise every time it opened. She hadn't figured out a way past it yet. She'd tried unhooking it on the way out, but Mom always found it and hooked it back up again.

So Mom was going to hear her coming in the back door, and she would probably be waiting there with the note. Again.

Sofi entered the garage via the small door and climbed the concrete step to the back door, sighing in resignation.

She just started to move the door when she heard Mom's voice. "Come in here, young lady." *Yep, just what I thought. So much for delaying the inevitable.*

Sofi opened the door and entered the kitchen.

Nadia sat at the table, her hands steepled in front of her face, as if in prayer. "Sofi, is there something you want to tell me?"

"Why would I want to say anything? You might as well just ground me now, and save us both the time wasted on discussing it."

Nadia dropped her hands to the table, and the note lying there. "Because I want to understand why you're behaving this way. You're failing classes when we both know how smart you are. You're skipping class, starting fights—"

Sofi remained standing just inside the kitchen door. "Why do you even care?"

"Who took the first punch?"

"Does it matter?"

Nadia rose to her feet. "Of course it matters. If you were just defending yourself, it's different—"

"And what if I was just pissed?"

"Watch your mouth, young lady—"

Sofi's hands balled into fists. "Or what, you'll ground me? Oh, now I've done it—"

Nadia's voice rose in anger. "We can't afford to stand out—haven't you figured that out by now? Do you *want* them to find us? What do you think will happen when they do, invite us to tea? They want to kill us, Sofi!"

"Anything's better than sitting here just hiding! I'd rather *be* dead than keep sitting around waiting for it to happen!"

Nadia stormed around the table. Before Sofi could back away, Nadia grabbed her by the shoulders and shook her. A strange, harsh light was in the woman's eyes. Her hands trembled even as her fingers dug in. "Don't you ever say that! Don't you know what it's like to lose—?"

"Yes!" Sofi screamed, "Yes! I watched them shoot my mother!"

Nadia's mouth worked fruitlessly as her hands dropped. The sudden release of pressure on Sofi's shoulders was almost as painful as the grip the older woman had on her. Nadia's face went slack, like some colossal idea just occurred to her, but then she just went blank. "M-mother…" Nadia staggered back, a distant, hollow look in her eyes. "Mother baby d-deer…"

The anger seeped out of Sofi, replaced by confusion. "Mom, what—?"

Nadia fell to the floor, her chest heaving. She opened her mouth and a strangled cry lurched from between her lips. Her head fell back, neck muscles tensed, and her limbs began to thrash. She kicked the metal and formica table across the kitchen. It crashed against the counter and fell over. Nadia's head slammed into the floor again as her back arched.

"Oh my God, Mom!" Sofi rushed to Nadia's side, knelt, and held her head steady so it wouldn't bang anymore. But she couldn't do anything more to stop everything else.

The thrashing continued for several more heart-jarring seconds before Nadia's body finally relaxed. She lay still, sucking breath after breath in a moaning delirium.

Sofi's hands shook. She couldn't stop the tears that welled up from her soul as the fear took hold. "Mom? Talk to me, please." She lifted one of Nadia's eyelids. The eye beneath wandered, uncomprehending of its surroundings. "Mom, say something."

The words were slurred, barely legible. "Deena? Deena, baby—"

Sofi stroked a sweat-soaked strand of hair from Nadia's eyes and felt her forehead. *She's so hot, what do I do?* "No, Mom, it's me."

Nadia's eyes opened. "S-Sofi—" she muttered. "Sofi, honey…"

"I'm here, Mom, it's me, I—" Sofi's breath caught in her throat. Nadia had bitten her lip during the seizure, and now—*Oh my God, the blood. The blood's white—*

Chapter Six

Jenna led the way up the stairwell of the Westlake Plaza Hotel in D.C., confident Phil had her back. This was a simple snatch job. The syringe Jenna had tucked away in her blouse pocket should be all they needed.

She didn't need to check her watch. Her internal timepiece was always accurate. 3:45 a.m. *Perfect. Now, if the room number is right, we'll be in great shape.* She pulled the card key from her pocket as they approached the door. Phil backed across the hallway, ready to charge should the privacy bar happen to be thrown. Jenna took a deep breath, eased the card into the slot, and paused. Closing her eyes to dilate the pupils, she nodded at each beat in the countdown. *Three, two, one, now!*

She snatched the card upward. When the lock clicked, she threw the handle down and shoved. The door opened easily. Jenna's world shifted into an eerie slow motion as she slipped noiselessly into the darkness beyond. A normal human would have been hampered without night vision gear, but to Jenna, the room lay suffused by a pale wash of light through the partially-opened shade. She picked out the shapes of the television stand, dresser, bed— *empty!*

A rustle from the left announced the shadow emerging from the closet. As she turned, the light from the hall flooded her eyes, but she could see enough to know this wasn't the one for whom they'd come. Just as her brain screamed *"Trap,"* the other raised a pistol.

Jenna dove to the right as the shooter fired. The silenced shot whizzed by her left shoulder and thudded into the wall next to the dresser.

Jenna straightened and sprang straight into her attacker's face, fists swinging as she rose. Her left hook made contact and a feminine grunt answered the sting in her knuckles. She tried to finish the combination with a right hand, but the punch whiffed through empty air. A smashing blow landed on her ribs and something hard slammed into her head. *More than one, there's more than one!* "Phil, I need—!" Another blow landed to her body, and a man's arms wrapped around her from behind.

She snapped her heel up into his groin and he let go with a sick grunt. Something moved to her left. Jenna's lunge punch hit something soft. The other woman fell onto the bed.

To her left, the open door beckoned. Jenna lunged for freedom, but a hand grabbed her ankle. The air left her in a rush as she landed. The woman was on top of her like a harpy, clawing at her face from behind.

Jenna rolled and threw a fist that crashed into the woman's face. Bone gave with a satisfying crunch. A shrill cry of pain bounced off the walls as her attacker rolled away. She lashed out with feet, found a throat, yanked away, and rolled, letting her momentum carry her to her feet. The other thrashed on the floor, strangling on her shattered windpipe.

A pistol cleared leather with a leathery rattle. Zeroing in on the source of the sound, Jenna charged, a whirling blur of fists, elbows, and feet. A shot went off. Something slammed into her body just as her elbow struck the base of the man's neck. There was a sickening *snap*, and a thud as Phil's body hit the floor.

Jenna staggered back into the hall, feeling the burn spread through her torso. No sound overrode the roaring in her ears. *Shot. Dammit, Phil, why?* Several other doors opened. Furtive, curious eyes followed her from sheltering shadows, not daring to let themselves be drawn into the deadly scene.

She couldn't breathe. At every inhale, spasms of fire shot through her torso. A hot stream flowed from the hole. Her mind raced. She had to remember what happened. *Phil and Gerda. A setup. I'm...* She made it to the stairwell at the end of the hall before collapsing in a broken, senseless heap.

* * * *

Jenna's eyes opened on a world of white. Some machine nearby kept a steady cadence of short beeps. Her fingertips were strangely numb, and her head felt like it was stuffed with cotton. *Painkillers. Probably morphine.* Even through the haze, Jenna hurt. The hard part was sorting out exactly *what* hurt, and what didn't. The left side of her head throbbed in time with every beep of the heart monitor on the wall. From her neck to her knees was a solid sheet of pain. But she was alive. That meant Gerda and Phil were dead.

So it was official. She was out, The Pinnacle's equivalent of being fired. *What day is it? How much time have I lost? I have to get out of here. They'll find me. They'll forge police credentials and check emergency departments for Jane Does with gunshot wounds. I figure I have—* A fresh spasm of fire shot across Jenna's abdomen, making her draw in a sharp breath. Squinting hard, she gripped the bars of the side rails and forced the agony back toward its cage inside her. *I have about a day before they find me. Well, I'm not going to be here when they come.*

She listened closely. The bustle of a normal day on a hospital floor was all that greeted her ears. The nurses' and aides' steps were brisk. Their loose cotton scrub pants made a distinctive *switch* sound with every step. Family and visitors walked more slowly by, and she could hear their low-toned mumbles as they sought particular rooms or discussed their loved ones' conditions. Another sound filtered through the bustle: A page turning, weight shifting in a folding chair, right outside the door. Probably D.C. Police. If they found out she was awake, she'd find herself talking to a detective about why she was wearing dark clothes and carrying a syringe of propofol, and walking around with no ID in the wee hours of the morning. *I'd best be moving on, then.*

Getting up would be the hard part. For one thing, she was hooked into IVs and monitors. If she disconnected, someone would be in here in a New York second, and she was in no condition to fight anything stronger than an angry kitten. For another thing, she was wired for stereo to that bank of monitors on the wall of her room, and no doubt there was a repeater at the nurse's station. Then there was the cop outside the door. The window wasn't an option. She wasn't sure what floor the room was on, but it was high enough, judging from the sound level of the street traffic.

Jenna shifted her grip on the bedrails and pulled herself up. She was already sweating from pain and exertion when she swung her feet over the edge. Fire branded her side again. She fought back a moan as she slid to the floor. Holding the rail for support, she stood for a few seconds. The bed invited her back in for a rest. When she took a step, the floor tried to make the same suggestion. Jenna compromised, sagging to her knees on the cool tile. Her head roared as her vision swam.

Her breath came in ragged gasps as she bit back the pain slashing at her side. Struggling to her feet, she fought to regain control. Her knees shook as she stood. *I can't...can't stay... Deep breaths, Jen.* She inhaled sharply. A fresh spasm of pain ripped her. *Oh, damn. Bad idea...*

A single, burning tear traced down her cheek, mingling with the sweat beading on her face. *Calm. Slow. Try again.* She tried again, drawing a slow, easy breath. It still felt like a tiger trying to tear her side out, but she managed, and sank further into her training. Moment by moment, one by one she overrode the pain circuits in her body. She couldn't get rid of it altogether, but she could function.

In the small cabinet next to the bed, she found gauze, tape, and scissors. She snipped the tape holding the IV tube to her arm and withdrew it, and then dressed the puncture with a gauze square and a strip of tape. *That's one thing. Now for these monitor lines.*

There was a small closet in the room just out of range of the lines and wires. A wire-framed chair sat next to the bed. She could reach that. An idea began to form in her mind. There was, however, one remaining problem. Her clothes were gone, and all she had on was an open-backed gown. *Great. I'll be sure to go far with my butt hanging out all over the place.* After another minute of thought, one thing was becoming abundantly clear. The pain med was beginning to wear off. Jenna was functional now. In another half hour, God knew what she was going to be going through. *Okay. One thing at a time. Let's rock.*

Jenna took a slow, deep breath and ripped the monitor wires from her chest and arm. Then she grabbed the chair and, with a monumental effort, slung it at the window. It crashed through the glass as she ducked, half-falling into the tiny closet. She barely got the closet closed before the room door opened and the hospital equivalent of the Keystone Kops poured in. Someone shouted, "Oh my God, she jumped!"

A half dozen others talked at once, adding to the pandemonium. "Do you see her?"

"Where is she?"

"It's straight down!"

Biting back the new rush of pain, Jenna opened the closet a crack and saw everyone's back. She slipped into the hall unnoticed and found the clean utility room a couple doors down and across the hall.

By the time anyone thought to call a lockdown on the hospital to find their missing patient, Jenna was already on the street in a stolen set of scrubs. At the corner, she oriented herself. Luck was with her. She was only a couple blocks from the hotel—and her car.

The spare key was still in its hiding place under the bumper. The engine started on the first try, and in another twenty minutes she was parked across the street from a company safe house in a quiet residential neighborhood. A single electric candlestick burned in a front window. The rest of the house was dark. *A single light. All clear, no active alerts. That won't last long.*

Jenna parked in the driveway and got out. The key was under the false stone beside the door. Inside, she turned off the candle before turning on the porch light to indicate an occupant. It would buy her a little time to gather herself. Just enough for another stretch.

The med had worn off completely, and the pain tiger was free of its cage inside her, tearing at her with burning claws. She had to crawl up the stairs to the bathroom where medical supplies were kept. With shaking hands, she prepared a syringe of dilaudid and gave herself a half-dose, just enough to take the edge off. Then she stripped. Starting with her abdomen, she took off her dressings. After cleaning the blood from the wound, she groaned out loud. She'd torn several sutures from where the doctors had opened her up to fix her. The bullet had hit her on the left, down low. It missed anything important, but her side was still an ugly, bruised mess. The front incision was about six inches long. Gritting her teeth at the stretch, Jenna put a hand on her back. There was an exit wound as well. "Dammit, Phil, why did they send *you?*" A sudden sob escaped her throat, the first crack in the dam of her will, and before she knew it, her soul was pouring through that hole like a summer flood through a Mississippi levee.

She didn't know how long she'd spent hunched over while the grief wracked her body. Every sob, every sigh, tensed her stomach muscles and ripped at her wounds afresh. But she couldn't stop. Phil was one of the very few people she'd ever called "friend." Upline had no damned business making him the hatchet man. Now he was dead, at her hands. Her own people wanted her dead, and she had no one else to whom to turn.

Presently, control returned. She fought the rest back, and turned back to the task at hand. A few improvised butterfly tapes tacked the incision back together. She packed two new pads on her abdomen, securing them with a fresh wrap of gauze. By the time she got around to her face, the meds were making her sloppy. She just left the dressings off once the dried blood was cleaned up.

The woman in the mirror looked like hell. A cut on her cheek ran through the middle of a huge purple bruise that covered the right side of her face. Her right eye flamed bright red around the blue iris. Her lips were twice their normal size, and she was missing a tuft of hair from above her left ear. Bruises and welts covered a good share of everything else. *Jesus, I'm a freaking zombie.*

A noise downstairs made her freeze, heart pounding so loud the neighbors must have heard. The front door creaked open under a hesitant hand. A floorboard creaked. Jenna counted, tuning her ear. *Just one.*

Her hand automatically went for the medical kit and came back with a scalpel just as the bottom step groaned under a careful foot. *About a hundred seventy pounds.* Her mouth went dry. Fear constricted her throat, quickly replaced by anger. *I swear they're going to know they had a fight before I go down.* Jenna crouched by the tub, adrenaline surging, ready to spring—

A figure crept up the hall and stopped in the open bathroom door. A kid, no more than eighteen, stared slack-jawed at Jenna. His hands hung limp at his sides. A dozen concepts fought each other across his face. Lust at the sight of her naked body, revulsion at her condition, fear of the blade in her hand, and when he looked into her eyes, they all came together and made his face a mask of shock. She couldn't blame him; for all he knew, he'd landed smack in the middle of the latest slasher flick. If it didn't hurt so much, she would have laughed.

Jenna rose, keeping the scalpel ready. "What do you want?"

His eyes darted nervously, avoiding her as if he'd just caught his own mother naked. "I, uh..." The teen backed away, flattening against the wall opposite the door.

A petty thief, then. A company man would have killed her without thinking twice. She took a step forward. "Get out, or I'll call the police." With her free hand she pointed to her broken body. "I'll tell them you did this to me."

His hands came up in supplication as he stammered, "No, okay? I'm goin'." He disappeared, and Jenna took a breath as his feet pounded down the stairs and out the door.

She "bumped" the painkiller with another shot and double-checked the deadbolts on front and back doors before sliding under the covers in the master bedroom. She set the TV to a news channel and lay back as the med kicked in. Bowman's talking head of the hour was just finishing his twist job on the attack at the hotel by painting it as a drug deal gone bad, and the screen faded for commercials.

The adrenaline was working its way out of her system, and her eyes drifted closed a couple times before she noticed the banner scrolling across the bottom of the screen. Something about the words caught her attention. Shaking her head, she read, instead of the expected local headlines, a personal message. "Miss Paine, I must meet with you. See me tomorrow, where we first met. JD." The message repeated several times before the banner was cut off. The talking head paused, looked off-screen for a moment, and then turned back to his audience. "Ah, we apologize for the, ah…technical difficulty. Now, back to the news…"

She could only assume it was for her. It was within Kalinsky's style to hack the network's banner feed and post something off the wall. "JD" could be Jon Daniels. But why would they want to talk to her? Daniels swore to arrest her the last time they'd met, and she would be powerless if he confronted her now.

On the other hand, she couldn't stay here more than a few more hours before The Pinnacle caught up with her. If she wanted to live, the only safe place was in the hands of her former enemy.

Mentally, she ran back the clock. The first time she saw Jon was at La Guardia Airport in New York. Jenna was part of the team sent to recover NADIA V when she went off the grid. They found her at… what gate was it? NADIA was near the gate for a flight to Baghdad, via London. Who else knew? Everyone else on that team was now dead. Daniels wasn't even considered a factor until some time afterward.

Jenna clicked the TV off and eased herself deeper under the covers. As she closed her eyes for the night, she thought, *Alive and busted is better than dead, I guess.* She set her internal alarm for seven o'clock and closed her eyes. In seconds, she settled into an uneasy sleep.

Chapter Seven

Terminal C, Gate 55 at LaGuardia International buzzed with the level of boredom only possible in an airport. Jon paced the concourse, occasionally running his fingers through his short brown hair or resting his chin in his hand. She had to come. *She'd better come. If she stood me up and sent some of her buddies, I may as well call ahead and reserve my casket. Did she even notice Bunny's message?*

The next flight to London wasn't due out for another forty-five minutes. A red-haired young woman curled up in one of the vinyl-covered seats, resting her head on her boyfriend's shoulder. A long-haired college student in jeans and a leather jacket typed away at his laptop. Other men in business suits worked at their own computers, talked on their cellphones, or read. Older couples passed the time, some in comfortable, intimate silence, and others in cold apathy.

Jon spoke into his Bluetooth. "Bunny, I don't see her."

"Maybe she didn't get your message."

"You must have rolled that banner fifty times before they cut it off. If she was within a hundred feet of a TV any time yesterday, she should have seen it."

"She's only ten minutes late, Jonny. Give her a few more minutes before pullin' the plug. Now shut up. You don't wanna spook her if she is there."

Out of the crowd rushing past, someone bumped into Jon. He turned, and a small girl of about twelve stood holding out a piece of paper to him. As soon as he took the note, she ran away. He unfolded it and read: *Ditch the phone and go to Gate A-47.* "Bunny, I have to hang up. Talk to you later." Before the other man could answer, Jon disconnected and pulled his earpiece off. His heart thumped harder. *She's here. Now, I only have to make sure I live through the rest of the day.*

At Gate 47 on the A concourse, he waited another ten minutes. A wheelchair approached him bearing a bundle of loose clothing in a wide-brimmed, veiled hat. The woman, face obscured by the veil, croaked, "Jonathan, it's been so long. Give your grandma a hug."

A chill slithered up Jon's spine. He scanned the area. No one in the crowd around them noticed, or paid any attention whatsoever. As he bent down, her voice changed. It was Jenna, but she sounded strained, tight. She whispered into his ear, "Get me the hell out of here, and if you aren't straight with me, I'll make you suffer before I kill you."

He whispered back, "Gee Grandma, you have such a way with words." Grabbing the handles of the wheelchair, he pushed it toward the main parking area. On the way out, he mumbled, "Long time no see. I suppose I should ask how you've been, but I honestly couldn't care less."

"Thanks for your concern," she said. Her voice was so weak Jon had to lean down just to hear. "We'll take your car. I assume you're still FBI?"

As he pushed her along, he scanned the crowd. No one paid any undue attention to them or changed direction as they passed. *We're not being followed. What's wrong with this picture?* "Actually, no. I transferred to Air Force OSI after our little party at Twin Oaks. It gives me even more super powers. So what have you been up to, Jenna? Conquer any countries lately? Maybe torture a puppy or two?"

"God, Jon, you are such an ass. Now I suppose you're going to try to arrest me again?"

"That depends on you. Let's just talk and see what happens from there."

At his car, Jon unlocked the doors and waited on the driver's side for Jenna to get out of the chair and climb in. She just sat in the chair in her disguise until he lost patience and came back around. He flipped the hat from her head. "Okay, you can dump the old lady act—" He took in her disheveled hair, the bruises and stitches on her head, her pale skin, and a hot wave of shock washed over him, mixed with shame. He tried to think of something appropriate to say, but all that come out was a gasp, followed by, "You look like hell."

"Way to compliment a lady, Agent Daniels." Her face twisted in a grimace. Her trembling hands clutched at the chair's armrests. "I need a little help getting up."

Jon opened the passenger door and helped her in, and then got in and started the engine. "Do you need a hospital?"

"No." She grunted, settling into the seat. "But if you could line me up with some painkillers and a place to lay low for a couple of days, I'll be a happier girl."

"Would you at least tell me what happened to you?"

"Bad day at work. Just get me out of here, will you? No hospitals. Can't be seen in public." Her voice was getting weaker; she was slurring her words. Sweat beaded on her forehead. Jon swerved out into traffic, and she moaned with the sudden movement. "You've a doctor workin' with you. Take me there."

"Okay, but I'll have to blindfold you."

"Don' worry," she slurred, "I'll prolly be unconjus in few minuz. Zis seat lay back?"

Jon stole a glance at her as he swung onto an entrance ramp. Her face looked like school paste and her jaw hung open. She was breathing, for now, but the last time he saw someone that pale, they didn't live much longer. *Dammit, girl, don't you die on me.* He put his magnetic rotator light on the car's roof and goosed the accelerator. As soon as he hit a clear stretch on the interstate, he called Donna Hermsen. "Boss Lady? We have a problem."

"What is it now? Are you followed?"

He double-checked his mirrors. "Doesn't seem to be an issue. Donna, I've got Jenna Paine—"

"And who's got who tied up this time?"

"Ha, ha. No, seriously. She's hurt, bad. I think she just passed out."

"What did you do to her?"

"I didn't do anything, she came in like this."

Donna's voice was tight with tension. "Make sure it's not a trick."

"Oh, it's no trick. She looks like hell."

"Well, what's wrong? Have you checked her out?"

"Hang on." He pulled over. "Okay, what do I do?"

"Weren't you a boy scout?"

"It's been a long time, Donna. You're a doctor—"

"A physiologist, not an MD. Hang on, Beth is here."

Jon clipped his Bluetooth to his ear as he ran around the front of the car and opened the passenger door.

Beth's voice sounded in his earpiece. "Okay, what's she look like?"

He felt her head. "Fishbelly white, her face is clammy. She's got fresh stitches on the side of her head and bruises all over the place."

"Check her pupils—make sure they dilate evenly."

Jenna didn't even twitch when he thumbed her eyelids up. "They look the same size. They react to light."

"There has to be something else going on. Is she bleeding anywhere else?"

"Hell, I don't know, she's dressed up in a huge grandma sweater—" He saw the stain on his car seat and cursed. "Beth, she's bleeding. Hang on—" He lifted the sweater and saw the dressing on her torso. "She's got a huge bandage on her waist, and it's soaked through with blood."

"Fresh, or clotted?"

"It's soaking with fresh blood."

"Dark or bright red?"

"It's bright red."

"How much is flowing?"

"It's just seeping right now."

"It's an active bleed, but it's not an artery. Okay, don't peel it away, but tell me what color is the skin around the edges of the dressing?"

"There's some bruising, but not too bad."

"Is the area hard and swollen?"

When he reached out to feel her side, Jenna grabbed his wrist. She looked straight into his eyes. "Wha' th'hell you doin'?"

"I'm seeing if you'll survive a four-hour drive."

"If I don', I prolly d'serve it. Le's go."

Beth said, "Okay, she's conscious. Listen—put more padding on top of that dressing. Do you have any way to secure it, to put pressure on it? Don't take it off for anything. Donna, Hushi, and I are going to take off right now. We'll meet you at the Virginia state line, at the welcome center on the southbound side. Meantime, I want you to push liquids, as much as she can keep down. OJ and clear soda, half-and-half. That'll keep her blood sugar up, and give us a little more time. Now haul out, and we'll meet you."

Jon hung up and took off his shirt. He packed it on top of the blood-soaked dressing and secured it with his belt before pulling Jenna's sweater back down over it. Then he jumped back in and pulled out onto the expressway. At the next exit, he found a quick stop and picked up a two-liter and some orange juice. *Now if I can get her to drink it...*

* * * *

It was dark when he crossed the Virginia state line. When he pulled in at the welcome center and opened the door, he looked over at Jenna. In the dome light's glow, her face was a mask of ghastly pallor. Her breathing came in ragged, shallow gasps.

He grabbed her shoulders. "Jenna? Jenna, don't you do this! Stay with me, do you hear?"

Her eyes opened halfway, glassy and blank. "Lemme th' hell 'lone, dammit."

"Don't leave us, okay? I need you."

Jenna brightened up. Recognition came into her eyes. "Y-you... wamee stay?" She grimaced and moaned. A tear squeezed from her left eye and caught on the side of her nose. Her hand fell slack as she passed out again.

Jon sat on the pavement, leaning back against the side of his car. He had expected a lot of things today, but a tear from Jenna Paine? He would sooner have expected Osama bin Laden to put on a yarmulke and sing *Hava Nagila*. He came out today ready to take up their rivalry from where they left off, with bullets and fists.

But something had changed. *Something? Hell, a lot of things had to have changed. Miss Paine, what in God's name happened to you?* Did her last target pack more than she could handle? It would be easy to say she deserved it. Hell, she was an enforcer involved in the world's most insidious hostile takeover bid. God alone knew how much blood was on her hands. But did anyone deserve to die like *this*, slowly bleeding to death, alone in the hands of the enemy? He almost felt sorry for her. Almost. Right now, all she was to Jon Daniels was a link to The Pinnacle's leadership. If she could be turned. If she lived long enough to turn.

Headlights approached, exiting the interstate at a hard pace. A plain white utility van appeared under the rest area's security light and screeched to a stop across his trunk, blocking him in. With a curse, Jon drew his pistol and rushed around to the front of his car as the side door slid back. A sigh of relief whooshed from his lungs as Beth scrambled from the back door and ran to Jenna's side. Hushi climbed out the van's passenger door.

Donna Hermsen shut the rental van off and stepped out onto the blacktop. A tall, slim brunette in her late forties, she bore the look of a woman who'd seen too much. She had a tired look about her eyes and a grim, tight expression, bearing the extra lines and silver streaks of a life marked by incredible stress demanded of leadership. "How's she look, Beth?"

Beth edged past Jon and crouched down next to Jenna. After a quick evaluation, she let out a soft curse. "She's in shock. Damn, we better get this blood in her ASAP. Jon, help us get her into the van. You lead the way back."

"How do you know that blood will work?"

Hushi spoke up. "Donna's O-Negative. The other bag is Oxycyte. Artificial blood. We're good. I hope. Let's get her in, now."

With some difficulty, they packed Jenna's limp form into the back of the van and laid her on a plastic covered mattress. Beth and Hushi climbed in with her. Jon lost track of who said what to whom as they traded information and orders. Beth hooked a bag of saline over a bar stretched across the vehicle's bed as Hushi grabbed a starter kit, and in seconds, they had an IV started in one arm and the O-neg flowing into the other.

At the same moment, Hushi shouted, "Done!" as Beth barked, "Shut it!" at Jon. He slammed the back doors closed and ducked out of the way as Donna threw the van into reverse to let him out.

He dove into his driver's seat and made rubber squeal on the way out of the rest area and back onto I-95.

Chapter Eight

The soft hum from the refrigerator resonated through the floor, nudging Nadia back to awareness. She fought a fierce battle with her eyelids, finally forcing them open to a world sideways from the one she remembered.

Her fingertips and toes still hummed and tingled as she teased her memory awake. Another seizure, and judging from the position of the table in the corner, it was a bad one. Her bottom lip throbbed in pain. Nadia brought a hand up to touch warm wetness, and then pulled back to show her alabaster blood on her fingertips.

Something shifted on the edge of her vision. Over by the refrigerator, Sofi sat huddled with her arms wrapped around her knees, trembling. An occasional soft sob escaped from her lips. When Nadia moved, she raised her head. "M-mom?"

Nadia's head vibrated with her own voice. A strange echo rang in her ears. "I'm okay, honey."

"No, you're not."

Nadia sighed. "Okay, maybe I'm not. I had a seizure. They've been happening mostly at night. But I'll be fine in just a little—"

"What's wrong with your blood?"

Oh Lord, here we go. "Sofi, how much do you remember about your mother?"

"Why are you changing the subject?"

"Honey, I'm not changing the subject. Now tell me."

"She was a doctor."

"What kind of doctor?"

Sofi's face scrunched up the way it did when she worked on her history homework. "She worked with Dr. Hamund at the lab."

Nadia struggled up to sit in the nearest chair. She locked her daughter's eyes before speaking. "Dr. Hamund and Dr. Spielberg made me."

"Made you do what?"

Nadia thumped her chest with her open palm. "Made *me*. I'm an artificial person." She waited while the concept sunk in.

Sofi's brow knitted as she struggled with it. "What, like a test tube baby?"

"No. Sofi, listen to me. You're twice as old as I am. I'm closer to Frankenstein's monster than a test tube baby. Do you know what an artifact is?" Nadia tried to read her daughter while she waited for the dawn of understanding to come. The girl looked every direction but straight at Nadia. Her mouth worked soundlessly before she buried her face behind her knees. As her shoulders heaved, Nadia wanted to run to her, sweep her up in her arms and comfort her. But something told her at this point it would not be well received. So she just stayed silent while her child cried to herself. *God, what does she think of me now?*

When Sofi's head finally came up, her cheeks were wet. "Why?"

"They built me as a weapon. I was supposed to kill someone."

"Who?"

"It doesn't matter. I didn't do what they wanted."

Sofi chewed her lip for a minute and stared at her adopted mom. "I don't believe my mother would want you to kill anyone."

"I don't think Anna wanted me to. But she didn't have any choice."

"Everybody has a choice."

"Sofi, could you make us some tea?" The girl rose from the floor. Her hands shook as she poured water into the teapot and set it on to heat. Then she stood at the stove, watching Nadia with timid eyes.

With effort, Nadia set the table back up and dragged it back to its place in the center of the floor. "It's okay. You can sit here with me. I won't hurt you."

As Sofi sat, Nadia went on. "Dr. Spielberg thought she was doing something good. By the time she found out Dr. Hamund was using her, it was too late to get out. She had no one to look after you if anything happened to her."

"You mean if they killed her? Would they do something like that?"

"She thought so. So she asked me to take care of you before they did."

"And then she killed herself," said Sofi in a soft voice.

They sat in silence until the teakettle whistled. Nadia set out the tea, honey, and cream, and sat again. After a couple of thoughtful sips, she looked at her daughter. Sofi's cup shook in her hands. The girl stared into her cup, her face a blank mask.

"Honey, are you all right?" Nadia knew the answer even as she asked. She just couldn't think of anything else to say.

Sofi put her cup down harder than necessary. She stood and backed away from the table. "No. No, I'm not all right. My mom's a… Okay, maybe not my mom. But you're a fake person? I don't know whether to say, 'oh, cool,' or run screaming down the driveway! Look at me—do I *look* all right?"

"You'd best get a handle on yourself, dear, because there's more I need to tell you."

Sofi halted long enough to throw her arms open helplessly. "Come on, Mom! What could possibly be worse than what I've already heard?"

Nadia sighed. *Oh Lord, help me now.* "Your mother made you, too. You're an artificial like me."

Sofi's face went pale. "This is *not* a good time for a joke!"

"I had a letter from your mother. The one where she asked me to take care of you. She said she made you in a lab."

"No! But my blood's red! Remember when I fell off the roof?"

"My blood is white because I'm a different kind of AP than you are."

Sofi began to back away, rubbing her arms in fear. Her face screwed up as tears rose in her eyes. "No. No."

Nadia got up and carefully approached her. "Look at me, Sofi. Honey, we're still the same people who came here together, okay? We came here to start over, together."

"Why didn't anybody tell me?"

"I didn't have time at first. Everything was happening so fast. And then when we got up here, I just wanted us to have a life, like normal people. That's all I wanted: to be normal."

"How can we be normal?" cried Sofi. "We're not normal! What part of this is normal?"

"Okay, you're right." Nadia took a couple tentative steps toward her. When Sofi didn't shy away, she came closer, arms open. "We're not normal. I should have told you. I'm sorry, Sofi, please forgive me. But tell me this—what difference would it have made? What different things would you have done in these last three years, knowing that we're not like anyone else?"

Sofi said nothing, just stared at the floor with her arms crossed tightly. She snorted once and wiped her nose with a sleeve. Nadia snagged a paper towel from the wall-mounted roller and held it out with a hopeful smile. Sofi didn't take it. A sob heaved from her throat and she leaned forward, falling against Nadia's chest. Nadia wrapped her arms around the little girl and kissed the top of her head. "It's going to be okay, sweetie. Just give it a little time."

* * * *

It happened again later that night. Nadia woke up with her face on fire, her brain tingling, her stomach threatening to empty itself. Her arms and legs felt like they'd been worked over by a large, ugly gorilla in boxing gloves. Her mouth tasted like someone stuffed it full of pennies, and then punched her in the jaw.

Sofi cried in the darkness nearby. "Mom? Mom, wake up…"

Nadia's arm felt like a ten-ton rubber tentacle. But somehow, she managed to raise it enough to touch Sofi's face. "Honey, I'm here. It's over now."

Sofi took Nadia's hand in both of hers. "Mom, what's going on?"

"I was hoping it was just a one-time deal, hon. I'm sorry."

Sofi crawled the rest of the way into Nadia's bed and snuggled against her. "I'm scared."

Nadia reached around her, pulling her close. "Me, too."

"What are we going to do?"

We. At least it's still we. If anything good came out of this whole mess, it was that Sofi seemed to become more like her old self. She wasn't the mouthy little renegade anymore. She was more like the sweet, gentle girl who moved with her mom to the UP to get a fresh start. The flip side, though, was that Nadia couldn't hide the seizures anymore. She didn't want to admit to herself that they were in fact getting worse with each one that rolled over her. She needed serious medical help, and there was only one place to go where she could hope to stay invisible.

Back to Virginia.

Back to Jon.

Did he even think of her anymore? Knowing him, he'd moved on. He'd laugh at her for holding on in her heart. His old FBI badge was still under her pillow, for God's sake. When Nadia woke up from one of her night terrors, she would imagine he was still there, holding her, stroking her hair, whispering in her ear. He was the only one who could get through to her.

But now what?

Nadia sighed and kissed Sofi's head. "Tomorrow, I'll get hold of a friend. We have to leave for a while. I know someone who can make me better."

I hope.

Chapter Nine

Jon paced the common room in the underground bunker, unable to sit even for a second. His legs ached, his back ached, and a large stone was busy exercising squatting rights in his brain case. He grabbed his coffee cup off the table as he walked by, and he raised it absently to his lips. *Damn. Cold again.*

Donna stepped in from the hall in blood-stained scrubs and a surgical cap. "You need sleep."

"When I know she's going to be okay."

"That girl is tougher than a Marine, and she's fighting for all she's worth. Get out of here and go to bed. I'll come get you when Jenna's out of the woods."

"And what if she doesn't make it? I need to talk to her. Maybe I can get some useful information before we lose her completely."

Donna took Jon's coffee cup out of his hand and set it back on the table. The care lines in her face looked deeper than they ever had, and the dark circles around her eyes made her look like she'd just gone three rounds with the heavyweight champ. But when she spoke, her voice rang firm and steady. "Don't make me sedate you. Jenna's unconscious, and will be for at least another day. It's a wonder she made it at all. If she were a human, I'd say she wouldn't have—"

"What?" Jon slumped into a thread-worn easy chair. "*Human?* Are you telling me she's a NADIA?"

"No. She's not a NADIA. But she *is* transhuman. Higher muscle density for enhanced strength, reduced liver size presents a smaller critical target. She has a spleen three times the size of a normal one, which means a larger emergency blood supply. Nerves twice as large for faster reflexes, faster thought—" Donna put a hand to her head. "She's definitely been engineered. It's most likely what kept her alive this long. Any normal human would have bled out."

"So how is she now?"

"Hushi and Beth are still working on her. She ripped out some stitches, and they had to close a couple of bleeders inside. She's lost a lot of blood, even with the extra capacity of her spleen." She sighed and poured herself a cup from the coffee maker. "It's going to be touch and go for a few hours yet. So get out of here before I fetch the dart gun. Go." She shooed him toward the stairs and went back down the hall to the treatment room.

Jon stepped out of Irving's shed and squinted in the sunlight filtering down through the trees. Jimmy strolled up, his rifle slung over a shoulder. His leathery face wore an uneasy, care-worn look as he scanned the area. "Well? How goes the war?"

Jon rubbed the back of his neck. "She's still fighting it. When was the last time you slept?"

"I'll be okay. I'm old, but I ain't that old yet." Jimmy looked back along the path down which he'd just come. "I sealed up the other end of the tunnel. If she tries to escape, there's only one way she can get out."

"If she does get out, I don't want you to hesitate. Put her down. I mean it."

Jimmy ran a hand through his hair and gave Jon a hard sidelong glance. "You sure it's gonna come to that?"

"She wouldn't think twice, buddy. I've seen her in action, and she is hell on wheels. In Vegas, she was chained in the back of a military police car between two armed men, and before they could get her off the flight line, she killed everyone in the car and escaped. Just watch it, okay?"

"Yeah, sure," the old man mumbled. "Hey, I gotta scoot. Catch you later, okay?" Before Jon could answer, Jimmy disappeared around the corner of the cabin.

* * * *

Jimmy ducked into the woods in front of the cabin. *Phone always hums at me when I'm in the middle of somethin'. We were better off before they invented the damned things.* He pulled it from his pocket and scanned the display. *Well, I'll be damned.* A warm feeling rose in his breast. He couldn't help but smile.

He hit the dial-back button and waited until Nadia picked up. "Hey, sweetie, it's me. Long damned time. What's cookin'?"

"Jimmy, we need to come back to Virginia. I'm having a problem."

The smile faded from his face. "Nothin' too bad, I hope. You want to talk to Jon?"

"Actually, I need Bunny."

"Ah, yeah, sure."

While Jimmy strolled over to the Kalinskys' home, he listened as Nadia caught him up.

"The seizures started a couple of months back. But they've been getting worse. I need Beth and Hushi to take a look at me."

"You still got the little one with you?"

"Yeah, but she's not so little anymore."

Jimmy paused at the door to Bunny's cottage. "I think we all owe you an apology for what happened."

"We were all afraid, Jim. But I had to protect Sofi. I know you understand."

"You want me to let Jon know?"

"Is he still an unbearable ass?"

Jimmy sighed and thought about his most recent talk with Jon. "Yeah, I guess so. Maybe a little worse."

"Then don't tell him, okay? The last thing I need is for him to get all worked up again."

The door opened a few seconds after Jimmy's knock. As soon as Bunny's head poked out, Jimmy said, "Okay, hon, I'll see you after a little bit then. Here's our transportation director." He handed the phone to a puzzled Bunny as he entered.

Chapter Ten

Nadia and Sofi grabbed their carry-ons and filed out through the boarding door past the smiling flight attendant. At the top of the jetway, Nadia spotted Hushi's Day-Glo red spiked hairdo among the mob gathered in the gate area. "Oh my God, Hushi!" Nadia laughed as she threw her arms around the tiny woman. "It's good to see you again!"

Hushi released Nadia and held her arms out to Sofi who shied away, clutching her duffel in front of her. Hushi looked questioningly at Nadia, who explained, "She doesn't like to be touched. It's okay, she's nervous about coming back here."

Hushi nodded to Nadia and bent over, looking eye to eye with Sofi. "Well, I *love* your hair, honey. I'd like to see what we can do with it." She straightened up and said to Nadia, "Bunny's waiting in the white zone. He's so cheap, he didn't want to park."

Nadia grinned and shook her head. "How are you guys doing, by the way? Catch me up."

In response, Hushi stuck out her left hand, showing off the wedding ring. "Okay, he's cheap, but he's not *that* cheap. Sofi, can I take your bag?"

"No, it's okay, I can carry it."

"Wait a minute," said Nadia, grabbing at Hushi's hand. "When did you two get married? That is so great!"

"Just over a year ago." Hushi turned and led the way up the concourse, rambling all the way. "I had a hot pink dress, and he wore a *real tuxedo*, can you believe it? Donna stood up for me. Papa and Beth made this awesome dinner. I have pictures…"

Part of Nadia wanted to ask about Jon, but she was more than happy to let Hushi prattle on about anything and everything else. It let her put off the inevitable just a little longer.

Maybe Jon had changed. Maybe Nadia had changed. Maybe they both had changed and just weren't compatible anymore. So much water had passed under the bridge since she'd last seen him, was there any way they could be what they once were?

At first, she was upset when he'd told her about sleeping with Sharon Buckmaster. She supposed she should have seen something like that coming. The Pinnacle had built Nadia as a single-use weapon system. They'd made no provisions for human female anatomy, replacing those organs with the ones necessary to control and trigger the forty-eight grams of quasi-stable antimatter caged in her skeleton. Her designers had never counted on her living long enough to develop relationships, nor did they care whether she might. It was only a matter of time before Jon felt as frustrated as Nadia did about their inability to consummate their relationship.

What made it worse for her was the memory she had of being in another body, and being able to experience physical love. So in a way, she found it difficult to place the whole blame on him, even though the circumstances were beyond both their control.

Still, he'd cheated. Sure, right and wrong make no difference to a person with no soul. But Jon had a soul, and he'd cheated anyway. He didn't cheat on her; he'd cheated on himself, on his own standards and morals. Could she forgive him for that, even after three years?

* * * *

Bunny gave Nadia a warm hug at the car. When he held out a hand to Sofi, she held hers clasped in front of her. Bunny didn't miss a beat. He raised his hand farther and rubbed the back of his head. "Well, okay, then. Let's get goin'."

As they pulled out onto the highway to Front Royal, Hushi fell silent for a space of time. When she spoke again her voice was lower. "We all missed you. Papa hasn't been well. He had a heart attack a couple months ago, and we almost lost him. We didn't have any way to get hold of you."

The blood left Nadia's face. She hadn't thought that perhaps Papa would die, and she would never have the chance to say goodbye to one who'd shown her such kindness. Shame replaced the shock a second later. What must he think of her now, after she'd deserted him? "Oh God! Is he all right?"

"Two arteries fully blocked. We got him to Stevens Memorial just in time. We've been treating him with that regen agent that Donna and I discovered, based on your healing ability. I think he'll be all right."

"How's Jimmy?"

"Still Jimmy. Gentleman on the outside, rattlesnake on the inside." Hushi brightened up again. "We had a group of hunters poaching deer out-of-season last year. Jimmy laid out a few surprises for them, nothing too serious. They got the message and quit."

The smile faded from Hushi's face. "Jon really wants to see you." She turned back around, facing the road, and Nadia couldn't read her face. "He's been kicking himself in the ass ever since, you know."

Nadia said nothing. *Sonofabitch deserves it.*

Hushi went on. "He hasn't been with anyone else, either."

For three years? I find that hard to believe.

"He'll be glad you're back."

"I'm not back. I'm only here long enough for you to fix what's wrong with me, and I'm leaving again."

Hushi spun back around, eyes squinted in confusion.

Nadia said, "I have a life now. We have a home—" She ignored Sofi's soft "Whatever" next to her—"and I've had enough of fighting giants. I can be normal there—"

"You can't be 'normal,' Nadia. That option was never laid out for you."

"We'll see, Hushi." Nadia looked out the window at the countryside rolling by and wondered if Hushi wasn't right.

* * * *

The yard was empty when they pulled in at Irving's cabin. Everything was just the way it was when Nadia had last seen it. The wood was a little more faded, but it felt like she was coming home after only a day, instead of three years. Even Irving's wooden rocker sat in the same spot it had always been.

She tapped lightly on the screen door and stepped inside. Irving sat in his recliner, watching the Boston Red Sox game. Nadia felt the blood leave her face when she took in the gaunt, pale shadow that used to be "Papa" Irving Ratzinger. His skin hung loose from sudden weight loss, eyes sunken and hollow.

When he looked up, though, the light behind his eyes hadn't dimmed a bit. The wrinkles in his aged face grew deeper as a happy grin split his face. "Nadia, dear! Come here and say hello."

"Hello, Papa." She felt hot tears on her cheeks as she knelt down to hug the closest thing she'd ever had to a grandfather. "I've missed you." She held him long, kissed his cheek, and stood. "You remember Sofi?" She pointed to the doorway, where Sofi stood picking at her fingernails.

"Of course I do. Welcome again, little one. I'm sorry I have no strawberry shortcake for you this time."

Sofi's hands stopped fidgeting and she looked up. "You remember what you gave me three years ago?"

He waved a finger at her and winked. "You remember it, don't you? There was only the one meal with us, and you made quite an impression." Behind his coke-bottle glasses, his eyes lost some of their levity even as he continued to smile.

He turned his attention to Nadia. "The rest of them are downstairs with our guest."

Nadia froze. "W-what guest?"

Chapter Eleven

Consciousness sifted back into Jenna's mind along with the searing pain in her abdomen. The fire grew in intensity as she became more aware, drawing an involuntary moan from her lips. The pain became a monster, feeding on her body bite by bite until she began to writhe in spite of her best efforts to control it on her own. Her wrists and ankles came up short against stops. In her semi-conscious state, fear shook free from its bonds in her mind, and the writhing turned into thrashing. Every movement made the pain worse, and every twinge of pain brought on an involuntary jerk of an arm or leg.

A woman's voice reached through the torment; a hand on her shoulder pressed her down into the bed. "Jenna? Jenna, stop. Listen to me!"

The sharp order got Jenna's attention, helped her to focus. She stilled, sank into her training, and opened her eyes. After fighting the pain tiger back into its cage, Jenna ran down her checklist. *First, evaluate your surroundings.* The light in the concrete block room was dimmed to a comfortable level. A faint musty odor stung her nostrils. *I'm underground. A basement...?*

A plump, freckled woman in her thirties with curly auburn hair hovered above the bed, both hands on Jenna's shoulders. Wrinkled blue scrubs rustled softly as she turned her attention to prepping a syringe filled with an amber liquid. "Do you need something for pain?"

Jenna forced herself to remain calm. *I was with Jon. I'm still alive; they didn't find us. Unless they did, and I'm going to just lay here and take a needle like a dog to be put down. No way in hell—*

The other woman seemed to know what was in Jenna's mind. She held up the vial from which she'd taken the serum so Jenna could see. "It's okay, just morphine. Please, let me help you."

Jenna didn't look at the bottle. She stared at the woman's face, reading everything she could. All she saw was open sincerity. Jenna finally nodded and sagged back against the mattress, sweat beading on her brow. The trembling in her limbs stilled as a warm sensation crawled up her arm. Seconds later, a fresh blanket was pulled up to her chest. As the painkiller took hold, she managed a weak "Thank you." That was when she noticed how dry her throat was. She could barely croak, "Water, please?"

The other woman stepped closer. The look in her eyes betrayed a mixture of relief and fear. "Y-yeah, sure, hang on." She stood and rapped on the door twice, paused, and then rapped once more. Jenna heard a man's voice on the other side, old and hoarse, but strong. The freckled woman said, "She's awake. Get Jon," before pouring some water from a pitcher into a glass and inserting a straw. After she helped Jenna to a few sips, she sat back down. "How do you feel now?"

"Better, I guess. I suppose it's out of line to ask where I am?"

The woman smiled a wide, nervous grin and said, "Why don't we start with some introductions? I'm Beth." She took Jenna's hand in her own. Beth's fingers trembled, but her smile was sincere.

"I guess you already know me."

"You're Jenna."

"Why am I tied up like a pig in a poke?"

"I'm sure you can guess. You're in a safe place, though."

"How did everything come out?"

"We worked on you for quite a while. You had a couple close calls. You lost a *lot* of blood. Can you tell me what happened?"

"Is it okay if I plead the Fifth for now?"

"Sure. More water?" Beth held the straw to Jenna's lips. Jenna drained the cup all the way down to the slurp at the bottom before she let go. "FYI, I'm not a cop. I used to work at the hospital in Twin Oaks Spa. On a scale of one to ten, how's the pain?"

"Three," Jenna lied. It hurt like hell, but she didn't want to be all drugged out anymore. She would need a sharp mind from here on out.

Beth looked into Jenna's eyes and stared at her for a few disturbing seconds. "Uh-huh." She nodded and pushed a syringe into Jenna's IV line. "I'm just going to give you a bump, anyway, to stay on top of it. Don't worry. I'm halving the dose. You'll still be reasonably sharp."

"For what?"

A knock came at the door. Beth spoke loud enough for the person on the other side of the door to hear. "We're good. Come on in."

A deadbolt slid back, a second lock opened, and the door swung in to admit Jon Daniels. He closed the door behind him, and the locks clicked back into place. *One nurse, Jon, and whoever is beyond that door. Probably a couple more upstairs. Outside, who knows? I might be on an Army base for all I know. Not that I'm in any shape to escape. A toddler could tackle me right now.*

Jon stepped up to the bedside, placing his hands on the side rail as he did. "Hey, Jenna. Sorry about the straps. I'm sure you understand."

"Under different circumstances, I'm sure it would have been fun. I guess I should thank you."

"I guess you're welcome. Thanks for agreeing to meet me."

Jenna stared at the ceiling. "Not like I had any other choice at the time."

"Who shot you?"

What do you care? "I was cleaning my gun and it went off."

"Nice try. The hit didn't quite go as planned, did it? Who was the target?"

"Is that what you wanted to talk to me about? Because the last I heard, you were a special agent for the FBI. As in, anything I say can and will be used against me—"

"You're not under arrest, Jenna. That's not what this is about."

"Then what's with the straps? Why am I being held underground? And who's outside that locked door? I know when I'm being held prisoner." Jenna tried to sit up. A spasm ripped through her torso. She squinted and flopped back down with a moan.

"You haven't exactly proven that we can trust you yet," said Jon, "and the stakes are too high to take any chances right now. Just take it easy and get better. We'll have time to talk later."

"We'll see about that."

Jon turned and left the room, leaving Jenna alone with Beth.

Beth checked Jenna's IV, and then drew the covers back. "Let's have a look at your incision."

"Can I at least have my hands untied?"

Beth looked at Jenna, and in her eyes, Jenna saw fear akin to a bird looking into the eyes of a cat.

"You know what I am, don't you?" asked Jenna.

Beth's hands trembled as she lifted up Jenna's gown and checked the dressing on her abdomen. "What you are doesn't worry me. It's what you can do that frightens the hell out of me."

"Does it look like I can do *anything* in my condition? Believe me, if I don't want to be tied up, I won't be for long."

"Did you kill Mark Boyle? The man who was holding us?"

The question took Jenna off-guard. She tried to find some safe way to answer, but couldn't think of anything to say that couldn't be taken the wrong way. *Damn painkillers.*

Beth broke the pause. "Because if you did, I'd say thank you. He…" Her lips clamped shut for a second. When she continued, her voice cracked. "He blew my friend's brains all over the floor, right in front of me. And he was going to kill us, too. Nadia said it was you. I… I don't want anyone to die. But he needed to die for what he did. So thank you." She covered Jenna back up. "Dressing looks good for now. We'll check it again in a couple hours."

So what do you say to that, Jenna? "Sure, no problem. Anyone else you want wiped out? I happen to be between jobs right now, rates cheap." *Yeah, right. It was an order, plain and simple. He was being cut loose. Just like me. The only difference is I made it out alive.* "Okay." Jenna closed her eyes and took a deep, slow breath, focusing all her energy on calming her pain receptors. With the added boost from the drugs Beth administered, she was able to quiet the spasms down, and drifted off into a fitful sleep.

* * * *

When Jon came out of the shed, Nadia was standing there waiting for him. His heart leapt into his throat as he blinked and shook his head. *Am I hallucinating?* Her curly blonde hair was cut short off her shoulders, but she still looked like he had last seen her, soft brown eyes so deep a guy could get lost in them.

Nadia took a hesitant step toward him. "Hi."

He wanted to run the rest of the way to her, sweep her up in his arms and never let her go. He wanted to grab her by the shoulders, shake her till her teeth rattled, and scream, "Why did you leave me like that?" But inwardly, he knew why. Was it too late to make it right?

"I missed you." She stood there, not saying anything, so he went on. "I've wanted to apologize for a long time—"

"For what, cheating on me in Prague, or threatening to shoot Sofi?"

"Wait a minute, I never threatened—"

"When the subject came up, you were awfully eager to volunteer, though, weren't you?"

"We were all terrified, Nadia. No one was sure if we were being set up. The Pinnacle could have planted her—"

"They didn't. Sofi is a *child*, Jon. She's not a weaponized AP. And you were ready to kill a child."

Jon sputtered in frustration. *This is not going at all where I expected.* He sighed and rubbed his neck. "Can we just back up to the point where I missed you and start again?"

"Only if I get to slap you for being such a jerk."

"How can I make this better, Nadia? How do I fix it? I've been sorry for three years, for everything that drove you away. I worry about you every night. I think about you every day. I'm sorry, and I wish we could be us again. But if I blew my last chance, I—" His voice caught as a lump rose in his throat, "—I understand."

She stood silent while they stared at each other. A gust of wind passed by through the trees, brushing a lock of hair across Nadia's brow. She ignored it. "Jon, I—" Nadia stepped back, clasping her hands in front. She looked away, and back again. "I'm having seizures. They started a couple months ago. They've been getting worse."

Jon's world swam in front of his eyes. "Oh my God—"

"I want to see if Hushi and Beth can find out why."

"Is there anything I can do?"

"I don't know."

All through the conversation, Jon had been trying to read her face. Most of their relationship, he had a pretty good record. Nadia was one of the most expressive people he knew. But every now and then, a mask would drop over her face, and to Jon she seemed more like a Barbie Doll than a real person. At those times, it was impossible for him to guess what was going on behind those brown eyes. Just like right now.

A girl's shrill voice from Irving's cabin yanked him out of his concentration. "Kiss her, you dope, she's scared witless!"

When Jon turned back to Nadia, her mask had dropped, letting him see how right the girl was. "Oh baby, I'm so sorry." He stepped forward, sweeping Nadia into his arms. She sobbed against his chest and clutched him to her, trembling.

Over the top of her head, Jon saw Sofi on the back porch, arms crossed and eyes rolling in exasperation as she turned to go back inside. "God, *grownups...*"

Chapter Twelve

John Bowman stood looking out over the Pacific from his office window. The sinking sun painted sky and sea in joyous splendor no fiesta could recreate, but the view didn't register in Bowman's mind; it was too busy with other matters.

Shrugging his shoulders to straighten the charcoal gray jacket on his beefy frame, he clenched his fists, fuming.

Jenna Paine was missing. Not dead, as he'd ordered. The bodies found in the hotel room after the set-up had been those of Gerda van Voght and Phil Batterson, the operatives who were supposed to eliminate Miss Paine. An ambulance had been called to the hotel by an undisclosed guest, and Miss Paine had been spirited away to the nearest hospital, where a bullet from Batterson's pistol was removed from her body. But before the police had an opportunity to question her, she had, in typical fashion, made her escape, and now God alone knew if she still lived, let alone where she was.

One thing Bowman prided himself on was his sense of timing. He knew when to cut and run, and this was it. The NADIA Project had proven successful to the degree where it had finally run its course. Therefore, all loose ends needed to be tied up, and here they were, the two ends no one could afford to leave loose: Nadia Velasquez and Jenna Paine. *Not dead.*

Bowman turned away from the sunset and addressed the only other person in his mahogany-paneled office. "Well, Mr. Frost, you trained Miss Paine. What's your assessment?"

Frost leaned back on the leather sofa in a corner of the office, cleaning his nails with a long-bladed stiletto. He was a lean, hard man with a face like a hatchet and a shock of white, close-cropped hair. His attention remained on his task while he answered, "It's difficult to say. Any normal human would have bled out and died before they even got to the hospital. But our Miss Paine performed true to her design and survived in spite of the extensive damage." He kicked his feet up on the coffee table and let an insolent grin slid across his face. "At least, temporarily."

"I assume the hospital's records on her have been expunged, then? It would be inconvenient, to say the least, if it got out that she's transhuman."

Frost slid the knife into a concealed scabbard in his jacket sleeve and reached for the glass of scotch on the coffee table. His voice carried the barest edge of a sneer. "Of *course* we took care of the records. We can't do anything about the staff's memories of her unique characteristics, but our team confiscated the X-rays and bloodwork reports, and recovered the bullet as well. She may as well have been a ghost."

Bowman sat at his desk and rubbed his eyes. He was always so tired, nowadays. *Must be lack of sleep. Stress. I need a good massage and a steam bath.* "What's next?"

Frost took a sip and set the glass back down. "Paine's an expert on staying invisible. We've been monitoring her credit cards and known accounts, and her last transaction was a cash withdrawal in Washington D.C., the same day she disappeared from the ICU at Madison Central. She's been lying low for the last couple of days, probably holed up somewhere licking her wounds. One area safe house showed recent usage, but was empty when we checked it. Local motels showed no activity under any of her assumed names, either. So wherever she is, no one cares about ID or computer records."

"I think I know where, Mr. Frost. Our 'friend' Agent Daniels managed to send her a message over the air. It was all I could do to stop it from repeating, and I own the damned network that aired it. I can only assume that our Miss Paine has figured out her standing with us and is now consorting with our most dangerous enemy." He glared at Frost. "My question for you is: do you have any idea where Daniels lives? We made you the security consultant for our enterprise because you convinced us you're the best man for the job. You've trained our enforcers and field agents very well, but with all due respect, your so-called 'skills' have yet to turn up the number one thorn in our side."

Frost bristled at the insinuation. His eyes narrowed to blue laser points and his mouth straightened into a grim line. "Daniels shows up only long enough to pound our face into the mud, and he disappears again, with every bit the skill our own people have. He has no known address. He has someone erasing his electronic tracks before we can get a fix on him anywhere. He hasn't set foot in any FBI facility for almost four years, and he's stopped reporting in. Where would you suggest I go from here, Mr. Bowman?"

Bowman spoke through gritted teeth. "Somewhere other than where you are, Mr. Frost. Investigation and enforcement are your specialties, not mine. I can tell you this: The Council will not maintain its patience in the face of such apparent inefficiency." He stared at Frost in silence, letting the dark hint soak in. *No one is safe, here. Not you, not even me.* He took a sip from his own drink before continuing. "That Hermsen woman who worked for the Bureau had her lab in Front Royal, Virginia, didn't she?"

"Yes, and we crushed that operation. If Boyle hadn't messed up, we would have had her to question, and this operation would have been brought to a successful conclusion."

Bowman leaned back in his chair. "That lab was associated with Daniels and his team. So is it possible they are somewhere in the Front Royal area?"

"It's very possible. I've had a team in town ever since the Boyle incident cooled down, watching for any sign of Hermsen or Daniels, and we've come up empty."

"Too bad they couldn't have backed up Batterson and Van Voght. We would have fewer headaches today otherwise."

Frost tossed back the rest of his scotch and set the tumbler down. "Or been two more agents short. Paine is beyond human in all capabilities. Our last hope of closing her out is to catch her out in the open, off guard. The only thing she'll never outfight is a sniper's bullet."

"And what are the chances of that happening?"

"Slim to none. But if we can draw them all out, we stand a chance of catching the whole sack of rats. We won't need anything as surgical as a sniper to cancel the project, then."

"All together, eh?" Bowman's mouth twisted in an ironic grin. "Tell me, Mr. Frost—have you ever heard the term 'critical mass'?"

Frost poured another drink from the crystal decanter on the coffee table and rolled the glass in his hands, waiting for the explanation.

Bowman smoothed his gray hair down and went on. "In the early days of research on the atom, scientists discovered that if they gathered enough radioactive material in one place, an uncontrolled nuclear reaction would occur, without any outside trigger. That amount, Mr. Frost is called 'critical mass.' In this instance, we have NADIA V, Jenna Paine, Jon Daniels, and his team, all in one place. One wonders how much more, if any, it would take for them to achieve their own version of critical mass, and make everything our group has worked a century to achieve crumble into the dust." He leaned forward, eyes boring into Frost. "We can't afford to let that happen."

Frost stood and brushed down his pants. "We'll just have to make sure they never get that chance, then." Using the glass of a framed print on the wall as a mirror, he straightened his tie. "John, I need two days to round up a crew and head east. I'll call you when I have a more specific plan." He picked up the tumbler and drained it in one swallow. "Thanks for the scotch."

After Frost left, Bowman turned back around, and really saw the sunset for the first time. "Spectacular," he muttered as the fading rays of the sun slid over the horizon with a last burst of brilliance reflected off the distant clouds. "Spectacular, indeed."

Chapter Thirteen

Sofi held the door to Jenna's room open while Nadia carried in a lunch tray. Hushi stood when they entered, checked Jenna's IV one last time, and then excused herself, carefully closing the door on her way out to make sure the deadbolt was in place.

"Oh, goody, the Ladies' Social Club is here," said Jenna. "Shall I clap my hands with glee?" She lifted her hands against the restraints on her wrists and waved them feebly.

Nadia thought about sending Sofi out, but reminded herself firmly that the girl needed to see Jenna for who she really was. It was time for her daughter's hero to step down from her pedestal. Nadia set the tray down on a bedside table. "Jenna, you need to understand how scared you have everyone. They're afraid you're going to kill us all in our sleep." She put a straw in a cup of warm broth and offered it. "You did try to kill me, twice. And you had Jon in a couple of bad places, too. Let's face it, you've built yourself a helluva reputation around here."

"Look at me, Nadia. Do I look dangerous to you? I'm busted up inside and stitched back together like Frankenstein. I don't have your healing ability. And I assume there are at least three security levels I have to pass before I can get out of here."

Nadia gaped. "How did you—?"

"Easy. This place smells like earth and roots, and there are no windows. That means I'm underground. So the first level is whoever is watching me here, and then that locked door and whoever's on the other side, probably some scared kid with a weapon who'll pop a cap in whoever doesn't answer with the secret knock, or the right password. Then, if I manage to fight my way past them, I have the cellar door and whoever's ranging around outside.

"I think I'm not in a city anywhere, because if I was, I'd hear traffic sounds through these walls, or at least feel the vibrations. So this is probably some place out, away on a farm or in the woods. Now that I recall, Jon's uncle had a cabin in some resort area outside Front Royal, Virginia. So I'll guess woods, probably not too far from where Roger Glass last saw you." She lowered her voice to a whisper. "Roger was crazy in love with you, did you know that?"

Nadia flushed in shock and shame. It was one of those things she'd never thought about. When Jenna said the words, Nadia had to face it, and the memories of all those anonymous letters and gifts from a long time ago came flooding back. He'd been posing as her personal assistant when she was a television journalist in San Francisco. She remembered the way he'd blush nervously every time she pressed him for more information on her "secret admirer" and how easy it was for the gifts and letters to get through the station's security process. But now he was dead, and she'd played a large part of it. When she finally found her voice, it came out with less reproof than she was going for. "Why share that now, Jenna? What good does it do?"

"Just FYI. In case you were too dense to figure it out on your own. You know, no one else knows what I know about this area. The men who found it out are all dead. Roger and David are dead, too. They were the two sent out here to recover you. I'm the only one outside of your little group who knows."

"And you kept it a secret. Why?"

"You never know when you could use some leverage. And knowledge is leverage." Jenna didn't speak again until Nadia looked straight into her eyes. "I need some leverage now. I'm out, Nadia. They've decided I'm not useful anymore. They tried to erase me."

"Why are you telling me this?"

"Because we were friends, once. Because we're more alike than you know. And because I'm useless, that means they think you're useless, too."

"What does that mean?"

"It means that, from now on, as long as The Pinnacle lives, the stops are out. They want every transhuman they made dead, and they won't let up for any reason until we are: You, Sofi, and me. They've left you alone because until now they've had more pressing things on their minds. But after I shoved that stick back in their eye this week, you can bet they'll pour everything they have into putting us out of their misery."

In the silence that followed, a small gasp brought Nadia's attention away from the bed. Sofi stood pale and shaking as the import sunk in. *Now do you see what I was protecting you from?* She wanted to give Sofi a good old-fashioned "I told you so," but thought better of it. The girl was scared enough as it was.

She turned back to Jenna. "So what are we supposed to do?"

Jenna looked at Sofi, and then at Nadia. "We hit them first."

Nadia took a step back, heat rising in her face. "What's with this 'we'? You got a mouse in your pocket?"

"I can't do it by myself, Nadia. I need a support team. I can make their eyes water for what they did to me, and to you." Jenna looked at Sofi. "Honey, I know who's responsible for your mother's death. I can make them pay. I've already started."

Nadia cut off any response from the girl. *Maybe it wasn't such a good idea to let her stay.* Of course, she wanted The Pinnacle to pay for their arrogance and deceit as well. But she was also trying to teach Sofi about forgiveness and mercy. "Why don't you concentrate on getting better? We can talk more about that later." She held out the cup of broth again. "Here, have some before it gets cold."

Jenna's head snapped up, angry, arms straining against her restraints. "I don't want broth, dammit, I want a *steak!* I want to taste blood!" She sank back against her pillow after the outburst, flushed from pain. "I want —" she panted, "I want those bastards to *pay*."

Sweat sprang out on Jenna's face. Sweat and—was that a tear? Nadia pulled a tissue from the box next to the bed and dabbed Jenna's eye. "It's okay. It's going to be okay. Just get better for now. We can talk more later." She offered the straw again. "Just for now. I'll talk to Hushi about solid foods, I promise." Jenna took some sips of broth and a few bites of gelatin. Then Nadia took Sofi by the hand and left.

On the way out, she passed Beth. "She needs something for pain." Beth nodded and went to prepare a syringe before going in.

* * * *

Late that night, in the still darkness of sleep, what began as a dream ended as another nightmare. Nadia felt it coming on as a thick, coppery taste in her mouth. The familiar twitches danced up and down her limbs. Before she could react, the fog covered her mind again. When it cleared, an overwhelming nausea twisted her gut. A tingling weakness paralyzed her limbs.

A light shone in her eyes. She clamped them shut. A gentle voice said, "Nadia, I need you to open your eyes for me."

There was a pressure on her hand. Other sounds reached her ears, and she identified them one by one. A child, crying softly. *Sofi*. Concerned voices murmured among themselves. *Beth and—what was her name?* "Diane?"

"Donna," corrected Donna. "You had another bad one."

Something soft pressed against the back of Nadia's head. Beth said, "Hold this for a second, hon. I have to go get a suture kit."

Damn, how bad could it be? "Just leave it, I'll heal in an hour or two."

"Not this one, I'm afraid. You need a little help. I'll just tack it for you, and by tomorrow you'll be good as new."

Gentle hands helped Nadia to a sitting position. Sofi climbed into her lap and snuggled close, an arm around her. Nadia's head began to throb. "Where's Jon?"

"We sent him on a run," said Donna. "He's picking up some meds for you."

"Donna? What's wrong with me?"

"Don't know, dear. But we'll find out, I promise."

Fourteen

If Jenna had plenty of one thing right now, it was time to think. During her years as a field agent for The Pinnacle, she'd been convinced that they were in the right. She'd also been given precious little time between missions to truly think about what she was doing, and why. She'd simply accepted that each operation was necessary for the final achievement of their stated goal, a lasting and true world peace.

But in the last four years, she'd begun to wonder if it was worth the trail of bodies they were leaving in their wake. And her first question had to do with Nadia Velasquez.

She'd known about Nadia from the first day Nadia woke up in Twin Oaks Hospital. She'd fed Nadia the lie that she was a journalist, and had helped to set her up for her "interview" with President Javad of Iran. That assassination never panned out because Nadia, ever curious about a past that never was hers to begin with, went off the grid before they could get her in position to set her off.

After Nadia disappeared, Jenna found out how powerful the weapon really was. Two megatons of yield seemed like overkill to take out just one sociopathic dictator. Tehran would have been wiped off the map. Javad would have been erased, but all those innocent lives, too, would have been gone, as if they'd never existed or mattered.

At the time, she justified it in the same manner she had since her first operation: it was to fulfill a bigger purpose. The needs of the village outweighed the needs of the one. The vision of world peace at all costs came first. The Council knew what was best. It wasn't her place to question "The Big Picture."

Then there was Tahiti. Anna Spielberg had told Jenna the group that had attacked them there had been a Pinnacle team. She began to put two and two together then, but there wasn't enough time to think, between protecting Anna and Sofi and getting captured herself. After she escaped, she went right back to duty, even though her main purpose was now to find out why her employers wanted one of their own liquidated. Was she anyone her dad would have been proud of?

That thought brought a shock of shame. A single, hot tear traced from her eye back toward her ear. *Daddy, I'm so sorry...*

"Are you all right, hon?" Beth's voice snapped Jenna back to the present. "Is everything okay? I mean, besides being tied up underground with a wound in your belly and a bunch of weird people around you?"

"No. Nothing's wrong." But she knew there was plenty wrong. How many people had she killed? And for what reason, other than to feed the very beast that tried to devour her as well?

"It's okay, you know. You can talk to us."

Jenna stared at her toes. "Gee, let me just tell you my life's story, then, and we can become BFF's."

Beth stood and examined Jenna's IV for several seconds before speaking. Her voice was soft with gentle reproof. "Don't you have eyes or ears, Jenna? You're the only one here who's been acting like a grade 'A' bitch. All we've done since you've been here is be nice to you—"

"So Jon can pump me for information." She raised her wrists against the restraints. "Look at this, Beth. Look at *me*. I've been tied in bed four days. I can't see the sun. I can't have regular food. I have to pee in a pan. I can't even wear real clothes. I haven't had a shower since I've been down here. And you have to *ask* why I'm such a miserable little bitch? I'm in deep kimchi, here, and I know it. Can't you give me *one thing* to help me feel like a woman instead of a freaking animal?"

Beth turned from the IV and stared at Jenna for a full minute. Her own face was an unreadable mask, a caricature of a china doll. "Let me see what I can do." She stood and left.

* * * *

Jon sat in Irving's kitchen, thinking about the choices before him. *It won't be easy getting out of this one. What's she thinking now?*

Sofi's eyes bored into her cards as she fanned them out. She peered over the top, fixing each of her opponents' eyes in turn.

Jimmy, sitting at her right, lifted one gnarled fist and brought it down once on the tabletop, signaling a pass.

Sofi pursed her lips, nodded, and tossed three red plastic chips onto the pile in the center of the table. Six more joined hers, from Irving and Jon.

"She's bluffing, you know," muttered Jimmy.

"Cost ya to find out, old man," she said, closing her hand with a sly grin.

Jimmy raised an eyebrow. "Got a mouth on you, too." With an easy toss and a good-natured elbow to Sofi's shoulder, he added his chips to the pot. "Let's see 'em, kiddo."

Sofi flipped her cards over. "Dead Man's hand: eights over aces. Read 'em and weep, boys."

The men tossed their cards in with varying degrees of disgust. Jon said, "You did it again, you little bandit. I'd swear you had one of those aces up your sleeves if you had sleeves." He reached over the table and flicked her nose with a knuckle, and she giggled in return, swiping at his hand.

Irving struggled to his feet. "I am cooking tonight."

Jimmy started gathering cards. "What's Beth gonna say about that—?"

He was cut off by a squeal from Sofi that pierced Jon's eardrums. She launched herself out of her chair and across the kitchen, toward a figure in the doorway.

The blood froze in Jon's veins as Jenna stepped into the kitchen doorway. She wore a sleeveless teal dress that on most women would have been seen as conservative, but on Jenna's curves it screamed, "Hello, boys!" Her cinnamon hair was clean and brushed, dangling onto her shoulders, her face was made up, and she was fresh, bright, and even more beautiful than the first time Jon had seen her.

Sofi skidded to a stop in front of the woman, throwing her arms around her waist. "Hello, Jenna." Jenna bit her lip and winced, but put a hand on Sofi's head, drawing her closer.

Jon was dumbfounded. "What the hell—?" he sputtered, looking around for anything that could be used as a weapon. "What's she doing —?"

Nadia's voice cut through the tension. "Jon, stop!" She stepped around Jenna, leading Beth and Hushi.

Behind them, Donna entered the kitchen. "Cool it, gents. This was my call, and I'm standing by it."

"Is that supposed to make me feel better?" asked Jon. "Do you have any idea what you've done?"

"Can it, Jon. You acted the same way when you first found out Nadia wasn't human, do you remember that? I've spoken with Miss Paine, and she's agreed to behave while she's under Papa's roof." Donna eyed Irving meaningfully. He nodded back and sat in one of the dining chairs. Donna continued, "You invited her here to talk to her, not hold her prisoner. She's not under arrest, so stop acting like she is."

Jon turned and headed for the back door. He was twenty meters away, striding through the dark woods, when he heard light steps behind him. Spinning around, he saw blonde hair outlined in the light from the screen door.

"It's going to be okay," said Nadia.

"Tell me how!" he hissed. "That woman is fully capable of killing every one of us with her bare hands!"

"And yet she hasn't." Nadia stepped closer. Her hands were warm on Jon's arms. "I knew her in San Francisco, honey. Jenna Paine is a lot of things, but she's not cold-blooded. We were friends for over a year before all this blew up."

"And she was a helluva liar, wasn't she? Surely you had no idea she was prepping you to kill three million innocent people. That sounds pretty cold-blooded to me."

"Do you remember the night I left here, Jon? When I brought Sofi home? I told you there was something different about Jenna. I still think there is." She looked back at the cabin. Her eyes shone bright in the light from the door. "She's not one of the good guys. But she's not one of the bad guys, either. Not anymore." Nadia stepped closer. Her hair brushed against his chin as her hands slid around his waist. She pulled him close, her eyelashes brushed against the soft spot of his neck. "Just give her a chance, for me."

Through the screen door Jon saw Donna and Hushi help Jenna to sit at the table. Her movements were slow, deliberate. He thought back to four days ago, when no one knew if she would even be alive in the next hour. *Either she's a better actor than Oscar ever imagined, or she still has a long way to go before she could pose any serious threat.* Nadia's scent wafted in his nostrils, and he closed his eyes. *So many nights without you, and now... Oh God, why am I such a sucker?* "You know I can't say no to you."

There was a smile in her voice as she answered. "You never could."

"I missed you." He kissed the top of her head, smelling her hair. "I was such a jerk."

"Yes, you were. Now, stop being a jerk and kiss me."

He did, and her lips tasted better than he remembered.

Chapter Fifteen

In a shabby little apartment on the wrong side of the tracks in Front Royal, Virginia, five men gathered around a table. Palmer Frost flipped a manila folder into the center of the table. "Here's our start, gentlemen. Let's open the case." He looked at each man, cracking a humorless smile. *This is a good team. We'll find them this time.*

Jack Verhoff opened a laptop and booted it up. His beefy hands showed deceptive nimbleness as he typed in commands. The chair creaked in protest as he shifted to take a swig from his beer. Walt Healy stood up straight and stretched his neck, making it crack a couple of times before setting his gaze back on Frost. He was short, but as wide as a truck and hard as a railspike. Rain Spooner, a tall, thin Oklahoma boy with long, stringy black hair, fidgeted with a large folding knife. Martin McVay spun a .50-caliber cartridge like a bottle in front of him as he listened. He was a hyper little kid, but Frost had seen him on operations, as cool as a snake in the shade. Patient, smooth, and efficient.

Frost continued. "We start by gathering the loose ends. Upline was so focused on the primary targets Velasquez and Daniels, they missed these little nuggets." He opened the folder and lifted the top page, handing the photo to Healy. "Dr. Donna Hermsen. She took over the downstairs crime lab at FBI Headquarters on the death of her predecessor." He held up another photo. "She and this woman, Holli

Hushido, opened a genetic research lab after NADIA V went off the grid. We sent in a probe team, and they screwed the pooch."

Healy took each photo and handed it around after looking closely at it. "I take it they found a connection to the primaries, though?"

Verhoff spoke up, reading from the computer screen. "They did. They were unable to secure the connection, though. Someone set the computers to lockout, and we ran out of time. Lost two in action. The third man, Mark Boyle, had to be removed before the police could interrogate him."

"The lab closed after that," said Frost. "Upline dropped the issue. We're here to pick it up again."

"Anyone else work for them?" asked McVay.

Frost smiled. "Good question." He fanned out some more glossies on the table, pointing to each as he spoke of them, "Jennifer Fowler was their receptionist. She was a casualty from the probe. Her mother, Sandra, lives in Front Royal. Elizabeth Ann Nelson is a nurse. She used to work for The Company, but as a loose contractor. She was on the outside operation in Oregon. She was co-opted by Daniels. He also recruited Oswald Kalinsky. You remember that news story about the man who hacked the Federal Reserve? He's the one they called 'Bunny.' He's been tracking us online for four years, and the little bastard's been giving Upline a severe case of the red ass."

"They have connections with Air Force OSI and Army Intelligence," said Verhoff. "There's been traffic on the IntelNet that's been making Upline nervous. They want this branch cut off and burned."

Frost said, "We know they were last seen here in town. Mr. Healy, pay a visit to Mrs. Fowler. You're a private investigator working for a pharmaceutical firm looking to do business with Genetek's CEO, Dr. Hermsen. See if you can finagle anything usable from her. The rest of you will observe around town. Keep an eye out for anyone in this folder, especially Hushido. She should be easy enough to spot, if she still dresses like a peacock on acid. If anyone catches a view, take no action other than to keep them in sight, and inform us on Channel Two.

Leave your weapons here for now. I don't want any trouble in town. Let's find where the rats live and wipe out the nest, there may be more than what we have in this file. This place will be HQ. Don't worry about reporting in unless something happens to report.

"Questions? Good. Catch some Z's. We move out at sunrise."

Chapter Sixteen

A cloud of gnats played at aerial dogfighting in Irving's yard a few meters from the porch rail. The woods lay quiet under the late summer sun, taking its midday siesta. A chorus of cicadas swelled from the trees, grew in volume and faded away, leaving somnolent echoes in the minds of the couple on the porch. Jon sat on a stump of log sawed off for a stool and leaned his elbows on the rail. Jenna, clad in one of Hushi's spare pajama outfits, leaned back in Papa's old rocker, her feet kicked up on the corner post. Neither spoke for some time, but sooner or later, someone was going to have to talk about the elephant in the room, namely, what they were doing there.

Jenna took another sip of cabernet. "This doesn't mean we'll be sharing mint juleps and talking about the good old days. As soon as I can travel, I'm out of here."

Jon watched a rabbit forage in the undergrowth fifty feet from the porch. "Then why did you answer my invitation?"

She gave a short, derisive laugh. "Think about it. I didn't have any other choice. It was take you up, bleed to death, or let them kill me. And I'm not done with this body yet. I've gotten quite attached to it."

"Were you someone else…before?"

"No. I was always me. Anna told me I was the prototype of the program." Jon looked over his shoulder. She was looking at him, and a shadow crossed her eyes. *Fear?* She took a breath and asked, "Are you going to parade me around as evidence, now?"

"If you would have asked me a week ago, I think I would have said yes. Now, I wonder if there's another way to bring them down."

"You're never going to touch them, legally, you know. They have ways around just about any charge you can throw at them, and you've seen what happens to people who get in their way."

Jon grinned. "I've been their biggest speed bump for about four years, and I'm still here."

"I think sheer dumb luck probably had more to do with it than anything else. Your uncle took your bullet."

The hair stood up on Jon's neck at the mention of Uncle Mike. "Leave my uncle out of this," he said with a growl. *Like you left him out when your sniper laid him out.*

Jenna pursed her lips and shrugged before taking another sip of wine. "Just saying. The sniper was aiming for you. And in Prague, you could just as easily been hit as Lt. Buckmaster." She penetrated Jon with an icy look. "Death follows you. It surrounds you. You, my friend, are the luckiest sonofabitch on the planet. Don't you think that if you became their top priority, they could have squashed you and everyone else here like bugs on a windshield?"

A cold chill slithered up Jon's spine. "I suppose you would know, wouldn't you?"

"I could have had you three years ago, Jon. I had Nadia in my hands. I could have made her bring me here, and finished off every one of you. Even that snaggle-toothed old wolf Jimmy."

"So why didn't you?"

"I'm done talking until we've made our deal." She tossed back the last of her wine and rose stiffly. "I need to stretch. I enjoyed our little talk."

"Wait a minute, what deal?"

Jenna said nothing as she eased off the porch and around the back of the cabin.

The screen door spring groaned as Jimmy came out and sat in the chair Jenna had left. "Ever get the feelin' you got a tiger by the tail?"

"More by the minute," said Jon. "I just hope we can get some kind of an edge before she decides to make her move."

"From what I've seen, boy, there's no way to get an edge on that. Sheer hell on wheels, that one. All we can pray for is that we ain't in her cross-hairs when she goes off."

* * * *

The common room in the underground complex hung silent with tension later that night after Jenna finished laying out her "deal."

Jon set his coffee cup on the side table before speaking. "What makes you so sure I'm going to let you walk away after we've bagged this 'Council'?"

Jenna lounged back, crossed her legs, and gave him a lop-sided grin. "Because you can't charge me. I'm technically not a person. And by the time you get the legalities of *that* straightened out, I'll have escaped anyway."

Nodding her head toward the corkboard, she continued. "This way, you get a shot at them. But if you don't play it my way, you go right back to square one, and we're all still on the run until they catch up with us."

"What you're suggesting is illegal anyway," said Donna. "Obtaining evidence the way you're suggesting would blow our case right out of the water. There's no court in the world who would buy it."

"But I'm not a law enforcement agent, Doctor Hermsen. You can't get it legally, but if it shows up on your doorstep, all wrapped with a pretty bow from an 'anonymous, concerned citizen,' that's another matter altogether. I take all the risks, you get the benefit."

"And you get off scot-free for I don't know how many murders?" Jon growled. "I don't think so."

Jenna pursed her lips. "Take it or leave it, babe. I can disappear, or I can remain your next to worst enemy. I don't think you want to fight me *and* The Pinnacle."

Jon rubbed his chin, gulping back the lump of fear in his throat. There might be worse things than having Jenna Paine for a mortal enemy, but at the moment he couldn't think of any. At the same time… "What about your victims? What about justice for them?"

Jenna leaned forward, her hands splayed on the tabletop. "Yes, Jon, let's talk about my 'victims.' Mob bosses, corrupt tyrants, mass murderers beyond the reach of the law. Face it, we're all better off without them. They already got their 'justice.' Besides, what good would it do? What's done is done. Look, I'm offering you a win-win, here. Are you going to take it all, or lose it all?"

Donna cut in. "I'm the leader of this team, and I'll make the call on it. Jenna, would you give us a minute? We need to discuss this as a group." She raised a hand as Jenna leaned forward to stand. "No, you just sit back and relax. We'll be right back."

Upstairs, Jon spun on Donna. "What the hell are you doing? We *had* her right where we wanted her! A couple more days down there, and she was going to break. But you decided she was a *guest*, and now *she* has the upper hand!"

"So what do you want, Jon? Do you honestly think you were going to get her to break? Then what? She'd turn into Sister Mary Confessor and spill everything she knows? Beg you to bring her to justice for her past misdeeds? Give me a *break!* You're lucky to get *this* deal. Why don't you get off this obsession with punishing this one person, and get back on the big picture. You don't want her nearly as bad as you want the ones who wound her up and sent her out." She turned and started back down the steps. "I'm taking the deal. Suck it up."

Jon punched the shed door on his way out. It swung out and slammed against the outer wall, bouncing back as he headed for the house. Flexing the pain from his knuckles, he breathed deep to release the anger. "She's going to regret it. We all are," he muttered to the darkness.

"Who's going to regret what?"

Jon spun to see a tiny shadow draw away from the corner of the cabin. Sofi stepped closer, her feet silent in the grass.

He wanted to tell her to mind her own business and leave him the hell alone. But something in the way she asked softened his anger. It wasn't her fault he was mad; she was just a girl who happened to be caught in the same wringer he was. A ten-year-old child in over her head. He shook his head and walked over to the porch, where he turned and sat on the steps.

She came to stand before him. The light through the back door made her eyes gleam. Jon found himself looking closely to make sure both eyes matched, but then chided himself silently. *Damn, I'm looking for a light trigger in a kid.*

Sofi rubbed her arms in the cool night air. "You're mad at Jenna, aren't you?"

"What makes you say that?"

"You don't say a whole lot to her, and when you do talk, it ends up with one of you saying bad words or hitting something."

"How old are you again?"

"Mom says I'm ten going on thirty. Whatever that means."

"I think I can see why. I believe it means you're smarter than other kids your age."

"Nice try. Mom only says that when she loses an argument."

"Nadia lose?" He chuckled. "I'd like to see that."

"So what's the deal? Are you going to let Jenna help you, or not?"

Wait a minute. What the...? "How do you know what she's trying to do?"

"I helped her come up with it. The plan, I mean. Me and her talked."

Jon rubbed his hands together. *How to approach this?* "Sofi, do you know what kind of person Jenna is?"

Sofi's eyes took a strange, distant shine. "I know she saved my life, and my mother's. The bad people wanted to kill us. Jenna killed them before they could. I know you think she's bad. But don't."

"And you think I should...?"

"She says she can help you make the bad people go away. Let her help, please."

"Why should I believe that she won't break her promise?"

The girl came closer and put a tentative hand on his. "She promised me. She won't do any more bad things. I know she won't."

He put his other hand on top of hers. "Well, maybe I'll think about it. For you."

She smiled for an instant, but then her face turned an odd shade of pale as she looked down at his top hand. His skinned knuckles were bleeding. She snatched her hand away and stepped back, unsteady. Her mouth hung open for a second before the scream came out.

Jon reached out, sweeping the child up before she could fall. The back door flew open as Nadia charged out, eyes wide in fear. "Where is she? What happened?"

Jon shook as he held Sofi. Her arms wrapped around his neck like a baby python. He had to pull his head back to speak. "I think she's just freaked out. I skinned my hand over there—"

"Oh Lord," said Nadia, stepping down to receive the trembling child. "She doesn't handle the sight of blood very well. I'll take her inside." She kissed the tears from Sofi's cheek and took her back through the door, which Jimmy held open for her.

The old man stepped down and took Jon's wrist. "You probably want to take care of that, son."

"It's nothing. A little soap and water—"

"I mean you need to keep your cool. Look at how she cringes every time you lose it."

Blushing, Jon looked into the cabin. The inside door was open, allowing a view through the kitchen and into the living room, where Nadia tucked in her daughter. The woman stroked Sofi's hair and cooed to her. As he watched, she cast a glance back in Jon's direction, and even through the screen he saw the fear in her eyes. He'd just gotten her back after three years, and already he was shooting himself in the foot again. "Okay, Jimmy. I'll take care of it."

The wrinkles deepened in Jimmy's face as he grinned. "Good man. That wound won't dress itself—let's go on in."

Chapter Seventeen

Nadia swam. The depths of the icy water threatened to rip the breath from her lungs; crushing pressure beat against her breast with every pulse of her heart. Her vision collapsed around the tunnel in front of her as a rippling ring of light—the surface—glowed before her, taunting, just out of reach.

Stretching out her arms, she grasped at the light as a muffled, bubbled scream escaped, and with it, her breath. Just as she lost awareness, a hand grabbed her wrist in an iron grip, yanking upward. The water rushed past her ears in a terrible roar. As her head broke the surface, something struck her. The hand clutching at her arm shook her violently, tossing her through the air like a rag doll.

She opened her mouth to inhale, only to have it seize shut against the frigid air. The impact as she landed tore what breath was left from her lungs. Something landed on top of her, crushing, bearing down...

Nadia opened her eyes to a dimly lit chamber in the underground complex. Cot springs squeaked and groaned under her thrashings. Hands clamped onto arms and legs as a mask pressed against her face. Cool breath was forced into her lungs in spite of the convulsions of her chest.

Donna's voice, calm and distant, issued orders to others in the room. "More lorazepam—push it in, Beth, and get that propofol ready. Hushi, keep that air going in— No, I have her arms. Keep it up, girls, she's coming around now— Okay, that's better. Nadia? Can you hear me?"

"Wh-what—?"

"I said, can you hear me? Do you know where you are?" As the convulsions calmed, Donna released her grip on Nadia's arms.

The last spasms left with the echoes of the roaring in her ears. A lingering soreness in her jaw and limbs told Nadia all she needed to know. She lifted an arm, hand open. It was received in a warm grasp.

Someone sat on the edge of the cot. Nadia opened her eyes again, and Beth was there, her expression fraught with concern. "Here, let's check you out."

The effort it took just to speak surprised Nadia. "Did I hurt myself again?"

"We'll know in a minute." Beth turned to Hushi. "Did you get it recorded?"

Hushi checked a monitor in a corner of the room. A series of multi-colored squiggles traced across the screen. Two of the traces ran as straight lines. Hushi checked the harness of spider-web-fine wires connected to the computer beneath the monitor. Satisfied with the connections on that end, she followed the cable back toward Nadia's head, where each wire terminated with a paste-on electrode. "We lost Channels 19 and 32. Not too bad, but that's information we didn't get this time. I'll check the scan. With any luck, they came off after the seizure started."

Beth finished checking her over. "You're good, babe. No ouchies tonight."

Nadia asked, "Donna? What's wrong with me?"

"We're getting there. I think tomorrow we'll have something to talk about. Meantime, it's two-thirty in the morning. Let's all get some sleep. Hushi, reconnect those leads and stay here with Nadia. Beth, let's go. Good night, ladies."

After the others left, Nadia lay still in the darkness. After some time, she asked, "Hushi?"

Hushi's voice was strained with fatigue. "Yeah?"

"They're getting worse, aren't they?"

Several seconds passed. A long, deep sigh in the dark said more than Hushi's words. "Hard to say, hon."

"I guess that's what Donna wants to talk about in the morning, then."

"We'll find out what's going on. I promise."

"But that doesn't mean you can do anything about it, does it?"

"No, it doesn't."

"Hushi?"

"Yeah?"

"I'm scared."

Hushi's hand found Nadia's in the darkness. "Me, too."

* * * *

Jon woke instantly with the light knock on his door. The cold spot next to him was all the reminder he needed about the sleep study they were doing on Nadia. He turned on the lamp next to the bed and sat up, rubbing his eyes. "Yeah, come in."

Donna opened the door a crack. "Are you decent?"

"Some would say I'm downright amazing, but yeah, come in."

She stepped through and sat in the corner chair. "You've been saving that one, haven't you?" she said with a tight smile.

"We can't let Bunny have all the zingers, can we? Now, you didn't wake me up in the middle of the night for snark drills, boss lady, what's up?"

"She had a massive seizure, Jon. They seem to be getting worse with each one. Worse and longer."

A shock of worry spread through Jon's bones. "You got it under control, right?"

"Yes, we stopped it with drugs again. But she stopped breathing this time." She held up a hand before Jon could say anything. "She's okay now. Hushi's going to stay with her to make sure she stays that way."

Jon stood and crossed to his dresser. "I should be there. I need to—"

"You need to get some sleep, Jon. There's nothing more you can do right now. If something comes up, I'll be sure to let you know."

"She needs to know that I'm here, too," said Jon. "That I care."

Donna patted his arm. "She knows. I'll tell her. I just came over because you wanted to know right away if anything happened."

"If she gets worse, I need to be there."

"Agreed, but tonight, she needs peace and quiet. What are you doing?"

Jon had a drawer open and was tossing clothes onto his bed. "It's a cinch I'm not sleeping anymore tonight. I may as well take a walk and get back to work from the center." He switched to his jeans drawer. "Don't worry. I won't bother Hushi or Nadia. I just need to focus on something, okay?"

"Just do it quietly." Donna stood and left as Jon pulled on a T-shirt.

How much time do we have before I lose her for good? Better make it count, Jon.

Chapter Eighteen

The sun rose cool on the streets of Front Royal. Pale, pink watercolor sky gradually replaced the sackcloth of night as the streetlights turned off one by one. In an alley off of Stevens Avenue, movement behind a dumpster sent a cat scrambling. A large sheet of corrugated cardboard shifted, and a figure beneath began to stir.

The man wasn't old, but the hard lines on his face betrayed a harsh life. A thin, scraggly beard glistened with dew. He emerged into the day, bones popping as he stretched. Crouching beside the dumpster, he pulled an energy bar from the swaths of rags that covered his filthy body and dined, chewing each bite thoughtfully. After relieving himself at a drain down the alley, he shuffled into the street and sat cross-legged outside a bank building.

He set out his hat, tossed a couple dollar bills in, hauled out a beaten-up harmonica, and began to play.

The sun was high, and he was halfway through his twelfth rendition of *The House of the Rising Sun* when he caught a flash of hot pink hair. It wasn't the first head of neon hair he'd seen that morning, or even that week, but it was the first he saw on a woman older than sixteen. She was cute, a tiny Asian woman in black tights and skirt with a blouse that matched her hair. A pair of little samurai sword-shaped sticks held her hair in a bun off her neck.

She tossed a dollar into his hat and smiled as she passed. He caught the aroma of Japanese Lotus.

When she disappeared into a pharmacy down the street, he mumbled into his sleeve, "One, three. Tango Four. Tango Four. Charlie-Charlie Five-Seven."

He heard the response through the tiny earphone, invisible beneath his tangled hair: "One copies. Three, stand by and observe. Follow at a distance. Two, heat it up. Remaining units, carry on." The other team members acknowledged. Three played on, watching the pharmacy out of the corner of his eye.

A few minutes later, the Hushido woman emerged from the pharmacy and turned down the street.

Three waited until she turned the far corner before he stopped playing and stood. "One, three. Tango Four is on the move. Southbound on Phillips."

"Keep her in sight, Three. Two, roll. Park on Western, south of Columbia. Remaining units, converge on Three."

Three rounded the corner only to see a flash of hot pink dashing around the next corner. "Damn, I think she made me! Pursuing." He broke into a run.

"Three, break off! Stand down, Team. Reset positions—"

Three didn't hear the rest of the transmission. Halfway down the block a long, skinny arm snaked out of an alley. The clothesline caught Three across the throat. His feet flew out, kicking helplessly against thin air. He hovered for a timeless moment before the arm forced him down, slamming him to the sidewalk. The impact knocked the wind from him, and he lay powerless as an old man with sad, sleepy eyes stepped over him.

He pointed a huge pistol in Three's face. "U.S. Marshal. Do *not* move, young fella."

Holli Hushido appeared next to the old man, chest heaving from her run, trembling with fear. There was something else in her face as well: anger. She bent down and yanked the false beard from his face. "How stupid do you think I am?" Reaching up his sleeve, she found the microphone cord and ripped it loose. "Now get in the car like a good boy, and no one gets his face blown off." Turning to the old man, she said, "Let's go, Jimmy."

They stuffed him into a small brown sedan. The old man held that pistol in his face while Hushido stretched his arms forward and secured his wrists to the passenger's headrest post with plastic zip ties. A black cloth sack was dropped over his head and they took off.

From the aroma of perfume, he surmised that Hushido was driving. The one she called Jimmy sat in the back and made sure he couldn't guess where they were headed. At random intervals, Jimmy grabbed Three's head and shook it violently for several seconds, disorienting him to the point of nausea. No one spoke, to him or to each other, until the car came to a stop.

They left him alone for several minutes. He could hear muffled voices as they spoke with someone outside. The temperature rose inside the car as they argued, or talked, or whatever. He began to sweat. The bag over his head became more stuffy. His lungs began to burn from the stagnant air.

A cool breeze brushed his skin when the door opened again. A woman's hand touched his arm, a soft voice said, "Okay, just a pinch." A needle pricked him, and a Band-Aid was applied. A minute later, he slipped into oblivion.

* * * *

Three came awake to a splash of ice-cold water. Sputtering, he opened his eyes and gasped for breath.

He was chilled to the bone. Goose bumps stood out on his naked skin. He was tied to a chair, stripped to his underwear. The room was a featureless, concrete-lined cube.

Jimmy slouched against the door. A younger man was with him, seated casually in another wooden chair. Holding a dripping metal bucket, a cinnamon-haired woman with an athlete's curves stood just out of kicking range. An amused grin lit up her penetrating, almond-shaped blue eyes. "Wakie, wakie," she sang in a cheerful voice. "Guess who's going to answer some questions?"

Three had been trained for moments like this. They'd pounded it into his head, through simulations, testing, and trials, until he understood exactly what to do, and why. It boiled down to two words: "Tell them." So he did.

"Joel Perry, corporal, U.S. Army. I'm trying to find the NADIA."

The woman pulled up a chair, parked it close on one side, and straddled it facing him, resting her arms on the back. In the harsh light from the single overhead bulb, he got the impression of a supermodel crossed with a cobra. Joel wasn't sure if she was going to kiss him or rip his heart out and show it to him as he died.

"Well, Joel Perry, corporal, U.S. Army, you are in a heap-o-crap. What you tell us next will determine whether you go home and have a nice family one day or end up next to Roger Glass and David Valdès out in the Back Forty."

"Ah, I wasn't briefed on those men—"

The younger man spoke up. "What other affiliations do you have, Joel?"

"None. I told you—"

The woman moved faster than his eye could register. She slapped him across the face, hard enough to rattle his teeth. *I guess that rules out the kiss.* "Who's your team lead? Who's your Alpha?"

"S-sergeant Villanueva. Look, I'm telling you—"

Another slap spun his head the other way before he could dodge. Stars sprouted in his vision. *That bitch packs a wallop.* The taste of blood in his mouth overrode the sting of the slap.

The man spoke again. "I'm Agent Daniels, OSI. What's NADIA?"

"I don't know—" Another lightning slap rocked his head. Anger finally boiled over the fear holding his mind at bay. "Look, lady, that's enough! I'm playing nice, Daniels. Now get her the hell away from me or I don't say another word."

"The lady just got out of a bad relationship," said Daniels. "She's still harboring some hurt feelings." He motioned to a corner. "Miss Paine, come on back over here and let's see if the corporal has any more to say."

The woman looked at Joel one more time. Her eyes betrayed a venomous rage barely in check. Her hand shook as she pointed a finger under his nose. "You lie one more time…" She stalked over into a dim corner and leaned against the wall, arms crossed. Throughout the rest of the session, he was keenly aware of her readiness to make good on her implied threat. If he didn't satisfy these people, he was going to die, plain and simple.

Not for the first or the last time that day, Joel wondered what side had captured him. He also wondered if it would matter in the end.

God, please keep her in that corner.

* * * *

A light breeze waved hello on its way past the front porch. Jon rubbed his chin with one hand, studying the cool water running down the outside of his beer bottle. "Damn, Jenna, I don't know who taught you how to question a man, but you need to leave some of his mouth intact for him to answer questions with."

She sipped her brandy and crossed her jean-clad legs. "You do it your way. I'll do it mine."

"I'm just glad you didn't use that technique on me."

"Judging by what you did to Steven, so am I."

Jimmy rubbed a sore knee and propped it up on the half-barrel table on the porch. "Who's Steven?"

Jenna answered, "Just my best friend. Oh, and the guy Jon beat to death back in Oregon." With an icy glare at Jon, she added, "With his bare fists."

Anger rose up in Jon again. *Oh, here we go.* "You want to keep score? Who ordered the trigger on my uncle?" he said, clutching his bottle tighter.

Jenna's jaw clamped at the insinuation. She sat easy, yet Jon saw her sink into herself, finding her fighting zone. But he wasn't about to back down. *Who opened the dance, anyway? I sure as hell didn't start this.*

Jimmy broke in. "Don't make me put you kids in a time-out. Jenna, did you recognize the kid?"

Jenna's cold eyes never left Jon as she answered. "No, I've never seen him before."

"Did he recognize you?"

"I don't think so." Her jaw relaxed. Her hand was steady as she took another sip.

"What about when we let your name drop? Did anything light up?"

"No. I think he's what he says he is."

Jon put his beer down and leaned forward, elbows on knees. "Maybe we should meet with his team leader."

Jenna stood with her drink. "Let's not, and say we did. I don't feel safe about it."

"I don't mean here. We can meet downtown somewhere. You can stay here. I think we need to know what the Army knows, and hopefully we can steer them away if we can't bring them on board."

Stopping at the door, she took a breath. "Maybe we want them to stay around town."

Jon looked up. "What happened to 'I don't feel safe'?"

"Put two and two together, Jon. If the Army knows you're out here, so do The Pinnacle. That means they're closing in. Let's finish our business tonight, because soon I need to leave."

"Like that's going to make a difference? Jenna, if what you're saying is true, we're as much a target as you are." He set his beer down and stood, offering his hand. "On our own, we stand a good chance of getting picked off. We could use an extra gun, and Sofi needs at least one of us around to watch her after everything's over."

Jenna looked at his hand, but didn't take it. "This is getting too complicated for me." She opened the door and went inside. The screen door slammed behind her.

Jon looked at Jimmy. "I don't know whose life you just saved."

Jimmy never looked up from his beer. "I got a pretty good idea."

"I'm going to let Corporal Perry get dressed and see if we can't get this whole misunderstanding behind us." Jon stood and stepped off the porch.

"Jon?"

"Yeah?"

"Don't get her spooled up, buddy. I'll bet my false teeth she ain't the one they used when all hell broke loose. She's the one they used when they *wanted* all hell to break loose."

A cold wave washed over Jon as the full meaning of Jimmy's statement sunk in.

Jimmy DeBartolo was a soldier for over thirty years, starting in the first days of Korea. He fought his way across frozen mountains, steaming rice paddies, and over dirt he couldn't even talk about. If Jimmy knew one thing, it was the art of war. And he could read a person.

Jon took a deep breath. *That was close, then.* "Okay, Jimmy. Thanks."

Chapter Nineteen

Donna opened her folder on the table in the common room. Spinning the top page around, she pushed it over so Jon, Nadia, and Jenna could see it. She was thankful for the dim light down here. She'd already had her cry, but her eyes still felt swollen. *Doctors aren't supposed to be so freaking emotional. I sure make a lousy physician.* She took a deep breath before she started. "Jenna, I wanted you here because this may pertain to you as well. I don't know enough about your modifications." Using a pen as a pointer, she noted all the facts as she spoke. "This is it, Nadia. This is the problem. Your blood levels are all off balance. Your grey nanobot count is way down, below the level where they can convert enough power for your antimatter stabilizer to be fully functional. The reds can't keep up with the rate of damage to your system. Fortunately, the blue ones— the ones that trigger the bomb— are within normal range for you. Not too many, but too many for my taste. Without enough grays to power it, your stabilizer is breaking down."

Nadia paled. "So what's causing it?"

"You have" —Donna's hand shook as she reached for her coffee cup— "Six tumors in your body. Two in your left lung, three in your abdomen, and one on the nerve connected to the trigger. The largest is about the size of a quarter."

Jon reached over and took Nadia's hand. "Okay, so what can we do about it?"

"Keep treating the seizures with dilantin, or lorazepam in case of emergency. Remove the tumors from everywhere but the nerve, and this one. The one in your nanobot factory." She took a deep, tremulous breath, feeling the lump rise in her throat. "We can try radiotherapy. I have no idea what type of chemo will work on your system, and I don't have time to come up with anything."

Nadia murmured, "But if you hit either of those with radiation, it could set me off—"

"We may have to relocate. That way, if the treatment goes badly, fewer people would be lost."

Nadia's eyes filled with tears as she gasped. "Oh, my God, I have *cancer?*" Jon pulled her to him, and she buried her face in his shoulder.

Jenna sat, still and paste-white, hands in her lap. Beneath the sound of Nadia's sobs, Donna heard her murmur, "pant creases."

"I'm sorry, what—?"

"Nothing." Jenna stood and strode toward the stairs. Her voice tightened in a strange, choked fashion. "Never mind."

Before Donna could figure out what was happening, Jenna was up the stairs and gone.

Turning back to Jon and Nadia, she said, "This isn't carved in stone. I intend to fight it, and I need you to fight with me."

Even as Donna laid out her plan, part of her mind was on Jenna and what could be going on with her.

* * * *

Jenna hit the top of the stairs and blundered out of the shed. Her head buzzed as she wandered the back yard in a daze. *Cancer. She has cancer. Just like Daddy.* Her thoughts shot back to another time, sitting next to her mom in the big room with all the people in black. Daddy was in the big box up front, lying there just like he was asleep. But Jenna knew better, even though she was only eight at the time. Daddy's *pant creases* killed him. Mommy explained it all, but it didn't help make her feel any better, and it didn't take away the big black hole inside her where Daddy used to be. The grief and sadness that had almost destroyed her as a child came rolling back in on her like a flood that threatened to break over Jenna's internal dam all over again.

Tears boiled over in her eyes as she thought about the horrible pain that wracked his body in those final months, how she sat and held his hand while he slipped away for the last time. Could she do the same for the closest thing she had to a sister?

No. Jenna gulped back a sob and balled her hands into fists. *I'm too strong for this. I will not break again.* Her knuckles glowed white under skin stretched taut from strain as the first drops trickled over the top of the dam. *No.* A sudden, overwhelming feeling swelled in her inmost being, something she hadn't experienced since her dad's funeral. Never since then had Jenna felt so alone in the world. No one could understand where she was, where she'd come from or why she was suddenly on the verge of crumbling into a helpless mass of emotion. No one except someone who'd experienced loss on the same level as she, someone who'd struggled through his own past.

Jenna's vision rippled through tears as she set off for the front porch.

* * * *

Jimmy was cleaning his Garand, an AK-47 leaning against the porch rail when Jenna rounded the corner of the cabin. She stepped up onto the porch and halted before him, trembling and pale. She opened her mouth to speak, but all that came out was a sorry little whimper.

He set the bolt assembly he was working on down on the half-barrel and stood, brow wrinkled in confusion. Scanning the trees, he reached over for the AK. "Somethin' wrong—?"

Before his hand found the barrel of the assault rifle, she threw her arms around his waist and clutched him to her like a lost child, shaking and heaving. "I—can't do this again. I can't be strong anymore." She buried her sobs in his shirt.

Jimmy just stood and let her pour out her grief and misery on him. After a few moments, his arms came up and wrapped around her, offering what comfort he could. With one hand, he patted her back. "It's okay, you don't have to be." *What the hell just happened?*

Presently, Jenna stilled. The sobs subsided. Jenna drew away and stepped back, leaning against the rail. She drew a shirtsleeve across her eyes and sniffed. He handed her a clean rag from his pile, and she took it, mumbling her thanks.

He sat back in his rocker, ignoring the wet spots on his own shirt from her snot and tears. "Can I ask what's wrong now?"

Jenna blew her nose. "I just got reminded of something. From a long time ago. I'll be okay now. I just needed…" She let the sentence hang unfinished.

"I understand."

Jimmy did understand. He'd spent enough frozen nights and hellish days hounded by his own demons as he fought to help his people maintain their sanity in a job no sane man would want. He'd talked them down from their terrors, listened to their confessions, seen them pick up their rifles and trudge back into the meat grinder, and he'd seen them carried off crying like children. He knew every person had their own breaking point. And he understood that, whatever had happened in the past five minutes, Jenna Paine had reached hers.

The color returned to Jenna's face, the washed out pale replaced by a blush of embarrassment he was all too accustomed to seeing on the face of a warrior trying to put themselves back together. Her voice was low, hesitant. "This is just between you and me, right?"

He nodded. "No worries."

"I need something to do."

He held up the bolt assembly. "Got a couple pistols need cleanin'."

Chapter Twenty

Carlos Villanueva stood at the edge of the parking lot and looked over Manassas Battlefield Park. Lifting the binoculars to his eyes, he examined the field below one more time. Joel Perry sat in jeans and a T-shirt in the grass at the edge of the meadow, looking at the ground and not moving a muscle. *Not another soul in sight.* "I don't like it, Tab. He's all alone, no one else to meet us. Daniels said he'd be out here, too."

Sergeant Tabitha Grubka sat in the passenger's seat of Carlos' coupe, tightening the laces on a combat boot. "Joel's probably being watched from the tree line. I bet Agent Daniels simply doesn't trust us. After what they've been through, I'd be pretty careful, too." Finally satisfied with the fit of her boot, she climbed out and closed the door. "Not that I'm complaining, but I'm way out of my element here. I'm a bit-chaser, not a rifleman."

Carlos turned around long enough to give her a good-natured smirk. "That's why the rest of the team have weapons, and we don't." He glanced at his watch. "Well, five minutes past H-Hour. I assume Joel's waited enough. Let's go."

They strode out of the parking lot, past the visitor's center, and down the hill, Tabitha occasionally rearranging portions of her battle uniform. Carlos glanced over his shoulder. He could barely see Erick at the top of the hill, watching the western side of the park. Dave Gunderson would be watching the other side. Not that Carlos felt any safer. *No weapons, no radios, he said. If I'm wrong, what'll they tell Tab's parents when they send her home in a coffin?* His stomach did a couple extra flip-flops for good measure as he stole a glance at Tab. Besides squirming in her bulky uniform, her face looked as pale as his felt. Her eyes darted constantly, looking for some undefined threat from the trees.

When they drew within a few meters, Joel raised one hand over his head. With the other, he held out a radio.

When Carlos took it, a short squawk came from the speaker, followed by a familiar voice, one he'd only heard on the phone the day before. "Sergeant Villanueva, this is Agent Daniels."

Okay, we play it this way. Carlos keyed the handheld. "Go ahead. This is Villanueva."

"Tell Corporal Perry he can stand up, and thank him for his cooperation. You can go now."

Carlos scanned the tree line at the edge of the field again. The late afternoon light made it impossible to pick out any details among the greenery. "I thought we were going to meet today, Jon."

"Maybe another time."

Carlos cursed under his breath. He wanted answers, not more questions. "What's NADIA?"

"Something you don't talk about on a radio."

"Jon, you can tell me what I need to know, or I can keep digging until I find everything out, including where you're hiding Bunny Kalinsky. He's facing quite a suite of federal charges, you know. What's it going to be?" He unkeyed the radio and motioned to Joel to go back to the lot. Not taking his eyes from the trees, he whispered, "Meet Dave up there. I have a recorder in my car. Start talking. Everything you remember."

Daniels' voice crackled from the handheld again. "There's a cannon fifty meters to your left, over toward the stone bridge. Look in the muzzle. Out."

Carlos' heart jumped. "No, wait a minute! Daniels, where are you?" Silence was his only answer.

Tab pointed. "There's the cannon."

"Hang on," said Carlos. "I'll go check it out. If it's a trap, get back to the car. Round up the others, and zero in on Daniels and his crew. Comb the damned woods till you find them."

"What then?"

Handing her the radio, he said, "Make 'em spill their guts."

He approached the cannon slowly, looking for wires or hidden antennas and mumbling to himself. His hands shook; he stilled them by force of will. "This is ridiculous, they're on our side."

His inner voice answered. *Oh, are they? What makes you so certain they're friendlies, Jéfé?*

He carried on the conversation with himself all the way to the cannon. "Because if they were working for the bad guys, they'd have popped me and Tab for even asking about NADIA."

Or they would have put one of their antimatter bombs in this cannon, ready to take out the whole park, right? Reach in—I dare you.

"Shut up, Carlos, they're the good guys like us."

How do you know?

He was at the cannon. "'Cause I'm going to find out right now." Shining a penlight down the muzzle, he saw a tangle of litter and several pop cans. "I hope there aren't any spiders in there." He took a deep breath and began to withdraw the trash one item at a time.

He unwadded the fourth candy wrapper to find a series of numbers scrawled in marker on the inside. After tossing the rest of the trash in the nearest can, he returned to Tab. "GPS coordinates."

She hugged herself and shivered in spite of the heat. "Let's just get out of here, Carlos. I get a bad feeling—"

"Tab, we're too close to breaking this open." He reached out and took her hand. "We can finally find out what this NADIA is. Do you have any idea what the implications could be?"

Pulling away, she said, "No. And neither do you. All I know right now is that *we're* the ones sticking our hands down the barrel of the cannon. These people may be on our side, or maybe they just want to make sure no one gets closer to NADIA. What price would *you* pay to keep a secret, Carlos? How scared do you think they are? Scared enough to commit murder on a back road?"

He scratched his chin and pursed his lips. Of course, she was right. At least, she was convinced she was right. And when she was this sure, she usually *was* right. He looked at the coordinates on the paper again. Maybe not this time, though. "Tab, you know those gut hunches I get?" He held up the wrapper. "I'm getting one now. It's never steered me wrong, and I don't think it's wrong now. I know it's asking a lot for you to trust me, and you don't have to come along. But I really feel like I have to do this."

"So what, then? So I can be a widow before we're even married? Dammit, Carlos—!" She bit back the rest of her answer and stomped around in a circle, jaw clenched. When she spoke again, her voice was tight with emotion. "All right. But damned if you're going to get killed all by yourself. Let's go, then."

"I can get Dave and Erick to follow—"

Tab wheeled on him. "Bull!" She punched him in the chest, and he was thankful she wasn't a bodybuilder. "They're *watching*, Carlos! Don't you think they can see the nice men with M-16s wandering through the park?" Grabbing his wrist, she turned back toward the car. "If you want in, you're going in all the way. And I'm going with you. But before you get our cans shot off, you're damned well going to know one thing, Carlos Villanueva."

At the car, she pulled him close and kissed him. "You're going to know I love you. Now, let's go. Let the others get back to the shop."

* * * *

Ten minutes later, Carlos pulled onto the shoulder of an unpaved road. After he and Tab got out, he locked the car and drew a small GPS unit from a cargo pocket in his BDUs. "Hang on—" He took a few steps to orient the unit, then turned and strode across the dusty road, boots grinding in the dry gravel. "This way. Just a short walk, now."

Tab muttered, "At least we're not wearing Class As," before following.

They walked along a deer path through hardwoods and poison ivy when Carlos heard the same voice he'd spoken with on the radio.

"That's far enough, Sergeant."

Carlos turned to see a mound of dirt move and rise into the figure of a man wearing a ghillie suit of rough, earth-colored rags. "Check'em out, Jenna."

"Right," a female behind Carlos answered.

As Carlos spun around, a compact young woman stepped out of the trees in camo BDUs. *What the hell, she wasn't there a second ago—*

Jenna seemed to read his mind. "That's okay," she said with a smirk, "I'm a sneaky little wench when I want to be." She hummed a random little tune as she waved a wand that looked like it was made from a curling iron in the air around his body. A steady static hiss came from a small speaker. She finished with Carlos and waved it around Tab. "Okay, no bugs, and they came alone."

"Sergeant Villanueva," said Jon, "I'll come right to the point. I want you to leave us alone. Don't contact us anymore, and shut down your investigation of NADIA."

Carlos looked them up and down for a minute. They didn't carry any long weapons, but that didn't rule out pistols. And the way they were just standing, it didn't look like they were in too much of a hurry to use them. But something about this Jenna woman nagged at him. Maybe it was just the casual, self-confident smirk she wore. But she was someone he did *not* want to make mad. All the same, he felt safe enough to respond honestly to the request to desist. "Can't do that, Agent Daniels. I'm under orders to get to the bottom of NADIA. You've been sheltering a known felon and using him to illegally obtain information—"

Jon said, "Are you a cop?"

"Huh?" Carlos' jaw hung open, caught open in mid-sentence.

"I asked if you're a cop. It's a simple question." Jon removed his hood and stepped closer, looking like a comical cross between Sasquatch and a homeless man with the rags hanging loose from his suit. "A yes or a no will do."

"No."

"Then shut down your investigation. It's a matter for the Justice Department, not the Army."

Tab said, "What's NADIA?"

Jenna stepped up, nose to nose with her. "Who's asking?"

"The United States Army, on whom you've been eavesdropping," said Carlos.

Jon said, "You could have closed the hole in your firewall."

"I peeked back through. It led me to you."

"It's also going to lead to you getting a bullet in your head, if you dig any further."

Carlos felt the hair on his neck stand up. "Is that a threat?"

Jon shook his head. "Not from me, Sergeant. But the enemy has moles everywhere. For all you know, the one who gave you the orders to find me, may have done so only so they could take us all out."

"Don't you think you're being just a little paranoid?"

"Do yourself a favor, Villanueva—start checking your superiors for connections to the Global Unification Alliance."

Jenna whispered in Carlos' ear, "Chapter Seventeen. Look for it."

Jon's brow wrinkled. "I'm sorry, what?"

Jenna stepped back. "Just keeping your ass out of the meat grinder, Jon. Let these guys handle that one."

"Are we going to have to have a talk when we get back?"

"No, dear." She gave Jon a sly grin as a flush rose in his face.

Carlos interjected, "So this...group will lead us to NADIA?"

"No, Carlos," said Jon. "It will lead you away from NADIA."

"Why?"

Jon looked around, shifted his weight nervously, and heaved a sigh. Rubbing the back of his neck, he said, "Carlos, you have to trust me. Finding NADIA will only lead to the last arms race that humanity will ever see."

Carlos thought for a minute. Was this man actually *pleading* with him? The implied threat was that NADIA could potentially destroy the world. The thought sent a cold chill up Carlos' spine. But he was duty-bound at least to find out what it was. "Are you asking me to ignore my orders, then?"

Jon fixed him with a desperate stare. "I'm asking a fellow human to leave well enough alone, for the sake of all our futures. If NADIA's secret gets out, no one on the planet will be safe. We're trying to make sure the secret dies where no one will dig it back up. I'm asking you to go beyond your orders, straight to the source of the problem."

Jon backed into the forest. "Leave us alone. Drop your investigation." He slid the hood back over his head and ducked down, and Carlos could no longer tell where the undergrowth ended and Jon began. He wasn't even sure Jon was still there anymore.

Jenna gave Carlos and Tab one last, penetrating look. "Take some big guns. You'll need 'em." She took off after Jon, so silent Carlos wondered briefly if she was a ghost.

Tab muttered, "Strange people."

Carlos whuffed a sigh of relief. "Scared people."

"What next?"

"Tab, I think we'll take a look at our own first. I want to see if Daniels' theory holds water." Carlos started back toward the car.

Tab waited a moment before hustling to keep up. "What if he's right?"

"I hope he's wrong. On everything. But if he *is* right, and we've got a rat in the woodpile, we're all in a heap of trouble. Let's go, Tab."

When he took her hand, it was trembling almost as much as his own.

Chapter Twenty-One

Bowman waited until the third ring to pick up his phone. It would never serve to seem too eager.

His assistant's voice was crisp and businesslike. "Congressman Brady on line two, sir."

"Thank you, Denise. I'll be indisposed for the next hour."

"Of course, sir. Here's the congressman."

A click on the phone told him the transfer was complete. "Walter, how are you?"

The congressman paused before answering. "John, I think we may have a problem."

Bowman took a deep breath. *As if we don't already have enough problems.* "I'm listening."

"Army Intelligence has been snooping around some of our lower level associations."

"Walter, you're going to have to be clearer. We have hundreds of 'lower associations.'"

There was another long pause. Brady spoke in a low, conspiratorial tone. "Chapter Seventeen."

A butterfly could have knocked Bowman out of his chair. "Chapter Seventeen is hardly 'low level,' Walter. What makes you think the Army knows about Chapter Seventeen?"

"John, come on. I do sit on the Armed Services Committee. One of my aides came to me twenty minutes ago and asked me about the Global Unification Alliance. He specifically mentioned Chapter Seventeen."

A burr of irritation worked into Bowman's voice. "Why is an *aide* asking about GUA Seventeen?"

"His girlfriend is an intelligence lieutenant."

"And he is still on your staff *why?*"

"Who was it who said, 'Keep your friends close; keep your enemies closer'?"

"That's a dangerous game, my friend. Leaks pass water both ways."

"I can handle him. If things get too sticky, he can disappear. It's happened before."

Bowman rubbed a temple with his free hand. "How do you think word got out on Chapter Seventeen? Has anyone found your records?"

"No, the ledgers and rosters are in my safe, and no one but me knows where it is. There's only one way I can think of. Miss Paine lives, thanks to the incompetence of Palmer Frost and his merry band of misfits."

"Are you so sure it wasn't Kuznetzov? He could have leaked the information to get rid of us."

"Get serious! We've always handled our differences in-house. No outsider gets involved. Kuznetzov has no interest in leaking Seventeen. Paine is a classic 'disgruntled former employee' seeking her own pathetic little agenda for vengeance. Well, it was your program. You sponsored NADIA, funded it, and pulled the plug when it was over. She's all yours now, Mr. Bowman, and I hope you're ready, because now *we're* on her list."

"Come now, surely you're making mountains out of molehills," said Bowman in a low, derisive chuckle. "Miss Paine is hiding. She knows what we're capable of, and if she dares to raise her head in public, we'll be waiting to see her out the door the right way."

"I wouldn't be so sure, John. She escaped once. What makes you think she won't do so again?"

"I have top agents tracking her down now. I expect to hear from them any day now—"

Brady's angry exclamation cut Bowman short. "Hey, what are you doing here? This is a private office, Miss!"

A feminine voice in the background said, "Good." Two soft pops in Bowman's earpiece hit like sledgehammer blows in his mind. A rustle on the other end told him the phone was being picked up again. The woman spoke in a bright, pleasant voice. "I'm sorry, the congressman has just been called away. Can I take a message?"

Bowman hung up, his lungs suddenly empty of air. *How could she do this? Walter wasn't a part of her excommunication, and neither was I. She should know I didn't want her killed. Surely she wouldn't come after one who'd supported her so faithfully. Surely she wouldn't—*

Taking a breath, he gathered himself. A panic would not help the situation. Not only was Jenna Paine still alive, but she most certainly was *not* hiding. She was in the open, flaunting herself in front of them all.

He buried his face in shaking hands. *Dammit all, she would.*

Chapter Twenty-Two

Jon nearly choked on his coffee when Walter Brady's picture came up on the newscast the next morning. As it was, he dropped his cup in his lap. The hot liquid soaked through his jeans, and when he opened his mouth to protest the pain, the mouthful he'd been holding ran down his chin and onto his shirt. He flew from the couch, sputtering and cursing.

Bunny came running in to see what the matter was, and stopped, slack-jawed, as the talking head on the screen continued his story.

Jon grabbed the remote and turned up the volume. "...Found dead in his office by an aide. Why he was targeted, and by whom, is still a mystery. For more, let's go to the scene with our own Kalita Famiano—"

The screen blanked out as Jon hit the button on the remote. "Where is she?"

"I guess I know better than to ask who," muttered Bunny as Jon bolted out the door.

Jon dashed through the woods to Irving's shed and leaped down the steps three at a time, ducking his head to miss the ceiling on the way down.

The common room was dark with the silence unique to empty space. *She wouldn't have the gall to stick around after pulling that stunt.* The shout was more to vent his own frustration than in expectation of any kind of response. "Jenna! Dammit, anyway!"

Rubbing the back of his neck, he spun around, releasing a stream of words that would have scorched the wood paneling. Three manila folders sat on the table beneath the corkboard. Walter Brady's photo was ripped in pieces next to them.

He stormed down the hall, pounding on each door. "Jenna!"

The armory door hung open. He hit the light switch, and his heart leaped into his throat.

Two Colt .45 automatic pistols were missing from their places in the rack, along with their spare clips and at two boxes of ammo.

Jon raced up the steps to the shed. Yanking his keys from the hook in Irving's kitchen, he dashed out to the drive. His and Jimmy's cars still sat in their usual places. He jumped behind the wheel of his coupe.

The starter pounded the engine futilely until he released the key.

He pulled the hood release and jumped out. One quick glance at the engine told him he wasn't going anywhere soon. "She took the plug wires," he muttered. With a curse, he slammed the hood down and turned around to see Jimmy and Irving on the porch, watching him impassively.

Nadia and Sofi were just coming out through the screen door. Bunny emerged from the tree line, following the path that led from his cottage.

"Jenna's gone," he said. "Who's seen her since last night?"

"Said she was gonna take first watch," said Jimmy. "Last time I saw her."

Jon took a step toward him, his hands balled into fists. "You let her take a watch on her own? I'm *so* glad you decided she was trustworthy enough to not slit our throats in our sleep!"

"Take it easy, boy," the old man grumbled. "She never was after us, and you know it. If you recall, she made a deal to act as your field agent. Seems to me you oughta spool down and let well enough alone."

Before Jon could open his mouth to bark back at Jimmy, Nadia spoke. "She didn't take either car."

"No," said Jon. "Jenna wouldn't do that, because we'd report it stolen, and she'd get caught in a heartbeat. She's too damned smart for that. Knowing her, she's probably hitching a ride to somewhere she can buy a car, probably with cash."

"It's too late to catch up with her now." Nadia drew out her phone. "What do you need to get these running? I'll see if Donna can pick it up on the way out."

"Have her file a missing person report on Jenna, too. Give her some kind of medical condition, amnesia or something. That always gets a better response."

Jimmy spoke up again. "That girl's probably gone five ways from Sunday already. You want my advice, I'd be lookin' at that board of yours, Jon."

"Why?"

"Those people pissed her off real good. She's probably gonna hit the next closest person on that list of yours."

Jon's jaw dropped. A cold chill hit him as he realized what she was doing. He started for the shed again. "Come on, Bunny. We'd better hope we can get someone arrested while there's still someone alive to arrest."

* * * *

Jenna was already a hundred miles away and making good time. The pickup was old enough to have been driven by Jimmy Carter when he farmed peanuts, but the engine was still sound, having been well maintained by its erstwhile owner. Jenna paid him an insane amount for the truck using cash money from Congressman Brady's "private stash" from the safe she'd found behind the bookcase in his office. The duffel next to her on the seat still held over seventy thousand dollars, plenty for what she needed to do next.

She fought back the lump that rose in her throat. There was a small part of her that wasn't surprised at what she'd read in Brady's files. After what they'd done to *her*, it fit their *modus operandi* perfectly: use whomever you can dupe for as long as you can, and then get rid of them as completely as possible. No loose ends, no "disgruntled former employees" left to blow the whistle.

Until now.

And this time, they were going to feel the full effect of their error.

Jenna stopped at a filling station in Pennsylvania, picking up a prepaid cellphone and a full tank of gas before continuing westward.

* * * *

Bunny pointed to one of the remaining photos on the Battle Board. "Here's the closest one, Jon. That Bowman guy who owns half the media outlets in the western hemisphere." He fired up a laptop and connected to the server from the common room. "You want I should send him a warning?"

"No, that wouldn't accomplish anything but drive these people further underground. We want them to think they're safe for now—"

"Don't you think Brady's murder would tip them off that something's up? Here's his ledgers with records of bribes collected and sent to all these groups" —he held up an ornate gold ring set with a huge ruby— "and we got this ring that matches the one Anna Spielberg gave Nadia before cackin' off. If their agents do any checkin', they're bound to put two and two together."

"I'm sure they will. That's why I want to visit Mr. Bowman personally, before Jenna gets there. Maybe I could convince him he can escape a similar fate, with a little cooperation."

Bunny whistled through his teeth. "You'd really threaten 'im with Jenna if he don't talk? Jonny-boy, that's hard-ball there."

"It's the only game in town right now, Bunny. Now, how about a ticket to San Fran? First class this time, that coach seating really sucks on long flights."

Chapter Twenty-Three

Bowman's voice shook as much as the hand that held his phone. "Mr. Frost, you have a new priority. Conclude your business at your current location and organize bodyguards for the rest of the Council."

"Do you want me to find his ledgers and ring?" asked Frost, speaking from his command post in the run-down house. "If they fall into the wrong hands, everything we've built comes down like a house of cards."

"No, not yet. See to the security of the Council and then worry about those items. Let the scene cool down before you return for those details."

Frost hesitated for a moment before answering. "Yes, sir. Of course, whatever you say. May I suggest at least that the Council take off their rings until everything blows over?"

"You may suggest." Bowman hung up and crossed his plush carpet. At the bar, he pulled out a decanter of caramel-colored liquid. After filling a tall glass, he took a sip and let the warmth radiate through his body. The shuddering stopped long enough for him to hold his remote steady. Turning the volume up on his FM receiver, he caught up on the latest from Washington.

How Miss Paine had gotten the names of the Council members was moot. The fact that she did have them was intolerable, unheard of!

He took another drink of Scotch. *I always supported the Project, didn't I? I always stood up against the majority of the Council on her behalf. Surely, she'll understand I'm on her side...*

* * * *

Frost slammed his phone shut before finishing his acknowledgement of Bowman's order. "Anything you say, you pompous bastard." He turned to the rest of the team. "Those records and that ring take precedence over everything else right now. Get to Brady's office and recover them. The man who brings them to me gets two weeks and my cut of the service fee. Mr. Verhoff, you and I are pulling the plug here and moving to another location. Let's *move*, gentlemen, you are wasting oxygen and daylight!"

Healy, Spooner, and McVay checked their weapons on the way out. Verhoff began to break his system down to be packed in airline cases.

Frost opened his phone again and dialed. "Miss Preston, this is Mr. Frost. I need to be wheels-up for San Francisco in two hours."

* * * *

Jenna pulled into the parking lot of a fleabag motel outside Cleveland. In the bushes at the southwest corner of the building she lifted the paver from beneath the downspout and dug through the moist soil until her fingernails scraped against a hard, flat surface. Prying around the edges, she pulled up a small metal box wrapped in plastic. Inside she found a brass key.

The room belonged to the Company. The master key was hers, a little extra she'd arranged on her own.

She walked around the back side of the building until she stood outside Room 211. There was no sound from within, and the lights were dark. Of course, they could have someone waiting inside, if they expected her here. But that was unlikely. The Pinnacle didn't have enough agents to cover every safe house between Virginia and California.

The door creaked open and she stood still for a moment, listening, reaching out with every sense for any sign of life. No sound of breathing or movement, no scent of cologne betrayed a would-be attacker.

Jenna slid through the door and closed it before turning on the light. A grin split her face as she thought of all the travelers and transients who'd spent nights in this room unaware what lay at their fingertips. The drawers all slid from the dresser. Against the back panel a .45 Colt automatic pistol was taped, along with two spare magazines. Around the pistol, the rest of the panel was packed with bundles of cash. These were collected and laid on a towel in the middle of the floor.

The bathroom was next. Jenna grabbed the medicine cabinet and lifted it straight up and off the bracket. Behind it lay the real reason she came. Three passports, one each for Trina Stevens, Linda Ballas, and Andi Reynolds, all bore her photograph. Inside each passport was a matching driver's license and a credit/debit card. Each account belonged to her, and as far as she knew, The Pinnacle was blissfully ignorant of these resources.

Ten minutes later, she was on the road again. She now had two hundred thousand in cash, untraceable IDs and access to all her private bank accounts. Jenna Paine was now officially off the grid.

At a small RV lot in Indiana, she picked up a camper shell for the truck and, a few miles down the road, a few hours' rest at a campground.

A grim smile played across her face as she swung out onto the highway the next morning.

They'll never know what hit them.

Chapter Twenty-Four

Donna clutched a handkerchief in one hand while she wiped the other on her slacks. She hated the way her palms sweated when she was nervous. Sitting outside the office of the Vice President of the United States was enough to make her wish she had a towel.

Vice President Gutenberg recruited her to lead the FBI's arm of the NADIA Project, almost five years ago. But Charles was no longer in the office, having been "removed" by Pinnacle operatives using a NADIA weapon in the form of the then-serving Secretary of State. His replacement hadn't called her since taking office.

The young man behind the desk in the outer office put down his phone and smiled at her. "Vice President Schiller is ready for you now, Doctor."

Donna picked up her briefcase and walked in on shaky legs. Charles was a constant, someone she had come to count on as reliable in an unreliable world. Linda Schiller was vice president for three years, and this was the first time she and Donna had met. Could she be trusted? *Should* she be trusted? Donna scolded herself for even asking. This was the Vice President of the United States. Surely she'd been checked out thoroughly. This wasn't some third-world dictatorship with a fourth-rate security system.

Mrs. Schiller came around her desk to shake Donna's hand. She was plump and short, with the soft, friendly figure of a grandmother, and the earnest demeanor of a fledgling CEO. She spoke over Donna's shoulder to her assistant. "Jamie, close the door. Make sure no one disturbs us." To Donna, she said, "Now, tell me why it took three years for us to have this meeting."

Donna sat and opened her briefcase. "To be honest, ma'am, I thought your predecessor would have left you with instructions on what to do if anything happened to him. This was a project high on his priority list. As for the three years, I must confess I've been a bit gun shy over the events surrounding Mr. Gutenberg's death. When time went by and you didn't contact me... This case is very sensitive, Madame Vice President. I had to be sure I could trust you. "

"Please, call me Linda in here." She knitted her fingers on her desktop. "How well did you know Charles?"

"Not very. The only time I met him personally was when he recruited me for this program. He wanted there to be a comfortable distance between us in case there were any incidents."

"And so, it seems, there was." Linda's eyes softened in thought. "And any instructions that may have benefited me vaporized along with him and Juliet Henderson."

"The secretary was an imposter, ma'am. She was a living weapon called a NADIA." Donna placed a folder on the mahogany desktop. The vice president opened it and read while Donna spoke. "It was an artificial person with a weaponized skeletal structure."

Linda's eyes rolled up from the folder to fix Donna with a hard stare. "So what happened to the real Juliet Henderson?"

"I'm sure she was dead before Charles was killed. They took her, copied her body, took her consciousness, and transferred it into the weapon. The real Juliet will have died during the transfer."

Linda leaned back and rubbed her temples. "Doctor Hermsen, I think you'd best start at the beginning and pretend I don't know a thing about what you're saying. Let's start with 'why.'"

Donna put on her glasses and put another folder on the desk. "A group calling themselves 'The Pinnacle' is behind it."

Linda nodded and motioned for Donna to continue.

"These people want to set themselves up as shadow rulers over every country on the planet."

One of the Vice President's brows rose slightly. She paused before speaking. "An ambitious plan indeed. So how do they intend to make this happen?"

"By manipulating economic forces to create chaos, they insert their agents into places of power around the globe. That way they can rule through their puppets. The ones they can't manipulate or recruit for their cause, they remove through assassination or scandal."

"Sounds like a pretty ruthless bunch, to hear you tell it."

"They tried to kill me and my associates on many occasions, for working to uncover their plot. They're behind the deaths of Charles Gutenberg, Secretary Henderson, President Bello of Nigeria, and countless others we haven't yet traced them to."

"Do you think they have designs against the United States or its allies?"

"Without doubt, ma'am. They already have moles in the Bureau and in every major investigative agency of this country, as well as Congress itself."

Linda straightened back up, her eyes wide in shock. "Who?"

"Walter Brady, for one. They were using him to strangle our self-reliance and keep us dependent on foreign resources."

"For what purpose?"

"To make sure we would have to play nice when the time came for the takeover, I guess. To promote their one-world agenda. To lower border tension so their people would be seen as peacemakers instead of conspirators."

Linda fixed Donna again with her eyes. For an instant, Donna saw the strength and drive the woman possessed, that had set her behind this desk. Despite her appearance, this was nobody's grandmother. There was steel in that mind. "You do know that Congressman Brady is dead?"

"Yes, ma'am."

"I suppose we should vet his successor thoroughly, then."

Donna pulled out another folder. "Check their background for connections to a group called the Global Unification Alliance."

The vice president nodded, her chin cupped in one hand. Donna allowed herself to relax a bit more, and she let Linda peruse the folders while Donna explained, "The GUA is The Pinnacle's front organization. Squeaky-clean from the outside, rotten as hell in the middle where we can't reach yet."

"Yet?"

"We haven't tied the GUA's senior leadership directly to The Pinnacle, but we know their major funding comes through seven of the most powerful and influential people on the planet."

"You have a list?"

"Yes, ma'am." Donna nodded firmly.

"May I see it?"

"I'm sorry, but all we have are suspicions right now. I don't want to compromise our investigation or slander innocent people until we have more solid connections to their subterfuge." Donna stood and began to gather her folders. "They've been very clever so far, working within most systems, and only going outside the bounds of the law when someone finds them out or gets in their way."

"If they're working within the system, where's the problem, Doctor?"

Gathering the last of her files, Donna closed her briefcase. "They're not being open about it. Their agenda is for a one-world government behind some golden curtain. On the surface, everything looks like business as usual, only without the normal international tension. But behind that curtain, the strings are all being pulled by this select group of non-elected rulers. Dictators, if you will. What will happen to freedom then? Liberty? Everything our Founding Fathers and every warrior in our history fought and bled and died for?"

Donna's nervousness gave way to the passion building in her breast. She placed her hands on the desk and leaned forward, her face burning. "I, for one, will not go gently into that good night, Madame Vice President. This country was founded on individual freedom and liberty.

We can't let this mob of megalomaniacs take away what we've spent over two hundred years building and defending."

She stood up, leaving moist prints on the polished desk where her hands had been. "I took an oath when I joined the federal service, to defend the Constitution of the United States against all enemies, foreign or domestic. You took that oath, too, ma'am. We need your continuing support to bring this investigation to a close and expose these would-be rulers, make them pay for the blood they've spilled."

Linda stood and smoothed her business suit. "Well-spoken, Doctor. That gives me much to ponder." She pointed to the briefcase in Donna's hand. "You may leave that here with me, and after I've made copies of your files, I'll return it to you."

"I'm sorry, ma'am. These are the only files in existence, and I want them to stay that way."

Linda stiffened, her lips pursed. "Very well. I'll have my Secret Service see you out, then." She smiled, although her face still had a drawn, tense look. "For security's sake, of course." She opened the door and shook Donna's hand again. "Thank you so much for coming, Doctor." At her call, two large men stepped through the door from the outer office. "Dave, Austin, please see Doctor Hermsen out." She smiled one last time at Donna. "Use the rear entrance."

Dave and Austin led Donna down a different way than she'd come in. She followed obediently, not knowing the way herself.

They weren't much for conversation. Each seemed lost in their own thoughts as they led her down hall after hall, ending up in a garage full of limos and sedans.

Dave pointed to a small black mid-sized sedan with a tan interior. "We'll use this one."

Donna stopped. "That's okay, boys, I drove myself. I just need to get to my car—"

A rough shove behind her knocked the briefcase from her hand. Before she could react, a rear door was opened and they stuffed her in, facedown across the backseat. Someone stretched out on top of her, clamping a rough hand over her mouth. His other hand wrenched her arm up behind her back. The weight of him pinned her down, unable to fight.

The front door opened and the other man got in. "I got the case. Hold her down till we're out of town."

Donna kicked and struggled. With every move she made, her arm was wrenched up higher. She couldn't scream through the massive hand covering her mouth. She pressed her face down on the seat, forcing some of the man's flesh between her teeth, and bit as hard as she could. In response, he only grunted and let go of her wrist long enough to beat her across the head. After the tenth blow, she began to feel reality leaving her. The driver called back over his shoulder, "Hey, not so rough! The Veep just called and said not to leave a mess in the car."

The Veep? Oh, my God, what have I done? Donna fought until she ran out of strength. But the mass of meat on top of her refused to budge. She fought to keep her mind under control. As long as she drew breath, escape was possible. She just had to wait for her chance. *Conserve your strength—you're going to need it when the time comes.* She choked back her tears, wondering if her chance would ever come.

An eternity later, the car stopped. The door opened, and the weight lifted from her back. A hand wrapped itself in her hair, dragging her from the car. *No! There won't be another time.* She twisted and yanked her head away, ripping loose and leaving him with a shock of hair and piece of her scalp.

The hot stream of blood pouring down her neck went unnoticed, masked by the same fear that kept her from feeling the pain. Donna screamed as she ran. Maybe someone would hear. "Help me—!"

Her shout was cut off by a sharp bang behind her. Something punched her in the back, and she fell. Her breath left her in a rush. She scrambled back to her feet and took off again. Behind her, she heard their footsteps as they raced through the undergrowth after her.

There was another bang, and a bullet buzzed through the air next to her head like an angry wasp.

One man stopped. She dodged to her right as the other came close enough to grab at her clothing.

She was running slower now. Her breath came in painful, awkward gasps.

Bang! Another bullet tore bark from a tree. Splinters sprayed her head. The next two missed.

Donna didn't hear the fourth one. It punched into her chest from the side, knocking her wind out and sending her to the forest floor again. She rolled to her back, unable to draw breath. The world grew dim as she saw the man standing over her, taking aim. She looked straight down the barrel of his pistol. A sudden calm washed over her, warm in her chest. There would be no more running. A peace flowed through her. The only shame was that she couldn't warn her friends. And poor Nadia… There was a flash, and a terrible sound, and she knew no more.

Chapter Twenty-Five

Jon finished packing his meager belongings and looked around the room he called home one last time. "Okay, that's about it." He turned to Nadia, standing next to him. "That's all I have."

"It's not much," she said. "Just one box of things to show for a lifetime."

"I'm just taking the basics. I'll settle down, eventually. When things get quieter, I guess."

He carried the box out and set it on the tailgate of the rented panel truck. Jimmy stood in the back to receive it. In a moment, it was packed neatly into a corner of the truck's bed.

Hushi came out with the last of her things, Sofi trailing behind with her duffel. When these were added to the cache, Jimmy sat on the bed and slid to the ground. "That does it, except what Doc wanted to take. Anyone know where she's at?"

Beth came around the backside of the truck, dangling car keys from her hand. "She went to D.C. this morning. She said something about checking in with her boss, whoever that is."

Jon said, "That would probably be the FBI director. Unless she answers to someone else for this project. She never did tell us who her supervisor is."

Nadia said, "She said it's safer that way. Suppose something happened? What if they were compromised?" A shadow of worry crossed her face.

"Don't go off just yet, babe." Jon took out his cell and dialed. After several rings, a click sounded in his ear. Donna's cheerful voice came on. "Hi, this is Doctor Hermsen. Leave your name and callback number, and I'll get back with you as soon as—" Jon slapped the phone shut. "She's probably in a meeting or something. Either way, we can't wait anymore. Beth and Hushi, tell us what to pack from the stores downstairs. If we need more, we'll have Bunny scrounge it up when we get there. Is everyone ready?"

"I just have to say goodbye to Papa," said Nadia.

Jon followed her down the path and up the steps to Irving's cabin. The old man sat on the porch with a blanket on his knees and a book in his lap. He looked up and grinned as they approached. "Off again, children?"

Nadia bent to hug him around the neck. "You make sure to take your medicine, and I'll see you when we get back."

He sounded weaker today. "Of course, little one. Get better quickly, now."

There were tears in her eyes as she released him. "'Bye, Papa."

When Jon gave him a hug, Irving whispered, "Take good care of her, Jonny. My Hilda, God rest her soul, she would say, 'Now there's a real person.'" He pushed Jon back and gave him a stern look. "Don't you let her go again, young man."

"Okay, Mr. Rats." Jon choked up as he let go and they headed back toward the truck.

Sofi and Jimmy met them on the path. Nadia gave Jimmy a warm hug. "Take care of him, please?"

He grinned at her. "Old war horses like us can take care of ourselves, young lady." With a wave, he took off through the woods toward Irving's.

After he left, Sofi asked, "Can I ride with Hushi?"

Nadia reached out to ruffle her daughter's hair, now spiked in black with pink tips. "Knock yourself out, honey."

"Cool!" Sofi smiled and took off at a run.

Jon watched the girl climb into Bunny's car and shook his head. "That kid sure has changed since she came here. Are you sure Hushi isn't corrupting her?"

Nadia smiled. "If she is, I hope it's permanent."

He paused again and pulled out his cellphone. Nadia put her hand gently on his wrist. "You think she's all right?"

There was a quiet desperation in Jon's chest, a feeling he didn't like. "It's not like Donna to go off the grid for so long. She knew we wanted to hit the road before dark."

"Wait a little longer before you call, okay? Give her a chance to finish up whatever she's doing." She wrapped her arms around his neck and pulled him close. Looking into her eyes, he saw that she shared the same concern, even as she reassured him. "I'm sure she's fine, wherever she is." Her lips were warm and sweet, and he found himself almost believing her.

She released him and started down the path. "I'd better take my Dilantin before we leave. It's going to be a long night on the road."

Grasping her shoulder, he turned her back around. "How are you doing, babe? Just between you and me, what's going on?"

The smile faded from her face, and she looked away. "I have cancer, Jon. I'm trying to stay on top of the seizures long enough for Hushi and Donna to find a cure for me before I destroy two hundred square miles. I throw up, I feel like the south end of a northbound elephant, and I'm freaking terrified. But I have Sofi, and I have you. That's what holds me together." She took his hand and they set off.

Jon turned back and looked at Irving Ratzinger's cabin one last time. The place looked tired, as weathered as the two old men they were leaving behind.

He felt terrible about dragging them into this nightmare, but was grateful for the assistance they'd rendered. Irving gave them a home base to operate from, and Jimmy had saved their skins on more than one occasion. If anyone could take care of Papa, it was Jimmy.

Jon sighed and waved one last time, wondering if he'd ever come back this way again.

He hoped so.

Chapter Twenty-Six

Arbor Hills, Colorado was the perfect community for security-minded people who could afford the extra frills that made them feel that little bit more protected. High stone walls capped with broken glass surrounded the entire subdivision. The only way in or out was through two massive iron gates with guardhouses, one on the east side of the compound and one on the northeast corner. The neighborhood was nestled on the outer fringes of Broomfield, between two other gated communities with their own private goon squads who patrolled the streets and kept the riff-raff at bay.

Unless the riff-raff could afford to move in, too.

Jenna had been camping in the hills around Arbor Hills for three days and nights, watching, measuring, stalking like a panther sizing up a deer.

At dusk on the fourth day she crept closer to the east gate, making no more noise in the undergrowth than a snake. At the edge of the tree line, she pulled out her binoculars.

Shift change occurred at a different time each night, but all happened within a one-hour window. The guards carried sidearms, but Jenna saw no long weapons. There was probably a shotgun or two in each gatehouse, if not an automatic carbine, but if there was, they were never taken out. Two men worked each shift. One rode around the streets in a golf cart while the other manned the east gate. The northeast gate stayed locked after dusk.

"No problem," she muttered as she slid back into the trees. She slithered back to the game trail before standing up and jogging to her campsite. Snuggled in a tiny clearing away from prying eyes, a dome tent hunched next to a small folding table and chair. A small sterno stove sat atop the table, making a fire unnecessary.

Jenna ducked into her tent to change out of her camo BDUs. Her plan needed another uniform.

She emerged a couple of minutes later in a snug, worn Grateful Dead T-shirt and a pair of Daisy Dukes. She kept her heavy socks and hiking boots. It was bad enough she was going to be cold, no sense giving up proper footgear. Guys found it sexy, anyway. Adjusting her shorts for maximum visual effect, she settled into her camp chair to wait for full dark.

Closing her eyes, Jenna steeled into her zone. The rabbit hanging from the tree behind the tent squealed and thrashed at random intervals. Far from a distraction, it helped her concentrate on her plan. The next few minutes, she mentally walked over every step, making adjustments and allowing for every possible variable.

She felt the darkness fall, heard the insects and night animals crawl from their burrows and warrens. Her eyes snapped open. It was time. She was the tiger again, the huntress, and prey was near. She stood and grabbed her pack. Just before she slung it on her back, she slid a large hunting knife from its sheath.

The rabbit's last cry was cut off as Jenna slashed its throat. She held the carcass above her and wrung it out, letting its blood pour hot over her shirt, her cheek, down a leg. She was back on the game trail when she flung her sacrifice into the woods for the wolves to find.

At the tree line, she hesitated, building up into her role. She took several deep breaths and tensed every muscle in her body, turning herself into a quivering, quaking heap. The knife had one more job. Holding it up for a moment, she examined the blade. *Careful, now.* The knife raised, halted, and came down, piercing her left forearm, just deep enough to show a wound, not too close to any major blood vessels.

Another thrust opened a small cut in her upper leg, just above the knee. Then the knife went sailing into the brush, its grisly job complete.

She took one more look to make sure every detail was in place. For a second, she wondered if hitting them from the "hot babe" and "Damsel in distress" sides at the same time was overdoing it. But for only a second. *Shock and awe, baby.* Nodding to herself, she closed her eyes and sank into that place in her mind where she was a coiled viper, ready for the strike. Then throwing her head back, her entire being erupted in a horrifying, guttural scream.

* * * *

The guard in the shack heard the scream and dropped his coffee cup. From the trees across Gordon Road emerged a nightmare, staggering toward him with outstretched arms and wide, terror-stricken eyes. She was petite and beautiful, a vision in shorts and tight shirt. And she was covered in gore. She bled freely down an arm and a leg and with that much blood, who knew where else she might have been hurt.

Running from the guardhouse, he pulled his pistol and, covering the trees, took the girl by the shoulder to guide her back across the road. He seated her in a plastic vinyl chair in the well-lit little shack and punched the key down on a base radio. "Mick, get in here. I think someone got attacked by a puma."

She was shaking and crying hysterically, her face buried in gore-covered hands. He grabbed a first aid kit from the wall and set it on the floor next to her. When he took a wrist and gently pulled one hand from her face, her shaking stilled. Her eyes rolled up to look into his, and behind those eyes, he saw something more deadly than a mountain cat. She wrenched her hand free from his shocked grasp and lashed out. Before he could react, she did something that made his neck explode in pain, and blackness took him.

* * * *

When Mick jumped out of the golf cart, the shack was empty. No one answered his call; the radio was silent. *What the hell—?* Stepping into the guardhouse, he saw signs of—something. No one was in the shack. The first aid kit lay open in the middle of the floor, supplies scattered. The orange visitor's chair was smeared with blood. Drops spattered the floor. A hiker's pack sat next to the chair. He keyed the radio again as he spun around, scanning again for his companion. "Danny, this is Mick—"

She came from nowhere. One moment he was looking through an empty doorway, the next his vision was filled with the blur of a nightstick. He ducked the blow, but her follow-up chop caught him across the throat. He tried fruitlessly to scream through his shattered windpipe as she dragged him into the bushes to lie next to Danny. Danny's lifeless eyes apologized as Mick's vision closed in.

* * * *

Jenna wiped her hands on his uniform before standing back. "Nothing personal, boys. You were just in my way." She grabbed her pack from the guardhouse and set off, recalling the layout from the map on the wall. The fresh pressure dressings on her cuts needed adjustments one time, but once she set them aright, they were good to go.

Once inside the neighborhood, the streets were dark. No one wanted streetlights shining through their windows. It worked well for her. It meant she wouldn't be disturbing anyone's dog, sneaking through backyards to stay invisible. She trotted easily along the sidewalks, confident no one would have reason to look out their windows at night.

Adrenaline pumped through her system, heightening her senses even more. The darkened streets in the full moonlight showed as clearly as on an overcast day. Sound reached her ears from each house she passed. The murmur of conversations, the clink of dinner dishes in the sink, children being tucked into bed, nothing escaped her attention. The breeze in her face brought smells of dinner cooking from a dozen homes, the rank odor of dogs or cats, the stench of someone's overflowing garbage container.

All those years in training, first with Mama-san, then with Steven, followed by Frost, confirmed in her now what she was, and would always be. And as it turned out, it was what she was born to be as well. They'd created a killer. They forged her, hammered her on their anvil, quenched and honed her, until she was what they'd envisioned before she was born, a perfect weapon. And now that they'd turned on her, they would find out what a splendid job they did, firsthand.

She found the house in the northwest corner of the subdivision, a red brick colonial with a white colonnade out front. Pale yellow light splashed onto the front lawn through one window. Subtle flickers and variations in the light pattern told Jenna the TV was on. She tried the door and found it unlocked. Slipping silently through the gap, she closed the door behind her and prowled over the plush carpet, down the hall.

She stopped off one side of the doorway to the TV room. Hugging the wall, she eased her head around the corner and saw her mother for the first time in nine years. Silver streaks graced her hair at the temples. The face showed more wrinkles. But there was no mistaking the way she sat stock-upright in her wingback chair watching Clark Gable murmur sweet nothings to Katherine Hepburn.

Jenna focused all her senses on the house, listening to every creak and groan. No other presence betrayed itself. The woman was alone. Steeling herself, Jenna stepped in. "Hi, Mother."

Meredith Paine froze. Her eyes widened in fear. A half-empty glass of Chardonnay trembled in her right hand; her left clutched the arm of her chair. "Oh my God, Jenna, what happened to you?"

"Bad day at work. I suppose they called you."

Mother's face softened. A smile tried to paint itself on her mouth, but utterly failed. Her voice was high, strained. "They who? N-no one called me. Who are you talking about?"

Jenna stepped into the living room. "You don't lie well, Mother. You never could. Can I trust you not to hit the panic button until after I've had a shower? I think you owe me that much."

Mother set the glass down on an antique end table and stood. "L-let me get you some towels. Are you all right, honey? What happened?"

"I'm all right. Just a couple of scratches. But I'd really like to clean up before I explain. And if you push the button, we'll never be able to talk. They'll take me away, and you'll never find out what I know."

"Like what, honey?"

"Like where Jon Daniels and his team are hiding."

Chapter Twenty-Seven

Jon pulled the little convoy into a truck stop on I-65 a little after ten. Clouds of mosquitoes and moths played tag with bats and night birds around the light poles. Sleepy-eyed truckers shambled across the lot, heading back to their rigs for the night. He shrugged his right shoulder to wake Nadia and stepped out onto the tarmac, which still radiated the day's heat into the damp air.

She took an extra minute to come around before swinging her legs out the passenger door. Jon wasn't so sure her pallor was due solely to the washed-out hue of the lights in the lot. When she gathered herself to get out, she stood uncertainly for a few moments, leaning into Jon's chest for support.

He stood back and took her hand, leading her to the restaurant door. "Hon, how do you feel?"

She gave his hand a squeeze and let go. "I really wish you'd quit asking. I'm fine. I just need to stretch for a minute before we sit down to eat, okay?"

At this late hour, only a couple of restless freight drivers browsed the travel store, and the restaurant was empty save for the weary little band of travelers.

The sign at the door said, "Please Seat Yourself." A cheerful voice from the kitchen called out, "Be with you in a minute." Bunny led the way to a large corner booth where they could all share the table. After they sat, a small, round grandmother paced toward them, pad and pencil ready in her hand. She beamed a wide smile around the group. "Hi, folks, I'm Shirley, an' I'll be Jane-on-the-spot tonight. Who wants coffee?"

Nadia said, "I suppose a double decaf mochaccino latte with a cinnamon stick is out of the question?"

Shirley shook her head wistfully, but didn't miss a beat. "How about a decaf espresso, hon?"

"Close enough."

After Shirley took drink orders and bustled off, Jon excused himself and went to the men's room, waiting until the table was out of sight before pulling out his phone.

Donna had to be home by now. *Why the hell hasn't she called yet? She has to know we'd be worried sick. Unless something bad happened...*

The phone rang twice, and someone picked up. Jon waited a moment for Donna's normal "FBI, Doctor Hermsen" greeting, but he was met with empty air, punctuated by a soft breath.

Red flags waved in Jon's mind, but he pressed on. Maybe she was sick. Or maybe she was in a situation where she was unable to speak. "Is everything all right?"

A deep male voice said, "Hold on." A series of clicks and muffled pops told Jon the phone was being handed off to someone else.

A woman came on. "Agent Daniels?"

What the hell? "Yes." Jon felt his chest grow thick with dread.

"This is Linda Schiller. Do you know who I am?"

Is that who Donna was meeting? "The vice president," he stammered. "W-where is Doctor Hermsen?"

"Missing. We found this phone, and were hoping it could lead us to the rest of her team. Where are you?"

"Ma'am, I don't believe—"

"Agent Daniels, this is *not* the time for foolishness about operational security! Doctor Hermsen was supposed to meet with me to discuss something of the highest importance to national security, and now she's missing. I want you to bring the rest of your team to my office, tomorrow. Do you understand?"

The red flags in Jon's head waved harder. Something about this just didn't jibe. "I'm afraid that's impossible under the circumstances, ma'am. We're in the field—"

"I'm changing your mission. As of right now, all priority is to be put on finding Doctor Hermsen. Am I clear?"

Fear chased its tail around his stomach for a few laps before he answered. *Whatever.* "Yes, ma'am, you are clear."

"I'll see you tomorrow, then. Bring the rest of your team in, and we'll hammer out a plan."

The line went dead. Jon slapped his phone shut. An icy spear of dread shot though his chest. *This can only mean one thing, and it sure isn't good.*

As he made his way back to the table, everyone was laughing at some wise crack Bunny had just made. Nadia glanced up, and when their eyes met, she paled and froze. "Jon, what's wrong, honey?"

The table went silent as he choked out, "They got Donna. We… we have to go. Now." He went on to tell them about the conversation he'd just had with the vice president.

"Are we going to go?" asked Beth, "To Washington?"

As Jon spoke, anger mingled with determination, steadying his voice and displacing the grief, if only temporarily. "Hell, no. They had Donna's phone all this time. My number is in it. Why didn't they call me?" He pulled out his phone again and looked at it. "And by now, they have our position. Everyone, give me your phones. I'll destroy them, and we can pick up new ones in the store."

Bunny stretched as he spoke. "Jonny, I doubt they can get agents here before we get a meal in. Let's just eat before we bug out, okay? I don' wanna get so busy dodgin' those mooks that we end up smearin' ourselves over the freeway. Know what I'm sayin'?" He pulled out his cellphone and added it to the others on the table.

"Get it to go. We're getting out of here." Jon held out his hand to Sofi. "How about you? Got a phone to add?"

She shook her head. "Nope."

"Okay, then. I'll get rid of these, and be right back."

As he turned with the handful of cellphones, the lump rose again in his throat as he realized they would never see Donna again. The strained sobs behind him fueled his own grief, and he was glad to be out of earshot while the rest of the group got it out. Someone had to be the strong one, especially now.

* * * *

Frost studied the screen over Verhoff's shoulder, his flint-hard eyes tracing the GPS coordinates of every call registered on the phone he had plugged into the USB. Verhoff pointed with a pencil to a set of numbers that repeated more than any others. "She received more calls here than anywhere else. And here is where Daniels is right now."

"Let me see a sectional map, Healy," Frost called over his shoulder. The map was produced and spread out on the table. Frost muttered as he read he grid coordinates. "That idiot Schiller rushed the job, or we could have caught them all together. Made my job that much harder… Aha, there it is!" He stabbed down with his finger. "Four years' worth of work for this. We'll find them here, gentlemen. Saddle up."

Chapter Twenty-Eight

Jenna wanted to stay in that shower for the next hour and a half, but there was no way in hell she was going to trust her mother any farther than she could throw the Chrysler building. She washed the blood off and toweled herself dry before throwing on a clean pair of shorts and a T-shirt from her pack. The old clothes she wadded up and wrapped in a plastic bag before stuffing them into the pack.

She carried the pack downstairs and found her mother in the dining room setting out a plate. "I thought you might be hungry—" Meredith gasped when she saw the cuts.

Jenna shrugged and shook her head. "Don't bother, they've already clotted."

Her mother said nothing. Her pursed lips and narrow-eyed silence said more than words could have as the woman marched past Jenna into a room off the hall. She came back with a first aid kit in a plastic toolbox. "They still need to be closed. Haven't you learned *anything* about infection yet?" Flipping back the lid, she drew out a suture kit. "Now hold still. This is going to sting."

Jenna sighed and sat. She knew better than to argue with her mother. It was a matter of natural law, as sure as gravity. In fact, Jenna wasn't so sure that if Meredith Paine wanted to fly, she would out-stubborn Newton himself. So she drew her pant leg up a little higher to give the woman some room to work.

Kneeling before Jenna, Mother started with the knee. "How did you get this?"

Jenna looked at the ceiling and gritted her teeth. "Just do what you need to."

Mother just smiled and shook her head. "Not too squeamish to cut yourself, though, are you? Now hold still."

Shame rose in a warm flush over Jenna's face. "How did you—?"

"I *am* a doctor. These cuts are too neat and planned to be a result of a fight. My guess is that it was part of your plan to get past the guards." A sharp tug and a snip later, she said, "There, that one's done. Now, let's see that arm."

Jenna winced as the needle dug into her forearm one last time. When she heard the snip, she looked down at her mother's eyes.

Mother gathered the scraps of her handiwork and stood. "You went through an awful of trouble to get in here. You could have just called, you know." She stripped off her gloves and squirted hand sanitizer into her palm.

"What, and have fifty security agents waiting for me when I got here?"

The older woman paused, a blank expression on her face that Jenna knew all too well. "What makes you say that?"

"How about the fact that you sold me out to them in the first place?"

The older woman backed toward the door, eyes wide. "What? I never—"

Jenna rose and followed her. Although she had to look up to meet her mother's eyes, she could see Meredith's will melting before her. "You knew Steven Olsen before he met me, didn't you?" Jenna didn't wait for the answer before plowing on, backing her mother out into the hall. "You arranged for my scholarship at Gradwell College. You pushed me into going there. I'll bet you even made sure Steven recruited me into Chapter Seventeen, isn't that right, Mom?" Jenna slammed her hand against the doorjamb. The explosion of sound made Meredith jump.

Meredith's back banged into the door on the opposite wall. Her hands rose to shoulder level as she shook her head. "Jenna, honey, listen to me. I never—"

"Don't lie to me!"

Meredith crossed her arms over her heaving chest as she shivered. "W-what are you going to do? Do it and go."

"I want to know why you killed him."

"Who? I've never killed anyone."

"You murdered Dad."

The grandfather clock on the landing ticked away the seconds while Jenna watched Meredith's face change from confusion to fear. "Jenna, he had cancer—"

Jenna's fist whistled through the air and smacked into the wall next to Meredith's head, burying itself up to the wrist. The smell of gypsum dust made Meredith choke. "I'm telling you the truth—"

"You gave it to him. I read it in Brady's ledger. You injected a virus into him that triggered pancreatic cancer. I want to know why."

"You wouldn't kill your own mother—"

Meredith reached out as if to take Jenna into her arms. If the circumstances were different, Jenna would have gladly gone to her, pulling the same comfort from those arms that she did the days following her father's death. But Richard Paine wasn't there anymore, and Meredith Paine was the cause of it. So now Jenna had no one. She stepped back out of her mother's grasp. "Don't you touch me. I know what you did. I talked to Anna Spielberg before she died. You're not my real mother. I have no mother." A disgusted sneer crawled across Jenna's face. "You were just an incubator, weren't you?"

Meredith took a deep, shaky breath and let it out before speaking. Behind her tears, her eyes changed from abject fear to indignation. "I carried you. For nine months you grew inside me. *My* blood nourished you. Don't you tell me who was or wasn't your mother."

"My mother isn't a killer," countered Jenna. "Why did you do it?"

Meredith's gaze wandered. The grandfather clock chimed nine o' clock. "Y-you wouldn't understand. Just…finish it, please. Make it fast."

Looking at her mother's face, Jenna sensed the lost, wistful soul standing there before her. All the way out here, Jenna had it in her mind to put a bullet through Meredith Paine's heart, to make her feel for that one moment of life she had left, what Jenna felt when her dad was taken away. Now, at this moment, something new entered the equation, something she'd never considered before. But it was so obvious, now that she thought of it. Jenna felt her anger crack and flake away, letting her voice soften. "They made you do it, didn't they?"

Meredith nodded. Her eyes met Jenna's, and a sob wracked her chest. "He was getting too…involved with you. He loved you too much. It wasn't what they wanted. They were going to kill you and start over."

"Whose idea was that?"

"Honey, I can't tell you—"

Jenna grabbed her mother by the collar of her blouse and slammed her against the bedroom door. The dull boom echoed in the room beyond, and down the hall. "Who gave the order? Tell me!"

"They'll kill me if I do."

"*I'll* kill you if you don't. And then I'll find out anyway. If you tell me, I might be able to finish them off before they get someone back here."

"It's too late for me, can't you see that? The Pinnacle's too big, too strong to take out that quickly. You were one of them, just like I was. You know they have moles, agents, all over the world. They run governments now. They have armies. If they want to get someone, there's nothing you can do to stop them." She locked eyes again with Jenna. "At least if you do it, I know it won't hurt as much."

Jenna pulled her back, and then threw her back into the dining room, where Meredith crashed to the floor. "Don't even go there," Jenna said with a growl. "I can make it hurt, too. You sacrificed your own daughter on *their* altar. Now, when it's time to pay the piper, you want to cop out."

Meredith tried to rise. Jenna lashed out with a foot to her shoulder, and the older woman crashed back to the floor with a cry of alarm.

Jenna stood over her, poking a finger into her quaking chest. "Your only hope right now—your *only* hope—is to tell me everything I want to know, and pray to God I find them before they find you."

"Jenna, don't do this—"

Jenna rocked back and placed a foot on the inside of Meredith's left knee, bracing it against the oak table leg. "Just one good, hard push and you probably will never walk again." She picked up a goblet of wine from her mother's place at the table and took a sip. "Let's start with the *who* in the equation…"

Chapter Twenty-Nine

Manitou City, Michigan wasn't so much a city in the expected sense of the word. It was more a loose gathering of properties around a central "downtown" that encompassed two gas stations and a log inn advertising a hot breakfast at the attached restaurant. One of the gas stations also housed the bank, and the other a post office. The school was a neat little one-story brick building just off M-78. Farther out along the two-lane highway, mailboxes marked driveways leading off through the pines lining the road.

Nadia had Jon turn at the third mailbox on the right. They bumped along the winding dirt drive until the car broke out into a small meadow of tall grass and buckhorn sprinkled liberally with wildflowers. At one side sat a neat log ranch home with a long covered porch and attached garage.

The group climbed from their vehicles into the yard and stretched. Jon leaned against the side of his car and listed to the sizzle and ping of the cooling engine. Nadia's arms slid around him as Bunny and Hushi came over with Sofi in tow. Beth followed close behind. No one said a word as they all joined in the hug, each with their own silent eulogy for Donna. It didn't take a club over the head to wake anyone to what must have happened.

It had been two days since his conversation with Linda Schiller, during which he watched his rear view mirror more than the road in front of them. The fact they had Donna's phone told him all he really needed to know; there was no way she would have given it up as long as she was capable of resisting. In addition, The Pinnacle as an organization was as thorough as they come. When a person disappeared, they did it for good. In his heart, Jon still tried to believe she might still live, but he didn't talk about it with anyone else. It didn't do any good to hold out false hope to anyone.

When they released their group hug, there was more than one moist set of eyes. As it was, Jon had a hard time swallowing back the lump in his own throat. He wanted to take that terrible loss, that empty spot, and fill it with a greater determination to see The Pinnacle brought down, their plot exposed.

He helped unload the heaviest articles from the truck and shared a bottle of soda with Nadia before taking her hand and leading her back out to his car.

"I only have about two hours before the flight out of Munising, babe. 'Frisco waits."

She pulled him close for a kiss. "Don't be gone too long. And be careful, okay? I still have to show you around."

"Take care. Do what Hushi says, and get better." After one last kiss, he was back on the road.

* * * *

Jon took a charter from Munising to O'Hare for his flight to San Francisco. Gazing out the window as Lake Michigan's coastline slid by below, he heaved a heavy sigh. He'd never felt so torn in his life. The last thing he wanted to do was leave Nadia behind with her health failing this way. In spite of Beth's and Hushi's reassurances to the contrary, he felt as if she could go critical any day. However, duty called. With Jenna on the loose, God knew how much time he had to round up The Pinnacle's leadership. He had to talk to someone while there was still someone alive to talk to.

In one corner of his mind, he felt like just letting fate run its course. *They* made Jenna; they could have her and reap whatever crop they sowed. But the more sensible side of him knew that just cutting the head off would be like Hercules and the Hydra. Cut off one head and three more would grow back. If Jenna killed all the kingpins, it would also kill the hours of work he and Bunny had put into discovering and tracing their trail. Hundreds more people were involved with this twisted plan for world domination. He would fall back to square one, and it would take years more to kill the beast. It might not even be possible.

For that reason alone, he had to beat Jenna to San Francisco. Logically, John Bowman should be next on Jenna's list, as he was the closest living member of the Seven. Then again, she might have elected an "island-hopping" campaign, to throw off The Pinnacle's security people. The one thing he could always count on from Jenna was that she would do exactly what anyone least expected. The only thing he was grateful for was that she no longer worked for The Pinnacle, and he wouldn't have to go through her to get to them anymore.

The flight attendant announced landing, and the little craft began its descent into Chicago. Jon would have just enough time for a quick lunch before the final leg to San Fran.

* * * *

Nadia remembered Beth's name about five minutes after she regained consciousness. As the last echoes of the seizure faded back into the mist of her mind, she brought a hand to her aching head. When she spoke, her throat felt tight. "Damn, this is getting old, real fast," she croaked.

Beth sat at her bedside, holding her hand. "It wasn't your worst, though. We can be thankful for that."

"Where's Sofi?"

"Living room, with Hushi and Bunny."

"Jon?"

Cloth rustled softly as a blanket was pulled up. "On his way to stick his head in the lion's mouth."

Nadia raised her head. The room flipped, and she sagged back into her sweat-soaked pillow. "W-what?"

Beth's brow wrinkled in confusion. "He left for San Francisco this afternoon. You kissed him goodbye, and he got on an airplane and left."

"Oh."

Beth flipped Nadia's pillow and stood. "I have to talk with Hushi. I'll be back in a minute, okay?"

"Beth?"

The nurse stopped at the door. "Yes?"

"It's getting worse, isn't it? The tumors?"

"Yeah, hon, the tumors are getting bigger."

Nadia turned her head to the wall so Beth wouldn't see her tears, but she couldn't hide the thickness of her voice. "So I'm going to die."

"Nadia, don't say that. Hushi's—"

"Hushi's not Donna. She doesn't know how to fix this."

"She's going to try her damnedest, Nadia. Give her a chance, will you?"

Nadia turned back to face Beth. "I've been thinking. I don't even belong here, you know."

Beth came back in and sat on the bed. "Now, don't say that—"

"I'm not supposed to be alive. I should have died with my family, as Alicia. *They* stole my mind and put it in this body. Into this…bomb."

"But whether or not you're *supposed* to be here, here you are," said Beth. "You're here, and you're alive, and we're going to make sure you stay that way. If we can reduce the tumors, you'll be just fine."

"No, I won't."

"What—?"

"Reduce the tumors. Get rid of them. We're still back at square one. I'm a two-megaton living weapon. Just the fact that I draw breath means that anyone within five miles of me is in danger. And here I am, trying to save the world…from *me?*" She gave a short, derisive laugh. "I may as well take a dive to the bottom of Superior and have done with it all."

There was a long pause before Beth spoke again. "When I first met you, you were strapped in a bed in a basement under the hospital where

I worked. I was there over ten years, and I never knew about that basement lab."

Taking Nadia's hand, she went on. "You freaked me out. I mean, finding out who—and what—you are. I could have run, right along with the rest of the staff. But I couldn't just take off and leave Jon and you. You needed someone to look out for you, and there was no one else. In the back of my mind ever since, I was always aware of what would happen if…you know. But I never left. And I never regretted it, either. Because in the short time I've known you, I learned more about medicine and friendships than I have in all my life before. Jenny Fowler didn't even know you, and she laid her life down for you. Me, Hushi, and Donna all were in that position one time or another. And we all stayed with you, through thick and thin. Now Donna's gone, too."

She pointed to the door. "Right now, you have one of the country's top geneticists working on a treatment to keep you alive for as long as you're destined. She hasn't slept for a week, poring over Donna's notes and anything else she could get her hands on. She's talking with cancer specialists from all over the world from here to Shanghai to make a chemo treatment that will work for you. We're not giving up on you. Don't you give up on us, okay?"

"I can't promise anything. I can't even guarantee there's going to be a tomorrow."

Beth turned toward the door. "None of us can. But we can fight for every breath we have given to us, and let none be taken away before its time. I'll let you know when dinner's ready." She left, closing the door behind her.

Chapter Thirty

Jon leaned his head on the cab's window, just to snag a moment's rest. His eyes burned from fatigue; his brain felt numb. But the adrenaline pulsing through his system drove him on. San Francisco was just a blur outside the window.

Half an hour later, he climbed out at a glass-walled skyscraper. Flashing his badge at the front desk, he didn't waste time making his demands known. "I need to speak with John Bowman. Now."

With trembling hands, the receptionist dialed her phone, and listened for several seconds before hanging it back up. "I-I'm afraid he's out right now, sir."

Okay, time to be a jerk about it. "I happen to know he's not only in the building, but he's in his office right now. You have exactly thirty seconds to round up a security detail and escort me up, or this station will be shut down. Do I make myself clear?"

While the receptionist scrambled, he gave silent thanks Bunny used his "back door" access to confirm Bowman's schedule in the studio's computer system. Bunny had set up his own user access to the station's secure server about four years ago, and Jon was amazed that it remained undiscovered.

Less than a minute later, a uniformed security guard appeared and led him to an elevator. Sliding a card key through a scanner slot opened the door. They stepped in, and the guard punched the top button of the row of five on the switch panel. *Must be the express to the executive floors.* He watched the guard's face for any sign of unease, any tension, but saw nothing that betrayed any hidden agenda or motive. If Bowman wanted to trap him, he could do it easily enough: just wait at the elevator with a couple more enforcers, and that would be the end of Jon Daniels. Just like his uncle. A familiar lump rose in his throat. *Just like Donna.* He shifted his shoulders, feeling for the familiar weight of his Glock 9mm in its shoulder rig.

The doors slid open to a white-carpeted, glass-and-chrome palace. Men and women in thousand-dollar suits bustled about, carrying clipboards and briefcases. A distant, booming voice droned, just low enough in volume that Jon couldn't make out any distinct verbiage. The guard led him through a glass maze and into an ivory-walled labyrinth hung with hideously expensive art. With each step, the booming voice became clearer.

"…No excuse for allowing that viewpoint to be presented on the airwaves—correction *my* airwaves! This station is *not* a sounding board for the Limbaugh-Hannity lunatic fringe—do you understand me? The next person who messes this up will be escorted from the premises by me, personally."

The voice paused for breath. "Now, on to other matters. Holdeman, you had a suggestion about an added feature…" The voice faded again as the guard led Jon past the meeting room and around another corner.

Bowman's office door opened at a swipe from the guard's card key. He held it open for Jon. "Mr. Bowman will see you as soon as his meeting's over."

"Ah…okay, thanks," murmured Jon as he went in. The guard let the door shut and left. Or so Jon supposed. He couldn't hear any footsteps walking away. *Come to think of it, I can't hear a blasted thing. This room must be soundproof.* Faint music played over hidden speakers as Jon surveyed the office. Everywhere else in the building was sterile white, ivory, chrome, and glass. Here, with the exception of one glass wall offering an awe-inspiring view of the Pacific, mahogany ruled. A black leather couch with a hand-carved mahogany frame sat primly against one wall. Two matching chairs were perched in front of Bowman's massive, polished mahogany desk. A liquor cabinet built into another wall boasted a dozen liquors Jon had never heard of, but must have been worth more than he'd ever made as an agent with the Bureau or OSI.

Jon scanned the room for cameras before reaching into his jacket pocket and drawing out a small black box about the size of a TV remote with two LED indicators on one end. He pressed a small button on top and walked around the room, watching the indicators change from green to red and back again. *It only fits that the room's wired like a damned recording studio. I'd lay odds there are cameras hidden in places I'd never think to look. So where are the secret panels the goons are going to leap out of?*

He thought he'd spotted a couple of likely candidates when the door opened and John Bowman walked in. In the moment the door was open, Jon glanced up the hall but spotted no guards or other people standing around.

Bowman's booming voice brought Jon's attention back to the interior of the office. "Mr. Daniels, I trust we can keep this short. I have a shareholder's meeting in fifteen minutes." Bowman had the liquor cabinet open, filling a tumbler from a square bottle of caramel-colored liquid. "Scotch, Mr. Daniels?" He plunked a couple of ice cubes in his own tumbler and drew out another.

"Yes, thank you. Straight up, no ice, please."

"Ah, neat," mused Bowman. "Straight to the point. A good business drink." He poured the drink and turned, offering it to Jon with a smile. "You can tell a lot about a man from the bottle he drinks."

Jon took the glass and smiled back. Inside, he thought he'd throw up any second. He knew he was grasping at straws, but he also knew he had to take this chance.

"Now, Mr. Daniels, to what occasion do we owe this little tête-a-tête?" Bowman strolled to his desk and sat down in his plush chair, setting his drink on a coaster. Even seated, Bowman's presence commanded a room. This man got things his way, by any means necessary. His eyes pierced straight through Jon's soul.

He felt as if he was being impaled on Bowman's will, yet another victim of his charisma. This wasn't supposed to be like this. Jon was the one with the upper hand, yet it seemed Bowman was the one holding all the cards. *Hold it together,* he told himself, *take the lead, now.* "I met a mutual acquaintance recently," he started. "I believe she may be on her way to visit you. I wanted to get here first."

Bowman beckoned with a gesture. "And this acquaintance, does she have a name?"

"Yes. I believe you know Miss Paine from some" —Jon took a deep breath to calm his heart— "previously contracted work she did for you."

Bowman had his tumbler halfway to his lips when Jon said that. His hand hesitated for just a brief moment, and when it continued, the hand trembled ever so slightly. Jon relaxed. He had control now.

"I'm...not sure I know the woman," said Bowman after the sip.

"Let's not pretend, Mr. Bowman. You have a shareholder's meeting in just a few minutes, and these games are wasting both our time."

Bowman picked up his phone and dialed four digits. "Miss Kingston, inform the shareholders I may be a few minutes late. Tell them it was unavoidable, and send my regrets. Thank you." Hanging up, he said, "What makes you so sure she hasn't already been here?"

Jon settled in one of the chairs, a grin he couldn't suppress spreading over his face. "Simple, sir. You're still alive."

Although Bowman's exterior remained flint-hard, his complexion paled a few shades. "Why do you think she means me harm?"

"She has this crazy idea you and your Pinnacle associates tried to have her erased. And after all she's done for you, too." Jon shook his head. "Tsk, tsk. What a waste of a perfectly good artificial person."

Now Bowman flushed red. "Why did you come here, Mr. Daniels?" he asked angrily.

"Actually, it's 'Captain Daniels,' sir. I'm an officer in the Air Force Office of Special Investigations." Jon brought out his OSI badge and showed it to Bowman. "I'm sure you've heard of me. I also happen to know another mutual acquaintance. She used to be your evening news anchor, until she found out you had other plans for her."

"That doesn't answer my question, sir!" Bowman stood and slugged down the rest of his drink, slamming the glass down on the desk.

Jon reached out. "You missed your coaster, sir. That's going to leave a ring—"

Bowman pounded his fist on the desk. Jon snatched his hand back. Bowman's voice lowered to a growl. "*Damn* the ring! Why are you here?"

"I want to give you a chance. Tell my people everything you know about The Pinnacle."

Bowman pointed a shaking finger at Jon. "If I did know about this organization, I wouldn't tell *you.*"

Jon sat and studied his scotch for a moment before downing the rest in one gulp. A warm glow spread from his throat into the rest of his body. "Then I would be unable to protect you, sir."

"So, you threaten me with assassination?"

"I can't control Jenna Paine any more than you can right now, Mr. Bowman. She did Walter Brady right under our noses. She has his ledger books and his ring. One that matches the one on your own finger." Jon nodded toward Bowman's left hand. Bowman curled his fingers into a fist. Jon continued. "I'm giving you an opportunity to live a long and happy life. You can begin again—get a brand new start under our protection. Just talk to us. Tell us what you know."

Bowman snorted and went back to the cabinet. "Protection, my ass." He refilled his glass and spun around. "Why don't you tell me how you're going to protect me from Jenna Paine?"

"We can discuss that after you've turned yourself in."

"For what? What charges, may I ask, are you preparing to level against me, and on what evidence?"

Jon sat silent for a while. Then he stood and put his glass on Bowman's desk. "I think you know we can't charge you with anything yet. I've been working for four years, trying to pin a dozen or so assassinations on you and your associates. Conspiracy. Bribery. Extortion. Probably fourscore and seven other charges. I'm not a prosecutor."

He held his glass up, letting the sunlight glow through the last few drops of his drink. "But I'm giving you this chance to get out alive. I know about your shadow group. I know they don't allow anyone to walk out alive. They've had their way for some time now, hiding in the shadows and plotting their takeovers. They say it's for peace, but you and I both know it's about power, don't we? Power to control others, to steer and direct the destiny of the world."

Jon locked eyes with Bowman. The drink had helped him to calm down, and now he was solidly in charge. "Well, the game's over. It's time to close the shop and go home. Help me, and I'll help you. Turn me away, and you know I can't save you."

Bowman took a sip from his drink and leaned back in his chair. He'd regained a little of his color and with it, his calm demeanor. "Your little group are the only ones who are even aware of our existence, Agent Daniels. What makes you so sure we can't simply wipe you all off the face of the earth and carry on with our plan for world peace?"

"Because, sir, you don't know how many other teams are probing your activities, putting two and two together. You know about me and my team. But there are others who know I'm here. Besides, if you were that confident you could wipe us out, you would have done so long ago." Jon reached into a pocket and drew out a business card. "My correct number is on the back. Thanks for the drink, Mr. Bowman. Let me know what you decide." He put his card down on the desk before turning toward the door. "You have a meeting to attend. I'll find my own way out, thank you."

He hitched a ride to the lobby with a group of executives on their way to lunch. Outside the building, he scanned the area carefully before setting off on foot. After several blocks, he looked around again. Satisfied he wasn't being followed, he hailed a cab back to the motel. He'd get a few hours' rest before flying back to Chicago that night.

Chapter Thirty-One

Jenna stopped in Denver long enough to buy another used truck as Trina Stevens. As soon as the camper shell was transferred over, she was on the way again. Driving north out of town, she kept the radio tuned to the news stations, listening for the inevitable uproar over the two dead security guards she'd left behind. Surely, they'd have been found by now. The question was whether her mother would take the risk and expose her. She rather doubted it, but one couldn't be too careful.

Meredith Paine was a research physician in The Pinnacle's medical division, part of the team headed by Dr. Petr Hamund. Meredith couldn't reveal their backers, but Jenna already knew one: John Bowman, the media giant. He'd established Nadia as a journalist in the first place, setting her in position as a pawn to take out President Javad of Iran. Jenna signed on as one of Nadia's handlers at the time, preparing her for her mission. Therefore, she wasn't especially surprised to see Bowman's picture on Jon's plot board.

She hoped everyone thought she was going after Bowman. *That should start their gears really grinding*, she mused as she passed the I-80 exit and carried on farther north. Bowman's turn would come in time. But she wasn't quite ready for her endgame just yet. She had other fish to fry first. Let them spin their wheels trying to outguess her. They would naturally assume she was after their leadership. Once she got them all herded together in their *sanctum sanctorum*, she'd drop the hammer on every one of them. Now was the time to hit their supply base. It was about time Gradwell College got a visit from one of their most esteemed alumni.

* * * *

The hunter's trail was right where she remembered. She and Steven Olsen had been down this lane so often, she could literally drive it blindfolded. Every bump and jar brought back its own memory from her college days, and her chest grew thick with echoes of Steven. He was her mentor, her friend, and more than she would ever tell. She stopped the truck and got out, leaving the engine running. The oak was still there. Holding a hand against the rugged bark, she circled the trunk to the far side, away from the trail, where a cryptic series of marks remained carved deep in the wood as the sole reminder of what they'd shared in this bed of ferns, so many promises ago. If things had been different, if they could have just been normal people in a normal world, with normal jobs… *Yeah, right. If.* She sniffed back a wistful tear and got back in the truck. It was too late to wonder "what if." All she had was "what now."

Jenna drove the path between the trees and undergrowth for a couple more miles before she reached the clearing she was looking for. Weeds, saplings, and thorny bushes strangled it, but a few minutes' work with a machete corrected that quickly enough. Soon she had enough room for a small fire pit and her camp chair.

The sun sank to an orange glow behind the ridge to the west, over toward the army post. It would be dark soon in this little valley, so Jenna wiped her brow, put the machete back in its scabbard, and washed up. There was much to do, and she wanted to be over with this part quickly.

Inside the camper shell, she set up a laptop, scanner/printer, card laminator, and digital camera on a tripod. She'd purchased these separately, from three different office supply stores using three different names to eliminate traceability. In ten minutes, she forged a perfect Gradwell College student badge for Linda Ballas. Thanks to her designers, she could dash on a bit of make-up in the right places and still pass herself off as a coed when she showed up on the campus in the morning. When she was done, she unplugged everything and heated a small meal in the fire pit over a sterno can. The moon filtering through the trees gave her just enough light to see what she was doing. Jenna smiled to herself as she licked the last of the meal from her spoon. There was something about being invisible so seductive that it brought to her abdomen a warm thrill almost better than sex. *Almost.* She allowed herself a sly little giggle as she snuggled into her bed for the night.

* * * *

The morning sun sent fingers of warmth through the cool early mist of the forest, caressing fern and fawn alike. Jenna had been up for over an hour before the light reached her camp, moving through her *kata*. It had been a good couple of weeks since she'd been shot and stitched up, but her abdomen was still tender, the muscles stiff. By the time she was ready for breakfast, she was trembling and pouring sweat from exertion and pain. But she had to push through, to make her body obey, to keep her edge.

Not far from her campsite a small mountain stream gurgled and rolled over rocks and under logs, carving out a few small trout pools as it passed through the woods. After stripping off her sweat-soaked clothes, Jenna stepped out into the frigid, swirling water, stopping when it reached her waist. As she scrubbed away the morning's workout, her fingers touched on the scars across her stomach, still angry and red. Reaching up to her temple, she felt the marks left by the fight in the hotel, when she'd killed Phil and Gerda. She'd called them friends once. They stood watch over her for more than three days while she was incapacitated by a drug reaction while on a critical assignment. And now they were dead at her hands, in blind obedience to the same masters she herself had once served.

A cold shock of realization slapped Jenna across the face, so hard she froze for several long moments. *Jesus, was I that blind, too?* The answer smacked her just as hard. As much as she didn't like Mark Boyle personally, he was a comrade. When the order came for him to be "cut loose," she pulled the trigger on him with nary a second thought. A chill colder than the water slithered through her. *They had me good. Brainwashed from the start. All this time, to be so wrong.*

Wrong. In frustration and anger, Jenna slammed her fist into the rushing water.

Wrong. A second time, she sent a wave into the air.

"Wrong!" The shout echoed through the trees, knocking her out of her thoughts. Biting back tears, she buried her face in her hands. *Later. Later, I'll fall to pieces. Not now.* Fists clenched, she brought herself back to the here and now, back on course. Looking furtively into the woods on either bank, she breathed thanks that no one was near to see her making such a fool of herself. She rushed through the rest of her bath, dressed in relaxed jeans and a sweater, and grabbed her book bag on the way to campus.

* * * *

Professor Greenstone's office was still in Woodbury Hall, on the east side of the Quad. Jenna flashed her ID at the receptionist and sat in one of the oak chairs along the wall of the wood-paneled foyer. Pretending to text on her cellphone, she let her hair hang in front of her eyes, concealing her face from anyone who might recognize her in spite of the adjustments she'd made to alter her appearance.

A few minutes later, the receptionist called her name. "Miss Ballas? Professor Greenstone will see you now."

Doing her best impression of a starry-eyed co-ed, Jenna stood and gathered her bag. She followed the older woman down the tiled hall. The receptionist's heel clicks echoed off the walls as she led the way to the third door from the end on the left, bringing back memories from Jenna's last trip down this hall, the day she'd met Palmer Frost for the initiation of her contract. Only nine years ago, but she was much younger then. And much more pliable, she thought with bitter disdain.

The dark-stained door swung open on well-oiled hinges, and Jenna stepped through. The receptionist closed it behind her as Miles Greenstone looked up from the paperwork on his desk through wire-framed bifocals. His eyes looked more tired, the wrinkles deeper now. His hair shone with more silver, but he still sported the same ponytail and beard she found so warmly quaint before. He smiled, and Jenna felt an icy spear of fear thrust through her chest. He knew her.

Chapter Thirty-Two

Five camo-garbed figures stalked through the dusk-darkened Virginia forest, advancing toward their objective with lethal stealth. Frost, taking the point, turned to check everyone's positions frequently, adjusting the formation with hand signals. The woods hung in breathless silence. Not even a whisper of a breeze dared interrupt their task. Even the birds seemed to know Death was afoot.

A faint sound to the front brought Frost to a sharp halt. His right fist shot up, pumped twice up and down. The team took cover, disappearing into the underbrush as if by magic.

Down the slope in their fore a rustic log cabin rested in a clearing. Behind it, a woodshed door hung open. Farther through the trees, in a tiny meadow, stood a gaily-painted cottage that reminded Frost of something from a fairy tale. On the far side of the cabin, a screen door opened and slammed shut with a protest of springs. A few seconds later an engine started with a cough and roar. An old pickup appeared, driving off down a dirt drive.

To Frost's left crouched Rain Spooner, a pair of high-powered binoculars held to his eyes. He spoke so low, Frost could only hear him through his earpiece. "One occupant. Looks like a male, older than fifty. No other movement down there, chief."

Frost stood slowly, the way a cobra rises, looking for a sensitive spot on its victim. He signaled the advance, and the others rose from the brush like zombies in search of fresh meat.

Spreading out, they surrounded the little cabin before Frost gave the sign to close in: two small coughs in his mic. Five automatic rifles cocked and locked as one, and they came together in a steadily shrinking ring, strangling the cabin and cutting off any possible retreat for its occupants.

* * * *

A hundred meters up on the far hillside, Jimmy sprawled in the brush, the lines in his face etched deeper than ever, his mouth drawn tight as a crossbow. Just under his right hand sat a small metal box with a single button and an antenna. It was the button he'd hoped he would never have to push, but the time was here. He wouldn't back down from what had to be done, as much as it hurt. A little red LED flashed eagerly next to the button. "Just another couple steps, ya filthy animals…" he muttered to himself. He counted them as they came out of the trees. … *Two, three, four…* Just as the first man stepped up onto Irving's porch, Jimmy's thumb mashed down on the button.

Irving Ratzinger's cabin rose up on a column of flame and exploded with a roar like a thousand thunders, sending logs, glass, and men through the air in pieces. When the smoke cleared, Jimmy grabbed the Remington Model 700 rifle at his side. Peering through the scope, he checked the scene for any movement. One figure writhed in slow motion, hands clutching his abdomen. *Two, KIA; one, wounded. At least one more at large. Sorry, buddy. I only need one prisoner…* He pulled the trigger twice. The rifle bucked against his shoulder. The single moving form jumped and lay still.

Jimmy crept closer, listening for any other movement. *They'll lie low for a while. Lemme see if I can get a little better view…* The spot he'd just left erupted in a shower of dirt and noise, rolling him over in the brush and grass. Shrapnel whistled overhead. Jimmy shrank down as low as he could. Fragments of memories from long ago shot by with the fragments of metal, memories from a hundred battlefields from Korea to Vietnam, to places no one ever dreamed could exist. *Damn, they came big, didn't they?*

Fear rose in Jimmy, the fear that kept him alive through times like this. The warrior in him nodded to the fear, embraced it, and kept it close. He had learned to focus the fear, let it keep him safe. Clenching his fists with the effort of concentration, he focused it like a laser, turning it back on his enemies. The words of his first platoon leader echoed in his mind. Was it Kipling he quoted? *All right, you apes—who wants to live forever?*

Looking around, Jimmy found the rifle and scrambled for it. A burst of automatic fire laced the growth around him. *They saw the muzzle flash. That's what they aimed the grenade at. They're not sure...*

A man in camo leaped up with an automatic rifle, about fifty meters away. Jimmy snapped a round at him from the hip, and the man dropped back into the undergrowth. A shot from his right whizzed past his head and smacked into the ground. A short burst from the direction of the first man whipped through the trees. *Crap! Bracketed!*

Jimmy popped a couple more rounds in the direction of the enemy on his right, guessing he might be the closer of the two. Then he rolled downhill just as the man answered with two of his own, missing by a meter.

A body rose and crashed through the growth as the first man rushed him. Jimmy dropped the rifle and pulled his .45 from his belt. Just as the man appeared above the bushes, Jimmy shot him twice in the chest. He didn't watch his attacker drop but rolled over as the second man rushed him from the other side. Aiming low, he squeezed off three more rounds at the running figure just as something punched him hard on the top of his left shoulder.

The man fell on Jimmy with a scream, pulling a knife from a sheath as they grappled among the bushes.

The stranger was stronger, and soon he was on top, the blade driving down toward Jimmy's chest.

Jimmy took the knife through his left hand. Groaning in pain, he directed it away from his chest. Before the other could wrench the blade free, Jimmy threw his right elbow into his chin once, twice, three times. The attacker grunted and rolled off, letting go of the knife. Jimmy swatted at him with his left hand, the blade still lodged through it. The tip caught in the man's chest.

The stranger reached up and grabbed the handle of the blade just as Jimmy drove in with his right hand, pushing the knife farther through his left and deeper into the other man's body.

A hand crashed into the side of his head. Jimmy felt the blow all the way down into his back. The fear drove him on harder, pushing the blade deeper in spite of the pain.

The other man howled. His hands quit beating Jimmy, and clutched at the ground, clawing fruitlessly in the dirt.

Jimmy grinned, his eyes burning with the adrenaline rush. He yanked the knife free with his left hand, and plunged it in again as the man started to move. Then he spun the blade around and clocked him on the side of the head with the haft end. The attacker slumped, unconscious.

With trembling hands, Jimmy cut a few strips from the other man's pant legs and tied his hands behind his back before fashioning some crude bandages, first for himself, then for his prisoner. Then he pulled out his cellphone and dialed. Irving answered before the first ring completed its twirring chirp. "Hey, buddy," Jimmy wheezed. "You better get back here fast. I'm on the hill with one of 'em." A fit of coughing overtook him then. He spat blood onto the ground and continued. "And neither one of us looks good."

He closed his phone and rolled onto his back to wait for Irving. "Damn, I'm gettin' too old for this."

But in his heart, Jimmy knew that there was only one way he would leave this world: as a warrior, kicking and screaming all the way. His coarse laugh was caught short by another coughing fit.

A soft moan next to him reminded him he still had a prisoner to mind.

Jimmy spoke into the trees above, too tired to rise. "U.S. Marshall," he said, panting. "You're under arrest. Anything you say can and most definitely will be used against you. So shut up an' lay still before I *really* get mad."

Chapter Thirty-Three

Hushi found Sofi sitting alone at the top of a stone promontory overlooking Superior, watching the massive lake as though they were sharing some secret, unspoken conversation between friends. The ten-year-old sat cross-legged with her hands in her lap, a still, black shadow except for the occasional hunch of her shoulders as she sniffed back her tears. A stiff shoreward wind tried to nudge Hushi away, but she leaned into it, insisting her way into Sofi's world. The crash of waves two hundred feet below them joined with the wind, rolling over and over in Hushi's mind in a powerful, rhythmic chorus that made human words seem a sacrilege.

As Hushi approached, she deliberately scuffed a toe on the rocks to announce her presence before taking a seat next to Sofi. Together they looked out over the water for several minutes, saying nothing. As much as Hushi wanted to put her arm around the girl, to wipe away her tears and tell her everything was going to be okay, she kept a couple inches of space between them. And she wasn't about to tell her that everything was going to be okay, because it wasn't.

Sofi gulped back a sigh and sniffled before she broke the rhythm of the lake's serenade. "My mom's going to die, isn't she?"

Hushi rested a gentle hand on Sofi's shoulder. When the girl didn't shrink away, Hushi wrapped an arm around her shoulder and drew her closer. "I hope not, hon."

"What are you doing for her?"

"Everything we can."

Sofi looked up into Hushi's eyes. "What does that mean?"

"It means I'm working on unknotting her genetic code, to engineer some nanobots that could fight the tumors for us. My husband is trying to reverse-engineer her neural schematic, to give us a surgical map if we have to operate—"

"What?"

Hushi released Sofi's shoulder and reclined on the smooth stone of the promontory, leaning on an elbow. "Humans are made of proteins. That's the basic building blocks of living things, as opposed to rocks and water and machines. Your mom is made of proteins, too, but she's been designed and built more as a machine than as a human. Her muscles and nerves are more like a machine's servo loops and wires, even though she's a living person like you and me."

Hushi picked up a pebble between her thumb and forefinger and flicked it aimlessly over the edge of the cliff, where it was swallowed by the sounds of the lake and the wind. "Bunny is trying to work out a wiring diagram that will tell us what nerves are closest to the tumors, and which might be part of her triggering mechanism. If we have to operate, we need to know what to stay away from. I don't want to do anything inside her until I have a better idea where I can't go." She looked hard at Sofi, wondering if anything was getting through. Nadia had told Hushi the girl was a genius, but that could have just been a maternal boast.

Sofi's eyes showed an almost frightening level of comprehension. She paused only a second, letting the concept settle. "But what if you can't find out soon enough?"

"Hopefully, we'll have enough warning..." Hushi's voice caught. Dammit, she hated to say it this way. "We should have enough warning to get you to a safe place."

Sofi turned her face lakeward and tilted her head back, letting the wind dry her tears. After a few more seconds' silence, she said, "She's not my real mom, you know."

"I know, hon."

"My real mom died in Europe. She didn't want me anymore, so she killed herself."

"Sofi, don't say that—"

Sofi's eyes flashed as she turned to glare at Hushi. "It's true. She made up this story about the bad people coming after her and handed me off to Nadia. Now Nadia's going to die, too." Pounding her chest with one hand, she cried, "What does that say about *me*? Why doesn't anyone want me?" Sofi tore a clump of grass from a crack in the rock. Her hand shook as a hard sob wracked her body.

Hushi sat up and took Sofi by the shoulders. "Now, you stop that, young lady!" Before Sofi could wrestle free, Hushi drew her into a hug. The girl buried her face in Hushi's breast and shuddered as she clutched at her jacket. "It's okay," Hushi crooned. "It's all right, let it go. I'm here, and I'm going to do everything I can for your mom." She let go long enough to look Sofi in the eyes. "And I can do a helluva lot."

Hushi's phone rang before she could get to her feet. Bunny's number showed on the display. "Yeah, babe, we're just on our way—"

Her husband's voice was flat, strained. He never sounded that way before. "Holli, get back here now."

Hushi's heart jumped. He *never* called her by her by anything but her nickname unless—"What's wrong?"

"Irving called. Him and Jimmy got jumped."

"*What?*"

"Jon's divertin' down to VA to get 'em. Jimmy's in bad shape."

Hushi stood on shaky feet, motioning to Sofi to follow. "How's Papa?"

"He's okay. There's another thing, too."

Hushi took a breath to prepare herself. "What?"

"We got us a prisoner."

"What are we going to do with—?"

"Dunno, babe. But we gotta get ready for a couple more guests. Talk to ya when ya get back."

The line clicked to silence. Hushi stood planted for several seconds, her body tingling with a disturbing mixture of excitement and fear. *Could it come to an end this easily? I don't think so. I just don't know.*

Sofi's voice at her side wrested her attention back to her surroundings. "What did he want?"

"Ah… we have to get back. I'll tell you more later."

"Hushi?"

"Yes?"

Sofi threw her arms around Hushi in a close hug. "Thanks."

Hushi hugged her back and took her hand. "Sure. Let's go, hon."

Chapter Thirty-Four

Professor Greenstone sat with his hands clasped on top of his desk after the receptionist closed the door, simply smiling and staring at her. Jenna began to feel a crushing pressure in the atmosphere of the room, threatening to squeeze the life out of her then and there. Something in her wanted to jump up and run away screaming. The other part wanted to crash a fist right through that smug grin. *So many lives, so many lies...*

Finally, the professor broke the silence. "Well, Miss...Ballas, was it? What can I do for you?"

"It's been a long time, Miles." Jenna forced his first name out. She'd never heard anyone call him anything but Professor Greenstone, and could barely imagine calling him anything else. But she had to change something about the situation. What was it Mr. Frost had said? *Change a variable, and you gain one more degree of control. It doesn't matter what you change; change something.*

He stood and fetched a bottle from a wall cabinet, along with a couple of glass tumblers. "I'd heard something terrible had happened to you." Setting the tumblers on the desk, he poured one half-full with an amber liquid. "I'm glad to see you're all right." He waved an inviting hand at the other glass. Jenna shook her head politely, and he set the bottle down before taking his seat.

"Do you ever wonder what happened, Miles?" The pressure began to release as Jenna said his first name again. *Another way to get control: ask questions.* "What happened, before Canada?"

Miles took a sip from the whiskey and swirled the glass around, watching the little wave chase itself around the sides. "I've told you the story. No need to repeat it, is there?"

"But you told me you always stood for peace. You were a pacifist. That was why you went to Canada."

"I'm still a pacifist, Miss Paine. Yes, I took a sabbatical from the United States for a couple of years. President Nixon sent me an engraved invitation to take part in his little party in Viet Nam, and I declined. But that wasn't the only reason I went north. Someone else gave me an invitation. The Weather Underground, The Black Panthers, The SLA, and a hundred other radical groups all had plans. Visions for a better world. They all broke a thousand laws for their petty little causes. This other group was the only one with a workable plan to change the world and end war forever."

Jenna nodded, completing the mantra she'd heard repeated so many times, so long ago. "'By uniting every nation under one flag of international brotherhood and harmony.' But what happened to your values?"

He drained the glass and set it on his desk. "The same that happened to yours. We trained you. Individual values have no place when the cause becomes bigger than the person." He poured another drink for himself. "Are you sure you won't have any? No?" Another sip later, he said, "So why don't you tell me why you really came?"

"I want your graduation rolls."

Miles leaned his forehead into a hand, shaking his head. "You know I can't do that, Miss Paine. And you also know why."

Jenna continued as if he hadn't spoken. "I also want you to stop feeding your graduates to Palmer Frost."

She was answered with a derisive laugh. "You aren't asking for much, are you?" His face darkened. Stabbing a finger at her, he said, "Haven't I taught you anything? You did it all wrong! You don't just march in and ask. You *take!"* He punctuated the statement by shaking a clenched fist in the air. "If you wanted those things, all you had to do was walk in with a pistol, blow my head off, and hack my hard drive."

"If I did that, The Pinnacle would replace you with some other burned-out ex-hippie and use them to keep brainwashing kids into doing their dirty work, while the Council sits off at a sterile distance and decries the same things they themselves do behind everyone's backs. I want the recruiting to stop."

"And if I don't?"

Jenna stood and leaned over the desk on both hands. When she spoke, it was in a low growl. "Then I'll park myself outside the campus gate, and I swear, Miles, I will kill every kid who comes out of here with a ring. Their blood will join that of every other student you sent out there, including Steve Olsen's."

"Why, Miss Paine, I do believe you're serious," Miles said in mock astonishment as he leaned back in his chair. "Is there nothing I can do to dissuade you?"

"You should know me better than to even ask. I'm giving you a chance to walk out of this alive."

The professor sighed and put his hands in his lap. Shrugging his shoulders, he said, "I was afraid you were going to be this obstinate."

That was when Jenna caught a familiar scent: fear. The man was terrified, in spite of his calm outward demeanor. *And terrified people do stupid things—*

She leaped straight up, her feet clearing the top of the desk just as the modesty panel flew away in a hundred shards. The shotgun blast tore the back off the chair she'd been sitting in, knocking the remains into a corner like so much trash.

Jenna landed in a sideways squat on top of the desk. Balancing on her hands, she lashed out from her coiled knee with a vicious kick to Greenstone's face. He flew out of his chair, crumpling to the floor in a heap.

Just as Jenna came down next to his inert form, the door burst in. Under the desk, Jenna could see the receptionist's legs standing in the doorway. The legs took a step forward. The slide of an automatic pistol rammed forward, chambering the first round. The receptionist spoke in a sharp, tense voice. "Professor? Are you all right?"

Attached to the underside of the desk was a double-barreled shotgun, sawed off to fit in the tight space. Smoke still rolled from the left barrel, choking the small space with the acrid smell of cordite. *I wonder what happens to the students he flunks*, thought Jenna, and she put her hand on the pistol grip, wrapping a finger around the trigger for the other barrel.

"Professor Greenstone?"

One more step to the left...

"Professor—?"

The blast caught the receptionist in the pelvis, knocking her back into the hall. The pistol flew from her grip and clattered to the floor. Jenna found a box of shells in the second drawer down. She thumbed the action open and reloaded as footsteps pounded down the hallway, accompanied by cries of shock and alarm. They stopped short of the door. One woman screamed when she saw the mangled remains of the receptionist. The noise in the hall continued in tense whispers. *They're calling campus security. I have about three minutes. Plenty of time.*

Fetching her book bag, Jenna reached in and pulled out a folding knife. She flicked it open, hacked through the cords attaching the professor's computer processor to its peripheral appliances, and stuffed it into the bag. Then, throwing the straps over her shoulders, she used the desk lamp to knock the glass out of his window.

Greenstone moaned and began to stir. Jenna slapped him hard enough to rouse him. Grabbing him by the collar, she pulled his face close. "I'll be watching you." Then she stepped up onto the windowsill and jumped.

The weight of the computer shifted when she hit, almost taking her off her feet. But she was off at a run before the first police car rolled up to the front of the admin building, and before they could organize a proper search, she was through a hole in the fence and gone.

Chapter Thirty-Five

Jon and Irving took over the small round end table in the corner of the surgical waiting room. Jon opened a deck of cards from the hospital gift shop, and they killed time playing Euchre with two other OSI agents brought in for additional security. He'd lost count of tricks played, games lost and won, cups of coffee drank, and hours spent in the cramped room.

A burly male nurse in purple scrubs entered through a door marked "Authorized Personnel Only" and approached Jon with a small blue plastic case. "Captain Daniels? I have the bullet we took out of your friend." He held out a clipboard. Jon signed for it, and the nurse turned to go back through the door.

"Hey, what about Mr. DeBartolo? How's he doing?"

The nurse pursed his lips for a moment. "I'll let Dr. Molari answer that. Your friend is still in surgery. As soon as we can, we'll get word to you." He disappeared back through the door.

Jon turned to Irving. "How you doing, Papa?"

"I'm all right, Jonny," the old man wheezed.

"Tell me what happened." The question went further than just concern for his friend. Jon had to submit a contact report back to Colonel Danson if he was going to get the additional security he wanted for the team.

Irving paused and leaned over the table. "The perimeter alert went off. We thought it was a deer, but it hit five times, at perfect intervals. Jimmy and I had a plan. I would leave in the truck and he would lie in ambush." He related the rest of the story. When he finished, his eyes were moist. "Losing that cabin was like losing my Hilda all over again, God rest her soul." The old man swallowed back a lump in his throat as Jon handed him a tissue.

"I know how you loved that place, Papa."

"I never thought I could hate anyone anymore. I thought I buried my hate in Korea." Irving bit back a sob. His fist trembled as he clenched it in Jon's face. "But those *yutzes* attacked me and my friends. They took everything I had left."

Jon reached to put a comforting hand on his friend's shoulder. "Where are you going now, Papa?"

Irving shook his head. "I don't know."

"Then you two are coming home with me."

"What about Nadia? Isn't that her place—?"

Jon held up a hand. "Papa, you put us up for four years. It's the least we can do for you. Besides," —he leaned closer to Irving, locking his gaze— "do you honestly think she'd turn you away? You know how much she loves you. You're the closest thing she's ever had to a grandfather."

Another nurse, a slim young woman, came in through the side door and motioned to Jon. When he stood, she drew back, inviting him to follow. Jon looked back at Irving, checked for the rest of the security team, and went through.

The nurse gave him a running report as he followed her down one hall after another. "Your suspect is in recovery now. He's waking up. The wounds were severe, but he's going to make it."

Jon followed her through two sets of double doors that opened when she held a card in front of a scanner. "In here," she droned, "Bed 17—" She stopped dead in the center aisle, her hands limp at her sides. Three federal officers and the staff nurse lay sprawled on the floor in widening pools of blood. Along the wall on the right side of the ward, a conspicuously empty spot where a bed should have been was strewn about with the refuse of haste: blood smears on the floor and walls, supplies spilled from their drawers and cabinets, an IV stand lying on its side.

Jon's hand leapt to the radio microphone clipped to his collar. "Pete, Will! Lock the hospital down, *now!* We have an incident."

His shout knocked the nurse out of her shock. She sprinted to a small panel on the wall and punched a large blue button. Before she reached the first victim, a smooth tone sounded through the PA, followed by a female's calm, practiced voice: "Code Blue, Station Two."

Kneeling down next to another of the inert bleeding forms, Jon checked the wounds: a single, deep slash across the throat. Bright red arterial blood was still pulsing onto the floor, though the strength of the spurts was weakening at an alarming rate. "This one's alive, but barely. How's that one?"

The nurse's voice was choked, hoarse, as if she'd been screaming inside her own head since they'd walked into this nightmare. "He's gone." She looked over at Jon. "Use your finger and thumb. Press on the arteries on either side of his windpipe. I'll be right there." She stood and yanked the top drawer open on a crash cart against the nearest wall. A second later, she was crouching next to Jon on the floor, tearing open a suture kit. "Okay, get out of the way. Check on Susan."

The doors burst open. In reflex, Jon rolled over. His pistol slid easily from his shoulder rig. The group running into the ward stopped dead, their hands raised as they saw the 9mm. Jon's heart pounded in his throat. As he recognized the scrubs and uniforms, he lowered his weapon, hands shaking.

Pandemonium erupted as the team flew into action. Jon stumbled over to a wall. His left hand came up to his face to cover the tears rising in his eyes, but he stopped when he saw the red blur. His hand was covered in Isaac Simpson's blood.

His legs collapsed and he slid to the floor amid the voices of the crash team, working on Isaac and the staff nurse. "O-negative over here,

I need blood *now!*" Another voice came from the other side of the room. "Susan? Susan, come on. Stay with us, hon. *Dammit, breathe!*"

The radio on his hip broke squelch. "Shots fired! Shots fired on the front lawn, officer needs assistance!" In the background, Jon heard the bark of pistol fire.

That snapped Jon back to reality. *Dammit, I'm done being helpless. Let's get these bastards...*" He fought back to his feet. The weight of the pistol in his hand reassured him as he walked, then ran toward the front of the hospital. Anger spurred him on, faster and faster. His feet pounding in the halls matched his racing pulse as he burst through the foyer and out into the front lawn.

Two agents were down, but they'd accounted for three of the enemy. Will Houghmaster hunched behind a low brick wall, ducking down as another hail of bullets flew from the two remaining Pinnacle attackers in hospital garb. A third was helping a gown-garbed man into the back of an SUV.

Jon never broke stride. He dashed across the lawn, making a beeline for the vehicle. The enemy agents turned their fire on him. He might have ducked, might have even run away, but now, he was too mad. He ran harder, his anger turning into a furious, heart-pounding rage. The man helping the other into the SUV was just closing the door when Jon crashed into him. The door slammed shut on the man's arm. He screamed at the loud, harsh crack as the bone gave way.

Kicking back from the SUV's side, Jon fired into the driver and ducked as bullets whined around him.

A loud wet slap to his left caught his attention, and he turned his head to see one of the remaining gunmen hit the ground under Will's fire.

Jon snapped off two more shots at the lone remaining Pinnacle agent. One of them hit home, and blood sprayed from the man's chest as he fired back.

Something punched Jon in the thigh. A moan crawled from his throat as he dropped to the grass. The dull pain in his thigh rose to a screeching crescendo as his own hot blood spilled over his hands.

Footsteps hurried across the grass. *More than one strike team... another attack—* Jon tried to raise his weapon, but it suddenly felt so heavy, he couldn't lift his arm. His vision closed to a tunnel. *Hurts...*

* * * *

Breathe, Jon...

Slowly, Jon's eyes opened. Someone pressed a squid over his nose and mouth. It puffed something cold and rubbery into his face.

"Ngah…" He tried to tear it away, but he was too weak to fight away the arms holding it there.

A woman's voice, tense with stress, urged him. "Come on, Jon, breathe deep."

"Sh'upp," he slurred.

His leg was on fire with pain. He reached down with a hand to put out the flames, but she stopped him. "Jon, just take it easy. Lie down and relax. Do you need something for pain?"

It took everything he had to nod.

"Okay. Just a poke." A sharp sting on his arm crawled up his arm, and his leg began to go away. As the pain subsided, his mind came back to the surface. "S-Shot?"

Will's voice, next to his head, said, "Yeah, buddy, you took one for the team. But we got the jerks. We got 'em."

"We got 'em?"

Fingers of darkness reached out and brought him downward. As his hearing faded, Jon heard Will's tired but confident reply. "Yeah, every one of the bastards."

Chapter Thirty-Six

The one U.S. city Jon had never visited was Detroit. He found himself wondering how it was, after almost twenty years as a federal agent, he had somehow missed this bustling, glimmering metropolis on Lake Erie. The medical transport touched down at Detroit Metro with nary a bump. The C-135's crew tended all their charges with practiced and efficient hands, making sure all were comfortable and stable throughout the flight.

The transport braked and taxied to a remote area of the Air National Guard base where a small fleet of cars and vans awaited. Outside the vehicles, a dozen air commandos stood ready with automatic weapons. Among the vehicles sat an armored personnel carrier, its weapons manned and vigilant.

Jon hobbled down the steps on his own, assisted by a cane. His leg was sore as hell, but he wasn't about to show any weakness. Irving followed, looking more drawn and tired than usual. The flight medical staff lowered the rest of the passengers on their gurneys: the lone remaining man who attacked Irving's cabin, and the two survivors from the attack on the hospital. These were loaded into the vans, one to each. The medical attendants from the flight crew split up and boarded the vans as well to tend them, accompanied by a couple of air commandos in each van.

Jimmy, assisted by two more nurses, came slowly down the steps, his right arm and hand swathed in bandages and supported in a sling. He let them help him into the front seat of a sedan. Irving and Jon took the back seat, and the convoy set off.

Through the afternoon and into the evening they drove north, crossing the Mackinac straits as the sun's last rays waved goodnight over Lake Michigan. Three hours later, they pulled up Nadia's driveway. A small collection of lights glimmered through the trees.

As the convoy drew nearer, a fuller picture emerged. A couple dozen men and women in work clothes carried lumber and hardware back and forth through the clearing. Three new structures were being thrown together to join the log home already there. One was almost complete. The roof was being finished as the vehicles pulled up. A stout wooden door hung open, and three large padlocks dangled from their respective hasps.

Hushi and Beth met Jon when he opened his car door. Hushi was snapping her gum furiously, and Beth chewed her bottom lip. Nadia was nowhere to be seen.

Jon grabbed his cane and fought his way out of the car. "Where is she? Hushi?"

"Lying down. She just had another bad one."

An icy wave hit Jon as the blood drained from his face. "How bad? Are they getting worse?" He limped toward the cabin.

Beth followed him. "We took a fresh MRI in Munising. The biggest tumor is pressing on the trigger nerve, but it's not wrapped around it, and hopefully the problem hasn't spread to the nerve tissue. We can buy some time by getting that one out."

Jon wheeled on her. "'Buy some time?'" The throbbing in his leg made him want to cry as it was, and this news wasn't helping. "What does 'buy some time' mean, Beth? Are you telling me we can't do anything else? Am I supposed to get ready to see her—" He couldn't finish the sentence. That thought was too much to bear.

Hushi touched his arm. "We're not giving up, Jon. We're working on a lot of options right now, but we have to get a little breathing room to see if any of the long-term ones are going to work. Just let us have a little space to do what we do, and you go in and cheer her up. She's been so worried ever since you called yesterday." She gave him a light push on his back to get him through the door and went out to meet the medical vans.

* * * *

Nadia lay in her bed under thick covers against a chill. She looked up as Jon entered, and he stopped, shocked. She looked so pale and weak he felt she would fade away and disappear before his eyes. But she looked up at him and knew him and smiled. She had a smile that always lit up Jon's heart with a warm and happy feeling that reached to his toes, even now. It's the kind of smile that wraps itself around whoever it's aimed at and hugs them until all their trouble is forgotten.

A mischievous gleam flashed in her eyes. "You look like hell, baby."

"Yeah. Aren't we a pair of bookends?"

She held her arms out. "Come here and give me a real hello."

Sitting on the edge of the bed, Jon helped her to sit up. Her arms around him personified her smile as they held each other. But Jon felt her chest heave as she sobbed, and it took all he had not to join her.

"I almost lost you," she cried. "Please don't ever leave me."

He kissed her ear and whispered, "Baby, you're so stuck with me. I'm too cussed stubborn to die on you." Releasing her, he stood. "I have to go see about some things outside. But I'll be back, and we can talk some more."

She lay back down and let him tuck her in. "Okay." As he straightened up, she stroked his arm with a fingertip. "I love you."

Jon couldn't suppress the smile that formed on his face. "I love you, too. Now get some rest."

* * * *

As Jon came back outside, Beth was neatly undoing a huge male military doctor with a stream of invectives that made some of the air commandos blush and turn away. She barely came up to his chest but looked into his eyes with the steady glare of the righteously indignant.

Her left hand was balled into a fist at her side; the right was waving and pointing like it had a mind of its own.

"Out beyond this swamp, *Captain,*" she spat, "you may call all the shots and get your way. But now you're on *my* turf. This isn't 'doctor-nurse.' This is 'yes-ma'am-no-ma'am.' And *I'm* the ma'am! Now, get those two patients moved into that building. Leave that one" —she pointed at the oldest of the three, a silver-haired man with a bruised, swollen face— "Right where he is. His room is almost ready. I'll let you know when and where to move him. Until then, that truck is his room. He is *not* coming into this house. Am I finally clear?"

The doctor's face flushed as he stammered, "Yes, ma'am," and walked away.

Beth turned and glared at the small group of air commandos and local workers who'd gathered to watch. "Don't you people have something to do?"

They all hurried away, lest they become the newest victims of her wrath.

Jon cleared his throat to get her attention. Her eyes still blazed as she wheeled around. "What! Oh, it's you."

Jon looked around at the bustle for a moment before asking, "Ah, where did all these people come from, and what's going on?"

"Right after you called, Nadia made a call to the tribal council. This is the Potawatomi equivalent of a barn raising. It seems our blonde mascot in there has a strong relationship with the local community. They've been out here since yesterday afternoon." She pointed at each building as she continued. "That one that's almost done is the holding pen for our two junior thugs. No windows. Triple-locked, solid pine door. Building 2 is our VIP quarters. That's for Mr. Big, and it's finishing up next. Nadia has room in the house for Jimmy and Irving if Bunny, Hushi, and I find our own places, and Building 3 over there is going to be a bunkhouse for the troops."

Jon shook his head. "I don't feel comfortable with so many people knowing about this, Beth. It could come back to bite us on the nose."

Beth stood, arms akimbo, and turned to face Jon directly. "And a dozen locals we know is different from a dozen heavily-armed men we don't?"

"I don't like any of it. The more people who know about this operation, the more at risk we are. I would think you'd be more gun-shy than any of us—"

She stuck a finger in his face. "Jon, don't go there. I've seen more weird crap in the last four years than the previous thirty-one. I can handle it. I watched a man blow my friend's brain all over the wall" — she pointed at the men being trundled into the lock-down hut— "And he was one of *these* animals. No one wants to end this more than me. So don't talk to me about being gun-shy." Walking toward the hut, she added, "Excuse me. I have to make sure our guests are comfortable."

Jon stood among the bustle of workers building pole barns, and military people setting up a bivouac. He never wanted things to get this big. Then again, he hadn't considered being in this situation. But at least now, he had a way to expose The Pinnacle's operation without having to bring Nadia forward. She could stay safely on the sidelines while Jon started with assault of a federal officer, attempted murder, murder, and about a dozen other major charges.

The last week had cost a lot, in lives lost and blood spilled. *But we won, by God. We won this round.*

His phone buzzed in his pocket. Puzzled, he pulled it out and answered.

The voice on the other end was cheerful, almost giddy. Considering whose voice it was, it sent a deadly chill through his blood. "Hi, Jon! How's every little thing?"

"Just fine, Jenna. Had a little wrinkle, but we got through it." He sighed. "I think we have to talk about some things—"

"We already talked. I assume you got the ledger. I have something else to send you, but I need a shipping address."

Chapter Thirty-Seven

Jenna leaned back in Bowman's plush chair with her feet propped up on his desk, holding a business card in front of her face as she smiled into her phone. "Well, not so much a shipping address, because I intend to deliver my gift personally." She loved tweaking people, and for some reason, Jon was her favorite person to tweak. He was just so... *tweakable*.

His voice on the other end was near frantic as he asked, "How did you get this number, Jenna?"

"I'm in John Bowman's office right now," she said, knowing it would unnerve him even more.

"You didn't kill him yet, did you?"

Jenna uncrossed her legs and swung the chair around, watching the last rays of the sun fade over the Pacific through the office window. *Beautiful. Just breathtaking.* "Not yet. Though the bastard deserves it, don't you think?"

"Where's Bowman?"

"On one of his boring business trips, I imagine. I just stopped by to have a chat and drop off a token of my esteem. Imagine my surprise when I found your card in his top drawer."

"Jenna, I want you to stop whatever it is you're doing and come talk to me."

She stood and smoothed her slacks with her free hand. "What *do* you think I'm doing, Jon?" Stretching her back, she reached inside her jacket and loosened the .45 in its holster under her shoulder.

Jon lowered his voice, as if someone else might overhear. "After what you did to Congressman Walters, I can only guess revenge. It's not the answer, Jenna—"

"Don't you pretend you know the answer!" she hissed. "You've been so clueless ever since I met you. Do you think you know these people? How they work? Who better to give them a taste of their own medicine than someone *they* trained?"

"What were you going to send me?"

Jenna looked at her watch. *Best be on my way.* "No offense, Jon, but I was actually thinking Bunny might be the one for this. But since his phone doesn't seem to work, I had to call you." She left the office, locking the door behind her, and made her way to the elevator. "So where do we meet this time? La Guardia was romantic, but I'm thinking someplace a little more intimate, maybe a little wine, candlelight—"

"Don't count on it, *dear.*" The rustling of paper through the speaker lasted only a few seconds. "Okay, how's Woonsocket, South Dakota, the day after tomorrow?"

"How did you come up with that one? Throw a dart at your map?" She snapped her free hand up, rubbing her eyes to hide her face as a security guard passed her in the hall. "Never mind, I can make it work. Give me a call when you get there, and we'll finalize it. Toodles, babe."

The elevator opened up as she pocketed her phone. Reaching into the empty car, she pushed the button for the ground floor and ducked back out, following the signs for the stairs.

Three flights down, a muffled *krump* echoed down the stairwell. Jenna pumped a fist in the air, whispered a harsh "Yes-s-s-s!" and counted on security flocking around an empty elevator while she made her getaway via the back entrance of the station building. It wasn't a large bomb, just enough to make a mess of Bowman's office and hide the fact that something was missing, something special indeed. *Think this'll get the Council together, Mr. Bowman?*

Chapter Thirty-Eight

Jon listened to the wind howl down Baker Street and scanned the horizon again, wondering what he was waiting to see. The highest point in town was the top of the high school bleachers, and from there he could swear he saw fifty miles across the prairie in every direction. What traffic crawling through on State Road 34 was as sparse as Irving's hair.

His pocket buzzed, and he hauled out his cellphone. "Yeah, Bunny, what now?"

"*Now* are you gonna tell me why you hadda drag me all the way to the Little Big Horn?"

"Jenna said she had to deliver something."

"What, she couldn't figure out how much postage for a dead body?"

"Actually, Bunny, she said it was for you."

A long pause preceded Bunny's response. "My birthday was two months ago. I don't think I want nothin' from her."

"I have a feeling we're going to need whatever it is."

"You know how she came by whatever it is, don't you? Don't it bother you she probably killed somebody to get it?"

Now it was Jon's turn to pause. Of course, it bothered him. There was little about Jenna Paine that *didn't* bother him. She flaunted the law at every opportunity, refused to treat seriously anything and anyone who didn't fit into her own twisted version of the universe. She made up new rules as she went along, and, thanks to the deal she'd cut with Donna, dragged Jon into playing this horrid game her way. Jon was used to taking the lead in every case he'd ever worked. The only reason he played second fiddle now was because she knew her way around the inside of The Pinnacle, at least enough to get the information he needed to shut them down once and for all.

He took a deep breath before answering. "Bunny, this is just until we finish our job. Whatever she has for us, we can hope it's enough to close out this case and end The Pinnacle's power grab. Then we can get her out of our lives once and for all."

"I still don't like it, Jonny."

"Just hang loose there in the car, Bunny. Let's see what it is before we get our hopes up."

"Hey, speakin' of hangin' loose, you better watch out. I think I just saw her headin' your way. A brown pickup truck with a camper shell just turned toward the stadium."

"I think I see her, Bunny. Thanks."

Jon slapped his phone shut and came down off the bleacher as the truck pulled through the gate onto the track and braked to a halt on the infield. It sat still, engine idling as Jon approached. He scanned the area apprehensively, every nerve on edge. Something was definitely wrong. He'd expected her to at least make herself known before his feet hit the grass. Coming closer, he thought for a moment that the truck was empty. Wondering how the hell she could have gotten out without him seeing, he reached behind his back for the pistol tucked into its belt holster there.

When he was ten feet away, something moved behind the steering wheel and disappeared below the dashboard. Coming around the side, he saw the bullet holes in the door.

Jon's phone buzzed again. *Dammit, what's happening?* "Bunny, can it wait? Something's happened—"

"Shut up and get the hell out of there, Jon! There's a half dozen cars comin' at you right now."

Jon whipped the driver's door open. Jenna lay across the seat, her face a deathly pale. Blood seeped steadily through her fingers from a wound in her thigh, soaking the seat and pooling on the floorboards.

"Bunny, listen. Go back home, I'll catch up. Just go now." He closed his phone and grabbed Jenna. Shoving her onto the passenger's seat, he climbed in. He ignored the warm blood seeping into his trousers as he put the truck in gear.

A movement in the side mirror caught his attention. Several dark cars entered the field through the only gate and fanned out. Goosing the accelerator, Jon spun out of the infield. "Hang on, Jenna." Aiming for a spot off the end of the bleacher, he rammed the chain link and tore off through the prairie surrounding the school, his pursuers hot on his bumper.

Jenna's voice was weak beside him, barely audible above the roar of the engine. "I'm sorry, Jon. I thought I shook them off." She seemed to recover a little, as if she were gathering herself, fighting off shock.

A ditch appeared in front of the truck. Jon whipped the wheel hard to the left, barely missing it. The car behind responded too late and skewed through the turn, rolling into the ditch in a cloud of dust. Its companions remained right on their bumper. "We have *got* to stop meeting like this," he grumbled as the truck bumped over the ground.

Jenna had a first aid kit out, and was winding a pressure bandage on her thigh. "Meeting like what?"

"Like you bleeding all over the front seat while I—" He swerved to avoid a dry buffalo wallow. "While I drive like a bat out of hell."

"A girl's got to get your attention somehow." She cinched the dressing on her leg and opened the rear window of the cab. "Get back on the road." Squirming through the opening, she disappeared into the camper shell.

Jon aimed for the highway and gunned it, tearing across the ground with five pursuers hot on his heels. He approached the highway berm at an oblique angle, launched across the ditch, and hit the pavement skidding and slewing. Another one of the chase cars hit the ditch at too steep an angle and crunched into it, an explosion of steam and smoke signifying the engine's failure. Jon snapped on his Bluetooth. "Dial Bunny." When the little man answered, he asked, "How's it going, friend?"

"Jon, where you at? It's all quiet here."

Gunfire erupted from the back of the truck. A squeal of tires and a crash accompanied Jenna's triumphant yell. Jon said, "We have four or five tagalongs. I don't know how much ammo Jenna's got, but I'm guessing it won't be enough."

"Bring 'em back through town."

"What are you thinking, Bunny?"

"Just do it, Jonny. Trust me." Bunny disconnected.

Jon shouted over his shoulder, "Hang on, Jenna!" Whipping the wheel to the right, he crashed through a fencerow, mowing through a wheat field as he swung around in a sharp turn. One of The Pinnacle cars cut inside, trying to head him off. He hit the accelerator and swung back left, drawing even with it. A burst of automatic fire raked the side of the truck. Jon ducked and cut the wheel back to the right. His fender caught the car on the front quarter and spun it out as he turned back toward the highway and the town. "Are you all right?" he yelled as he gained pavement again.

Jenna called from the back, "Hold your ears!" Moments later, an explosion rocked the truck, followed by another yell from Jenna.

Jon fought it back under control and hit the pedal. "What did you do?"

Another round of gunfire answered him back as Jenna emptied another magazine at their pursuers. She poked her head through the window, a grin splitting her face. "That was my gas camp stove. Wasn't it cool?" She squirmed back through the opening and slumped down in the passenger seat. Her face was horridly pale. Beads of sweat rolled down her temples, slicking her hair down. Her jaw trembled from pain and blood loss. But her eyes gleamed with excitement. "They backed off, but they're still following. Out of range for now," she panted. "Where are we going?"

"Back through Woonsocket. Bunny has a plan."

"Good for Bunny." She dropped the empty magazine from her pistol, slid a fresh one home, and released the slide, letting it snap forward. "You have some good friends."

As they approached the town limit, the cars began to close in again. Jon dialed Bunny. "I hope you're ready, because we're coming in now. Eastbound on 34."

"Got ya covered, Jonny. Come down the main drag… Okay, I saw ya! Hang on…"

Jon caught a movement in the side mirror. A brown blur exploded from a side street and slammed into the lead chase car, knocking it sideways in the narrow street. The car behind crashed into them both, scattering parts and steam into the air.

Jon screamed, "Bunny! What did you do?"

Silence was his only answer.

Chapter Thirty-Nine

Carlos was on his way to the parking lot when his phone rang. He paused to look at the caller ID and frowned. *No one I know...* "Charlie Company, Sergeant Villanueva, how may I help you?" He twirled his car keys in his other hand as he crossed the lot.

He was sure he'd heard the woman's voice before, but there was something different about it: she sounded strained, sluggish. "Have you looked into Chapter Seventeen, Sergeant?"

The keys flew from Carlos' hand and jingled their way under an SUV. He froze in place, pulse racing. "Who is this?"

"I have a present for you. The Grand Hotel on Mackinac, tomorrow at dusk. Take the ferry from St. Ignace." The line clicked dead.

Frantically, he hit the dial-back sequence on his phone. It rang twice, and the recording said, "The number you have dialed is no longer in service. If you'd like to make a call—"

He cursed and slapped his phone shut, then opened it again and dialed. "Tab, pack for a week. We're going west...as soon as I find my car keys."

* * * *

The truck pulled up the driveway after dark. A nervous air commando waved Jon through after verifying his identity. Jon spoke loudly enough for Jenna to hear from the back of the camper. "We're here."

Hushi waited on Nadia's porch, a camp lantern in her hand. In the harsh glare of its light, Jon found her face impossible to read. He climbed out and stood as she came off the porch.

Her voice was strained. "Jon, where's my husband?"

"Hushi, I said I don't know—"

"Why?" She stepped closer, her voice rising in volume. "Why did you have to take him with you?"

"I thought we'd need him right away—"

He could have blocked the slap; he'd seen it coming. But something told him it would have been worse if he did, so he let it come without raising a hand. As it was, she hit him hard enough to make a hundred colored pinpricks explode in his eyes. When his vision cleared again, she still stood in front of him, tears streaming down her face.

"He's dead, isn't he? If the wreck didn't kill him, they will, won't they?"

Jenna's voice came from behind Jon. "Not necessarily." She made her way forward, leaning against the truck as she came into the light of Hushi's lantern.

Hushi gasped at the sight. Jenna was pale, trembling as she staggered on her bad leg. The bandage she'd tied around her thigh the day before was soaked in red. Her whole pant leg below the wound was black with dried, crusted blood.

Jenna continued, her voice weakening as she spoke. "They want him alive. His skills are priceless to them." She stumbled and held her hand out, too weak to recover, and fell to the ground. She mumbled, "I don't feel good," before her eyes closed in a faint.

Hushi yelled over her shoulder, "Beth. Get out here!" Then she pointed at two nearby air commandos. "You two—go get Captain Watts and tell him to meet me in the ambulance. He has a patient." With quick, efficient movements, she checked Jenna's leg and helped Beth get her settled on a stretcher. As the medics carried her away, Beth walked alongside, holding Jenna's hand.

When she turned back to Jon, Hushi's chin trembled with emotion. "Get him back. You go and bring Bunny back home."

"I promise, Hushi. Whatever it takes. I'll get started as soon as I can."

"You'll get started *now!*"

Jon grabbed her shoulders. "Listen! I don't know where he is. Someone's coming in tomorrow who should be able to tell me. But tonight, all we can do is rest and hope. Trust me. I'll make it right." Hushi let him pull her in for a hug. She buried her face in his shirt and cried while he rocked her. "It's going to be all right," he murmured. He just hoped he could believe it himself.

* * * *

An hour before sunset, Carlos and Tabitha pulled up to the tollbooth at the southern end of the Mackinac Bridge. He handed the attendant the toll and took the receipt, which he handed to Tabitha without looking twice at it.

They were through the gate when she said, "Hey, Carlos, there's a note here on the back side."

He looked in his side mirror to see the attendant nodding back at him.

Tabitha read as they crossed the straits. "They're latitude and longitude numbers." She plugged the data into the GPS mounted on the dash. "Guess what…We're not going to Mackinac."

He smiled at her. "You sound disappointed."

"Hey, a night at the Grand Hotel, on Uncle Sam's dollar? Would you pass that up?" She slouched in her seat with a pout. "With our luck, they'll be set up in some bivouac in the woods and we'll spend the week dodging bears and snakes."

Carlos reached over to take her hand. "Don't worry, honey, I'm sure they have motels up here, too." He took a couple extra turns in St. Ignace to make sure they weren't followed and set off for the Simi Stretch and points west.

* * * *

Nadia and Beth were with Jenna in Nadia's back bedroom when Jon came in to check on her the next morning. "How's she doing?" he whispered.

"Not too bad, considering how many bullets she's taken in the last month," said Jenna in a hoarse voice. "I'm awake, Jon. How are you?"

"Not too bad, considering how many times I've been bled all over in the last month."

Jenna's smile was soft and sincere, quite unlike her usual coquettish smirk. "That's two I owe you." She held up a hand for Jon to squeeze. "Thank you." When Jon let go, Jenna held on tighter. "You have *gorgeous* eyes."

A hot flush rose in Jon's cheeks as he looked to Nadia, who blushed and smiled back, shaking her head. Looking back at Jenna, he asked, "Ah… Are you on drugs?"

"No, thanks," she purred, "I already had some."

"Then I suppose now would be a bad time to discuss what you brought us, and why?"

"Yeah." Her eyes drifted closed, and Jon turned to leave when she opened them again and stopped him. "Jon? I'm sorry. About Bunny."

"Yeah, me too."

Nadia followed him out. When he stopped, she circled around to his front, arms crossed and a lopsided grin on her face. "You know, you *do* have…gorgeous eyes."

He rubbed the back of his neck, heat rising again in his cheeks. "Look, babe, seriously, nothing happened—"

She stepped closer, looking at him from beneath her brows. "She is kind of cute, you know. And you two do have a history—"

"Nadia, look at me." He took her shoulders in his hands. "You know you're the only one for me. You *know* that, right?"

She snuck her hands up under his shirt and tickled his ribs. "I know that, silly. I just like to see you squirm once in a while." With a chuckle, she said, "She is so zonked, I seriously doubt she'll remember anything she said."

He held her close, relishing the feel of her against him, the smell of her hair. Then he kissed her, long and deep. "Promise me something: promise me you'll fight for every last breath you can take."

She gave him a squeeze and released him with a smile. "Okay."

"How's Sofi handling it?"

"She's at the shore with her friend Sammi. Handling it in the best way she knows how, by hiding from it."

"I figured she'd be in there with Jenna. Those two have a connection that goes way back—"

"Sofi refuses to talk about it. I think it has to do with something that happened before I met her. You have to admit—asking a ten-year-old to handle everything that's been going on around here is a bit much."

Jon took Nadia by the hand, guiding her toward the path to the lake. "She's going to be in counseling for a long time, isn't she?"

One of the air commandos stepped up to Jon and stopped with a crisp salute. "Captain Daniels, I have a message from Sergeant Stephans. He just made the handoff, and he's coming back."

Nadia said, "What's this about?"

"We need help finding Bunny. Jenna said what she had was for him, so I'm assuming it's something to do with computers. I just called in the only man I know who could come close to Bunny's skill with a machine. In about three hours, he'll be here. If he can fill in some blanks for us, we should be able to round up our little cybergeek before anything too bad happens."

Her mouth fell open, and her eyes glistened with hope. "Does Hushi know?"

"I tried to tell her, but she doesn't want to see me right now. I can't say I blame her."

Nadia turned back to the house. "Give her a little time. She'll come around."

"Yeah. Maybe."

Chapter Forty

Sammi tossed another pebble over the cliff, watching it shrink into nothing just before it hit the lake's surface with a tiny white splash far below. Superior swallowed it, uncaring, and slammed another wave against the cliff base. "So how's your mom?"

"Not so good." Sofi lay on her back, watching puffy white clouds scud across the sky. A chill breeze came ashore carrying the cries of gulls and the roar of the waves below.

"What's wrong with her, anyway?"

What's wrong? Sofi took a deep breath and let it sift out through her nose. *What's not wrong? My mom's dying, and if we're lucky, she won't take the town with her. If you only knew what was wrong, you'd run away screaming.* "I don't know. The doctors are trying to figure it out."

"The Potawatomi have been out to your place a lot lately."

"Mom needed a shed built. She does a lot of stuff for the Tribe, and they help out around the place."

Sammi tossed another pebble over the edge, rolled over, and sat up. "Where did you go? You never even called me."

"I forgot."

"Are you okay? It's like you're someone else, all of a sudden."

"Maybe I am," Sofi muttered under her breath.

The redhead stood and brushed grass from her knees. "What?"

"Nothing."

"You know, we used to talk about all kinds of stuff."

"Yeah, well..." Sofi let the response trail off into nothing, so Sammi wouldn't hear her choke up. She didn't ask for any of this. She was dragged into existence at somebody's whim, a science fair project. And because of this, her first mother died. Her second mother was dying. She lived with soldiers and spies, among secrets and guns. The Bad People were getting closer, and now it seemed there was nowhere else to run. It was too much to take. She was smart enough to know if she opened her mouth, Sammi was going to be in just as much danger.

As Sofi's mind raced, the clouds overhead lumbered across the sky like a herd of gigantic airborne beasts. "That one, right there. It looks like an elephant."

Sammi paused and glanced up. "Yeah, whatever. Well, if you need to talk about anything, let me know." Sammi strode off down the path to town, swiping at a low branch as she passed into the woods.

Sofi sat up. "Wait, where are you going?"

Sammi's voice floated from the trees. "I'm going home. You want to come? We could play some online games."

Rising, Sofi brushed herself off and trotted after her friend.

Chapter Forty-One

Carlos pushed on past mile after mile of desolate jackpine swamp as he watched the numbers on his GPS dwindle closer to the numbers programmed into it. He stopped for nothing, so determined was he to get to their destination.

He stole a glance at Tabitha Grubka in the passenger's seat. She was catching a couple of winks as the afternoon lolled on. The convertible's windshield allowed the occasional errant gust over the top to play with a lock of Tabitha's hair, tossing it mischievously around her face as she slept. If he hadn't been so worked up over this whole mess, he probably would have been sleepy himself. But as it was, adrenaline and caffeine pushed him on harder than ever.

His heart quivered in his chest as he drove on. This could be a trap. The voice on the phone could have been someone from The Pinnacle. Maybe they noticed his probes into their network and activities, even as subtle as he'd tried to be. He was good, but he didn't have the resources his enemies had.

Or, it could have been an invitation from Daniels to join the party again.

After that red-haired woman told him about Chapter Seventeen, he and his small team did dig into the Global Unification Alliance's networks and chapters around the world. Chapter Seventeen was a ghost at first, seemingly another dead end at the end of fifty other dead ends. But under Carlos and Tabitha's more determined searches a pattern began to emerge. The first thing they noticed was that the GUA refused to even acknowledge its existence. That chapter, they were told, had been disbanded due to financial difficulties. No one would even say at which college campus it was chartered.

Then last week, a news article about an incident at Gradwell College caught his attention. There was a shooting. What struck Carlos as strange was the press seemed to be on a tear lately about every little disturbance at any little college, especially any incident involving a gun. It was almost as if the news people covering this story would much rather have said nothing about it and let it go away on its own, a quiet little death among the cacophony of national news for that day. Two people were involved, one of them a secretary who'd been nearly cut in half by a shotgun blast, and a professor who was listed as not seriously injured. What slapped Carlos was the mention of the professor's role at the college. He was the student advisor of the local GUA chapter: none other than Chapter Seventeen. Witnesses described a woman running from the scene and disappearing into the woods around the college. The police searched the area with dogs and found nothing.

Carlos had to wonder if the person they were looking for was the same woman who'd shown such incredible stealth in the Virginia woods not that long ago. She would have had plenty of time to mount an operation at that campus.

And the voice on the other end of that strange call he'd received, now that he thought about it, could very well have belonged to her. Was she trying to disguise her voice? Probably not. She could have used some other device and made it totally unrecognizable. She didn't have to play childish games like trying to sound like she'd been gargling razor blades. So it was probably her.

Just in case, though, he'd packed two M-4 carbines and five hundred rounds of 5.56mm ammo, hidden under a jacket on the back seat.

As they passed the last turn to Munising, a shadow in the road ahead caught Carlos' eye. Moose, maybe? He thought about waking Tabitha, but by the time he opened his mouth, the shadow grew into a vaguely box-shaped vehicle parked across the road a couple of miles ahead.

He eased up on the accelerator. "Tab? Honey, wake up. We have company." Glancing again at the GPS, he noticed they were getting closer to the position given them at the bridge tollbooth.

Tabitha opened her eyes and squinted at the truck ahead, the only other vehicle on the road. "Looks like a military truck."

"Yeah. Get in back, will you? Stay low and get those M-4s ready to rock."

Tabitha climbed over the seat. Seconds later, Carlos heard the metallic sound of a magazine sliding into a receiver, followed by the *slick-chick* of a charging handle. The routine repeated as she loaded and charged the second carbine.

Slowing as he approached the truck, Carlos felt beneath his shirt for the symbolic comfort of his Kevlar vest. He pulled to a stop a couple hundred meters short of the truck. Several figures stepped out from the trees on both sides. One man came forward, holding his hand in the air. Cradled in his other arm was a combat shotgun, pointed away. No one else advanced, though every man held their weapon at the ready.

Tabitha's voice trembled as she asked, "What's the deal?"

Carlos kept his hands on the wheel, his head facing forward. "Take it easy," he whispered. "We're just out of easy range, there's only one guy coming toward us. Stay frosty, but be quick if you get the word."

Fifty meters away, the soldier pulled out a camera with his free hand and took a picture. A few seconds later, he held up a hand toward Carlos and stooped down, laying his shotgun on the road. When he stood, the others behind him lowered their own weapons. It felt like a huge, collective sigh of relief as he smiled and walked toward the car.

Carlos' knuckles cracked as his hands relaxed their grip on the wheel. He blew a cleansing breath into the air. "We're good, Tab."

The soldier stopped a few meters in front of the car. "Sergeant Villanueva, I'm sorry for the inconvenience. If I can take your shotgun seat, I'll take you to Captain Daniels. He's waiting for you."

* * * *

Jon eased into the wooden rocker on the porch and stretched his sore leg out, resting his foot on a wooden fruit crate. Nadia's front yard-cum-bivouac had settled into what passed for its normal rhythm after the excitement of Jenna's return to the group, and the impending arrival of his newest member. It gave him time to breathe, for the first time in some weeks.

Jimmy pushed the screen door open with his back, right arm suspended in a sling. Clutched between the fingers of his left hand, a pair of cola bottles sweated cool drops of condensation. He held out the hand to Jon, who took one with a grin. "Thanks, old man."

"S'matter, boy? Got a hitch in your git-along?" Jimmy creaked down into the straight-backed chair next to the younger man.

Jon took a pull from his cola. "Aren't we a real pair of bookends?"

"Yeah, that'd be a crackerjack library." Jimmy laughed a low sardonic chuckle. "We took a hellacious beatin' the last couple of weeks, my friend."

"Yeah. It's kind of hard to tell who's kicking whose ass anymore."

"You knew it was gonna get messy, Jon. These kinds of ops always do."

"But we lost Donna. You and I are both wounded, Nadia's still sick, and Bunny's missing in action. Hell, they may have even killed him by now. We don't know."

The screen door opened again, and Jenna limped onto the porch carrying a folding tray. Behind her, Nadia came out with a plate of sandwiches. She set the plate in Jon's lap, took the tray from Jenna, and set it up between the men. Then she stooped to kiss Jon and patted him on the head before turning back to enter the house.

Jon stopped her before she got away. "You're extra bright today."

Nadia smiled in a way that she hadn't in a long time. "I have a meeting with Hushi and Beth. They said it was good news. I'll see you when I get back, hon."

Jenna sat on the rail, arms crossed. "Well, if it isn't Frick and Frack."

"You're looking good, yourself, there," said Jon. "You want to sit down?" He made as if to give up his seat, but she waved him off with a wry smile.

"I need to stand for a while, if it's all the same." She took a breath before continuing. "I want to see who you have in the holding shacks."

"A couple of your old buddies. You should count yourself lucky you're not in there with them. What the hell were you thinking, invading the whole western seaboard like that?"

Jenna managed a twisted little grin. "Quite the field trip, wasn't it? I can hardly wait to see what we can use out of those little presents I brought back."

"You know I can't look at it, whatever it is. I have to be able to use the information in court, and you hardly had a warrant—"

"Warrant? You want to play by the rules all of a sudden?"

Jon fought back the wave of anger rising in him. "Jenna, I don't like the rules, but if I want this case to stick, I still have to follow them."

Jenna laughed derisively. "Then you're going to lose, Captain Daniels. Who do you think owns the courts now? Who are the ones making the rules? The very people we're trying to bring down, can't you see that? If you keep playing by the rules, they are always going to win. They'll find some loophole, some technicality, and have the whole thing thrown out. The only way we're going to beat them is to refuse to play by their rules."

She slid off the rail to stand over Jon. "Besides, I wasn't operating at your behest, so whatever the cat dragged in on those hard drives is open season for you. For all you know, the equipment showed up on your porch, and you had to look inside to find the rightful owners."

Jenna turned to look at the shacks again. "Have they called yet to make a trade?"

"Not a word, so far."

"Has he told you anything yet?"

"He just keeps staring at the wall and grinning like a sick possum."

"You should let me talk to him. I know how they're trained. Whoever it is, I'd bet I can break him in an hour."

Jon's phone rang. Before he could rattle off his normal greeting, a man on the other end said in a jovial tone, "How's everything going, Captain Daniels?"

His heart jumped. "Who is this?"

"Your friend wants to say hello." In the background, Bunny's strident voice: "You mooks are gonna pay for this, I swear! Do *not* piss off my wife—" A sharp crack cut off the remainder of his shout, and the man spoke again. "Let's talk trade, Jon. I have your IT god. You have someone we want. Let's make this easy."

Jon's mind raced. *What to do?* "I'm listening."

"We want you to return our people. In return, we'll guarantee Mr. Kalinsky's safety. Now, that's a generous offer. You have three days. Think about it. We'll be in touch." A click announced the end of the call.

Jon slapped his phone shut and struggled to his feet. "I think it's time we took a new look at who we have in the hoosegow. Jenna, let's take a walk."

Chapter Forty-Two

The two air commandos in camo BDUs snapped to attention when Jon and Jenna approached the door to Shed 1, holding their rifles angled across their chests in salute. Jon returned a non-committal wave as he pulled a key ring from his pocket. With a mechanical click of the padlock and a jangle, the chain fell away. Before he stepped up onto the plank floor, he held out a hand to Jenna. "Do I need to cuff you, or do you promise not to kill him until after we've had a chance to find out more about him?"

Jenna put a hand on her hip, leaning on the single crutch. Through a sly grin, she purred, "If cuffs are involved, I can guarantee they won't be on me." When she winked, a flush rose in Jon's cheeks.

He stood, trying to come back with something, anything, but his brain was too busy going in directions that led to other parts than his mouth. Finally, he simply raised a hand and motioned her in. "Ah… yeah, right." His ears burned at her stifled giggle as she passed.

The laugh was cut short when Jenna saw who was tethered to the two-by-four upright in the corner. In two lurching bounds, she was across the shack and lashing out with both fists, a stream of obscenities pouring from her mouth. The hapless prisoner had barely enough time to bring his arms up to cover and restricted as he was, he was unable to mount any kind of counter to Jenna's assault.

Jon grabbed her by the waist and wrestled her to the floor as two unarmed guards came in to help drag her outside.

As the door swung shut, the prisoner yelled, "You keep that bitch out of here!"

Jenna stopped struggling under the weight of the two beefy men who had her pinned to the ground. Her face betrayed the pain she was feeling from her exertion but still she managed a smile.

Jon slumped to his seat, panting. "So...former boyfriend?"

"Not exactly." She held out her hands out in surrender, and the guards backed away. "That was the man who signed my death order."

"Then why are you grinning like the cat that ate the canary?"

Jenna shook her head slowly, the fire in her eyes kindling afresh. "Because that felt so *good.*" One of the guards grabbed her outstretched hand and helped her to her feet as the others retook their positions outside the door. "Plus, I'm willing to bet you couldn't get him to talk at all. Know how to get someone to talk, Jon?"

He fought to his feet, gritting his teeth against the spasm in his injured leg. "I suppose you're going to tell me."

"First, you scare the holy living hell out of them." She started back toward the house. "He wasn't afraid of you, because you play by the rules, and he knows that."

"So, slapping the man silly…"

Jenna spun on him, fixing him with a sudden glare. Jon's blood froze as he stopped dead. She poked his chest with every word. "Changes the routine." The glare disappeared, replaced by an impish grin. "Get it? He has no idea what we're going to do to him next." Her gaze wandered to the other holding shack, and she nodded toward the armed guards at that door. "Now, who's our next contestant?"

Jon shook his head. "Not a chance. I want them alive to face charges."

Jenna opened her mouth to say something more but stopped when a red sports convertible pulled up the drive and stopped in front of the garage. "Oh, I see they got our invitation. We may not need our VIP after all."

"Correction—we need him to trade for Bunny. That phone call was from our Mr. Big's buddies. They want him back, and they're offering Bunny in return."

Jenna grabbed his arm. "You have *got* to be kidding! They have no intention of letting you or Bunny out of there alive. Don't you know by now, Jon? These beasts eat their wounded!" She stabbed a finger back at the shack they'd just left. "Palmer Frost is the man you have in there. He's their chief of security. He has a bullet waiting for him, just because he's been seen. This 'deal' being offered to you is just their way of getting you to expose yourself to them, on their ground, and on their terms. If you play by their rules, you're signing your own death warrant." Spinning on her heel, she limped back toward Nadia's porch. "You'll also be killing Bunny. And that'll be the worst shame of it all."

Jon's leg throbbed, and he stood for a while, rubbing the ache. "I don't have any other choice. There's nothing more I can do. I pulled Bunny into this, and I have to give him a chance to get out."

Jenna sank into the vacant cane chair next to Jimmy. "If you want to give him that chance, we're going to have to change the rules."

"How?"

"Have they called you back with details on the rendezvous yet?"

"No."

Jenna picked up Jon's soda and took a sip, letting her lips linger on the bottle's mouth just a second longer than proper. She tipped it toward Jimmy and said, "Let me and this old wolf handle that part. You go meet our guests and show them to the back of my truck."

Chapter Forty-Three

Jon looked again at the sheet of paper on the table before him and clamped his mouth shut before he said anything loud and stupid. Jenna and Jimmy sat on the other side of the table, the overhead light cutting deep shadows across their stony faces. All the other lights in the house remained off, the hour being late. Outside, a chorus of cicadas filled the void in dialogue.

Finally, Jon found his voice. "This is nuts. You two are crazy. I won't let it happen." They sat in cold silence as he ripped the paper to shreds and heaped the pieces together. "Give me another plan by sunup. One that doesn't involve Nadia."

In response, Jimmy's wrinkled fingers gathered the scraps and swept them off the table as Jenna put a fresh copy of the same plan in front of Jon. Her voice was firm. "This is it. We're not asking for permission. We're telling you what we're doing."

"You'll never get the commandos to agree. Jimmy, you're not in their chain of command—"

Jenna cut him off. "Don't you see the way they hold him in awe, Jon? They'd follow Sergeant DeBartolo into Hell, if it meant ending this mess once and for all. He's a freaking *legend* to them."

"Do you have any idea what would happen to them if they did go? They'd be court-martialed, every man-jack of them."

"Not if no one knows, Jonny," croaked Jimmy. "I've run a lot of dark ops. I can make sure this one doesn't get out."

Jon sputtered helplessly for a second before answering. "You've run ops with men who had all been cleared for black ops, Jimmy. How do you know you can trust these apes to keep their mouths shut? What about Dr. Watts? He doesn't seem exceptionally happy about being any part of this. If he says anything—"

"Already handled, dear," said Jenna. A predatory grin slid over her face, and she raised a conspiratorial eyebrow. "I had a little chat with him this afternoon."

"I can only imagine how that went."

She examined her fingernails under the light from the overhead lamp. "I just explained to him the physical benefits of discretion."

Jon paused, fixing her with ice in his eyes. "Well, at least you didn't come out and *tell* me you threatened to tie him to an ant hill and pour honey on him. I'd have to arrest you for extortion."

Jenna met his glare evenly. "Who said anything about ant hills?" Several tense seconds passed before she pointed to the paper in front of her. "The Pinnacle will set up before we get there. It'll be an ambush—"

"And you want to take Nadia into *that*? You're crazier than I thought!"

Jimmy said, "Beth and Hushi removed the worst of the tumors. She's already healed enough to go—"

"Right into a death trap," Jon hissed. "You're going to get us all killed. All it would take is one bullet—"

Jenna put her hand on top of Jon's, pinning it to the table. "They won't dare take the shot. They're dedicated, Jon, not suicidal. If they kill her, they'll never get clear before she destroys twenty square miles of earth, and anything standing on it." Removing her hand, she added, "If she doesn't go, we'll all be dead for sure. Tell you what—we'll keep Nadia as our 'ace-in-the-hole.' She'll stay back with me as long as things go by the book. If you need us, we'll be there on the spot."

Jimmy squinted and raised one eyebrow in surprise. Nonetheless, he stayed silent, contenting himself with leaning back in his chair, arms across his chest.

Jon took advantage of the moment. "Jimmy, you look a little put out. Is this all okay with you?"

The old man pursed his lips before speaking. "I think we could still make it work."

"Has anyone asked Nadia what she thinks?"

Jenna nodded toward the doorway behind Jon. "Ask her yourself."

Before he could turn around, Nadia's voice said, "I said yes." She ambled past John in a fluffy white bathrobe and opened the refrigerator. "You people make enough noise to wake the dead. Funny, I thought I had some Coke left in here. My sugar level is atrocious. I need something…"

Jon sighed and rose. "Sit down, babe. I'll get you some OJ."

She reached up to give him a quick kiss as they passed. "You're a doll."

"And you're nuts for going along with this," he muttered. "But it looks like I'm outnumbered."

Nadia slid into the chair Jon left. "Honey, if you have something better in mind to get Bunny back and get out of there alive, I'm all ears."

"What makes you think Bunny will even be there?" Jon set a glass down in front of her and filled it with orange juice. "Here, slug that down and I'll top you off again."

A knock at the back door made Jon jump. "This time of night, what the —?" He opened it to admit an excited Carlos Velasquez. His face betrayed the fatigue of the task given him, but his eyes were wild with energy.

"Hey, Captain Daniels! You want to come out to the truck, or shall I just spill the beans here? Never mind." He stepped into Nadia's kitchen waving a perfunctory salute. "Where did you get those computer drives?"

Jon looked hard at Jenna before answering, "They just showed up on our doorstep. I was hoping you could tell us who the rightful owners are, so we could return them."

"Yeah, right." Carlos laughed. Noticing the others in the kitchen, he stopped. "Is everyone else in the loop, or do we need to leave?"

"You can tell us all, son," said Jimmy. "What did you find out?"

"Cracked the code, Sarge." Carlos pulled out the last empty chair, leaving Jon standing. "I have lists of graduates from the Global Unification Alliance's Chapter Seventeen, and about half of them have spent time on the FBI's 'Most Wanted' list, going back to the Weather Underground, the Earth Liberation Front, Symbianese Liberation Army —just about every militant radical group you could name. There's some other stuff on there, too, but we didn't have enough time to get into it all. Hey, you got a beer lying around not doing anything?"

"Check the fridge, Carlos. What was on the other one?"

"How about several very incriminating emails? Names, addresses, titles. This guy was into fixing elections, interfering with government investigations, racketeering, conspiracy to murder, you name it."

Nadia held up a hand. "Wait! Did you say 'addresses'?"

"Well…yeah—"

Jenna cut in. "Jon, how long did they say we had to make the exchange?"

"They didn't say. But they're going to call in three days to set it up."

"So they didn't set a date or place. That means they probably need some time to get their crap together and set the ambush. They'll only call us after they have the trap set."

"Must mean they ain't set yet, themselves," said Jimmy. His hard eyes shifted to Carlos. "Sergeant Villanueva, if you can tell us where their command center is, we might could hit 'em before they have a chance to prepare."

Jon said, "Fine. A suicide attack on the headquarters? What do we have, a dozen air commandos and us? Plus, there's no guarantee that's where they're holding Bunny."

"Then leave the commandos out," said Jenna. "We four will handle it."

"How?"

"Let's let Carlos find the place." She shifted her attention to the young sergeant. "You have until morning to find that command center. I'll make some coffee for you and bring it out."

"And what makes you think that's where Bunny is?" asked Nadia.

Jenna put a hand on her shoulder. "Because of the time lag between his capture and the call. If you have a VIP prisoner, you don't hold him in a field office. You go to where you think your enemies will never find you."

Jon tapped on the tabletop. "Why does this sound like it's going to get harder?"

Chapter Forty-Four

Nadia lay in the dark next to Jon. His soft snoring mingled with the swell of cicadas outside her window. Snuggling up behind him, she slid an arm over his middle and pulled him tight to her. He moaned and put his hand on hers, subconsciously knitting their fingers together. She kissed his shoulder, and he slept on. It always amazed her how he could sleep, no matter how stressed or upset he was when awake. The only sign that betrayed what was going through his mind was the occasional twitch of a muscle in his shoulder or hand. Tonight, he was twitching more than ever. But he slept, deep as the night outside.

Memories from years ago, of a night spent together in a faraway place, crept into her mind. He'd held her through the fear of a terrible nightmare then, and the warmth of his body comforted her, just as much as it reminded her now of what she could not share with him. Physical love was the one thing they lacked in their relationship.

Just as she was then, she still was now: no one, nothing more than organic hardware, an assassin's tool meant for a single, horrific use. *Expendable. I wasn't supposed to live more than a year or two.* She counted to herself. *Almost six years. If I had a shelf life, I'd be growing mold by now.* A bitter realization swept through her mind. *That's what's wrong. I'm not growing mold, I'm growing tumors. It's time I stopped pretending I'm like him. I don't belong here.*

With a soft sigh, Nadia rolled away from Jon and slipped from under the covers. Feeling through her drawer in the darkness, she found a well-worn pair of sweatpants and a T-shirt, and drew them on before making her way through the house and out into the yard.

Dim shadows drifted through the moonlight, sentries on the prowl. The faint green glow from night-vision goggles each wore made them look like alien monsters as they made their rounds through the compound. As each passed Nadia, they nodded in silent acknowledgement, and she made her way through the compound like a queen of phantoms.

Nadia thought she'd gotten away clean when she brought Sofi up here to start a new life for them both. She'd hoped then they'd gotten away from The Pinnacle altogether, far from plots and plans, from weapons and insidious, underground battles for the souls of nations. But this haven she'd created was now violated, drawn back into the corrupted world of the silent war. As long as she existed, peace was a lie.

Crossing to the far side of her yard, she found a shadowed spot under an ancient oak. The gnarled roots on one side formed a sort of natural chair. She liked to come here and take in the woods around her, to restore her soul in prayer or meditation. When she rounded the trunk, however, someone had already taken her seat.

Nadia bit back the remark sitting on her tongue like an electric shock, and barely managed to keep her voice from shaking. "I…kind of need to sit there. Now. Please."

Jenna's voice answered from the shadows. "Oh, I'm sorry. I didn't realize this was yours." She made no move to vacate her place. "Something you want to talk about?"

"Why would I feel like talking now?"

"We used to talk. Remember? Besides, it's two a.m. and you're walking around outside. I'm betting you could think a little better out loud. And you sound like you could use a Special."

Nadia let out a whuff and sat down, leaning back so Jenna could rub her neck and temples using her own unique style. There was no name for it. Nadia just came to know it as a Special. "It's crazy, isn't it?"

"Could you be a little more specific? There's a whole load of crazy sitting all over your lawn." Jenna's fingers shifted. "Oh, there's the spot. You're tight as a banjo string." She pressed with one finger on Nadia's neck. "Tense up here, and then let go."

Nadia complied, allowing Jenna's fingertips to ease some of the tension from her mind. After some moments of silence, she asked, "What comes after?"

"After what?"

"If this goes the way you want, The Pinnacle won't exist as a threat after tomorrow. What's next for me? Do I keep on fighting this cancer, lose, and die? Even if I beat the cancer, I'm going to die someday, Jenna. Then what? I'm going to go up like a nuclear bomb. Sooner or later, it's going to happen."

"Don't have an answer for you, babe."

"What about you?"

One of the patrolling commandos stalked by, green eyes glowing in the dark. Jenna rested her chin on top of Nadia's head, crossing her arms around her friend's shoulders. "I don't know," she murmured.

"At least you could find a job—"

"Doing what? Nadia, you do know what I do for a living, right? I kill people. I infiltrate, I steal. I'm better than anyone else on the planet. You know anyone hiring for that?"

Nadia patted her knee, trying to be reassuring. "You're a bang-up physical therapist. You could do that."

Jenna's hands dropped away. "Stop."

"What?"

"Stop trying to fix me."

"But you at least have a future—"

"Do you want to know how many people I've killed?" Before Nadia could respond, she rushed on. "Forty-three. And that doesn't take into account the number of assassinations I've taken side parts in. That makes me one of the most prolific serial murderers in history. What kind of a future do you think that would make for me?"

She slid out from behind Nadia and stood. Her voice thickened as she continued. "I can't go back. And there's nothing for me to go on to. The best thing that could happen for me is if I don't make it out of there alive. It's no wonder The Pinnacle's retirement plan is a bullet. It's the only humane way out. Once you're broken, you can't be fixed." Jenna turned and disappeared into the darkness, moving as silently as a spirit through the trees, farther away from the house.

Nadia settled back against the bole of the old oak, letting Jenna's words steep in her brain. *Once you're broken, you can't be fixed.* Hot tears welled in her eyes as the familiar lump rose in her throat. *I was broken from the time I opened my eyes. I've just been pretending that I wasn't.*

Thoughts chased each other around in her head. A plan began to emerge. It was time to end this, once and for all.

Jon, please don't be angry with me...

Chapter Forty-Five

Cool morning mist hung in the trees the next morning as Jenna strolled across the yard with her burden. She set it down and nodded to the commandos on early watch before knocking on her camper's back door. "Breakfast, guys," she sang out.

Tabitha's sleepy voice answered. "Unless you have coffee, go away."

Jenna opened the door and handed her the thermos before picking the cooler up and setting it on the bed of the truck. "How's it going, if I can ask?

Tab rubbed her eyes and motioned to the laptop on the little table. "Not easy. Not fast. But I think we're getting somewhere."

A beep from Tabitha's laptop momentarily snatched her attention away from the conversation. She held up a finger. "Hold on…What do you know about a place called Baron Lake?"

Jenna craned her neck in, trying to see what was flashing on the screen. "Never heard of it. Why?"

"Seems our Mr. Bowman mentions it in a lot of his emails to his friends, and especially ones to little Mr. Frost over here," Tab said, jerking her thumb toward the detention shed. "Bowman Communications owns three corporate jets. I'm collecting registered flight plans and matching them up to dates and times of his meetings at

Baron Lake. I should be able to triangulate its location, but I was hoping someone could tell me where it is without a load more hassle."

"Wish I could help you. Here." Jenna handed her the cooler. Tabitha thanked her and closed the door. Jenna turned and started back toward the cabin, her mind buzzing as her heart thumped in her chest. *Careful what you give away. Prison is not an option.* It was bad enough with Jon riding her tail. Sooner or later, the question would come back to whether he was going to try to arrest her again. Without Donna's deal to protect her, Jenna was a sitting duck. There was a fine line between what she could reveal, and what she needed to hold to herself.

Even if it helped her own endgame.

The commandos lining up for breakfast in the yard served as another reminder of Jenna's precarious standing. Her entire career was based on making their kind obsolete. She'd been at war with the militaries of every nation since her own basic training, and just being around a dozen air commandos twenty-four-seven gave her creeping willies. If they only knew how many of their comrades came out on the short end of encounters with her, they wouldn't be so friendly every time they saw her. The only people who'd accepted Jenna Paine for who she really was no longer wanted any part of her. For the first time, she was truly alone.

Hushi stumbled out onto the porch as Jenna came closer. When the tiny Japanese looked at her, Jenna stopped dead. Hushi's face was as gray as ash. Her cheeks were wet, her eyes swollen behind her glasses, hands trembling as she clutched at the rail. "Papa," she choked out, "Papa's dead."

Aw, dammit. Jenna stepped up and wrapped her arms around the petite brunette, resting her chin on Hushi's shoulder. She didn't waste her time trying to say anything; nothing could be said. Jenna didn't know Irving like these people did, and she never got comfortable calling him "Papa." But he was someone whom she'd come to respect greatly in the short time she did know him. She could feel the love they all had for him, and wished there was someone in her life she could look up to like that. The closest she'd come was her own father, and he died when she was eight.

The memory stung her, and she held on tighter, letting her own grief blend with Hushi's. Hushi sagged back against her and let Jenna guide her to a chair.

The door creaked open again, and Beth came out, followed by Jon, Nadia, and Jimmy. They all gathered around Hushi, and Jenna backed out. This *wasn't* her circle; she was still an intruder. No one had asked her to come here.

She reached the first step on the porch when a hand on her arm turned her attention back to the silent congregation. Jimmy's gnarled fingers held her sleeve in a gentle, but firm grip. His eyes, normally flint-hard, were soft and kind, though red and swollen along with everyone else's. He said nothing, but nodded back toward the group. Jenna let him draw her into the circle. Nadia's arm looped out, bringing her in close for a group hug.

In spite of the grief of the moment, a warm feeling rose in Jenna's chest. It was something she hadn't felt since college, only this was somehow *more*. There were no lies here, no manipulation, or steering. Just this group of friends, being together, and they wanted her here, too. It was her first moment of really belonging. They wanted *her*.

Chapter Forty-Six

Bunny looked up from his novel when the door opened. A plump, pleasant woman with short brown hair carried a tray in and set it on the bed table. "Hi," she chirped. "How's the leg today?"

"Still hurts like hell," he grumbled. "Thanks anyway."

She lifted the lid off the plate and waved the aroma at Bunny. "Maybe some pot roast will help you feel better. I made cheesecake for dessert."

"Yeah, sure." He went back to his book, determined not to acknowledge her kindness.

The woman stood for a beat, a hurt and confused look fixed on her face, before turning and leaving.

Bunny heard the lock set with a sharp *snick* before her footsteps faded down the hall.

He'd seen only the inside of this room since he came to after the wreck in South Dakota. He wasn't banged up too badly: a concussion, a couple broken ribs, a bruised thigh bone, some cuts and bruises. *Jon owes me big-time after this little party*, he thought wryly. *Gettin' shot with a friggin' buffalo gun, chased across the country, hidin' like a field mouse, and now this.*

It had been almost a week now. They tended his medical needs with quiet precision and fed him in a way that Papa would have envied. Once a day, someone came to talk to him, but there were no interrogations in any way that he expected. He almost felt bad about ramming their cars so Jon and Jenna could get away. Almost. There *was* the matter of all that shooting going on, and the fact that these people were every one of them cold-blooded killers when it advanced their agenda.

To be honest, he wasn't sure how to handle all this damned politeness. He would have preferred they hauled out the thumbscrews and gut-hooks. At least then, he'd know where he stood.

Escape didn't seem to be an option. As banged up as he was, he needed a walker just to get to the bathroom. Even if he got out of this room, he could just picture trying to hobble out of this place in his boxers and T-shirt. *Shortest damned chase in history is what it'd be.*

It would have been easy just to give up and let them do what they would do anyway. That was, after all, how he'd survived school, and how he'd done business with the Mob. It was also how he'd made it through five years in a federal penitentiary. He just gave up, because he'd never had anything to lose. Until now. He'd never had anyone like Hushi in his life before. He couldn't bear to think what she would be feeling right now, let alone if he never came home. Therefore, the choice was now made. He had to take this bull by the horns. *Okay, so what would Jenna do?*

He answered his own question a moment later. *Probably punch through the wall with her bare fists, break the guards' necks, steal their guns, and wire the whole place to blow on her way out. Well, that's out. I can't punch my way through a wet paper bag, and I hate guns. What about Jimmy? He'd just turn into a ghost and float through the wall, break the guards' necks just by lookin' at 'em mean, steal their guns, and shoot the "big red button" from five thousand meters without a scope, and blow the whole place on his way out. Yeah, right. My best "Chuck Norris" look makes Hushi giggle and I still hate guns.*

Bunny sighed and tried to get back into the book, but the aroma of that pot roast seemed to grab him right by the nose and wouldn't let go. When he stole a glance at the plate, the potatoes still wafted steam through the melted butter that ran through every crevice and soaked into the carrots, onions, and celery. A tall wedge of cheesecake drizzled with chocolate sauce and topped with a dab of whipped cream made the temptation unbearable. He sighed and put the book down. *It's boring anyway.*

Ten minutes later, he was finishing the dregs of the iced tea when the door opened again. In walked a squat, middle-aged man with a short bristle brush of red hair, carrying a tackle box of medical supplies. "Hey, young man, let's see those ribs today."

Bunny set the glass down. "Can I ask you something, Mitch?"

Mitch set the box on the foot of the bed and lifted Bunny's shirt to check beneath. "Sure, go ahead."

"How come you guys are treating me this good? I mean, it's not like we're old kindergarten buds or anything."

"Would you rather we put you on a rack and flayed the skin from your quivering body one strip at a time? We're not barbarians, Bunny. If you want us to know anything, you'll just tell us. Roll onto your side for me so I can check your back. No, this way—toward me."

Bunny grimaced as the medic's fingers probed a tender spot. When his eyes straightened out again, he found himself looking at Mitch's belt. On it, in a holster at his hip, was a cellphone. *Oh, hey there, beautiful.* An idea presented itself to Bunny then, a wicked little glimmer in his mind. There were worse things a kid learned growing up in Brooklyn.

He waited for another touch on his back, and feigned a gasp of pain. "Oh, cheese-and-rice!" He moaned through gritted teeth, and grabbed a fistful of Mitch's shirt.

"You need to stay still, buddy. I just need to—"

"Got dandruff, some of it itches!" Bunny made his move, and before Mitch rolled him back over, Bunny had the phone beneath his pillow.

Mitch backed away. "Do I have to get some help?"

"No, no. It's all right. I just had a cramp. Come on, man, do your worst."

A few minutes later, the bandages were changed, the bumps were all checked, and Mitch was on his way to wherever he worked when he wasn't poking Bunny.

Bunny wondered how long it would take Mitch to notice his phone was missing. *I better hide this thing before he misses it and comes back.*

Cameras. Crap. Scanning the ceiling and walls for concealed devices, Bunny was relieved to come up empty. The ceiling was a plain drop-in type with large foam tiles suspended in a flat metal framework. A single fluorescent fixture lit the room. The walls were all smooth, and there were no windows. No telltale glints from lenses showed from vents or corners anywhere he could see. It didn't necessarily mean there were none, but he was willing to bet his life on it at least for now. The worst that could happen was they would find that he'd stolen the phone, take it back, and kill him.

If they were going to kill him, though, they would have done it already and spared the expense of taking care of him at all. They never even roughed him up. Yet. Who knew, if he became enough of a nuisance, maybe they'd have to show him who was boss. *Ah, hell. I grew up on the short end of the stick anyways. I got the dogsnot beat out of me for breakfast.*

He pulled the phone from under his pillow and checked the display. *No bars. Damn!* He almost threw it against the wall. *What kind of idiot has a cellphone in an area where they can't even get a tower signal? Wait, no tower signal?* He checked the phone again and found the 3G setting disabled. After turning it back on, he waited. Again, no signal. *Where the hell am I?*

Okay, play time's over. This thing's been on long enough. He thought about laying it on the floor and waiting until Mitch came back to claim it; it wasn't any good to him anyway. But, he had to concede, it was something; and something was better than nothing.

Turning the phone off, Bunny ran over options on where to hide it. Under the pillow was just plain stupid. *I deserve what I get if I put it there.* In the bedside table was just as dumb. *Might as well just set it on the table.* The ceiling. Struggling to stand on the bed, he reached up through the pain, trying to touch the tile above. *Still too damned short. Whatsa matter, Dad? Couldn't spare a couple extra genes for height?*

He scanned the room, finally locking his eyes on the walker. The legs were adjustable for height. Within seconds, he wrestled two of them out of their support tubes and crawled back onto the bed. After poking a ceiling panel loose, he tossed the phone up into the hole and onto the next panel over. Then using the walker legs again, he maneuvered the panel back. It refused to drop back into place. Poking it did no good. *Dammit! Footsteps...*

Flopping back down, groaning against the shock of pain, he tucked the walker legs under the covers just as the door opened. Mitch stepped back in, a sheepish blush on his face. "Hey, I didn't forget anything when I was in here, did I?"

Bunny hoped his face didn't betray the fear that leaped into his throat. "No, I...don't think so," he managed to croak out.

"Okay, then." Mitch took an unobtrusive glance beneath the bed and around the floor before closing the door on his way out. Bunny heard him muttering to himself as his feet faded away. "Could've sworn I had it. Patrick's gonna kill me..."

Bunny almost felt bad for him. Mitch didn't seem like such a bad guy. Then again, most of these people weren't necessarily bad *guys*. All the rotten apples were probably on the top of the basket. But Mitch still bore a certain accountability in all the blood shed by The Pinnacle. So Bunny didn't feel all *that* bad.

After reassembling the walker, he flopped back into bed and closed his eyes, waiting for his pulse to return to normal. *Hushi, I'm gonna try, hon. Don't know how, but I'll get outta here and come back home to you.*

* * * *

Walker, a beanpole with a hawkish face, smiled at the monitor screen. "Sneaky little ratbag, isn't he?"

Behind him, another figure spoke in the shadows of the surveillance room. He droned in a bored baritone. "Resourceful. Given time, he could be either one of our best assets, or one of our worst problems."

"Want me to tell Mitch where the phone is?"

"No. He should feel bad for a while. Besides, I think I have an idea that may bring this whole mess to a close." He leaned down next to Walker's ear. "Put a tracer in Kalinsky. Then let him send up his smoke signal. If Daniels' team does come for him, we'll take them down. If Kalinsky does escape, we'll just follow him back home and wipe out the whole nest of vermin once and for all."

The figure turned to leave but stopped at the door. "I'll call off the swap. Let's just see what falls out of the tree."

Chapter Forty-Seven

Nadia sat behind Sofi at the cliffs, her arms wrapped securely around the girl she'd brought home as her own. The ever-present wind off the lake blew Sofi's scent back into Nadia's face, and she relished the moment. There was only one other time that Nadia had been so aware of everything around her. Every sight, every sound, every smell was sharper for the significance of the moment. She'd felt like this only once before. Her life hung in the balance there, also.

Sofi leaned back against Nadia's breast. It was a rare thing when she allowed anyone to touch her. It said a lot about how much stress the girl was feeling. Sofi's voice was almost drowned out by the waves and wind. "When are you leaving?"

Nadia fought back the lump in her throat. "Tomorrow, early."

"Is Jenna going with you?"

"Yes."

"Jon, too?"

"And Uncle Jimmy."

"Will you come back?"

Honey, if you knew... "Hushi will take care of you while I'm gone."

Sofi turned and locked eyes with her mom. "You didn't answer my question."

Nadia hugged her closer. *Having a genius for a daughter isn't all candy and cartoons, is it?* "Because I can't tell you. What we're doing is very dangerous, baby. There's a chance none of us will come back."

The child stared out at Lake Superior. "Then why do it?"

It was a long time before Nadia answered. "You asked me once if we could stop hiding. This is so we can."

"But what if…" Her voice grew thick. "What if you get killed?"

"What if I don't? Then I come back here and die of cancer."

"Don't say that." Sofi stood. When she turned to face Nadia, her cheeks were wet. "Don't you say that!"

"Honey, listen to me." *God, how do I say goodbye without saying "goodbye"? No easy way. Just do it.* "I'm dying. I can't do anything about that, and neither can you." Nadia reached up to take her daughter's hand.

Sofi backed away a step. "So you're going to leave me, too? You just gave up, and now I have to be alone again!"

Nadia stood and brushed the grass from her jeans. "I…I didn't give up. I just—"

"Why do you hate me so much? What did I ever do to you?" She took a step back and turned as if to leave.

"Stop," Nadia barked. "You stop right there, young lady!" She darted forward before Sofi could dodge, grabbing her by the arms so the girl couldn't squirm free. "I don't hate you, dammit!"

Wrapping Sofi in a tight embrace, Nadia felt her floodgates burst open. "I love you. I love you more than if you were my own real daughter. I don't want to leave you, don't you know that?"

She held Sofi away and looked her in the eyes. "Your mother knew the bad people were after her, and they wouldn't quit until they'd killed her and anyone who was with her. She did the only thing she knew to protect you. If she was already dead, then they wouldn't have any reason to come after you."

Sofi sobbed and sniffed. "Why does everyone leave me?"

"Honey, I'm doing this so there will be no one left to hide from. I'm going to end this, once and for all. No more soldiers, no more Pinnacle, no more running. Can I do this for you?"

The child's voice came muffled from inside Nadia's embrace. "But I don't want you to go."

Nadia fought back her own tears as she kissed her daughter's head. "I'll make this whole mess right, I promise."

She wasn't about to tell Sofi how hard this goodbye was for her or share her own doubts whether she was actually "making things right," or just copping out. But one thing Nadia knew: this was going to end now, and on her terms.

* * * *

Jimmy sat on the porch, watching the dull routine of the afternoon in front of him. The air commandos not on guard sat in the shade of Nadia's lawn for lunch, weapons within easy reach. Those on duty at the detention shacks stood their watches, ever vigilant against any attempted breakout. The occasional fly or wasp buzzed by, its hypnotic drone lulling the man in the wooden chair. The pain med Watts had given him was just starting to do its work, and the ache in Jimmy's shoulder was finally at a tolerable level. But on the downside, that warm, sleepy feeling Jimmy hated so much was just beginning to creep in and steal the rest of his afternoon.

The old warrior's eyes had just drifted shut when the screen door opened with a protest of springs. The steps on the porch were light and favored one side. The soft scent in his nostrils confirmed the identity of the other party. "Afternoon, Miss Paine," he mumbled through the painkiller's haze. Another smell, cool and yeasty, wafted to him and he held out a hand to receive the cold bottle offered, his eyes still closed.

He couldn't resist his own grin at the smile in her voice. "You must have sonar, you old coot." The chair next to Jimmy's creaked as Jenna settled into it. She clinked her bottle against his and took a pull.

The first swallow went down good, so he took a second before speaking. "How's the leg?"

"Better, thanks. A little stiff, but I can work with it."

"Good. Wouldn't want ya to miss out just 'cause ya got a little hitch in your git-along."

"Jimmy, I wouldn't miss this if I had a whole leg off."

"Big deal, eh?

Jenna looked out at the yard for a while before answering. "They lied to me. I don't like being lied to."

"But do you still believe in what they want? World unity and Kumbaya, and all that crap?"

Jenna tensed and clenched her jaw at the offhand remark. "When you kill someone, what do you feel?"

Jimmy bristled at the question. "You're kidding, right?" *Feel? How the hell am I supposed to feel? What kind of stupid question was that?*

Jenna's eyes narrowed with passion. "I want to know what you feel when you pull a trigger and put a bullet into another person, and let their life spill out. In whose name did you do it? Yours? Your country's? And how did it solve anything?" She looked away. "That wasn't even enough, was it? You had to teach others how to kill, too. For a border. An imaginary line on a map."

She paused long enough to take a swallow. "So before you label someone's beliefs as 'crap,' just think about what it felt like every time you killed someone for that imaginary line."

The hair stood up on Jimmy's neck. *I swear, if you were a man, I'd pin your ears back...* As it was, there was no way he was going to let that one go. It had been a long time since he needed to shift into sergeant mode, but the shift was as smooth as his last class of recruits.

"Young lady." He struggled through gritted teeth. "I didn't kill anyone for a line. I killed to save an idea. That idea was that free men should be able to defend themselves from oppression and tyranny and help other men to live free as well. Them poor jackwagons who stood in the way of that idea were the ones I killed. And to tell you the truth, I don't feel a damned thing for 'em. That line on the map you're goin' on about is the line that says, 'on this side you're free to choose your own destiny.' And I'll spill as much blood as I have to to make sure it stays where it's at."

Jimmy sniffed and set his bottle on the small table between them. "Look at you, giving me the 'baby-killer' speech. How many bodies have *you* left behind? Why don't you tell me what *you* felt when you stood over the bodies of the people you laid out for a lie?"

He gave her a cold smile then and watched the steel in her eyes melt away. "I'll grant you, hon, you ain't any worse than me. But you sure as hell ain't any sight better."

Leaning his chair back, he said, "Now, I'd be willin' to bet your vision for this earth ain't too far from mine. We just ended up thinkin' about it from some different places." He fixed her eyes again with his. "I do know if I'd have had a half-dozen more of you on my team, we'd have buried less of our boys and more of theirs."

Jenna broke her gaze away and looked across the yard. In the silence that followed, Jimmy imagined he could hear the gears working inside her head. He just hoped that, whatever she decided in the end about whatever it was she was pondering, it wouldn't affect her edge when it came down to brass knuckles and billy clubs.

Things were going to get bad enough as it was.

Chapter Forty-Eight

Bunny waited until the lights went out and the hall was quiet before slipping out of bed. In the wan glow of the night light, he parked the walker on his mattress. After gathering himself, he stepped up into the rungs of the side supports, holding onto the handles for dear life in an awkward squatting position until he found his balance. Slowly, he rose up until he could reach the ceiling tile next to where he'd stashed the phone.

After the third poke from his fist, the tile popped loose, and he groped around the edge until he felt the small plastic case and pulled it down, clutching onto it for dear life as he lowered himself back to the bed. After turning it on, he checked the signal, not expecting to see anything usable, but still… His brows knit as he blinked in surprise. *I got bars. What the…?*

With trembling hands, he dialed out.

* * * *

On the control room monitor, the shadowy figures watched Bunny juggle the ceiling tile back into place and settle under his covers.

Walker said, "That's it, Mr. Pritchard. The smoke signal's up."

A beefy, middle-aged man yawned and rubbed his eyes. "Kill the repeater, Mr. Walker."

Walker pressed a lighted switch on his control console, and the light went out. "Okay, no more signal. Do you think that was enough?"

The other figure stretched. "Oh, yeah. I'm sure it was. I just don't know how much time we have to prepare the welcome committee."

The door opened, admitting the silhouette of a stocky man in an expensive business suit. His rich bass voice filled the dim control booth. "What news of our guest, Mr. Pritchard?"

Pritchard snapped to nervous attention. "Good evening, Mr. Wilkes. Gabe just killed the cell repeater. Kalinsky made his call but didn't say anything. It must have gone to voicemail."

"Are you sure?" asked Wilkes. "He may have keyed in some secret code of his own."

"Even if he did, sir, that wouldn't make a difference. He doesn't know enough about this place to compromise its precise location from where he is."

"And how exactly does this give us back Mr. Frost?"

"Well, sir, we use Kalinsky to draw out Daniels and his companions. I'm betting that he's going to come bringing every combatant at his disposal. We can catch them all when they show up on the east road, as long as we have enough personnel to do it."

Wilkes' face screwed up in contempt. "Our field agents are scattered all over the world, Mr. Pritchard."

"Yes, but sir," said Pritchard, rubbing his neck nervously, "we have twenty-four agents in-house now, and I can have another thirty here in two days."

"Is that enough time, Mr. Pritchard? And will that be enough manpower?"

"I think so. Sir, may I show you something?" Pritchard touched a dimmer switch, bringing the light level in the room up a few lumens. He sat at a computer terminal at one end of the main console and pulled up two pictures from driver's licenses. "In Oregon, Daniels recruited a woman named Elizabeth Nelson and a man named James DeBartolo, a couple of locals. Nelson was a nurse at the hospital. DeBartolo is a retired insurance salesman, but an asset in the Army turned up something else."

The pictures spun away, replaced by a pdf image stamped "EYES ONLY" across the front in huge red letters. Pritchard went on. "U.S. Army. Korea and four tours in Viet Nam. In 1974, he was selected for a Joint Special Operations Command position. By the time he retired, that old codger saw more action than Audie Murphy. In the Front Royal operation three years ago, he eliminated two of our three agents, causing the eventual loss of the third as well as a collapse of the operation in general."

Wilkes cut in, impatient. His proper British accent made him sound even more demanding. "You've a point, I assume?"

"Yes sir. Please bear with me for just a moment. Daniels has never been involved in any force of numbers. Of all the people he's gathered around him, most are non-combatants. Why would he risk their safety by involving them in any operation against this facility? NADIA will stay under whatever rock Daniels has hid her. Nelson is a non-factor, as is our current guest. At the most, we can expect two operatives, unless somehow he's managed to round up Jenna Paine as well. But I seriously doubt they've hooked up."

The older man lit a cigar and puffed a cloud of acrid smoke into Pritchard's face. "Now, I'd be very interested in knowing *how* you came to that conclusion. He did send her an overture on national television, as we know. They may have formed some unholy alliance, and even now be pooling their resources against us. Now, Daniels has been enough trouble on his own. With this antique war machine, he's given us fits. If he and Miss Paine have managed to put their differences aside, there could be a good deal of trouble." He tapped the ash from his cigar and poked a screen with one thick finger. "And you seem to have forgotten how Mr. Kalinsky became a recipient of our most gracious hospitality." Sticking the stogie between his teeth, he puffed around it, a malicious, lopsided grin punctuating his disdain. "She escaped our clutches in his company. So let us assume the worst. Do you still have enough manpower in your little plan?"

Pritchard stammered a couple times before looking back at Wilkes. This was not a man in whose presence to show one's weak side or make a misjudgment. "Yes sir, I believe we do."

"Very well. Continue."

"We draw them here and engage them with overwhelming force."

"I see," said Wilkes. "We capture them and make them talk."

"Actually, sir, we only need one." Pritchard nodded to the sleeping figure on the monitor. "He'll talk easily enough if he thinks he can save his friends. When he tells us where they're holding Mr. Frost, we can safely retrieve him, eradicate the rest of the vermin, and recover NADIA as well."

"Well, then, if we only need one, you have my permission to do with the rest as you see fit." Wilkes puffed another acrid cloud of smoke into the air and turned toward the door. "Oh, and Mr. Pritchard? Make sure everything goes as planned. I don't have to tell you how bad it would be if you'd made a muck-up of it. Good evening, sir." The control room door closed with just a little more force than necessary as the Englishman made his final exit.

Chapter Forty-Nine

A gentle tap on Nadia's bedroom door roused her in the dark of the predawn. She sat up and ran a finger gingerly down the fresh wound on her abdomen. The tingling was almost gone. The scar would be also, before noon. Hushi said the surgery was as successful as it could be, under the circumstances. The largest of the tumors was gone from her "nanobot farm," and with it, the seizures, for the time being. *That should at least get me where I need to go.* She rose and grabbed her robe from the hook by the window, wrapping it loosely around her body before opening the door.

Jimmy stood, awash in the dim glow of the hall night light. "Time to get movin', kids," he whispered before ambling on toward the kitchen.

"Thanks." Nadia turned the light on and sat by Jon as he opened his eyes. "Good morning, sunshine," she murmured, bending low to kiss him awake.

"Who needs an alarm clock," he said with a smile. Curling around Nadia's waist, he laid his head in her lap, letting her stroke his hair for a few seconds before rolling back to let her up. "I suppose we ought to get some breakfast before we hit the road."

Nadia shrugged into a blouse and picked out a pair of jeans. "I think Jimmy's idea of breakfast involved MREs in the Hummer, babe."

"I was thinking closer to steak and eggs, with hash browns and an English muffin. Oh, hey, what's this?" Jon picked up his phone and touched the screen next to the blinking call indicator. "No number I know…" He touched the icon and activated the speaker.

Bunny's whispered voice greeted his shocked ears. "Hey, Jonny. Still here, buddy. Play this for Hushi." Eight short beeps followed, a click, and the message ended.

Jon's eyes snapped open as he shot to his feet. He jammed his legs into a pair of BDU cargo pants, ran down the hall, and into the yard. Pounding on the door to Jenna's camper, he shouted, "Carlos! Tab! Get up."

The door flew open and a light came on. Carlos stood in a pair of boxers, rubbing sleep from his eyes.

Jon held out the phone in a shaky hand. "Here. Can you backtrack a cell number?"

"Only back to the nearest tower," he said, "but it should be close enough. Let me get that number." Taking the phone, he wrote the number on a slip of paper and handed it to Tab.

Tab powered up the laptop. A few keystrokes later, she asked, "What service do you have?" Jon told her, and she called up a screen. "Okay, give me a little bit. If it was an Android phone, the GPS may have been disabled. That'll make it a little harder to pinpoint."

Carlos handed the phone back. "Don't let us hold you up. Go ahead and start out. I'll call you as soon as we have coordinates on the last tower."

"Thanks, guys." Jon ran back to the house to finish getting dressed. *Bunny, I knew you'd come through for us.*

* * * *

Jimmy took first shift at the wheel. They were in Wisconsin before the sun came up. Tearing open an MRE, Jon shot Nadia a wicked glance. "Never knew you were psychic, too." She just smiled and handed him her salt packet. Military rations in a moving vehicle didn't count as an official breakfast for Jon but it would have to hold him over until they could stop somewhere for a decent meal.

"Hey, Jimmy, you plan on stopping anytime soon? I know we need to hurry but my back teeth are floating."

Jimmy didn't even acknowledge Jon or his attempt at levity. He didn't seem amenable to stopping for anything other than fuel or to switch drivers. Great, Jon thought, all I need—an old man with kidneys of steel and no appetite. At the same time, Jon understood the need for haste. They had to push hard for Wichita to begin their move against The Pinnacle and to rescue Bunny. Jimmy and Jenna had agreed that was the best place to start. It was centrally located, and if their objective was farther west, they had a head start. If it was back east, they wouldn't have lost enough time to make that much of a difference one way or the other.

Flying was not an option; they would not be able to pass their weapons through security, and having them packed in checked luggage left them vulnerable to an ambush at either end of the flight.

So as Jon crossed his legs and watched the telephone poles race by, he resigned himself to the "are we there yet?" seat in back next to Nadia while remembering the last cross-country trip he took. It was just he and Nadia on their own, in a rusted-out beater of a car that left them stranded in Colorado. That trip ended in Oregon, and very nearly cost them their lives. He couldn't see this one ending any better.

He'd wanted no part of this from the start but he went along, partly because Nadia had already agreed. But he also couldn't see any other way out. There simply was no better plan he could come up with given the short time they had.

The feeling kept nagging at Jon's mind that, in spite of every shred of will he possessed, he was being dragged along to meet his ultimate fate, and all he could do was sit here in this cramped, packed Hummer and let what fate would happen, happen. He found himself struggling with a mixture of dread and elation. What began as a law enforcement issue had turned into a combat operation. Yet there was the hope that when this was over, The Pinnacle would no longer pose a threat to human freedom. It was the one thing that kept Jon from panicking.

Nadia became more quiet and introverted as the trip progressed, and in her turns at the wheel, seemed to drive more slowly the farther west they drove. Jon thought he saw tears on her cheeks a couple times, but she muttered something about ragweed and wiped them away with her hand. *Maybe she's just getting tired.* God knew how much this was taking out of all of them. This was also the first time Nadia had been away from Sofi since bringing her back from Europe. Any one of a hundred things could have been bothering Nadia, making her withdraw from everyone around her. Jon reached over once to give her shoulder a reassuring touch, but she shied away. After that, he just let her be. If she wanted to talk, he would be there. Surely she would know that.

Jenna and Jimmy shared what passed for them as light conversation. Most of it was the various merits of different guns. Jenna was more relaxed, more talkative now. She was less of a flirt factory and more of a team member. But occasionally, Jon still saw a shadow pass in her eyes, like some dark herald of the intent still lurking in her mind. Was she as scared as he was, in that corner of her that hid behind the warrior's armor?

As they crossed the state line into Iowa, Jon's phone rang. Carlos' voice was tense and drawn. "Okay, I can get you pretty close. They scrambled the routing, but we traced the call to a tower in Nevada, just north of Vegas."

"Hold for a second, buddy." Jon set the phone down long enough to pull out a dog-eared road atlas. "Okay, where's the tower, and what kind of radius are we looking at?"

Jon wrote the map coordinates in the margin of the Nevada page. Then Carlos gave him the bottom line. "We have about a twenty-mile radius from that tower, and God knows if the signal came in scrambled from another somewhere up the line. But my gut tells me that's the ball park."

"Thanks, my friend." Jon snapped the phone shut, fingers tingling from excitement. *One step closer to ending this. If you're right, Carlos.* Using the grid numbers on the sides and bottom of the map, he plotted the tower's approximate location and marked it with an "X."

"Jimmy, the drive just got longer." Jon plucked the GPS from the dashboard mount and entered the numbers. "Let's pick up some more snacks and empty the trash from this bus."

Chapter Fifty

Hushi pulled her hands from the sink and grabbed a hand towel when Jon's ring tone cut through the video game noise from the living room. "Girls, turn it down, please." Grabbing her cellphone from the counter, she slid her finger across the display to activate it as she raised it to her head. "This better be good." She growled, retreating to the far corner of the kitchen for privacy.

Jon's voice was tired, drawn, but determined. "Hushi, I have some information, but I don't feel safe talking to you over the phone like this. I have a message for you. I practiced it 'till I got it. Hang on…"

Hushi listened while the eight-tone sequence from Bunny's message played, and she nearly dropped the phone before it was done. The anger and fear she'd been harboring dropped from her like an old shroud, and an excited thrill washed over her entire body. The sequence was a code that she and Bunny had developed and played with. There are only three different notes on a touch-tone keypad, but she and Bunny had sent this same code to each other so many times, there was no mistaking the notes for "I love you." There was no way Jon could have known it; they'd never shared the code with anyone else. So somehow, that crazy, screw-brained husband of hers had found a way to contact them. *He's still alive…*

A hopeful tear slid down her cheek as her hands shook. Jon's voice kept her from passing out with relief. "Hushi, are you still there?"

"Y-yeah. Jon. I don't know what to say."

"We're going to get him and bring him home. Just like I promised you."

"Where are you?"

"I can't tell you that. I'm also going to drop off the grid for a few days. I'll get back in touch when I can."

"Jon?"

The pause was so long, Hushi thought he'd already disconnected. "Yeah?"

"Thanks." Hushi swiped her finger on the screen to disconnect and set the phone down before burying her face in her hands.

She'd been a faithful agnostic so many years, before this whole situation reared its head. It wasn't that she actively defied any belief in a god, per se; she just never took the time to make up her mind, and there were so many unanswerable questions. Besides, she'd done pretty well for herself without any outside help and looked forward to just living her life the best she could. Wasn't that what everyone was preaching about, anyway? Be a good person, love your fellow man, and seek justice for the beaten-down. You don't need a god to do any of that.

The first time Hushi prayed, she was performing surgery on an active antimatter bomb. She didn't receive any special "bolt from the blue" or anything. She wasn't even praying to anyone in particular, let alone expecting any kind of answer. She just didn't want to be wrong, in case things went bad. Something Jimmy had said once passed through her mind: "There ain't no atheists in foxholes." It was funny at the time. Now, she understood the meaning so much more deeply.

Sofi and Sammi cheered each other on in the living room, oblivious to anything outside their cyberworld. Hushi edged into the corner of the kitchen next to the broom closet, her lips and fingers numb. Sinking to her knees, hands shaking, she murmured, "It's me. I know we haven't been talking, but it's not…" *Get to the point, girl, he's busy.* "Bunny isn't Billy Graham, and I'm no Mother Theresa, but—" A weak sob rushed from her throat before she could stop it. "I love him. I've never met anyone I even liked before." She sniffled and looked to the arch leading to the living room. The television threw flashes and shadows against the walls as the girls continued their war against psycho zombie hordes and wind-up doomsday devices. Hushi clenched her trembling hands and whispered, "He could really use some help. If it's not too much. Please."

Sagging against the broom closet door, Hushi buried her face in her hands and wept. Here, at the end of herself, maybe there was room for just a little—she struggled to find some word, some term, that fit her current paradigm, but none came to her fuddled mind. Maybe those late night discussions with Nadia were starting to get to her. All that mattered right now was that Hushi had reached out a desperate hand and found faith.

Chapter Fifty-One

Jon left Las Vegas on US-93 North, skirting the Red Rock Canyon area and heading out into the badlands. False dawn glowed dim on the horizon, an angry bruise across the eastern sky. Jimmy stirred in the front passenger seat and opened his eyes. Worn joints cracked and popped as he stretched and yawned. "How far now?"

Jon glanced at the GPS glowing on the dash. "Almost there. Probably another twenty miles."

The older man pulled up a thermos and filled two styrofoam cups with coffee, handing one to Jon while he sipped the steaming brew from his own cup. Jon drove on as the women slept, leaning against each other in the back seat.

After ten minutes, Jimmy tossed back the last lukewarm drops of coffee from his cup and said, "This is good enough. Pull off the road." He guided Jon down into a draw. Jon stopped the engine and they got out. No one said anything for several minutes; three hard days on the road had taken its toll on everyone. Jimmy opened the rear of the Hummer and started hauling out packs, tossing each onto the ground with a heavy thud and cloud of dust. Drawing a machete from one of the packs, he said to Jon, "Find some brush. We gotta hide the truck."

Jon and Nadia set off, and shortly found several scraggly, sun-parched bushes clinging to the rocks at the base of a cliff. A few hard machete strokes later, they had enough brush to bundle up with a length of rope and drag back to the draw.

When they got back, Jenna and Jimmy had already strapped on their packs and were checking their weapons. Jenna was ooh-ing and aah-ing over a wicked-looking shotgun cradled in Jimmy's hands. It was obvious that this weapon was never intended for sport hunting. Every angle, every line, betrayed its design and purpose: inflicting massive amounts of damage to whatever or whoever got in the way of its bearer. It had a squat, triangular shoulder stock. A stout pistol grip protruded down from behind the breach. A massive drum magazine clipped in front of the trigger guard, and the barrel was short, for close-quarters combat.

Jimmy slung it over his shoulder as Jon and Nadia approached and nodded in approval at the pile of sticks and scrub they dragged behind. A short minute later, they left the Hummer concealed under the scrub and set off into the hills.

Jimmy took the point, followed by Jenna and Nadia. Jon came last. The straps of his pack dug into his shoulders as the day dragged on and the sun beat down. The band of his boonie hat soon soaked with sweat. He took frequent sips from the tube running over his shoulder from the bladder of water tucked into a pocket on his pack.

They trudged on as the sun climbed to its zenith, taking shelter under an overhanging cliff in the desert. After a quick lunch of MREs warmed in their packages, Jimmy announced an hour's rest, and the group stretched out on the sand. Jon hadn't walked this much since his Boy Scout days, and he felt it right to his bones. He could only imagine how tired Nadia must have been, never having had the experience of an extended hike on ground such as this, let alone after three hard days on the road. But she never complained, not even when the sweat ran down her back and soaked her fatigue shirt.

It seemed like he'd just closed his eyes when a boot in his ribs nudged him awake. Jimmy grinned down at him. "Come on, sleepin' beauty. Time to roll on. We gotta make that tower before nightfall." Jon fought to his feet, settled his pack in place with a groan of pain, and they set off again, climbing higher and higher into the desert badlands.

They found the tower at the peak of a bare promontory several miles away, overlooking two hundred square miles of the most desolate land Jon had ever seen. The sun sank low in the western sky, beckoning the night with rich red and amber shades in bands from north to south, deepening toward the east to black, speckled with a million diamonds. Jimmy had them set camp at the base of the hill, in a narrow gully hidden from prying eyes. In weary silence, they laid out sleeping bags and settled in for the night.

Jon took first watch, sitting against the cliff wall with a cup of cold coffee in his hand and an M-16 across his lap. When Jimmy relieved him two hours later, he stumbled to his bedroll and no sooner did his head hit the ground than he was fast asleep.

* * * *

A gentle nudge at Jon's shoulder awoke him just as a pale rose glow welled into existence in the eastern sky. Jimmy was already packed and ready to go. "Up an' at 'em, buckos. We got some ground to cover. Change your socks and tighten your boots."

Jon rolled over and touched Nadia's shoulder. When she didn't show signs of stirring, he placed a hand more solidly on her and shook gently. A low moan answered his ministrations, and he shook her again. She sat up, rubbing her eyes, and smiled weakly at him. He helped her to her feet and they began their day.

They secured their bedrolls and broke fast on energy bars and a swallow from their canteens. Jimmy shoved a handful of hot cinnamon jawbreaker candies in Jon's pocket before they set out. "Helps the water last longer." A pale dawn colored the rocks around them as they stretched the night chill from weary bones. A gray lizard skittered from under Jon's pack as he grabbed the strap. He kicked Nadia's pack, and a huge, hairy spider crawled out. It issued forth a tiny growl of irritation before stomping off across the rock floor.

Jimmy took Jon's sleeve and tugged him toward the cliff wall. "No word from the bad guys? Deadline's supposed to be up."

Jon checked his phone. *No messages, no missed calls.* A feeling of dread rose in his chest as he checked for reception. "Damn, Jimmy. You're right. I don't see where they've tried to get hold of us at all."

Jimmy's voice lowered. "You're the cop. What does that mean?"

Jon hesitated before answering. "In the kidnapping cases I worked for the Bureau, it usually meant there was no longer a need for an exchange."

"Like a dead victim?"

"I don't want to go there. I promised Hushi we'd bring Bunny back home—"

"But you opened the door to it. We have to think of every possibility."

Jon fought back the fear trying to swamp his brain. "So give me another possibility, Jimmy."

The old man's brow furrowed in thought. "The Pinnacle could be planning a move of their own."

"Like what? Talk to me, buddy."

"We could be walking into a trap. Think about it. They could have let him make that call, tricked him into making it, or even forced him."

"He wasn't forced. His voice was too calm, and he whispered, like he was sneaking the call."

"Tricked, then. He ain't no idiot, but this bunch managed to keep their existence a secret from the whole world until just a little while ago. They're clever."

Jon rubbed his neck. "So what do you suggest?"

"Play it out. Let's keep going. We still have two aces up our sleeve. I'm betting they don't know Jenna's here, and we still have Nadia. They won't take a chance on blowing themselves up by taking pot shots at us."

"If they catch us before we get close enough to be a threat, they won't care. They'll just put one in Nadia, 'retire' another agent or two in the process, knock the dust from their hands, and keep on keeping on."

A tired grin crept onto Jimmy's mouth as he slapped Jon's shoulder. "Let's get close enough to be a threat, then." He raised his voice so everyone could hear. "Gear up, folks. It's gonna be a *lovely* day."

Jimmy and Jenna spread out and took the lead, trudging along with their heavy packs strapped onto their shoulders. Jon glanced at Nadia, three meters to his right. She looked out of place, garbed in desert camo and combat boots, her blonde hair tucked up under a boonie hat to ward off the harsh sunlight. But she lugged her own pack with stoic determination, even as her face showed her discomfort.

The only thing Nadia did not carry along with the others was a weapon. When Jimmy offered her a rifle from the collection in the Hummer, she paled and refused. She reluctantly accepted a KA-BAR, but only after Jimmy convinced her she might need the wicked-looking knife as a tool.

The coolness of the night air quickly gave way under the sun's onslaught, and the temperature drove upward with every step he took. Jon's wounded leg began to throb after the first half hour. Jenna did only slightly better. A noticeable limp was making itself more pronounced in her step. Jimmy was slowing as well. A dark stain crept from under his right shoulder strap, which surely must have been digging into the wound in the old man's shoulder. The group slogged on, determined to get to the tower. God alone knew how much more time Bunny had, and they still had no idea if they were chasing a red herring in the Nevada badlands.

They broke twice before noon, taking ten minute breaks to gather their strength for the next miles. The way got rougher the higher the group got. Jon briefly wondered why they weren't moving at night and resting during the day, but he soon reasoned through it. Their heat signatures at night would show up on any infrared sensing devices The Pinnacle may have spread out in the area. They were much harder to spot against the desert, with their brown mottled camo outfits.

Late that afternoon they broke out on top of the ridge. Jimmy consulted his hand-held GPS and swung around in an arc, settling on a heading just off of North. Shading his eyes, he squinted against the sunlight. "There it is. About five more miles along the ridge."

Five miles as the crow flies turned into twenty by the time they worked along the ridge, through the rocks, and over the scree. Sunset dyed the horizon rich scarlet and purple before they stood at the base of the cell relay tower marked on Jon's map. On any other day, the vista would have taken Jon's breath away. Today he attributed the lack of breath to fatigue, dehydration, and muscle cramps. Collapsing in a panting heap on a concrete footing, he tried to rub life back into his legs as Jimmy and Jenna scanned the area. Nadia slumped next to him, laying her head on his shoulder.

Jon's ears caught at Jenna's voice, carrying just over the wind. "How far away from Chicago would you say this is?"

Jimmy punched the screen on his GPS. "'Bout eighteen hundred miles, give or take."

"Three to four hours. That about fits, then."

Jon struggled to his feet. "Fits what?"

"I think I was there once." Jenna shaded her eyes against the sunset and pointed across the valley. "There's a dry lake bed. Jimmy, does that look like a runway to you?"

"Hold it," Jon said, his voice tightening. "You were *where?* When were you going to tell us?"

She shrugged. "I figured about now would be good."

Jon advanced on her, his scalp tingling with anger. "And why would you wait that long to tell me you've been there?"

"Because you'd assume that I knew where the place was." Jenna squared off to face him, arms loose at her sides. "Just like you're thinking now. For your information, I was blindfolded from the time I took off in Chicago. The flight lasted about three hours, and I deplaned inside a closed hangar. They stuck me in a limo and took me to a building with fifty floors. I remember the elevator. But I knew it was their headquarters, because there was this room—"

Jon waved an arm around. "Okay. Show me a building with fifty floors."

Jimmy broke in. "We could be standin' on one. Who's to say they have to build when they could excavate and stay outta sight?"

Jon and Jenna held each other's gaze for an instant, and then he spun to look at the old man. He stared through a pair of high-powered binoculars, locked on a target across the valley, a strange grin plastered on his face.

A tiny black dot appeared on a small road that stretched between the two ridges and crawled across the dry basin like a flea creeping over a china dinner plate. About halfway across, it turned toward the far cliff wall. As the team watched, a dark spot appeared at the base of the wall and the car disappeared through it. The mouse hole then closed, leaving no trace of its existence.

Jimmy's voice rasped just over the wind. "Someone gimme a compass. We just found us a rats' nest."

Chapter Fifty-Two

The last embers of daylight faded beyond the ridge as two dark-garbed shadows belly-crawled to the peak of the rock. They settled in just below the summit to avoid skylining themselves. One of the figures lifted a pair of binoculars and squinted through them across the lakebed. He spoke just above a whisper, as if afraid of being overheard, even from this great distance. "They must be out there still. There's something over there."

His companion replied in the same low tone. "Could be antelope. Maybe goats."

The first one shook his head, barely perceptible in the dusk. "Nah. Antelope move on. These blips stayed around the tower most of the afternoon."

"How many?"

"Three, maybe four." He lowered the binoculars and brought out a pack of cigarettes. Sitting up with his back to the valley to shield the spark, he stuck one between his lips and struck a lighter.

"Those things are going to kill you, Harris."

Harris blew out a stream of smoke and chuckled. "Like I'm going to live long enough to get cancer."

The other one took the binoculars and lifted them to his eyes. "That's not funny, you know."

Harris took another puff. "Wasn't trying to be funny, Kyle. Haven't you been watching? All hell is about to break loose, and we're stuck in the middle. Bowles is recruiting, I hear, and paying premium."

Kyle humphed and adjusted his focus. "He'd have to. That old jackass is hell to work for."

"Can't say Bowman is any better." Harris stubbed out his smoke on the rock and field stripped the butt, shredding it and tossing the pieces to the night wind. Then he patted his friend's shoulder. "Let's get on inside. It's too dark to see anything anyway."

Kyle lowered the glasses, but his gaze stayed locked on the peak of the opposite ridge, outlined below the flashing red obstruction lights of the radio tower. "But they're still out there somewhere."

"Too far away to do any damage tonight, if they are. They're still two miles across the lakebed, on foot and outnumbered. We'll catch them in the open tomorrow, and this will be all over and done with."

"We should probably set out a few recon teams in the passes, huh?"

Harris took a deep breath of night air. "Don't think we can afford the manpower. We know where Daniels is coming. It doesn't matter what approach he takes. The only thing that matters is who he has with him."

The sun's last glory faded as night took hold over the desert. Kyle sat up and stretched. "We can assume he has the old man, what's his name?"

"DeBartolo. Dude may be old, but Mr. Pritchard says he's still BA."

"That leaves maybe two more people."

"At best, they're probably Special Forces. Maybe air commandos, with Daniels' current connection. At worst—"

Kyle huffed a breath. "We don't have enough agents if Paine's with them, you know. By herself, she's ten pounds of trouble in a five-pound sack. If we have to fight all of them, that's going to be a bad day."

"Not to mention who may have that fourth slot."

"There's another possibility, sir."

Harris turned, the question in his eyes hidden in the darkness, but his pause invited Kyle to continue.

"They could be just hikers."

The other man snorted. "Yeah. And I'm the next president of the Council. Come on—let's grab a cuppa. Tomorrow's going to be busy."

* * * *

A distant coyote called to its mate with a high, keening howl that carried over the miles that separated them in the still of the night. Nadia lay awake, watching the stars dance their way across the black sky. She never thought she'd seen so many in her life, and was glad in her heart that she saw this sight. At the same time, however, was the undercurrent of sorrow of knowing this was the last night sky she would see. Rolling over, she snuggled closer to Jon, relishing the smell of his musk. No, they hadn't bathed since they left Michigan. Yes, she probably smelled like the rear end of an ox to him, and yes, his odor was stronger than it had been since she knew him. But it was *his*.

The soft scuff of a boot sole on the rock nearby made her twist to see the shadow looming over her. Her eyes picked out Jenna's outline against the faint moonlit glow of the sky, and Nadia slipped silently from under her cover to stand next to her companion. Jenna touched her on the shoulder and stalked off into the darkness. Nadia followed as quietly as she could, tiptoeing across the rocky terrain. A misplaced step dislodged a small stone, sending it rolling and tumbling down the steep hillside. She froze, cold sweat moistening the small of her back, as Jon mumbled and turned in his sleep. Farther away, Nadia could hear Jimmy snoring in his sleeping bag. She stayed still for another minute, knowing that old man would be instantly awake if any note sounded off-key in the symphony of the night. Presently, confident the camp remained still, she started again, and caught up with Jenna behind a dried, scraggly bush too stubborn to wither completely away in this harsh land.

The moonlight in Jenna's eyes made them seem to glow with a vindictive fire. Her whisper, though low in volume, came out in an urgent hiss. "What are you willing to do to get Bunny back?"

"What do you think? I'm ready for this, Jenna. Why would you think I'm not?"

"A lot of people are going to die tomorrow—"

"Don't tell me about that!" Nadia put her hands over her mouth and looked over her shoulder, afraid her voice carried back to the men. "I don't want to think of it like that."

Jenna touched her shoulder. "You have to. Those are people down there. Every last one of them at this level has to know what the real agenda is, and they're on board all the way. They're twisted, and they're evil. But they're still people."

"Why do I have to know that?"

The redhead took her hand away. "The first thing a modern army does in warfare is to dehumanize the enemy, make them appear as raging animals that want to eat our children in front of us. It makes it easier for a normal human being to pull a trigger on another normal human being."

"Why are you telling me—?"

Eyes narrowed, teeth clenched, Jenna leaned closer to Nadia's face. "*We* aren't 'normal human beings,' Nadia. We never were. And we're not normal human beings because of *them*. They made us." Jenna's eyes became baleful, glowing orbs in the night. "They made us to kill other humans, because they don't have the guts to see their own plans through. After all, hon, they're just 'normal human beings,'" she said with a sneer. "If they can't dehumanize the enemy, they can dehumanize the people they send into the breach. And that's us."

The coyote howled again twice before Nadia spoke. "Do me one thing. Take care of Sofi."

The answer was blunt, and carried a hard edge. "No, I won't." A tense pause later, she said, "I'm not a mom. Sofi's been through enough. I can't take care of her."

"But I need to know she's safe."

The other woman sat again, warm at Nadia's side. "Have you seen how much Hushi loves that little girl?"

Nadia's throat thickened with emotion. "I'm never going to see her again."

"She'll be all right."

A realization alit in Nadia's mind, and the words were out of her mouth before she could weigh them. "With Bunny for a dad?"

"Oh. My. God," said Jenna, stifling a laugh. "That would be so…"

"Do you still think Sofi's going to be all right?"

"I think I'd be more worried about Bunny."

Nadia couldn't hold back a laugh. At least, it began as a laugh. Five seconds after it started, something changed, and her body began to tremble. Tears rose in her eyes, and the chuckles turned into sobs. She collapsed against Jenna, clutching her clothing. "I'm so scared. Make it stop. Make this stop, please."

"I can't stop this, only you can." Jenna held her close, pulling away when the shaking stilled. "The sun's going to be up in a few hours, and then you'll make it all stop." Reaching into a pocket of her cargo pants, she pulled out two round objects and pressed them into Nadia's hands. They were baseball-sized, hard, and cold. "Let's get you set up."

Chapter Fifty-Three

Hushi backed away from the microscope and rubbed her eyes. Somewhere among the mountains of records and data, the tissue samples and blood work, was the answer. Whatever was causing Nadia's tumors to spread, she had to find it. It wasn't behaving like cancer. Not *exactly*, anyway. The tumors themselves weren't consuming Nadia's body the way cancer would. They were just growing in size, occupying space. Putting pressure on surrounding tissues and organs.

She was analyzing the largest one right now, the one she'd removed from Nadia's abdomen. Hushi was convinced she'd gotten good margins, but that was only a guess. Nadia's physiology was still an alien concept. A scientist with more training and knowledge than Hushi would still spend years trying to decipher the complex genetic and protein breakdown of the world's first living weapon design.

Leaning back in her chair, Hushi stretched and then reached for her favorite teacup. Oolong always helped her to think. She brought the cup to her lips and savored the aroma before taking a sip. *Cold again.* She stood to refill the cup when the door at the top of the basement stairs swung open. Beth's legs appeared. "Hushi? You down there?"

"No. But since you're invading me anyway, bring down my box of tea and another gallon of water from the fridge, will you?"

"Sure." A few seconds later, Beth came down the stairs.

A lighter set of steps accompanied her. *Wait, too heavy for Sofi! Beth, what the hell are you doing? Who*—? Hushi scanned the room frantically, trying to decide what to hide first. When she turned back around, she was staring Tab Grubka in the face.

Hushi's heart leaped into her throat. Memories of another time, another intrusion, sprang to mind. Jennie Fowler's head exploding from the bullet's impact. A cruel beating inflicted without mercy. She scanned the basement for anything she could swing.

Beth grabbed her shoulders and shook her. "Hushi, listen to me! I brought Tab down here. It's okay."

Fists clamped into rock-hard clubs, Hushi stood trembling. "Why the hell didn't you call me first?"

"Because you would have said no."

"Of course I would have said no! I don't know anything about her, or anyone else stalking around this case in the last two weeks. Why the hell would I trust her enough to allow her in *my* lab?"

"I want to help," said Tab. "Beth and I were talking, and I have an idea—"

Hushi stabbed an angry finger at Beth. "You *told her?*"

Tab took a step forward. "No. I figured it out. I am a spy, after all. Now, can I see one thing?"

Shaking herself loose from Beth, Hushi stalked to the far wall. Her knees almost gave way before she could turn and lean against it, arms crossed over her chest to still the shaking. *This has to stop. For Jenny—and Donna, too. Too much blood, too much fear. This has to stop now.* "What do you want to see?"

"An electroencephalogram."

"An EEG." Hushi's jaw hung open in disbelief. "Why? Are we a neurologist all of a sudden?"

Beth touched Hushi on the shoulder. "It's all right. I thought I saw something and I wanted Tab to look at it."

"You should have talked to me beforehand."

"We may not have much time. Please?"

Hushi took a deep breath to finish calming down and dug a CD from the middle of a stack on her desk. After loading it into a computer, she called up the file. A series of erratic lines scrawled across the screen against a white background. "What are you looking for?"

Beth pulled up a chair and sat next to Hushi. "Words. Pull up the first EEG we ran on Nadia." Hushi complied. Beth touched the screen at several points. "See these discharge points? They pop up too regularly to be normal brain waves. I thought they were a subtle form of epilepsy, just as you and Donna did. But something occurred to me this afternoon." She straightened and rose to let Tab take her place, speaking over her shoulder. "Nadia's personality was loaded into her by a digital process. With a computer."

A thrill began in Hushi's chest. She manipulated the mouse to expand one portion of the screen. "I think I see what you mean. Tab, can you make any sense of this?"

The blonde squinted and leaned forward. "Yeah, I can see a definite pattern there. It's almost hidden in the random noise, but this here" — her finger stabbed out—"This is a sixteen-bit binary word. Does it repeat in any kind of pattern?" She scribbled a series of ones and zeroes on a notepad while Hushi copied the screen shot.

Two hours later, they'd established a solid pattern of repetition of the digital pattern. After switching to a more recent scan, Hushi's eyes grew heavy. But she was too excited to stop. Here, finally, was something new to look at. Two pots of tea later, Tab, suddenly shouted, "Stop!"

Hushi's hand shook as she released the mouse. "I think I see it."

"It's the same word, I know it," said Tab. "But it looks like it's been corrupted. Here, it's got a stray 'one' where there should be a 'zero.' It changes the whole command for this sub-routine."

"So can it be fixed?"

Tab rubbed her eyes. "It could be rewritten, but we need the equipment to access her brain at the right point—"

"We have the designs for the gear they used to program her," said Beth. "It was in that notebook she brought back from Prague—"

"And we have the original file!" said Hushi. "Could it really be that easy? How do we know what's causing the tumors?"

"Look at the channel it's on," said Beth. "That's the part of the brain you said communicates with her nanobot factory. Everything that's been going wrong is centered there."

Hushi's breath caught in her throat twice before she could speak coherently. "We have a cure," she finally fought out. "My God, I have to call her!"

* * * *

A thousand miles away, in the bottom of Nadia's pack, her cell phone buzzed urgently, four times, and then fell quiet again as the call was routed to her voice mailbox. A minute later, Jon's phone hummed and also recorded a message heard only in the ether of silent airwaves.

Thus the old saw remains true: a chain is still only as strong as its weakest link.

Chapter Fifty-Four

Jimmy squatted on the hilltop in the early dawn, the sky behind him just showing a rosy glow on the eastern horizon. Soon the sun would warm his back, and ease the aches and creaks of age. He took another bite from the macaroni and cheese in his MRE and glared across the dry lakebed at their objective. All was quiet now, but soon there would be plenty to do. He just hoped he had the right people for the job.

Sipping from his canteen, he scanned the camp area. From the end of one sleeping bag sprayed a shock of cinnamon hair. He had no doubt Jenna could do what she had to. But in her drive for revenge, could she be trusted not to endanger the rest of the group? He wondered what kind of leash he could pull on to keep this stick of dynamite from exploding and killing herself and everyone else in the process.

Jon rolled over and heaved a snore. Nadia moaned in her sleep and snuggled closer to him. Jon was as out of his element as a guppy on Mount Everest. He was a helluva cop, but this was way beyond cop work. He had a history of pushing the edges of the envelope, but in two hours, the envelope wouldn't even exist. He would have to throw out the rulebook and just shoot to kill. Orders would have to be obeyed on the spot, and he wasn't one to follow any orders but his own.

Nadia had the simplest job, and the most critical. Jimmy had no doubt she would do what needed to be done. As long as she didn't lose her nerve and run like a scared deer. He had to confess, he'd never seen her in action when the chips were all on the table. He wasn't in Prague, and didn't see how things went down. But she'd come through that ordeal all right, and even had the composure to see Sofi to a safe place. So maybe she had more in her than anyone thought, especially one old silver wolf.

He sure couldn't leave himself out of the equation, either. He didn't get to live this long by missing details or giving anyone a break for circumstances. Either his team did their job, or they died. It was always that simple. This op was no exception. Just because he had the most combat experience didn't guarantee he could perform when the rubber met the road. He wasn't getting any younger, and the odds rose against him with every operation he undertook.

The Army had been good to him, but he knew when the time came to cash out and walk away. A soldier can't lead a team when he's the slowest member. Now, here he was, thrown back into the meat grinder in spite of his best efforts to put his rifle down for good. All that blood, all that death... Jimmy looked up at the sky and allowed himself a solitary tear for the kids he'd brought back home in metal, flag-draped boxes. "I tried," he said under his breath. "I tried to make it right with You, and leave it all behind. I can only get forgiven so many times, you know. And I keep gettin' pulled back in. I don't know how to end this so I can stop for good. I'm gettin' too old for it. The weight's too heavy. I can't carry it no more."

Jenna's boot scuffed on the rock behind him before she spoke. "Am I interrupting?"

Jimmy hurriedly brushed his eye with a calloused fingertip. "Nah, I was just thinkin'."

"This is the Last Op," she muttered, squinting across the valley.

"There's only one Last Op, you know."

"The one you don't come back from," she finished. "Yeah, I've heard that one."

"You're gonna have to get 'em outta here if I get zapped."

"Who says you're going to buy it today?"

The old man struggled to his feet. "Maybe. Maybe not. But I been through enough, my odds are pretty low. It don't mean I'm just gonna give up an' let one of them snot-nosed kids pop a cap in me without knowin' who he's tanglin' with." He turned to face Jenna, touched her arm as he fixed her eyes. "But I ain't kiddin' myself, hon. I ain't as fast as I used to be. I got a bum shoulder an' a bad hand. If these kids are all half as good as you, we're in a heap of trouble."

Jenna reached up and touched his cheek. "For your information, old man, there isn't one of them who's as poison-mean as you are. You know what they say," she said with a grin, "'old age and treachery beat youth and vigor every time.'" Suddenly she grabbed his face, pulling him closer. Before Jimmy could react, she planted a soft, warm kiss on his mouth. "For luck. Now, let's go get Bunny," she said, and strode off to gather her gear.

Another soft chuckle rumbled through Jimmy's throat as he turned to wake the others. As he glanced back over his shoulder, Jenna was just turning away. A strange, distant smile was just fading from her lips as she strapped on her gun belt. *Girl, if I was fifty years younger, I'd curl your toes. Ah, well. Let's get to work.* "On your feet, kids, let's go."

As the group prepared, he issued orders. "Drink all your water now. Leave everything but your weapons and ammo. Clean and clear weapons before we leave." He went to each one, checking gear and making sure all was ready before issuing the command: "Move out."

* * * *

The sun was high overhead when they reached the bottom of the ridge and stepped out onto the dry lakebed. Jon's leg was aching fiercely with each step, but he dared not utter a sound. Jenna limped on, a defiant, hungry look in her face. At his side, Nadia reached out to give his hand a reassuring squeeze before she wiped sweat from her forehead. Something about her look disturbed him, but Jon couldn't pause long enough to read her.

Jimmy spoke up, his voice ragged from the rough climb down. "All right, it's about three klicks across the lakebed. There's only one way we're gonna make it across alive, and that's to make sure they have somethin' to lose. We gotta get as close as we can before they stop us." He caught up to Nadia and Jon, and waited for Jenna to close up from the rear position before he went on. "Nadia, at the first sign of trouble, you have to raise your ticket high. Everyone else, stay as close as you can to her. That way, they can't shoot at us without risking hitting Nadia. Everyone clear?"

Jon said, "Wait a minute. 'Ticket'?"

"This," said Nadia, pulling a round, green object from her BDU blouse.

A shock of terror rolled through Jon's body. The blood rushed from his face as he grabbed for the grenade. "No! You never said anything about this!"

Jenna stepped between them, grabbing his wrist. "It's okay, Jon. It's a dud. I disarmed it myself."

"Then what's it for?"

"Insurance. They should see it if she holds it up. They won't dare shoot at her or us, or they'll be killing themselves."

Jon pointed a shaking finger at the grenade. "So that's useless?"

"It's a red herring, that's all," said Jimmy. "C'mon, we gotta move out right now."

They started out at a trot, trying to get as close as they could before being stopped. Before long, however, everyone's aches and wounds began to take their toll, forcing them to slow. Jimmy's breath came in ragged gasps. Jenna struggled along, her limp becoming even more noticeable. Jon's leg felt as though it were on fire with every jarring step. No one said anything; they were all just trying to close.

Jon looked up after several minutes. It seemed they had barely started out onto the flat of the dry lakebed. The ridge with the hidden door was just as far away as it was from their camp of the previous night. They weren't close enough, and out on the flat like this, they would be picked off by sniper fire before they got close enough to pose a threat to anyone buried inside that mountain. Even two megatons of NADIA couldn't cause that much damage to this massive a fortress. They'd lost before they even fought. Any minute now, the snipers would open up from the mountain. Any minute, the bullets would begin spraying the ground around them. Any minute, he would feel the round that would take his life, and The Pinnacle would simply take over everything. There would be nothing left to stop their insidious conquest.

The only sound was the slog of their boots across the flat, and the torn, forced breathing of the tired party. They were all on their own now. No water, no supplies. They'd left all back at camp, except for a couple packs of ammo. Jon carried a M-16 assault rifle. Jenna packed a brace of pistols with a bandolier of magazines for them. Jimmy carried that wicked-looking shotgun, and a pack of extra magazines.

Jimmy held up a weathered hand. The party came to a halt while he pulled out a compass and took a bearing on the door. They carried on at a brisk walk. Jon took a position just to Jimmy's left, slightly ahead of the women. "If I didn't see that car come through here last night, I would have sworn we had the wrong site."

"They're just waitin' for us to get within rifle range."

"I've always been the operational leader of this team. I made the calls, up to now."

Jimmy marched on, his eyes locked straight ahead. "This ain't a job for law enforcement anymore, buddy."

"That's what's bugging me, Jimmy. This *was* a legal matter until Jenna roped us into this 'Rat Patrol.'"

"For your information, sonny, this 'Rat Patrol' was my idea. Jenna helped me polish the plan."

"Jimmy, we don't have to do this. I can call Colonel Danson. He could still dispatch a team and we could arrest everyone in there."

"Been through that already. These jackwagons write the laws now. They make their calls, and every one of 'em walks. Then we get to do this again. Is that what you want?"

"I want to come out of this with a clean conscience."

The old man stopped long enough to fix Jon with a hard stare. "It's a war, son. No one gets out clean."

A single, silent puff of smoke on the mountain jerked Jon's attention away from his friend. Seconds later, a whooshing sound sliced through the air, followed by an explosion of dirt thirty meters in front of them. Jimmy held up a hand. The party halted. "Nadia! Get yourself up here."

Nadia came forward, the dummy grenade held high above her head in a trembling fist. "What makes you think they won't shoot first and look later?"

"If we're wrong, we'll never feel it, and neither will they," said Jimmy. "But I think we're right. Look."

Ahead of them, the mouse hole had opened in the mountainside. A squadron of black vehicles rolled through and fanned out as it approached them. Jimmy unslung the shotgun. Jon took the cue, swung his M-16 around and pulled the charging handle, reassured only slightly by the *shack* sound of the first round sliding into the chamber.

"Ah, Jimmy? Are you sure this is part of the plan?"

Chapter Fifty-Five

Five vehicles emerged from the mouse hole. Once in the open, they wheeled into a precise box formation and charged across the lakebed, kicking up a rooster tail of dust as they came. Jimmy raised the shotgun to his shoulder just before the convoy came into range, and the shotgun barked five times in rapid succession. A half-second later, five spouts of flame and dirt exploded into the sky as the mini-grenades detonated.

Jon raised the rifle to his shoulder, sighting in on the lead vehicle. Every heartbeat hammered in his ears. His finger tightened on the trigger as his thumb switched the safety catch to "automatic."

Jimmy's hand shot up. "Hold fire! Close up around Nadia."

Nadia raised her fist again, clutching the grenade high above her head. Her mouth was a straight, grim line. Desperate fear shone in her eyes.

The convoy split into a "Y". Two of the black trucks swerved left, two right, and the center vehicle came straight on. At the same moment, all skidded to a stop in the dirt less than a hundred meters away. Doors flew open, and two dozen black-suited figures spilled out, fanning into a semicircle. All but one raised their weapons, training them on the team.

Jon's mind raced. *Are we close enough to threaten them? Do they even know who Nadia is? Worse yet, do they even care?* His mouth felt as dry as the inside of a coffin. Sweat poured down his brow and off the end of his nose. He broke away from the sights of his M-16 to glance at

Jimmy. The old man stood as solid and still as a Joshua tree. The back of his leathery neck turned a darker shade of red, the only hint of his stress. Jenna planted herself behind Nadia, one arm around the blonde's shoulder and across her chest, the other pointing one of her pistols at the enemy. The look in her face was grim and fatal. She was ready to die, even if her eyes betrayed a suggestion of fear.

The Pinnacle agents approached in a skirmish line, closing the circle to surround them. *Now? Do I fire now?* Jon swung the rifle wildly, finding one target, and then another, trying to decide who was the biggest threat.

Jimmy spoke up again, a harsh croak that carried over the wind. "That's far enough, boys." When the enemy ignored him, he racked the bolt on the shotgun, sending a shiny round spinning from the breech through the air. "I said, ENOUGH!"

The line stopped. Everyone froze, stock-still. Jon could see their eyes, and part of him relaxed. They knew. They knew if they fired on anyone, they ran a risk of hitting Nadia. And no one wanted to conceive what would happen next.

"Jonny-boy, you're up," murmured Jimmy. "I think we got their attention now."

With shaking hands, Jon lowered his weapon and stepped forward. Gathering himself, he slung the rifle and clenched his fists to still the trembling. He stopped five feet in front of Jimmy. "Who's in charge here?"

A slight, wiry man stepped forward, holstering his pistol. Jon hoped he looked as calm as this guy. Maybe half. Even half as calm would look good. Of course, the runt had twenty-three armed guards to back him up against two women, an old man, and a wounded ex-cop.

Jon went on. "You know who we are. You have a friend of ours. We want him brought out."

The other's voice was smooth, with a light, continental French accent. "What do you have to trade for him?"

"This isn't a trade." Jon motioned for Nadia to come forward. She came up and stood by Jon, the grenade still in her fist at her side. "I think you know what happens if this grenade goes off."

"But your friend, he will die as well."

"Concerned for him, all of a sudden? Since when did one man's life ever concern you people?"

Jenna stepped up, too, holstering her pistol. "Here's the deal, Jean-Jacques. Nadia and I go in to address the Council, face to face. I know they want us. I went through a lot of trouble to make it so. In return, we escort Mr. Kalinsky back out here."

Jean-Jacques pointed to the grenade in Nadia's fist. "Not with that. And no one addresses the Council. You know this, *traîtress!*" He spat the last word out like poison, finishing the statement by flicking his thumb against his top teeth at Jenna.

Jenna tensed, a low growl rising in her throat. Jon took her wrist in a soft grip. When she turned to face him, a quiet fury flashed in her eyes, barely suppressed.

"Bunny," whispered Jon. "We get Bunny first."

Jenna swapped glances with Jon. Her eyes bore within them a cold, still rage, waiting to be unleashed. For a moment, Jon pitied everyone in the world named Jean-Jacques, because when she finally uncorked on this dude, they'd all be feeling it for a week. The moment brought to him a calm. He spoke to Jean-Jacques. "Buddy, I'm betting you don't have a choice here. You people have been after Nadia since she woke up and walked off your plantation, and here she is. Now, you know as well as I do that she doesn't stand a chance on your terms. She's coming on *her* terms, and I'd like to see you stop her. Keys, please."

Nadia followed Jenna into the No-Man's area between the two groups. As she passed Jon, she reached out and brushed her fingers across his hand. He didn't have the time to respond, but he managed to whisper, "I love you."

Jon and Jimmy fell in behind the women as they closed with The Pinnacle agents. Their opponents retreated, all except their leader, who paled as Jenna strolled up to him with her hand out. Her eyes locked his with a withering stare. As if he were merely an automaton under her mental command, he held out a set of keys. Jenna took them and climbed into the nearest SUV. The others followed suit, and as they took off, Jon looked back through the rear window. Jean-Jacques was talking with someone on a cellphone and glaring holes through the SUV.

Seconds later, the black-clad agents recovered from their confounded stupor, scattering like a flock of angry crows. They boarded the remaining four SUVs and swung around in pursuit.

Jenna's voice dragged Jon's attention back to the front of the vehicle. "Jimmy, don't let them get too close. When we get to the door, you men will stay and keep the way clear. Nadia and I will get Bunny."

"Just make sure you don't stop for tea. I don't know how long we'll be able to keep these jackwagons at bay." The old man leaned out a window and sent a couple more grenade rounds flying back at their pursuers. Jon followed suit with a burst of automatic fire that sprayed dirt into the air in front of the nearest chase vehicle. A couple of short bursts from the chase cars answered back, but the response was cut short as the enemy realized the danger of hitting Nadia.

Ahead in the cliff wall, their entrance to the mountain became more evident. The mouse hole hung open, waiting for them. Jenna heaved the wheel hard to the left and the SUV went into a sideways skid that stopped with them across the door, blocking it to any other vehicles and against closing. Nadia bailed from the front seat with Jenna hot on her heels. Jon and Jimmy climbed out and took cover behind the SUV as their enemies drew nearer.

Jon checked the M-16 and pulled a couple extra magazines from his pack while Jimmy grabbed the extra ammo for the AA-12. Jon's hands shook as he turned to sight over the hood of the car. Jean-Jacques and his troops had just pulled up in a horseshoe formation, cutting off all escape routes and pinning Jon's team against the cliff. He rapped a couple times on the metal of the truck. The hollow, ringing echo that answered did nothing to ease his trepidation. "Jimmy, I don't know if this thing is armored."

Jimmy drew a pistol and blew out the truck's rear side windows to clear his firing path. "It's better than toilet paper, boy. Just make sure you hold fire until you have a target. Let *them* waste their ammo killin' a truck."

Just then the enemy, reassured the women were clear of the SUV, opened up with a withering volley of rifle and automatic fire. The sound, amplified by the cliff, surrounded the pair in a sonic fury that threatened to drown them in waves of pressure. The tires on the far side of the truck disintegrated. Glass from the remaining windows sprayed across the dirt and onto the concrete of the entryway. Jon frantically scanned the edges of the doorway, hoping to find a more secure place in which to shelter from the storm of lead and steel threatening to overcome and destroy him. The urge to run away nearly overwhelmed him. He'd never experienced this volume of fire before.

Then he saw Jimmy, hunkered down behind the rear wheel. His face was drawn tight, lips cutting a grim, straight line across his face. But the old man stayed stock-still. No trembling or fear showed on the sergeant's countenance. There was something else there, someone else who had come to the surface of this aged warrior. A fire Jon had never seen, stoked to a hellish heat, and controlled by years of training and experience. As rounds pinged and ricocheted all around them, Jon drew strength from the man who had seen countless others through wars and rumors of wars, and would see him and his little team through this as well. Jon's heart calmed, his hands steadied as he took a deep breath to clear his mind and re-center himself.

The cacophony stilled as suddenly as it started. Jimmy's voice came out as a harsh, tight croak. "Here they come." The old man rose enough to fire through the empty windows of the truck, and he sent five more grenade rounds down range in a wide arc that made the advancing agents stop dead in their tracks and scatter back behind their own vehicles. "What say we make this a little more interesting, buddy?" Jimmy raised his aim a little, pulled the trigger on full auto. The shotgun barked five more times in rapid succession, and two of The Pinnacle SUVs exploded in flames and shards of metal and glass. Several dark figures moved around the outside edges of the horseshoe barricade, but Jon squeezed off a short burst at each end, and the figures retreated again.

Jimmy spoke again, barely heard above the ringing in Jon's ears. "Keep count of your rounds! When in doubt, drop it out!"

"What?"

"It means reload, ya pinger!" The silver-haired warrior rose again and dispatched another black SUV with a couple more rounds from the shotgun. The effect on their enemy's morale was obvious. They cowered behind whatever pathetic cover they could find, only firing sporadically when they did find enough courage to brave Jimmy's aim.

A sound behind Jon brought him up short. Footsteps echoed from somewhere deep in the gloom of the passageway they currently blocked, reminding him they were only at the entrance of a nest of hornets. He swung the rifle around to face the new threat, straining his eyes to see in the darkness. *What do you do when you've got a tiger by the tail?*

Chapter Fifty-Six

Nadia couldn't still the shaking in her knees as Jenna took the lead into the gloom of the entrance passage. They rounded a corner to a larger space just as the first burst of gunfire erupted behind them. Jenna broke into a trot. Nadia lost sight of her in the darkness. "Wait a minute. Slow down."

"It's all right. Just stay on my tail and follow my footsteps." Their echoes rang back after a long pause, indicating how massive a cavern they were passing through. The floor stayed smooth and flat beneath Nadia's feet, allowing her some small measure of comfort as the women left the desperate firefight behind.

Lights flashed on overhead, bathing the cavern in an industrial wash. Nadia ran into the back of Jenna, who had drawn up short. A sharp cry from a few meters away hacked through her jangled nerves, and she nearly dropped her grenade. It would have been the end of their bluff, far too soon.

"Halt!"

Nadia turned toward the source of the shout. A half-dozen armed sentries advanced on them from a side passage, rifles and pistols trained. Jenna grabbed Nadia's wrist and raised her hand high. "Stop! Or she drops this grenade."

The cohort of enforcers stopped dead, weapons still level but their aim began to waver as the import of the statement sank in.

"The Council is here," said Jenna. "I know about the meeting. Now take us to them."

A beefy woman with a buzzcut stepped out, lowering her pistol. She held a hand out in a calming gesture. "We don't want to hurt anyone. We just want you to give us the grenade."

"I can't," said Nadia. "I lost the little pin-thingie." She took her hand back from Jenna's grip, clutching the steel ball to her chest. The cool of the small bomb felt strangely comforting against her breast, still hot from the desert heat outside as well as the stress building inside. Her vision shrank to a sharp, pinpoint focus directly in front of her. *If I don't faint, I'll get through this. Please, God, don't let me screw up.*

Buzzcut stood in front of Nadia with her hand out. Jenna stepped between them, locking the woman's eyes. "No. Elevator. *Now.*"

"I can't take you there. No one brings weapons to the Chamber."

The edge faded from Jenna's voice. "What's your name?"

Buzzcut faltered, confusion wrinkling her forehead. "Barbara."

"Well, Barbara, you could shoot us both right now. But you'd be dead before you knew what happened. You could try to block us. But, I'd probably break your neck. Then your buddies would shoot us, and everyone is still dead. The worst part is, a two-megaton antimatter reaction would rip this mountain from its foundation, and your leadership, everyone from the high king to the last pauper in the dungeon, dies. Is that what you want?"

The radio at Barbara's hip squawked. "Miss Cornell. Bring our guests to the Chamber."

She grabbed the radio and brought it to her mouth. "But sir, they're armed."

"This standoff will not be solved in the hallway. Miss Paine is as stubborn as she is rebellious, and the NADIA doesn't know better. Bring them."

"Yes sir." Barbara heaved a sigh and motioned down the hall, behind Nadia and Jenna. "Okay, ladies. We're going this way."

* * * *

A chill slithered up Jenna's spine and settled around her mind like a cold, tentacled thing from a nightmare as they passed through the doors into the Council Chamber. It was just as she remembered from the last time she was here. The red and gold carpet lay across the expanse of floor, so soft beneath her boots she felt as though she was desecrating something by her very presence in this place. The horseshoe dais rose in three steps around the outside walls, and the podium at the far end was the same dark, richly carved wooden pedestal. The only difference was that this time, every seat was filled, all three rows along the side walls and every chair behind the podium.

Solemn figures in red silk robes glowered from under deeply shadowed hoods at the women as they entered, followed by Barbara's team of armed agents, who fanned out and surrounded them.

One shrouded and robed figure rose from the center of the mass with a smooth, easy grace borne of power and privilege and mounted the podium. "Miss Paine, why do you come before us thus armed?"

Aside from the robe, he sounded like Jenna's middle school principal, imperious and demanding. Jenna struggled to remember his name— Mr. Crowder, that's who it was. Ricky Blanton had stuck his hand in Jenna's blouse, and she'd punched him, dead in the face. The hall monitor reported her for fighting, and she found herself sitting in Crowder's office. He pointed his fat finger right at her and blamed her for the whole incident. When she tried to tell him it was Ricky's fault, he wouldn't even listen. She'd gotten three weeks' suspension. Jenna swore from that day forward that *no one* was going to talk to her like that again. Council or no, this man wasn't going to get away with it. She was done being their puppet.

Jenna met his gaze evenly. "At least we have the guts to show our faces here, instead of hiding behind those tacky bathrobes," she retorted. "We both know full well if we didn't have an ace up our sleeve, we wouldn't be alive now."

The man threw his hood back to reveal gray hair trimmed close around his ears. His clean-shaven face was care-worn and drawn, the wrinkles deep around his mouth and neck. But deep within the blue eyes, passion and drive burned like an unquenchable fire. "So be it, then. Now, what do you want? Our time is precious."

"Have I finally got your attention, then? Begin by having your thugs leave our friends at the gate be. Then bring Bunny Kalinsky out here and turn us loose."

"And in return, Miss Paine, what do we get?"

Nadia stepped forward. "You get me."

The man sneered back at her. "What would we want with you?"

"You've been chasing me around the world for four years, Mr. Bowman. All my life I've been on the run from you, and now you have the gall to tell me you don't *care* anymore?"

Bowman looked back at his compatriots. "Someone tell me why this *thing* is talking to me."

Nadia flushed, her brown eyes blazing. "Because I have *this!*" She brandished the grenade above her head. A collective hiss rose in the chamber, suddenly cut off by a sharp motion from Bowman. Nadia said, "Bring Bunny up here, *NOW!*"

A smaller figure behind the podium stood and advanced to stand next to Bowman. A smooth, feminine voice spoke in a clipped accent. "John, there is no need to be so rude. They don't understand." She drew her hood back and smiled at Jenna. She was everything Bowman was not: small, tawny-skinned, dark-haired. And gentle. "You look familiar."

Still on guard, Jenna said, "I attended your lecture at Gradwell College."

"I spoke there many times."

"You signed my book afterward."

The sirdar's smile broadened. "Yes, I remember."

"Your lecture on world peace didn't include underground hostile takeovers."

"And yet you were very much in favor of our plan and vision, were you not?"

Jenna flushed and looked down in shame. The sirdar was right. This little chickadee had followed the trail of breadcrumbs right into the cat's mouth all on her own.

The sirdar spoke again, to one of the field agents surrounding them. "There is no need for further violence here. Please bring our guest here so he may be on his way."

Jenna's head snapped up. "Just like that? You'll let us go?"

"Not you. Just Mr. Kalinsky." She watched the agent nod and leave the chamber. "You and Miss Velasquez cannot leave, I'm afraid. Neither may your friends at the gate."

"We have another chip for the pot. Palmer Frost is still in custody."

"Mr. Frost is damaged goods, Miss Paine," said Bowman. "Anna Spielberg had a daughter—"

"She's a *child!*" blurted Nadia. "She doesn't know about you, and doesn't care. Why kill her, too?"

Bowman turned his diamond-hard gaze on her. "Great vision requires great sacrifice. Of course, I wouldn't expect *you* to understand that."

"I understand about right and wrong. I'm only five years old, and I understand that very well. You don't throw people down the toilet when they become inconvenient for you."

"Right and wrong are relative terms, NADIA. They aren't carved as deeply in stone as some outdated belief systems would have you believe. They're dictated by the leaders of cultures, not any fixed standards. Here and now, *we* say what's right and what's wrong. We've spent over a hundred years as an organization trying to change the world paradigm on that antiquated philosophy. Don't dare to lecture me on morals."

The hot wave of anger prickled the hair on Jenna's neck. Before she could stop herself, she blurted, "So how about you lecture *me* on why it was right to murder my father? Your kind makes me sick, you pompous, arrogant, miserable—"

A touch at her elbow stilled the outburst. The surge of anger, defying suppression, made itself another outlet in the tears that squeezed unbidden from her eyes to roll, hot with her hate, down Jenna's cheeks. At her ear, a whisper. "I got this. Get Bunny out." Nadia's voice trembled, but when Jenna turned to look into her eyes, she saw a fatal confidence. With a short nod, the redhead clamped her mouth shut. Her bridges would be burned soon enough.

Bowman droned, "The Council will overlook your outburst. This time." One arm rose in a grand gesture. "*Ecce homo!* Behold the man." Jenna followed the movement to a side door of the chamber heretofore hidden by the gloom of shadows.

Bunny stepped hesitantly into the room and descended the dais to stand next to the women in the middle of the room. He mumbled from a corner of his mouth, "Can someone tell me just *what* the hell is goin' on here?"

Nadia nodded at Jenna, squeezing her hand. She looked at Bunny. "Bye hon. Go with God."

Jenna whispered to Bunny, "You're going home. Just make sure you stay within five feet of me. Let's go." Taking a deep breath, she spun on her heel and struck a brisk pace toward the big double doors at the far end of the chamber. She was reaching for the handle in the shocked silence when Bowman's voice rang across the room.

"Where do you think you're going?"

Her heart leaped into her throat. Through a mouth suddenly dry as hot sand, she said, "We're leaving. You and Miss Velasquez have some things to discuss."

"Stop," he ordered. "Someone stop them!"

Nadia brandished the grenade again and barked, "Let them go, or I drop this!"

Jenna took off, reaching behind her back for the pistol tucked in her waistband. Bunny's footsteps right on her heels told her he was doing his best to obey her order.

"Do you even know what you're doin'?" he wheezed. "What about Nadia?"

She slowed down to grab his shirt sleeve and slung him ahead, snapping off a shot down their back trail as they passed through the outer office. "Shut up and run!"

Chapter Fifty-Seven

Sweat poured down Jon's forehead as he hunkered behind the truck. He seriously regretted emptying his canteen that morning. The truck behind which he and Jimmy crouched was reduced to a shattered heap of smoking scrap metal across the opening in the cliff wall. He dug in his pocket for another jawbreaker with a trembling hand, but found it empty. Maybe Jimmy had one?

The old man was locked in position, propped over the hood with the barrel of the assault shotgun pointed at the one SUV he hadn't blasted to shredded wreckage with grenade rounds. A tight grimace pinched his pale face as he swung the weapon to cover a shadow that dared to show around the barricade of twisted skeletal SUV remains. The shotgun barked twice. A scream of pain answered as another enemy agent fell wounded. Jimmy ducked as a long burst of small arms fire tore through the hood of the truck. He grinned at Jon, an ugly leer stained with carbon and memories. "They gotta run out of either ammo or soldiers sooner or later."

"If we don't first," muttered Jon. "Think we can save that last truck for us?"

"We'll find out, soon as the others show up. It'll take a fast rush. You up to it?"

"Yeah, I think so."

"How you fixed for ammo, boy?"

Jon counted the magazines laid out in a neat row along his right leg. "Five mags."

"How many in your weapon?"

Jon thought for a long moment. He'd sprayed a couple long bursts before recovering his fire discipline and switched the selector toggle to the semiautomatic position. He couldn't honestly say how many rounds he'd fired. His gut wrenched with the realization.

Jimmy seemed to know what he was thinking. "Switch magazines, boy. Put in a new one." He punctuated the order with another fusillade, scattering dust and rocks in front of the enemy just to keep their heads down, covering Jon while he dropped out the magazine and rammed a fresh one home.

With a silent rebuke at himself, Jon vowed to keep count from here on out. God knew his life could depend on that knowledge.

* * * *

Jenna led the way out the elevator and into the parking garage, pistol at the ready. *So far, so good.* She motioned for Bunny to come out. Before the doors closed, she dragged a grenade out of a cargo pocket by the pin and slung it into the elevator, watching the priming lever pop off as it bounced off the back wall. She gave Bunny a shove and dove the other way as the doors blew open in a cataclysm of noise and smoke. Hands grabbed her shoulders. She twisted the shadow in a reflexive throw, bringing the pistol to bear as Bunny struggled to his feet. "Don't do that again!" she barked. Bunny's mouth worked in a desperate demand Jenna couldn't hear above the ringing anyway, but she could guess what he was saying. There was no time to answer or explain how Nadia would get out, so she clutched his shirt and shoved him again, down the hall toward the entrance door.

* * * *

Time. Buy time. Nadia's pulse raced as she brought the grenade back to her chest. Shifting nervously on her feet, she tried to think of anything to say. Her knees wobbled. She was past the point of no return now. That was firmly established when she heard the dull *krump* of an explosion somewhere in the distance. There was only one way out for all of them now.

Bowman softened. "There's no further need for that weapon, NADIA. Just give it to us, and we can talk about whatever you want."

Nadia took a deep breath to calm the buzzing in her breast. "Forgive me for being so callous, Mr. Bowman. I suppose I should feel thankful to you for the time I've had on this earth, but let's face it—I'm here because of your incredible hypocrisy and gall."

"Harsh words from someone in your situation."

"Why wouldn't I deserve the right to speak my mind?"

Bowman's eyes widened. "By all means, speak your mind—" Then he leaned over the podium, his face darkening into a mask of disdain. "Somewhere else. Here, Miss, we demand respect. In this august chamber, you will address no one by name. You have not earned that right—"

"The *hell* I haven't!" said Nadia, stamping her foot on the carpet. "You dare stand there and tell me what I have and have not earned, you who breathe poison into the ears of your puppets? You who throw people away like trash when they no longer serve your twisted purpose?"

"What purpose would you assume, NADIA? A purpose for ending war? For healing a broken and dying world? What's so 'twisted' about these ideals?"

"Your methods." A sound reached her ears, a whisper from behind. Her left fist shot out and whipped back in an automatic response, landing with a soft *pop* in a windpipe. Someone dropped to the carpet with a strangled gurgle. "Keep *back*, people! You don't think I'm serious?"

The circle around Nadia widened in answer. Five guns rose to bring their muzzles to bear on her. Anger and fear made every nerve in her body sing with energy. "I DARE YOU TO SHOOT!"

* * * *

Jenna stopped short of the corner, stabbing a fist in the air. Bunny, oblivious to the signal, ran right past her. She snagged his shirt just in time and swung the little man back against the stone wall with enough force to elicit a grunt as the wind left him in a rush. "That means *stop*," she hissed in his ear.

"C-cool."

She drew out a small mirror and angled it out into the hallway, checking both left and right before sliding around the corner. "Through the double doors at the end and turn left. Keep your head down; I'll be there in a minute. Now, run!" Giving Bunny a shove to get him going, she retreated up the hall they'd just left, listening hard. Sure enough, there it was. *Four, five... more. Damn.* She'd been outnumbered worse before, but these weren't normal soldiers. They were Pinnacle agents, trained as she was, by the same instructors. She was good, but was she *that* good? Her edge would have to be in the enhancements with which they'd built her: speed, vision, and strength. She moved into an ambush position and tucked her pistol away. It would be useless for what she had in mind.

* * * *

Jon spun when a door opened in the distance behind him, whipping the barrel of the M-16 into position as a shadow emerged from the gloom of the passage. "They're trying to flank us!"

"Hold your fire 'til you know who it is, boy!"

Clutching the rifle in hands numb with fear and fatigue, Jon fought to a crouch and moved where he could cover the opening better. "Federal agents. Come out with your hands up!"

A familiar voice came back to him through the sweltering heat of the entrance cavern. "I dunno if I want to, Jonny! The last time you said that to me I ended up doin' five to ten."

A wave of relief washed over Jon as he lowered the weapon and scooted back into his place beside Jimmy. "Bunny, you scared the hell out of us!"

Bunny strolled into the passage. The older man swung a glance over his shoulder. "Where are the girls? I wanna get outta here— Duck yer head, you ape!" A burst of automatic fire ripped through the opening from the agents cutting off their escape.

Bunny dropped to his knees, eyes wide and jaw clenched.

Jon looked back up the passageway. "Bunny? Where are they?"

"Jenna's just behind me. I don't know about Nadia."

"Why? Where is she?"

Bunny's face fell. "I don't know, Jonny."

A shock of realization slammed through Jon's chest. "Oh God, no." Fighting to his feet, he took off into the darkness of the passage. Behind him rang Jimmy's voice "Get back to your post, dammit!"

* * * *

Jenna waited until the second Pinnacle agent rushed past the corner before she reached out and punched the third in the throat. Then, leaping across the hall, she kicked off the far wall before landing in the midst of a half-dozen of the enemy. She was right smack in the middle of them all before the first one thought to cry out. Grabbing someone's head between her hands, she wrenched it hard and was answered by a sickening *crack*, and another body slid to the floor.

That was when the free ride ended, however, as the remaining agents caught up with what was going on. They tried to withdraw, but Jenna headed off each retreat with a punch, a kick, a grab. She dodged, parried, and blocked as her victims began to strike back in desperate fury.

She didn't care who she hit. She tuned her hearing to ignore the grunts and moans of those around her, listening for the rustle of clothing, the whistling rush of a fist through the air, the stomp of a foot to tell her when and where to strike. She ducked to let a kick whiff past her head and smiled when it connected with someone else's body. She followed it up with a lunge punch that broke something and a back elbow that landed somewhere soft. Someone grabbed her arm, and she clamped down with her teeth, the hot taste of blood filling her mouth as a ragged scream of agony filled her ears.

Something connected with Jenna's abdomen, driving her back against a wall as a flurry of fists rained down on her head. In the seconds it took to draw a breath, several more hard shots landed on her body and face. Her lip split as a punch made contact. One more attacker fell back under a desperate, wicked chop, but there were still plenty of enemies left. A knee rode up into Jenna's breadbasket—

The hall rang with explosions, sharp and close, then all was still and quiet. Jenna slid down the wall, her head and body singing with pain. She struggled to inhale. Through the tunnel of her vision, a silhouette advanced on her. She caught the line of a rifle barrel...

"Wake *up*, dammit! Where is she?" Jon shook her again, his fists wrapped in her shirtfront. Sluggishly, her body began to respond to commands. She managed a weak grunt as he lifted her to her feet. He backed her against the wall. His face hung before her eyes, a mask of anger and fear. "Where's Nadia?

"She's gone."

"What?" His fists clenched tighter, lifting her off the ground. "What did you say?"

Jenna shook her head to clear the cobwebs and evaluate her situation. She was... she was... *Wait a damned minute!* Her left hand came up, and she used her right as a fulcrum. With a yelp of pain, Jon dropped her, his arm a limp rag. She shot out with a hand, grabbed his collar, and pulled his face close to hers. "You will *never* handle me like that again!"

"You owe me! I have to find her. I have to—"

She took his arms and locked his gaze in the dim light. "Do you really want to die like this? She's giving you your life, Jon. Don't throw it away." Leaving the heap of bodies behind, she swung around the corner and back toward the garage.

"Jenna?"

Stopping to lean against the wall for support against the pain, she looked back. Jon stood there, the rifle held by its pistol grip in one hand. The look in his face told her what he knew. "S-she's going to do it, isn't she?"

"She didn't see it ending any other way. Sooner or later it was going to happen." She pulled out her pistol, checked it, and turned away. "We have to get clear."

An explosion shook the floor. Jon took off with a groan. "Jimmy's alone up there!"

"And whose fault's *that*," grumbled Jenna as she followed.

* * * *

As they rounded the corner into the entranceway, another rocket slammed into the truck parked across the entrance. Sparks, fragments, and smoke filled the cavern as the noise died away. No answering fire came from the figure lying off to one side like a discarded rag doll. Frantic, Jon looked around for Bunny. The man was nowhere to be seen. With the truck blown away, the entrance now lay open, no longer barricaded against the rush of agents converging on it from the outside.

With a curse, Jon rushed to the entrance, raising the rifle to his shoulder. The first agent to approach the entrance took a short burst to the chest. The others faded back to their defilades behind the other vehicles and opened fire.

Jenna dove for the shotgun next to Jimmy's body, sweeping it up and checking it as a new sound came from behind them. An engine revving hard echoed through the dark passage. A black stretch limo skidded to a stop in the middle if the chamber. The driver's window rolled down, and Bunny's head poked through. "Your chariot awaits people. Let's roll!"

Jenna shouted, "Get Jimmy!" and laid down covering fire as Jon dragged Jimmy to the car. She dove in as Bunny goosed the accelerator. They shot through the entrance into a hail of fire. Bullets played *Wipeout* against the armored sides and glass of the VIP limousine as Bunny crashed through the barricade and across the dry lakebed.

Jimmy lay on the floor, pouring blood from a half dozen ragged wounds. Jon tried to find the worst, to find somewhere to apply pressure, but most of the bleeding seemed to have stopped. "Jimmy, don't you leave me, man."

"Turn right, Bunny. Right!" Jenna manipulated the window switch. The pane refused to budge. "Dammit!"

Jon looked up from Jimmy's limp form. "What's wrong?"

"The safety circuit's cut in. I can't roll down the window." Jenna opened her door. Hooking her right arm around the frame, she leaned out and fired the shotgun off-hand. The remaining black-garbed agents scattered in the stream of explosions, and then converged on the lone remaining SUV as a huge black dragonfly zoomed overhead. "Damn, they have a helicopter!"

The helo gunship wheeled into a steep, climbing turn and swooped back upon the limo like a hawk after a mouse. Flame spouted from one of the twin pods mounted under the belly, and an instant later, the limo rocked as the rocket went off mere meters away. Jenna ducked as the spray of shrapnel spacked against the side of the car. Rising again, she braced a foot against the door and took a bead on the retreating aircraft, adjusted for motion, and pulled the trigger. Five rounds pounded from the barrel before she released it.

The chances for a hit on a moving aircraft were normally slim to nil, even as highly modified as were Jenna's reflexes and coordination. But combined with chance, the difference was good enough. One of the explosive rounds hit a rotor blade, blowing it in half. The engine, now horribly out of balance, took only a second to rattle itself to pieces under the force of the remaining blade, and the helpless craft spun into the ground with a sickening crash and roar of flame.

Bunny swung the wheel hard, dragging Jenna off balance. "Guys, we got company. Jenna, get back in here!" She landed with a grunt on the expansive floor of the limousine.

Jon glanced up, looking out the rear window at the vehicle gaining on them. "Gun it, Kalinsky." He went back to working on Jimmy, pawing through the bloody rags to find what wound was the worst.

Jenna rolled over and put a hand on Jimmy's chest. The old man lay still, his face ashen. The lids lay limp over half-open eyes. She pressed her fingers to the soft spot on one side of his throat, feeling for a pulse. When she looked up, her eyes had a cast that sent a horrid wave of anguish through Jon. Despair and grief wrenched her features into a grimace he could read without words. *It's my fault. Jimmy's dead and it's my fault.*

The rattle of lead off the rear window brought their attention back to the situation at hand. Jon barked, "Bunny, there's a roadway up here somewhere. Turn right and goose it."

"Got it, boss. Hold on!"

The limo jumped a small berm, landing with a crunch of scraping metal on the pavement as Bunny wrenched on the wheel. The ungainly, armored car swung wildly back and forth as he fought it to a straight course. Hot on their trail, The Pinnacle truck fishtailed and steadied, gaining still. Another burst flared from the passenger's front window, answered by a trail of fresh spider cracks across the limo's rear window as the glass began to weaken.

Jenna leaned out the door again, laying down fire with the last rounds from the shotgun just as another burst rattled from the SUV. The SUV took two high-explosive rounds, one blowing off the right front wheel and the other passing through the window as it swerved. The truck spun sideways and rolled, over and over, until it came to a stop upside down, a steaming, smoking wreck.

Jon looked back one more time to make sure no one else pursued them. With a sigh of relief, he sagged back in the seat. Then he saw Jenna lying half out the open passenger door. Her head sagged toward the ground rushing by underneath. One arm hung loose outside the vehicle. Reflexively, he grabbed her belt and dragged her in. Her left hand was a mess of road rash, pouring blood through ragged gashes. She coughed, and more blood sprayed from her mouth. "Ah, dammit, Jenna!" He snatched a multi-tool from his belt and went to work with shaking hands. "*Drive,* Bunny!"

Chapter Fifty-Eight

"NADIA, I grow weary of this pointless conversation," Bowman said. "Surely, you have some further purpose for standing here thus than waving a grenade in our faces? Or is this some senseless power trip for you?"

Nadia shifted weight to relieve a cramp in one leg. "I was just going to ask you the same thing, Mr. Bowman. What is it you get out of manipulating the world like this? Place your puppets in the seats of power so you can pull their strings with no responsibility?"

"Aren't you tired of all the killing in our world? Have you had enough of all this organized terrorism they call war?"

"And yet you wage your own war against everyone who stands in your way. You slaughter people like animals if they dare to disagree with your methods, let alone even find out about your existence. Do you really want to know what I think?" She turned to face the rest of the gallery. "You're all cowards. You hide in here, in your secret tower, and you force policy on a world that would drag you all into the street and lynch you if they could only figure out what you're really up to! Do you honestly think you're doing anyone a lick of good from in here? You place yourself so far above everyone you rule, you're out of touch, and you're terrified to admit you have no idea what you're doing."

Bowman leaned back, a smug grin on his face. "Is that so?"

"If you know so much about how to run things, why not come out and run for office? Why all this James Bond crap with the stupid robes? I bet your Halloween parties are a real hoot. Does everyone wear the same costume?"

Hattangadi spoke up. "Miss Velasquez, we have seen what happens for century after century of rule from public office. Those who are elected, are put in place not on the merits of their ability, but on how well they can lie to the electorate. The monarchs of the world care only for how much they can wring and extort from their subjects. We place our support behind kind and just leaders who have in mind and heart only good for their people."

"And yet you kill with such callous abandon?"

"At times, it becomes necessary to remove an obstacle, NADIA."

"It's *murder*, Bowman!"

"No. Murder implies a personal hatred of the individual. We hate no one. All decisions are made for the good of society at large."

"And who are you to make such decisions for the rest of us?"

"We are the future, NADIA." Bowman nodded in Nadia's direction. A sudden dread filled her chest. *Jon, run faster...*

A whisper of movement behind Nadia was the only warning she got before a rough hand grabbed her wrist. Iron-strong fingers clutched at the grenade, holding the priming lever against the case. Someone else grabbed her left hand, and together they pulled her to the ground. She found herself face-up, staring into the face of a large, red-haired man. He kneeled on her right arm, pinning it to the floor. With both hands around the grenade, he lifted it in triumph. "I got it, I got..." Nadia watched his expression change from gleeful victory to puzzlement at the wire running from the grenade, to the pin now dangling from the other end, freshly pulled from the second grenade tucked in her shirt.

Just over the hiss of the fuse, she said to Bowman, "For the good of society."

The last thing Nadia Velasquez felt was the *whoomp* of the charge going off against her chest. It didn't even last long enough to hurt.

Forty-eight grams of antimatter, no longer held in stable form, unleashed itself on its creators in a final flash of vengeance.

* * * *

The ground shook beneath the limousine speeding south on Nevada Route 168. Jon felt the shock through the center of his soul even as the purple-blue flash filled the sky behind them. The mountain lifted, dissolved, and fell back to earth, crumbling in on itself like some eerie magic act. A part of his mind wondered if David Copperfield would appear along the road, making the last nimble hand gesture to tell everyone it was part of the show. The rest of him prayed it was all just a horrible dream, that he could wake up and Jimmy would be there, grinning that grin of his. Jenna wouldn't be bleeding to death in his hands. Nadia would be… *Nadia. My God, Nadia.*

Bunny fought the car back onto a straight course. When he spoke, all the irreverent humor was gone. His voice was flat, dull. "Jonny, I used the car phone and called ahead. They got a medevac chopper on the way to meet us."

"They won't get here in time." Jon didn't even care if Bunny saw him crying. He just let the tears flow while he tried in vain to stem the flow of blood from Jenna's wounds. He'd cut away her shirt with the multi-tool and found two holes in her upper chest, just inside the shoulder, and one lower down. She still bled from her mouth, and every breath came with a rasping gurgle. Every so often, she would cough, and pink foam would ooze onto the floor of the limo.

He rolled her onto her right side to keep her left lung from filling with blood, too, and applied pressure to the wounds as best he could. But she was senseless and pouring her life out fast.

"Dammit, Jenna, don't you die, too." She *deserved* to die for what she did. She was a murderer, a paid thug for those bastards that built Nadia. But for some reason, he couldn't let her go, not now. Not like this. She'd paid in her blood, to save Bunny and him. She was a stubborn, infuriating, backstabbing, selfish—

"J-Jon."

"Shh, don't talk."

"Did she—?" A wracking cough shook her, and she spit more blood onto the floor. Her face was drawing pale.

"Yeah. She did it. She made them all pay."

"Nothing left." She said with a sigh.

"Nothing left for what?"

Jenna's eyes rolled back and then fluttered closed. She exhaled and lay still.

"Jenna?" Jon took her shoulders and shook her gently. "Jenna!"

The car began to slow. Jon looked up. The helicopter sat just off the highway, its medical crew standing by with a gurney. He barely recalled the limo pulling to a stop, or the jump-suited medical crew pulling Jenna's form from the car. In fact, he didn't remember much of the next week. He debated whether it wasn't better that way.

Chapter Fifty-Nine

The yard lay empty, the trampled grass and bald spots all that remained to remind Sofi of the previous two weeks' activity. She sat on the porch, feeling dark and empty. She'd listened at the other extension, a hand clamped over her mouth to smother the sobs as some colonel something-or-other from Las Vegas told Hushi about what happened. Hushi was too busy crying to hear Sofi drop the handset on the carpet and run to her room. She'd buried her face in her pillow and bawled like a baby.

Any minute now the Weesaws' old Chevy would pull through the trees up the drive, and Bunny would get out. Just Bunny. No one else was coming back.

The Air Force people all shouted for joy, packed up, and went home with smiles on their faces. The world was safe for democracy and all that. They took that creepy Mr. Frost and his buddies with them, too. They got what they wanted and left. *That's cool. Everyone else is totally geeked. I'm the only one who lost out here, and no one gives a—*

The front door opened with a protest of springs. Hushi stepped out and stood next to Sofi on the porch. "George Weesaw called. They're turning off of M-78 now." Her voice held a nervous hope.

"I suppose Carlos and Tab are leaving, too." Sofi tried to fight down the lump in her throat and failed miserably. It made her sound like she was talking through Jell-O. When she looked up at Hushi, she knew her eyes were wet again. But it was okay. At least Hushi understood a little.

Hushi sat in the old chair that Jimmy used to sit in all the time, the rickety white rocker that popped every time someone rocked back. Just like Jimmy's knee used to pop all the time. Only Jimmy wasn't going to sit there anymore. Jimmy was—

"Actually, Tab's talking Carlos into staying around for a while longer." Hushi reached out and took Sofi's hand. "If that's okay with you?"

"Why should it matter whether it's okay with me?" Sofi mumbled.

Hushi took a deep breath and looked out over the lawn. The pause stretched out while a blue jay's ragged *scraw* sounded once, twice across the clearing where the sheds had stood until this morning. "This *is* your place now. Technically, you could give them permission to stay, if you want—"

"They can do what they want."

The blue jay called again to its mate. Hushi inhaled before going on. "Bunny was talking with Tab. She found a code, hidden in Nadia's brain pattern..." She trailed off and looked around. "Jenna lost a lot of blood, honey. She almost bled out before they could get her stable—"

"I heard them tell you, remember? I heard about the brain damage. I don't want to talk about it anymore."

Hushi grabbed her hand tighter. "Listen to me. We think we can bring Jenna back. But we need your help."

The honk of a car horn made Sofi jump. Hushi turned, and her earnest, serious expression transformed instantly to one of tearful joy. A small, red Chevrolet sedan pulled up in front of the garage, and the back door flew open. Bunny stepped out and stretched his arms wide. His shout echoed through the trees. "Stick yer lips on me an' make me like it, baby!"

Hushi's response was an unintelligible combination of sobs and shouts of laughter as she flew off the porch and across the lawn. She knocked Bunny back against the car, covering his face with kisses and happy tears. He finally pushed her back with trembling hands. "No more, now, Hushi, you done used up all your allowance of mushy stuff for the week." Then he pulled her close, and she buried her face in his chest.

They held each other and cried while George climbed out and walked around the car. He caught Sofi's eye and started toward her with a casual, soft stride. When he stepped up on the porch, he held one tawny hand out. "How you doing, sweet cake?" She didn't take it but looked away. He backed up and leaned on the rail, facing her with his arms crossed. "It's okay, you know. It's okay to feel bad, even if those two"—he nodded toward the couple in the driveway—"can't see how much it hurts." He paused, locking her gaze. Why hadn't Sofi ever noticed how kind his eyes were before? "We all loved her, too. She was part of us, the little time she was here. That means you're part of us, too. And when one of the tribe hurts, we all share it. We want to help you say goodbye. Is that all right?"

Sofi stood, a sudden flush of anger washing over her. "Why does everyone need my *permission* all of a sudden? What's wrong with you people?" She couldn't stop the fresh flood of hot tears that sprang unbidden from her eyes. "*You're* supposed to be the grownups, not me!" She stomped into the house, slamming the door behind her.

* * * *

Hushi knocked lightly at the bedroom door and waited five full seconds with no answer. Unsure, she looked back up the hall to her husband. Bunny just nodded and urged her with a silent wave to try again. She eased the door open with a curious little creak and slipped through. The blacklight in the corner lampstand threw its eerie purple glow over Sofi's Day-Glo graffiti. The dark lump under the blankets shifted. A single pathetic snort betrayed the girl's presence. Hushi used that sound to figure out which end was which and climbed in, pulling Sofi close against her chest. Nothing she could say would make this broken little girl feel better about anything right now.

The sounds of Beth Nelson puttering in the kitchen floated down the hall and through the open door, a hollow pretense at normalcy. Hushi only prayed that somehow it would help to comfort the child in her arms. Sofi lay still and miserable, a rag doll. An hour passed. Hushi nodded off. She came awake when a soft whisper tickled her ear.

"What's wrong with me?"

"Baby girl, nothing's wrong with you."

"Something's wrong with me. Everyone keeps dying." Hushi listened as she went on. "Mother died. Mom died. Jimmy died, and Papa Irving died. There's no one left."

Hushi caressed Sofi's hair. "I'm still here. Bunny's here."

"You better go, or you're going to die, too."

With a soft chuckle, Hushi sat up and drew Sofi's head into her lap. "Not a chance, baby girl. The bad people are all gone now. Your mother *and* your mom both saw to that." She brushed Sofi's hair with a gentle hand. "Even if they were still out there, Bunny and I would be here. Someone has to keep you out of trouble, young lady. Someone has to be here to love you—" The words got choked off by the lump in Hushi's throat. She gathered the child into her lap and they shared their sadness, their misery, their mourning, until Beth tapped at the doorframe to announce dinner.

Sofi sniffed and wiped her eyes. "Stay with me?"

Hushi kissed her cheek and hugged her closer. "Always. I promise."

* * * *

Sofi took a deep breath and settled back in the cot. The sting from the IV was still fading from her hand. Beth took a moment to explain again. "Now, this tube is in case anything gets uncomfortable for you. I can give you something to help it get better, okay?"

Hushi hooked up the last probes to Sofi's head, double checked her connections, and nodded before stepping back.

Beth asked her, "Are you sure we know what we're doing?"

"Have we ever been sure? This is new territory for just about everyone." Hushi took Sofi's hand. "We wouldn't be doing this unless we had to, baby girl. But if we want to help Jenna, we need to know what Dr. Spielberg loaded into you."

"Will it hurt?"

Bunny pushed his coke-bottle glasses up on his nose between keystrokes. "If it was going to hurt, we wouldn't even try." His twisted grin held more than a little wistfulness. "I double-checked the notes from Anna's book, and if Tab's right, we can trigger that little capsule inside you to give us what we need right here." He patted the computer in front of him half-reassuringly.

The room fell quiet. Everyone was looking at Sofi. She wanted to melt away under their stares and disappear. She knew they were waiting for her. She would give the word to start. That's what Beth said.

Sofi debated whether to just get up and leave. She could; they'd told her she could. They'd also told her what it could mean if she let them go ahead with this. Jenna lay in a coma halfway across the country. Her mother had implanted knowledge inside her that was supposed to trigger itself into her brain when she hit twenty-one years of age. Knowledge that could bring Jenna back and make her whole again. Sofi knew in her heart how much she owed that woman. She had saved Sofi's life on more than one occasion. Here was her chance to repay her debt to Jenna.

Before she could talk herself out of it, Sofi squeezed Hushi's hand and nodded, a brave smile (she hoped) on her face. Bunny touched a key. A soft beep answered him from the system.

A warm tickle began in Sofi's scalp. She thought it was just the gel Hushi used on the leads, but it grew warmer by the second, more intense. It was as if something was reaching, probing deeper into her head. Something *connected* inside her like a switch being thrown, and a shock shot down her spine and into her left thigh. It hit so suddenly, she yelped and jumped. Her eyes rolled back hard, and her back arched.

"Hungh!"

"Sofi?" Hushi leaned close, her voice near panic.

Beth said, "Pushing fifty milligrams." A hot feeling crawled up Sofi's arm, and the feeling diminished. She felt woozy but remained conscious. With a moan, she sagged onto the cot.

Bunny said, "Hey, I'm gettin' somethin'. There's a file— Holy— It's *huge!* How's she doin', ladies?"

Sofi was dimly aware of a spongy clip being attached to a fingertip. A speaker began sending out a regular pattern of beeps. A touch here, a caress of her forehead. *Warm, hot, burning up*, she couldn't speak, couldn't move, couldn't—

Bunny crowed, "Got it!" at the very instant something new happened in Sofi's mind. It felt like a cool wave, starting at the top of her head and splashing down like diving into a pool on a hot day.

And Sofi knew. She *knew* how to fix Jenna.

The connection shut down inside her. The fingers stopped reaching from the leads on her scalp. She felt winded, like she'd run from her house to the cliffs and back again, like five times, on a fall day. Someone laid a cloth on her forehead, and she realized how much she'd been sweating.

Beth whispered in her ear, "Honey, do you want to sleep?"

She didn't want to sleep. She wanted to jump up and run around the room like a raging maniac. But she was just so *tired*. She'd jump around like a maniac tomorrow. Sleep sounded like a good idea after all. Sofi kept her eyes closed, and managed a weak nod. Someone started to pull the leads from her head. Someone else kissed her cheek and giggled. The last thing she felt was a happy warmth as she drifted off to an easy sleep.

Chapter Sixty

Jon signed the papers and slid them back across Colonel Danson's desk. The colonel took them and added his own signature next to Jon's. "Thank you for serving your country, Major. Allow me to be the first to congratulate you on your promotion and on your retirement." He snagged a rubber stamp from among a half dozen dangling from a little metal tree on his desk, and thumped a date on four different color copies of Jon's orders, setting two aside before handing the others back. When Jon reached out to take them, Danson held on. "There's one more assignment I want you in on. If it's convenient, Major?"

The colonel released the stack, and Jon slowly withdrew them, his curiosity piqued. "Sir?"

"Bowman's computer drive yielded quite a few names, dates, and cold, hard facts. There are teams out rounding them up now. At least, the ones who haven't disappeared mysteriously over the last week. How are you doing, by the way? That was one hell of an action report."

"I guess I'll be all right," Jon lied. *Eventually.*

"Anyway, that information, along with something else, leads me to believe you'll want this one bad." Danson paused before continuing. His mouth worked as he cleared his throat. "A couple of hikers found a woman's body in the woods outside D.C. A Bureau forensics team identified the remains as Donna Hermsen." He handed Jon a thick manila envelope. "There's more intel in here, and you can read it on the way. Your new team's waiting."

* * * *

The last time Jon was at the White House, the West Wing was a shambles of broken masonry and shattered lives. The physical repairs were seamless, but he still couldn't shake the image of smoking rubble, fire rescue crews and police. He felt a grim satisfaction that he was even now visiting the site of The Pinnacle's most devastating handiwork to bring their own doom back down on their heads.

A marine guard waved casually at the receptionist in the outer office and swung the door open. He paused before stepping through as Linda Schiller looked up, startled. "What's the meaning of this?" she demanded.

Jon fought the urge to march across the office and punch her face in. At this point, he didn't really care if this was done right. But technically, Jon was still on active military duty, and she was his vice-commander-in-chief, at least for the next four or five seconds. The office warranted respect, even if the woman holding it was a contemptible worm. He stood at attention in front of her desk as his team fanned out around the office. Steve Mrosinski and Allen Kirk stepped up behind her as she stood, her face framed in fury. Jon announced, "Madame Vice President, you're under arrest for conspiracy to murder, high treason against the Republic, and sedition. Place your hands behind your back, please."

Schiller's mouth worked in futile anger before she found words. "How *dare* you! I'll have your commission, young man." Her voice lowered as she continued. "I will ruin you."

Jon turned to look back to the outer office. The Chief Justice was there with a Bible held out. The Speaker of the House was being sworn in as interim vice president in front of a shocked assistant. He waited until the oath was administered before turning back around to face the woman who'd murdered his friend. "Lady, it's over. Dr. Hermsen's body turned up."

"I don't know what you're talking about," she hissed. But her face turned white, proving the lie.

Jon held up the packet he'd read on the way over. "Ballistics matched the bullets in her body with the service pistol of one Adam McLeach, one of your personal bodyguards." He leaned closer and a smug grin eased over his face. "Agent McLeach also had Donna's cell phone in his possession. It had been picked through pretty extensively. It also had your fingerprints on it. The boy squealed like a pig to get out of a needle. What are *you* willing to sell us?"

Her shocked eyes bored into his. "This isn't over. You know we make the laws now. We own the courts—"

"Can the pep talk." Jon said with a growl. "Yeah, you'll probably get some slick bloodsucker to get you off the charges. But you're damaged goods now. Even if any of the leadership survived the raid on their facility, you're known now. You'll just end up like your man Whitfield, face down on your carpet with a bullet through your own brain. Or," he said, stepping back, "you could plead guilty. Spend your remaining days all warm and safe in a federal pen. Your choice." He smiled at Allen, who deftly applied the cuffs to her wrists.

Linda's shoulders slumped. Sweat began to bead on her forehead as she looked down, shaking. "I m-may have some information for you..."

Jon passed the file packet to Steve as they walked out. "I'm done, guys. Go ahead and take it home, will you?"

At the curb, he flagged a cab. Twenty minutes later, he sat in the grass in front of a black marble stone, one of five in a row. "Alli, we did it. You—" He fought back the lump that rose in his throat—"*You* did it, honey. The funny thing is you don't even know it. But that part of you that carried on, turned out to be the best thing that happened to me."

He rubbed his eyes and lay back on the manicured lawn. "I'm sorry I never came back here on my own. I just couldn't take the thought of you"—his breath caught—"lying there, like that."

Closing his eyes, he said, "I miss you. But I think I'm going to be okay now. She took good care of me. And she was good." Jon paused long enough to take a deep breath. "She was very good."

He watched a cloud meander across the sky for several minutes. A rustle of feathers nearby brought his attention back to the stone. A red-winged blackbird perched atop it, its head cocked to one side as it eyed him cautiously. Then with a trill, it took off again.

"I'm going to forgive myself for Jimmy. I've second-guessed myself a hundred times, and there's nothing I could have done. Jimmy died. If I hadn't been there to save Jenna, we would have all been dead. I can't take back time, so I'm going to let it go. As soon as I can convince myself, I'll be all right." *As soon as I can convince myself.*

He sat up again and ran his palms over his face. "I'm going away. Uncle Mike had some property out west. It's mine now, I guess. I really need to sort some things out."

Jon stood and touched the stone. "Goodbye, Alicia. I promise, when we meet again, I'll have a fair accounting of the time I have left."

* * * *

The sun set in front of Jon as he pushed west out of the city. A full tank of gas, Hell behind him, the world ahead. For the last four years, every waking moment had been focused on one thing. Now it was over.

Now what?

It was something he'd been trying to figure out since he walked out of the White House. The initial triumph after he arrested the vice president was replaced with a hollow kind of buzz. He felt like he should be still doing something, turning over one more stone, finding one more loose end that needed to be tied into something. But what?

Long into the night he drove, the question still echoing across the hollow space where his purpose had been. It was still smoldering in his mind when he pulled off the road.

He had dinner and checked into a mom-and-pop motel within shouting distance of the interstate, lying awake as he listened to the trucks "jake" their engines down the backside of the grade.

What was next? The question might be there for a long time before he figured it out.

With a sigh, Jon rolled over and turned out the light.

He had time.

About the Author

Cyrus Keith is the fortunate by-product of an Englishman who one day happened upon a charming young lass of Irish origin. The world has never quite been the same since.

* * * *

Did you enjoy Critical Mass? If so, please help us spread the word about Cyrus Keith and MuseItUp Publishing. It's as easy as:

•*Recommend the book to your family and friends*
•*Post a review*
•*Tweet and Facebook about it*

Thank you
MuseItUp Publishing

THE NADIA PROJECT

Becoming NADIA

Unalive

Critical Mass

CPSIA information can be obtained at www.ICGtesting.com
Printed in the USA
BVOW05s2215270815

415522BV00001B/10/P